Anna Richards was born in Essex and currently lives in London. This is her first novel.

LITTLE GODS

Jean Clocker is conceived by her mother, Wisteria, to entrap a First World War veteran into marriage. But when she fails to rid herself of the now-redundant snare, Wisteria visits maternal tyranny on Jean. Born into a body as epic as the life she will live, Jean spends her early years avoiding her mother's blows and striving to be a little less extraordinary. She is finally released from servitude at the start of the Second World War. Orphaned, she thrives in wartime whilst fearing the return of normality and conformity. Then Denny, a GI, facilitates her second liberation, as he takes her across the ocean as his bride. But in California he disappears without warning, and Jean is again required to negotiate the world alone.

ANNA RICHARDS

LITTLE GODS

Complete and Unabridged

CHARNWOOD
Leicester

First published in Great Britain in 2009 by
Picador
an imprint of Pan Macmillan Ltd., London

First Charnwood Edition
published 2009
by arrangement with Pan Macmillan Ltd., London

The moral right of the author has been asserted

British Library CIP Data

Richards, Anna.
 Little gods.
 1. Mothers and daughters- -Fiction.
 2. Abused children- -Psychology- -Fiction.
 3. World War, *1939 – 1945*- -Social aspects- -Fiction. 4. Marginality, Social- -Fiction.
 5. Self-actualization (Psychology)- -Fiction.
 6. Domestic fiction. 7. Large type books.
 I. Title
 823.9′2–dc22

 ISBN 978–1–84782–881–1

Published by
F. A. Thorpe (Publishing)
Anstey, Leicestershire

Set by Words & Graphics Ltd.
Anstey, Leicestershire
Printed and bound in Great Britain by
T. J. International Ltd., Padstow, Cornwall

This book is printed on acid-free paper

For my family and my love

Acknowledgements

Victor Navasky's *Naming Names* for its vivid depiction of political persecution in postwar Hollywood. Jean's experiences are not based on those of any individual, but the sense of period evoked by the book was invaluable.

The February 16, 1946 edition of the *Picture Post*, containing the article 'To America with the GI Brides' (text Lionel Birch, photography Zoltan Glass), a wonderful description of four hundred and fifty-seven British women (including one Mrs Curnalia, whose surname I have borrowed, with thanks) on their way to the complete unknown.

The poem referenced on page 552 is 'No Coward Soul is Mine' by Emily Brontë. 'I sing the body electric' is gratefully reproduced from *Leaves of Grass* by Walt Whitman. 'Euclid alone has looked on Beauty bare' copyright © 1923, 1951 by Edna St. Vincent Millay and Norma Millay Ellis. Reprinted by permission of Elizabeth Barnett, Literary Executor, The Millay Society.

Thanks to
My parents, Linda and Robert Richards, my husband Jamie, Jane Hill, Rachel Calder, Ursula Doyle, Sam Humphreys, Corinne Beaver, Lucy Rowan and Paul Talan.

1

Hours before dawn, on not quite the forty-seventh day of the war, a nineteen-year-old girl was curled up in a too-small bed, looking like a doll that had been sold with the wrong cot. The room she slept in had been decorated for a baby — a stranger to her, long since grown and gone, along with those that cared for such things as decorating and babies. On the walls, small pink roses were being eaten by large pats of green mould. The girl's feet twitched, deep in a dog dream in which she ran fast, straight and light; a soft hum escaped her. It might turn into a throaty snore when she was older but now it was just a contented song of sleep.

The bomb tore through the still night like birth, and landed like a foundling on a dark suburban doorstep. Every window in the street was blown out but only one house fell. It was so clean as to seem personal. The front two rooms were ejected straight out of the back, nothing but ash and splinters. The blast carved new corridors in seconds, sending slicing fragments of wood and glass hurtling along them. It cut a path straight to the attic, throwing floors and walls behind it. The girl was on top of a volcano; the building under her rushing to turn itself inside out. There was hardly any time; the scream of its arrival to the end of everything could be measured in a breath.

If time could slow, she could have opened her

eyes and seen air gather like a fist and punch in the door. Seen it rake her with the grit it held in its tail and seen the blood bloom under her nightgown and know that it wasn't fire that swept over her though she saw flames swirl behind her eyelids and felt her skin scorch. All in a breath.

The faded roses bubbled to life as air rushed behind the paper, flaying it from the wall and casting it up to the roof, which had been torn off and was capering down the street. A funnel of brick and ash formed in its place, a gateway to Oz into which the house flew on a thread. Then the walls billowed like bedsheets, the floor fell away like wet sand and the girl sank faster than hope into the room below.

Before the house was exploded, no one near it had known that blood could take to the air and stain it, hanging heavier than the smell of cooking or the sea. A great fountain of it was released. It splattered the dust that, for days after, would seek out people's noses, eyes and mouths, that coated their hair and crept into their houses through closed windows. It hit the pavement with the force of thick rain and streaked through the rubble as if the building itself had veins that were open and running.

The girl was not alone in the air, in the whirl of it; eight others rolled through the night. They settled on the earth in hard and soft layers, masonry and flesh. The cyclone of brick and blasted air scooped them up and threw them down again like dough, kneading the bones out of them, stretching and tearing their soft bodies.

The house came down in waves, plunging the nine into moving currents of brick and water; they drowned in plaster, were dashed against beams and torn by glass. Arms and legs kicking against the tide, the women and children spiralled down into the house that drew itself over them and settled in a calm black mound. Nothing had travelled across their minds past the first few seconds when they struggled to recognise death: a racing cloud come suddenly over, turning everything dark.

Everything falls apart uniquely. A bomb could leave a house three parts standing, as open as a dolls', photographs still hanging on the back walls, a washstand balanced on three floor-boards, the jug not even chipped. This house was turned over like soil, a hill of dirt and brick crowned with shoes, pieces of furniture and food. The inside looked like an ant farm, little tunnels forged by cascading bodies led to separate chambers, each containing a broken human, splayed out like French tapestry men with odd-angled arms and surprised eyes. Petrified in the act of swimming away from the monster that would devour them, the children were delicate enough to be cave paintings, their little white nighties and pale slender arms bright against the dark sludge and soot that held them fast. At the edge was an egg, a pearly white case with a life inside. As the building had sunk back into the ground, the body of a nineteen-year-old girl had slithered under a bathtub, which closed over her and kept her, like a spider in a matchbox. Jean.

Part One

CREATION

2

When Jean was born for the first time, her mother said it split her like a rail and was done on the topic. Some mothers do not love their children, but most at least forgive them.

The battle of her birth raged for two days. For the first few hours, Jean's mother had been reluctant to uncross her legs, insisting that it was a bad pie and would pass. Awkward in conception and growth, the child had not gone according to plan. It inflated as well as inhabited its mother, terrifying the host body with its demands, draining while drowning it. Two early efforts at ending the pregnancy with a gin bath had left the mother with scalded skin and a sick hangover but no release. The child swelled enormously after each assassination attempt and fought its expulsion with blind vigour. After two days of labour, Jean's mother succeeded in evicting her daughter from her womb, but the child snatched victory with its first breath.

Jean sat in the hospital scales like a prize marrow, shiny and full, while her mother bled on the table next to her, her face an expressionistic rendering of pure horror — all eyes and angles, pointing towards the ceiling. After a few minutes, the doctor attempted to coax the new mother's face downwards with a little ammonia. She snorted back to life and lunged for the coat that shimmered in front of her, the white of it interrupted by splashes of her own insides. Her cracked hands reached for the lapels and hooked them, she lifted her head though it sent fire all the way down to her toes to do it and after a couple of dry gasps managed to speak.

'How many?' she panted. 'How many?'

The doctor tried to unsnag himself from her as if she were a tiresome piece of foliage.

'One,' he muttered as he picked at the red, stringy hands. 'Just the one, Mrs Clocker.'

The agony told her he was lying, and blood watered the fast-growing horror in her mind. Pain and fear fed the muscles she needed to draw the doctor down to her face, to where he could see the scabs and fresh tears on her lips, the skin caught in her teeth. She managed to whisper, 'Heads? How many ... heads?' And then fell a hundred feet down into the darkness.

While the mother was swabbed and stitched, they took the child away to find a cot, the ward sister worrying she might have to grease the sides. Eugenia was the name that had been agreed upon for the mighty newborn, should she live, but it was soon after shortened to Jean. Inhibiting her, in whatever way possible, was paramount from the start. She was taken home from the hospital in an ancient pram that was deep and wide enough to hide a man on the run.

★　★　★

Jean's mother was thirty-four when her first and only child was born. She herself had entered the world at the height of the floral craze. Against a

8

bed of Violets, Lilies and Roses, she was named, by a mother with a botanical dictionary and seemingly the gift of clairvoyance, Wisteria — a tough, twining climber. Only she never flowered. Gums of lemon rind and teeth of pure alum couldn't produce anything to rival the malevolent arsehole of a mouth Wisteria sported. Disappointment was her drug of choice and she was a good way through a lifelong bender.

At twenty-eight, Wisteria gazed long and hard into a scratched mirror and decided that life had promised far more than it had delivered. Her eyes were pale and watery, her hair clung to her scalp in ashy licks and her colourless skin indicated its intention to gather in folds with unmistakable clarity. She looked as though she needed to hang upside down for a while. If only she'd been beautiful, she thought. That's all it would take. She had spent years waiting to become so; it had proved to be an exercise in futility. Wisteria believed there was nothing in the world a well-shaped nose couldn't bring her; it had not arrived, and neither had a change in fortune. The injustice of it was like lit matches between her toes.

Wisteria's father took the long walk after cigarettes that does not lead to the tobacconist when she was nine years old. Wisteria went to work not long after that and spent every day being reminded of the gap between her life and a comfortable one. At fourteen she started in the laundry of a seafront hotel and didn't progress far from it. In every well-dressed woman who came into the hotel she saw what she should have been. Wisteria became expert at leaving ink marks on beautiful clothes, slipping tiny flakes of fish under the uppers of shoes, adding vinegar to perfume and extra starch to underthings. These women had everything that should have come to her; all she possessed was absence, she was made of it. It made her wicked.

If Wisteria's life had been a fairy story she would have been rescued by romance. Wisteria had only once believed herself in love, and had found it to be the fastest way yet to make a person despise her.

He was twenty-five to her twenty-eight, and on him it was still youth. He had come to the hotel for one season and slept in one of the staff bunks kept for itinerant workers. The laundry provided the linens for these rooms as well: scratchy towels the size and thickness of envelopes, and striped sheets dotted with cigarette burns. Wisteria had been asked to show him the room and bring clean bedding. He had thanked her, taking her hand in his, and smiled as he told her his name. Thomas. Her cold hand had for once felt warm in his grasp; the smile was one meant for a kinder face than hers; by giving it to her he had conferred fairness upon her. She wanted to earn that smile again, to be made different by it.

She took the softest linens for his bunk and made sure that she alone stripped them on washday, when she breathed in the scent of his hair oil on the pillow slips. He was tall, fair and unmarked; beautiful in a way that could make even Wisteria reel. She forgot her antipathy to surprise — which she viewed as life making a

10

mockery of her — each time she saw him and was reminded of what could exist so near to her. She felt that to own him would be like owning the most wonderful coat; it would cover her and make her elegant and desirable, all the shabbiness would be underneath. He could change her. He was her chance.

Wisteria pursued Thomas with the delicacy of a Cossack, not seeing the contempt build in him with each clumsy new advance she made, as she tossed her hair and bared her brown teeth. She had waited too long to want and now was grasping and wild with it. She had truly forgotten herself, defining herself only by what she wanted, not what she was. She was vindictive, pathetic, dishonest and cruel in her pursuit. Each rejection lit a new horror in her as she strove for his recognition.

After some weeks, Wisteria felt her desire grow strong enough to overpower him. She followed Thomas into the narrow cupboard where the guests' footwear was cleaned and polished, and cornered him. Wisteria was convinced that her passion had become so strong as to act as a kind of romantic purgative, forcing heretofore well-concealed desire out of him in a torrent.

As she closed the door carefully behind her, she failed to see Thomas's look of surprise turn to recognition, disappointment and then disdain.

'What do *you* want?' he asked. Wisteria couldn't answer, she could only look at him. 'I've got work to do, can't you see?'

His voice was quiet but soaked in loathing. The others ragged him mercilessly about this

11

droopy old maid; her attention angered and humiliated him. To be found with a woman, even this one, in the boot room could mean his job; it could never be worth it with her. Wisteria was mute and still, wetting her lips with her narrow lizard tongue. The words that she ran through her head so many times a day had yet to come from his mouth. But she could wait.

'You can't be here, you have to go.'

He wouldn't even look up from the boot he was polishing.

'Thomas. Can you not look at me?'

'What for? I know what you look like.'

Her heart surged a little at the thought he had memorised her features, as she had his. She was about to entertain the notion that he might have practised kissing them in a mirror or window, when he finished his sentence.

'More's the pity. Give me nightmares, you do.'

He was not the thing that turned her; Wisteria was curdled long before. But he was the thing that reminded her of who she was, when she was about to forget.

'Look, stop bloody following me, all right? You're always there, mooning about. Don't you know what people say about you, don't you know they laugh at you? Laugh at me because of you. I'm sick of it! I'm sick of you! Why can't you just . . . piss off?'

In that moment, Wisteria regained her lost senses and saw herself clearly. She saw the past weeks in minute detail: the eye rolling, the gestures, the whispers that followed her. The background suddenly came into focus. She felt anger course through her; a flash flood of rage that threatened to knock her down. Her neck grew warm. She saw her own ridiculousness, and it appalled her that she had been led to this point, that she had been tricked. Her breathing became wild, and she was sweating; Thomas was eyeing her as one might a small, trapped animal, unable to judge whether superior size or viciousness would win out.

'Look, now, if you just go, go right this minute, no one will be any the wiser. I won't tell a soul, I swear it. Just bugger off, all right?'

He took a step towards her, his hand held out in a placating gesture that only enraged Wisteria further. She took up the nearest pair of boots and blindly hurled them. He yelped and jumped backwards, covering his face with his hands. She had cut him above the eye, and to see his beauty marred gave her an exhilarating feeling of retribution.

'You mad bitch!' he screamed. 'You've cut me, you bloody cow!'

Wisteria launched another pair of boots. Thomas gave a cry of pain as they hit his elbow; blood from his eye was now running between his fingers. He picked up a wooden tray and held it in front of his face.

'Stop it, you lunatic! I'll have the bloody law on you!'

His voice wavered, and he sounded scared; Wisteria felt her old self-possession returning. It was as if he had drugged her, and she had shaken off the effects of the potion; her head was clear, and her anger was righteous. She hurled a delicately heeled ladies' boot at his torso; he batted it away with the tray, and as she scrambled for another missile, he lunged at her. Before his hand could reach her, her own was at her throat; Wisteria grabbed the material of her uniform and began to pull, her eyes bright with provocation.

'God, no!'

He took a step backwards and held up his hands. 'Don't.' His voice was pleading, his movements submissive. He edged to the back of the cupboard. His near blubbering disgusted her, and she rejoiced.

'Don't. Just let me go. I never touched you, I never did.'

And he never would, so she would make him pay. Wisteria kept her hand at her throat; she looked at him steadily, letting him know she was considering his fate. If she continued to pull at the fabric, if she screamed, he would be ruined. As she now was. Tears and sweat mingled with the blood on his face; he was cowering in the darkness, out of reach of the light. Wisteria felt her humiliation lessen as his grew. She couldn't make him want her, but she could make him disappear and take the creature she had been for the past few weeks with him.

★   ★   ★

All that was known was that Thomas had left halfway through his shift, taking several good pairs of boots. They later turned up in a pawn shop about as far from Wisteria's home as she could manage in one fair walk. Wisteria told her mother that Thomas had been sent away, having previously told her she was in love and to be married. She cast herself as the pitiful victim in a melodrama, abandoned by a callous man who had attempted to breach the sanctity of her virtue.

Her mother just put her bread and dripping in front of her and poured the tea.

'You'll lose that job, you know. And get no references.'

Wisteria shrugged and waggled her head to show she didn't care, moving the hard bread around her rotten teeth.

'No one can say I did anything improper,' she simpered. 'He took four pairs of boots, so anyone could see he was a wrong 'un.'

The money from the pawn shop felt warm in her pocket; she decided to spend it on cakes that she would buy and eat on the way to work, a walk she took alone. Wisteria took a mouthful of tea and let it dissolve the food that clung to her gums.

'Well, that's that then, isn't it?' Her mother sighed. 'We're for the workhouse, and I'm for a pauper's grave. What you've saved wouldn't bury a cat. I've seen worse than you married, I don't know why you can't manage it.'

Wisteria looked at her sharply and then pushed her tea away and took a cigarette from a tin box. Worse than her had married, it was true, but she wasn't far off bottom. Poverty had aged her quickly and ground whatever might have been good in her to dust. She studied her mother as she sat drinking her tea. She could see herself in a not-too-distant old age in the creak of the older woman's elbow, the roll of her mouth when it was full of liquid, the lack of life in her. Wisteria saw defeat and despised it. She could feel her wheels spinning; she would just sink now in the ruts of her own making. The only paths left to her were marriage or madness.

'It's not getting them,' she announced to her mother. 'It's not letting them get away with it.'

She was twenty-eight and would have to wait another year before the world gave her the circumstances she required.

3

War would prove to be a great force for change in Wisteria's life. The declaration of the Great one caused a marriage-rush strong enough to sweep even her along. The hotel filled with men celebrating their last nights of freedom, the streets were strewn with the fallen after closing time. Even Wisteria might find herself grabbed and kissed before a man really knew what he was doing. A shrewd judge of the moment, she accepted three drunken offers of marriage and settled back to see which of the trio would return to claim her. If there had been time for a ceremony she would have made it legal with whichever one was sober enough to stand.

Wisteria saw no danger of a farcical reunion of all four in a marriage dance. By the time she became engaged, the decimation of the first pals' battalions had begun. With the skill of a street-corner bookie, she calculated the odds of three pieces of cannon fodder returning to make good their pledge. She needed only one, which was still something of a long shot. She sent socks instead of the photographs they asked for, and in return extracted written promises from her doomed youths.

All three survived. The places they had been became new names for death, given in answer to an enquiry after the health of a son or brother. Two of them had fought next to each other, advancing as men fell to their left and right. Tipsy with life they returned — still intent on marriage — to a vague memory overlaid with hopeful details cribbed from other girls. The three were brought home on the same troopship and by the time they docked had discovered themselves to be trousered lots in a Dutch auction.

Wisteria received three handwritten notices advising her of a death in action, one scrawled on an advertisement for a digestive tonic. Faced with defeat, she regrouped and rethought. She, for one, had learnt the lessons of the war and would never fight on three fronts again.

There were many veterans' associations, and Wisteria threw herself into volunteer work at various functions, which she cruised like a salvage merchant looking for wrecks. At the church hall one summer Sunday afternoon, a bingo game was in full swing for veterans. Wisteria was stationed behind the tea urn, a hyena at the watering hole. Jean's father came closest to the dark waters and stayed longest, his one arm causing the fatal delay. A handwritten note was pinned to his pocket, 'Clocker, Arthur'.

'There's a dance later tonight. For your lot,' Wisteria announced over the offer of a sandwich. The soldier flapped his empty sleeve by way of explanation.

'Still got your feet though, haven't you?' she snapped. 'I don't see your trousers pinned up 'n' all.'

The soldier raised his eyes to take in the owner of the souring voice. She held his gaze and dared

18

him to look away, the distaste she felt for him pouring out of her and mingling with the desperation that hung around her. He saw a plain woman alive with hatred and disgust. She wore on her face what he carried in his gut. He had given an arm to stop fighting, but what this woman required for the cessation of hostilities was him entire, the honouring of a debt he hadn't personally run up. The tired survivor looked at the woman with the cruel mouth and the grasping bony hands. This is punishment, he thought, and nodded.

★ ★ ★

'I thought: at least he can hold his own cup of tea,' Wisteria told her mother that night. 'If not a plate of sandwiches at the same time.'

★ ★ ★

He had his pension and some money from a dead family that he seemed not to remember. Enough for Wisteria to live on. She would take no chances this time and managed to get herself pregnant at the first attempt. Her own efficiency pleased her, and she was grateful she wouldn't have to try again. Wisteria initiated the coupling, then held her body rigid while he moved inside her. They were between two gravestones in a cemetery that was full of new plots for the war dead who had managed to make it home before expiring. He wept afterwards, while she wiped her legs with a towel taken from the hotel. They

19

were married once the pregnancy was confirmed, and moved to a new set of rooms a little
closer to the sea; Wisteria felt the fresher air
might benefit her complexion, though this belief
did not extend to her opening a window. Arthur
was exiled from the marital bed immediately and
slept on two chairs in the parlour, the trenches
having prepared him for sleeping within sight of
the enemy. Wisteria continued to share a room
with her mother, leaving a room in the roof that
she did not expect to be filled with anything but
pigeon mess. There was also an indoor, shared
bath, though Wisteria brought in the old tin one
from outside when she tried to abort Jean.

Wisteria was surprised when her body refused
to give up the child; she certainly had no further
use for it. At five months she had to concede
defeat and sat back to await the birth with a
queasy attitude of defiance and a careful
disregard for the dangers of strong drink. This
early rebellion did not bode well, but on the
better days Wisteria reassured herself of her
ability to retain sovereignty. On the bad ones she
loitered at the top of the stairs. From this Jean
came, with a vengeance.

⋆　⋆　⋆

The hospital had a policy for married woman
— they were to want their children. Wisteria
begged to stay there, hoping for a reprieve
— that the baby might come into contact with a
disease that would leave it mute and manageable, or be snatched by one of the childless

20

lunatics that were said to roam the wards. But it wouldn't sicken, wouldn't shrivel, wouldn't waste to an appropriate size. And so Wisteria went home, pushing the heavy pram. The sea behind her; shit-wiping, screaming, puking motherhood ahead; her insides feeling as though they might drop out. Once, Wisteria's body had done more or less as it was told; after Jean, she felt like a badly made puppet. Too-short strings ran from her groin through her stomach and heart all the way to the back of her ears. Everything left in her was afterbirth, waiting to follow the child out and slither away into uselessness.

Wisteria resented Jean as she would an assailant. Her child, even in its supposed innocence, had tried to murder her. She watched its seditious head, that had left her legs in separate hemispheres, loll from side to side, keeping time with her efforts to push the gargantuan vehicle onwards. She muttered, 'Bitch, bitch, bitch,' as the bar pressed into her soft, stretched belly, forcing her to piss herself a little each time.

Watching the pitch and roll of her daughter, Wisteria contemplated the child's every inch, every alien feature. If ever there was an infant less well-shaped for the world, she had yet to see it. Something like her might once have delighted Wisteria, had she belonged to someone else. Having always been morbidly self-conscious, she would scan the streets for someone whose legs were twisted, whose clothes were of a material rougher and greyer than hers, whose skin was

21

more marked by the scars of acne past — anything that made her feel better. She would have allowed herself a smile at the poor woman she saw pushing this around and would have thought to herself: 'Won't catch me in your shoes. I'll have more sense.' The baby swung from side to side as the carriage creaked on. It didn't look like anything that could have come from her, from anyone right; it wore its illegitimacy like a flag. Wisteria felt shame burn behind her ears and wet the back of her neck. The child's existence mocked her; it had already been too hard and cost too much.

She did not know what she was going to do. It was not a feeling she was used to, and it left her watery and weak. Wisteria looked back down the hill at the promenade, the shut-up shops that came alive only for people from outside, the railings and finally the sea, the flat green glassy sea that reached out towards nothing in particular. That was behind her. The row of houses containing her home was in front of her, perched on the top of a steep hill, the view of a patch of brine no longer sought after now the salty air had rotted the window frames, bleached the brick and choked the odd tree the council had bothered to drag up there. It was a hard place for an old woman to live, not many places she could go once her legs went. Wisteria wondered how she would get around. She felt the pram's weight against her body. The body was still hers, pain told her that, though birth had rendered it unfamiliar and obstinate. The carriage was pushing at her, trying to get back down the hill, wanting to fly into that smooth sea. What if, she asked herself, she just stepped out of its way?

Wisteria looked down at the child in the pram, and she knew the returns would be poor. The pram pushed at her still.

'You want to go, do you?' she whispered. 'Got somewhere better to be, have we? Got an appointment?'

Jean made a mewling, kittenish sound, sending another shudder through her mother. The pain rippled out from Wisteria's groin, washed over her spine and ran down her thighs. Her mantra ran through her mind: 'Why me?' It circled her brain and tightened like wire; why me? 'Why not you?' the baby seemed to say back to her with each heavy breath. Why shouldn't you have been ruined by me, what good were you anyway?

Wisteria felt a coldness inside her head where rage had recently been boiling. She slowly turned the pram to face downhill and loosened her hold on the bar until the pram was held back with just the tips of eight curled, reddened fingers, her thumbs aloft. The vehicle's insistence on being on its way was clear; cords stood up in Wisteria's hands, like the tough sinews of chicken's feet. The strain was painful. She wasn't sure how much longer she could stay like this.

She could be found in a faint at the crest of the hill, she thought, the heavy pram at the bottom. Her grip would have failed as she slid to the floor; she could even cry out, 'Save my baby!' There wasn't a soul to witness it; no one in the houses could make it on to the street in time. You might as well try to stop a bowling ball on a greased slide as catch this fat little number hurtling down towards the prom. She could do it. It was self-defence, after all. Then Jean opened her eyes.

She looked directly at the woman contemplating her demise. Her eyes were almost all iris, impossibly dark with tiny slivers of white at the corners. Her gaze was without emotion, or pleading. She simply looked. Wisteria felt the pull of gravity through her wrists and arms; the carriage wanted to be away. Jean's gaze was deep and unflinching, Wisteria could make out nothing in it, not even fear. Jean looked at her mother for another few seconds and then closed her eyes, returning to sleep. Wisteria gripped the carriage bar and twisted her hands, its rough covering scouring her palms. They would know. Whatever she told them, they would know. They would only have to look at her.

'Fuck you,' she whispered. 'Oh, fuck you.'

Bitterness spilled out of her eyes and wet her cheeks as she whispered again and again to the child: fuck you. She put her head down on the bar and wiped her eyes on her sleeve, then tipped the carriage towards her and turned it on its hind wheels. With her back to the sea, she pushed on up the hill.

Wisteria told herself it was a choice; the wait would be long, but she would have her reward. She would have some return. The child would be of use at least, a peg to hang it all on. She would claim something back. At least it had been a girl; shouldn't be too hard to shrink down. She'd feed it loathing mixed with milk, and its bones would warp; it would become twisty and small and ashamed. She had dreamed of a servant all her life. Strengthened, Wisteria pushed the pram up over the kerb and turned into her street.

The pram was left in the hall, where it became the enemy of getting in the front door. Clasping one hand between her legs, Wisteria lifted Jean with the other, then straightened her aching spine and held the baby, like a bedroll, under her arm. She used the rail to pull herself up the stairs, to the top floor where this third generation would share three rooms and a kitchen with the other two, her husband and mother. The door was ajar; she could see her husband turning nervous circles in front of the fireplace, as if he had popped out of a clock and, finding no weather at all, couldn't get back or go forward.

Wisteria lowered herself into the armchair. Jean nestled in her lap, still fast asleep, pressed so deeply into her mother's stomach there was no need to hold her. Wisteria slumped in the chair — her chin set into her chest, a collapsed hat pitched forward onto her sweaty forehead — eyeing her husband like a murderous pasha, waiting for offence to be given so that a favourite punishment could be exacted. With each second under her glare, her husband's doomed revolutions became more frantic. She was met with silence, when she wanted recognition.

'Fine, thank you,' she snapped. 'Back from the brink of death, as you can see.'

She watched him for a reaction, for an acknowledgement. His eyes flicked her way, then back to the window. He had given up so quickly, there was barely anything left of him after just a few months of marriage. It was as if he had held on long enough to be found by her and then gone entirely to pieces as soon as she had got him home. She felt cheated even in him, angry at herself for seeing only the lack of an arm. She cursed not being able to see the true rot inside.

'Go on, look,' she jeered, watching the sickness surge through him, the sickness that had gone through her and emerged in a fat packet of skin and bone.

'See what you've done. See what a mess you've made of it.'

Jean's father placed a hand, his only, on the mantelpiece, anchoring himself; his feet moved forwards and back in a solitary jive but the circles had stopped. He marked time with his eyes, which bounced towards the mother and child before returning to rest on his shoes. She watched him sidle and fret, working out his approach to this unknown quantity, then lost patience and snatched up her hat and threw it at him; it fell uselessly short. He tried to quiet his internal dance; he trod on his own foot, pressing one down hard on the other, keeping them both still while his kneecaps leapt to an unheard beat.

'Go on, look!' Wisteria roared, her mouth thin and white with years of anger and days of pain. 'See what you've done to me!'

He let go of the mantelpiece and launched himself into the room. He approached them in turns and circles, as if trying to confuse an enemy. His wife watched him, her body tense,

26

hands gripping the arms of the chair as if she might launch herself out of it at any moment and go for his throat. Her eyes glittered terribly as she watched his nervy progress. Reaching them, he peered at the baby on her stomach as it breathed deeply then yawned. Jean woke, and her father saw himself reflected in darkness as her brown eyes held him; he reached out his hand, the fingers twitching with indecision on their way to her face, the memory of tenderness refusing to enter them, the memory itself mothballed up somewhere at the back of his mind, behind the war, behind something, as vague as scent from a long-ago letter. Wisteria held her breath. His brain tried to give shape to the shadows that roamed its corridors, hoping one might be the feeling he was reaching for. But as he approached so he passed through them, boating through mist.

His hand hovered then darted forward, stopping an inch from the infant's face; he had taken a run at her, trying to wake some instinct, but the suddenness hadn't brought clarity, just as the shock treatments hadn't worked on him either. He couldn't remember. He pressed the end of Jean's nose with his index finger as gently as he could, as if testing a loaf, watched his girl twitch her face in response, and danced back to the wall.

Wisteria saw him confirm her own disgust; he didn't recognise it any more than she did. It was a distillation of their crimes, nothing more. Her mother appeared in the doorway holding a cup of tea and a plate with a small, dry piece of cheese on it. She placed the refreshments next to Wisteria and looked at the grandchild denting her daughter's lap.

'Well, well,' she muttered. 'That can't have come out without a fight.'

Wisteria threw back her head and howled.

4

There are degrees of burial. Jean survived the confinement of her mother's womb because, try as she might, Wisteria could not prise her daughter loose before her time. But in her mother's house, Jean was so held so deep and so fast that only a bomb could get her out. There were lessons to be learned at least; a wanted child would not have been as prepared.

Jean landed in her family like an albatross in a nest of sparrows. Her enormity at birth signified intent, not some temporary inflammation. She started as she meant to go on; she did not spurt, she did not fall down a hormonal rabbit-hole and emerge as big as the house. She progressed, slowly and steadily, on a path of uniquity.

Wisteria found Jean's physical excesses quite shameless, as if the child were deliberately drawing attention to herself, and she suspected Jean of some monstrous, concealed vanity that she did her best to wring out of her. She starved her and kept her constrained in too-small clothes until Jean burst out of them like overcooked sausage. But the girl was unstoppable.

Jean would grow to be a great, loosely strung together thing topped by a mass of dark hair that started in a dense fog about her head and radiated out in a fluffy wave, seemingly independent of gravity. Magnificently large, she did not waver in the breeze like those who have been stretched on nature's rack. Spun beyond their capabilities, they are small people taken to an extreme, elongated rather than exponential, as thin and precarious as pulled toffee. Jean would inhabit every inch fully; her chest wasn't sunken or her legs spindly, her fingers did not look like melting wax, drooping palely downwards from overburdened wrists, her face wasn't as long as a sermon, ending in a dull point. Robust and quite heroically proportioned, in a former life she would have guarded a temple — or pulled one down on herself. It was a miracle, considering the odds.

★ ★ ★

Jean's first few years were the most precarious, as she served little purpose. She could not work, brought no pleasure and was possessed of no talent to entertain or engage. Childhood diseases seemed unable or unwilling to ravage her, so the final word on her survival was Wisteria's, and Wisteria could wait. She had a deadly patience for things she considered her due. Jean was fed and bathed by her father and, at night, positioned next to him in a box in the front room to keep her cries from waking the rest of the house. Though she never cried. When she became mobile, she was sent to the attic room, and Wisteria put down tacks outside the doorway to discourage any ideas Jean might come by of feeding herself up in the night, or escaping.

Jean survived this fallow period because she brought in more than she cost. Wisteria had no fear of charity, unlike many of her generation. She revelled in the idea that some do-gooder would finance the upbringing of her idiot child. She wheeled and then walked Jean round the various societies with practised tales of deprivation and depravity, claiming money for food, for clothes, for moral re-education, whatever was going. As Jean's eyes rolled in her half-starved head, panels of adjudicators would take one look at her and hand over the money, pitying the poor mother who had to bring up such a useless thing. A child for life, Wisteria would sigh.

Though she was permitted life, Jean was not permitted much of what makes life endurable. Emotionally, she was feral — even a child raised by wolves would at least get its face licked every once in a while. Wisteria had decided that she would raise a stupid, obedient child who would experience exactly as much misery as she had. Perhaps more. She saw no possibility beyond that.

Jean was occupied by the physical. Trained like a monkey to perform tasks, she earned days of life with each one accomplished, buying a month or two by mastering the collection of bread, perhaps as much as a year with her ability to wash clothes. Every spare ounce of concentration was put into controlling the arms and legs that seemed to shoot out from her body like anchor chains plunging into the deep. She had to keep her expanding form from damaging the household, or all ground won would be lost. Jean stepped deliberately, full with the knowledge that anything beneath her foot was halfway to becoming a fossil. When she fell, she fell like a rotted beam. She wasn't slow, she was in another time. As someone without sight marks out every groove in a board, navigates by every tear of wallpaper, Jean could measure the distance between herself and anything that could be broken. She was surrounded by a haze of caution that would condense around objects; they would glisten in her sight, and she would breathe in around them.

Wisteria allowed Jean to attend school after it became a condition set by some of the children's societies she drew upon; the six-year-old Jean put on the pinafore of a dead ten-year-old neighbour and began another kind of education. Her attendance was erratic — she never knew when she might be required to scrub steps or appear in front of a charity board — but she somehow managed to learn to read and write, though recitations would always be beyond her. Her life had been one of silence against the roar of her mother's rage. When called upon in class for the first time, she made noises like the crying of a loon as her vocal cords vibrated under unfamiliar stress. She hadn't spoken more than a sentence in the month beforehand; paragraphs were rare, and her vocabulary small. Jean knew the words of her mother's disgust, she felt them when they were spat against her skin, but she was backwards in her understanding of what it was to communicate. To Wisteria, parenting was a soliloquy, not a conversation; 'I like' was a revelation to her six-year-old daughter, its application almost beyond her. Wisteria warned

Jean not to get too clever to be of use; she tried to navigate her education accordingly and managed never to shine — dutifully becoming the dulled automaton of her mother's dreams.

By the time Jean was seven, Wisteria had become quite creative with her tortures. In the summer of that year, she took her daughter to a circus, a Victorian throwback where glands hyperactive or lazy had conspired to produce women with wispy beards, men with protruding eyes and batwing ears and little people of both sexes, the genetic opposite of Jean. Wisteria wanted to go for herself, but thought something useful might be had from the day for Jean: a lesson for her future. First they saw a pretty girl in a flesh-coloured suit, spangled with sequins, who rode a dappled pony and could stand on its back. Wisteria saw Jean look up at the tiny figure, and down at her own already solid physique and sigh. The thrill of it made Wisteria giggle. But the real treat was the curiosities area. She expected her child to cry, to scream for mercy and forgiveness. To shrink. Jean had stared in wonder at the pony girl, at her shimmering form, but she didn't feel the pull until she saw the sad, dark stalls that housed the beings who were a little too wondrous; who pushed at the bounds of the possible from the wrong side. The freaks. Along with the expected fear of confinement and naked display, Jean felt a little tug, an urge to slip behind the rope and take her place among them. But she had no idea how.

Wisteria had done her job well: Jean seemed entirely ignorant of the possibility of freedom.

Theirs was not a household from which there was parole. Jean inhaled resignation and swallowed defeat, unconsciously absorbing the fact that there was nowhere to go but around. She felt it from her father, who had left an arm in France and all hope elsewhere, and even her ferocious grandmother, who had long accepted her dependence on the whims of another.

Jean's grandmother had no intention of being left out of the sham marriage her daughter had made — or the house she had gouged from it. They shared both a bedroom and a distaste for Wisteria's husband and child. In the day, the old woman occupied a corner of the parlour with the tenacity of dust, her greasy black clothes shining like oiled feathers beneath her weathered, beaky face. She passed the time in silent contemplation; realising after an hour or more that she had no idea what had been going on in her mind for that hour, marvelling at that for a few minutes and then drifting back to the blankness. She didn't like to think on any specific thing, she might dwell on some unpleasantness that would then tie up her digestive system for a while. (Thinking of her missing husband tended to do that to her, making her feel bloated and ill at ease — though as a memory he was little more than a pale shadow on a wall these days, having left without being persuaded in front of a photographer.) Her slices of cake and her cups of tea and the wireless provided a meaningless but not unpleasant accompaniment to her inertia. It was a full day before her first stroke was noticed.

Only one arm was left fully functioning. She didn't like to drink her tea when Wisteria's husband took his, as she felt he mimicked her like some impudent comic or fairground mirror — though he had been one-armed first.

To this wizened woman — four foot ten with corsets, four foot eight without — Jean was something she shared space with, but could never acknowledge as anything to do with her line. She suspected Jean of having been brought back from an expedition to darkest Africa, as the girl was oddly reminiscent of the subjects of a photograph seen in an article about a great exhibition (an event Jean's grandmother judged to have been full of dangerously foreign ideas and superfluous English ones). She would think of the group of elegantly lofty warriors captured by the camera, peer at Jean's wavy hair and prodigious length, shake her head and mutter, 'Hottentot,' under her breath. Jean didn't know what the word meant, and worried that it was a curse that, should it land on her, would transform her into something very small that the old lady could keep in a jar.

Successive strokes whittled away at the old woman's flesh and speech; she was left mute and dribbling by the time Jean was ten. The penultimate explosion tore through her brain mid-mutter, the word 'Hottentot' collapsing in on itself until it became something like 'Tottenham', then she fell silent and remained so. But her eyes became eloquent. She would fix the child with a coruscating stare that left Jean feeling coated in blame. She would always be amazed by her capacity to startle her own family. They never did seem to get used to her.

The year of her grandmother's silencing would also be the year of her father's death. Jean thought of him as winding down rather than dying; while alive he seemed in perpetual, degenerative motion, diverted by barked commands from Wisteria as to where he could and could not sit, stand or drink his tea. Jean's abiding memory was of him moving slowly and lightly about the house, a ghost in carpet slippers with toast crumbs speckling the front of his waistcoat like fine beading, a pinhead of stray dripping as an occasional pearl.

He became less precise as the years went by, seeming to float from room to room. Too insubstantial to open a door if it happened to be closed to him, he would take another turn about the room he was in and wait for someone else to tackle the tangible so he could cross the threshold and continue on his circuitous journey. He never seemed to be at rest for more than a few seconds, until he was found dead one day in his chair. He had stopped moving and could not be started again; like a drumming toy he had worn himself out.

Jean would not be able to remember feeling particularly upset when he died. It was as if a neighbour, to whom one waved every morning, had suddenly moved to another town. Her father passed her often on his way to or back from some part of the house and would look hard at her round face, as if close to remembering the acquaintance who had first introduced them. His regard for his daughter was characterised by polite bemusement. Fellow voyagers on this ship of fools, they had merely booked passage with a bad agent and could only, in the English way, roll their eyes when confronted with another bad meal they had paid too much for.

The death of her husband did not seem to calm or satisfy Wisteria; she embraced the tragedy with the vigour of spring-cleaning, throwing open the windows on her resentment and letting the gloom pour in. She took a perverse pleasure in being left in 'circumstances', as she described them: a war widow with a dependent mother and retarded daughter. Shopkeepers would shrug and add another potato, a couple of carrots, a rasher or two. Wisteria took back little bits from the world, a piece at a time, with the glee of an amateur conning a professional. This was part of her war of attrition. She battled life for all she could get from it, which was small beer indeed. When true war came again, it made equals in suffering. For Wisteria, with her store of resentments, slights and deprivations, it was like scaling the summit only to find no room for her flag.

Over the years, Jean was worn smooth by the unceasing stream of deprecation and chastisement, offering no resistance. Her life was an interpretative dance of avoidance; she sought the edges, where she could do less harm. The brief time at school was her one opportunity to be a child, and she had no idea what to make of it. Her attempts to join in school games often led to injury and exile; she skinned the insides of legs by holding skipping ropes too high; cleared hopscotch in a single bound; had an unfortunate habit of misjudging leapfrog and was just far too terrifying to be allowed to join in any chase. She had no friends. Until Gloria.

5

The daughter of a confectioner inhabits a special place in seaside society. This one could have collected friends as easily as collecting powdered sugar with a wet finger; but instead she collected causes.

Gloria Smith's father had owned a sweet shop inland, where he made a modest living. Except on holidays. His shop faced the bus station, and as he watched the daytrippers stagger from their charters, noting the sugar-glazed eyes of children, the pained expressions of bloated women and the embarrassed air that hung around grown men who had made themselves sick on ice cream, he wondered why he was wasting his time with penny bags and valentines.

Jean's rather poky and peeling resort town had worked 'end' into its name as either a warning or an admission, and was not the most favoured on the coast. It had little money to advertise itself and usually gained mention in the newspapers only after the hottest day of the year, when people driven mad by the sun were pictured braving the icy waters that sluiced its stony shores. The rest of the time it was home to a shapeless, shifting population of brush salesmen who occupied its promenade hotels, the smell of bad breakfasts and disappointment spreading back over the town from there. But it could be reached in a day from the city, and so Mr Smith bought a shop in the commercial street and leased a stand on the promenade. Gloria rode into Jean's life on a wave of sherbet.

By the time she was eleven, Jean was seen not so much as a prepubescent child of average intelligence but a moronic adult who had failed to progress. She was treated as such and rarely called upon. A new table and chair had to be requisitioned from the staff room for Jean, her eleven-year-old legs having been so constricted under the tiny child's desk that they were often completely dead when she tried to stand; she had fallen a few times, occasionally dangerously close to other children. The new table was delivered to the classroom and for the first time since she was eight, Jean sat down and took her first full-lunged breaths, letting the trenches that the child's desk had dug into her stomach and thighs fill with cautious, tingling flesh.

Jean's teacher, Miss Gormast, did not respond well to this silent challenge to her status. She was a small woman with tight hair and loose tweeds who drew what power she had from furniture. Her desk and chair, set on a level above the rest of the class, conferred the rule of the room on her. She felt Jean's equally imposing fixtures drawing it away. Her eye line had remained uncluttered for thirty years, and it unnerved her to be caught in Jean's liquid gaze. Miss Gormast took to populating her table with a fearsome array of weapons, including sharp metal rules and a frayed cane. (She tried sitting on a cushion to elevate herself above the head of her tallest pupil, but this only gave rise to a rumour about piles, and the white-knuckle hold she had on the class began to erode.) Jean began a conscious effort to retract herself, but the more she attempted to slide from view, the more her fluid spine was seen as a challenge to order and decency. She and her teacher developed the relationship of eager dog and erratic master. 'Sit up!' when Jean started to melt across the furniture, 'Get down!' when she rose into Miss Gormast's eye line. She was always between commands, never able fully to complete a move, and so she vacillated between levels, her spine twisting painfully. After too many days of this, Miss Gormast ordered her to stay down and Jean gratefully slumped in disgrace. Like an old beaten collie, she raised only her sad eyes from then on.

The relaxing of Jean's posture soon spread to the others, the boys first; they discovered the exquisite joy of going against the grain. As they had shared their measles and their colds, the virus of slouching seeped into them all. Eventually unravelled by this silent opposition, Miss Gormast decided to take action.

She slapped the palm of her hand with a metal rule, causing bottoms to inch back onto seats, arms to discreetly withdraw under desks. Jean did not know what to do: to sit bolt upright was a challenge as direct as a slap in the face but to continue to slide was outright defiance. She was caught.

'If you cannot sit up straight, I will have to teach you how to sit up straight.'

Miss Gormast snatched a bundle of long

41

wooden rulers from her table, and, pulling back the jumpers of the first few unfortunates to be within her reach, roughly shoved the rulers down the gap between skin and fabric, staking them to their chairs from waistband to neck.

'You will not deviate one eighth of an inch from the line of that ruler, do you hear me? If you do so, you will all stand against the wall all day, is that understood?'

And with a final flourish she plunged the last ruler down Jean's back, not noticing it was shorter than the others. It was swallowed up like a lolly stick by a sack. Incensed, Miss Gormast gave an anguished roar and tore out of the room. She reappeared a minute later brandishing a large cricket bat. Jean blanched, she was to be beaten to death before lunch, and not even by her own mother.

'Lean forward,' Gormast hissed. She held the bat up like a spear and repeated her demand. 'Lean . . . forward.'

Jean blinked, fat tears pooling on the crest of her cheeks, and obliged; to oblige was her purpose after all. Tearing the pinafore from Jean's back, the teacher thrust the bat down, scraping skin from bone. She then took a tie from one of the boys, fastened Jean's head to the handle and left her there like an early Christian. It was at this moment that Gloria Smith arrived.

Gloria had a fondness for Bible stories, gleaned thirdhand through garishly coloured illustrations from annuals bought by her busy parents who bagged sugar and cleaned shelves on Sundays and had no time for church. She was possessed of a sentimental bent that led her to envision herself as a saviour of fledglings, kidnapped heiresses, babies from burning buildings and so on. When she entered her new classroom for the first time, she was greeted by the extraordinary sight of a real-life martyr trapped, apparently, in an agony of stoicism. The wordless Jean, bound to her stake, was too much for Gloria to bear; she fell instantly in love with the suffering of this outsize creature and — her imagination flooded with an illustration from one of her favourite stories — longed to remove the thorn from its paw, or in this case, the cricket bat from its back. Gloria was in the orbit of a lost cause and surrendered fully to the pull. She took the place next to Jean, turned to her, blue eyes rippling with tears, gently touched her grubby sleeve and smiled.

Gloria instructed Jean to wait for her after school and secured her with the offer of a boiled sweet (which Jean wouldn't eat but instead take home and secrete under the wallpaper where, a few days later, she found it had melted into the wall). At the end of that first day, Gloria took Jean by the hand (which alone made her dizzy with sensation) and led her to an empty patch of ground close to her parents' shop.

'What do you play?' she asked, as they scratched pictures in the dirt. Gloria's was of a princess hat with a flowing veil; Jean's was of a cat. She had never been allowed a pet, and Wisteria threw lit matches at strays.

Jean shrugged. 'Don't know. I'm not really allowed to play with the others.'

43

Gloria added a mass of ringlets. 'Who says?'

'The others,' Jean admitted. 'I broke someone's arm once when I fell on them.'

'You can play with me.' Gloria leaned over and changed the mouse snout on Jean's cat into something more feline and made the tail bushier. 'I can tell you what to do.'

And so Jean became Gloria's cult of one. For a glorious half-hour that afternoon, Jean had stones thrown at her. Gloria was not always entirely accurate and occasionally one would bounce off Jean's shoulder with a sharp sting, and she would wince. Although it occasionally hurt as much, this was different from the other times stones had been thrown at her after school. It was a game she was part of at least.

'They don't hurt,' Gloria explained. 'You're Goliath. When you're dead I'll tell you, but up until then you don't get hurt. The next one won't get you. I promise.'

Jean nodded and continued to wave her arms above her head in an approximation of violent rage. Despite having witnessed more than her fair share of this, she was deficient in reproducing it. She already suspected that her meaty arms could unleash more than she could repair.

'All right then, die!' Gloria shouted, and Jean dropped to the floor with a satisfying thud.

'Hurrah!' Gloria whooped and ran over to the felled giant. She lay down next to Jean and rested her head on the wide expanse of her friend's stomach.

'That was very good. I had a friend before

44

who was quite good, but she didn't like doing the man parts and she was as small as I am, so I was never very convinced.'

'I don't mind,' Jean quickly answered. 'I'm very tall. And big like a boy. I can do all those parts, if you tell me how.'

'You can be Samson tomorrow,' Gloria offered. 'He dies too.'

Jean laughed and bounced Gloria's head up and down. 'I can do that. I can do anything you like.'

It was a matter of luck that Gloria never came across anyone she wanted killed.

The game made Jean late, something she had never been before. Wisteria wouldn't suspect she had a friend; it would be some years before Gloria's name was mentioned in the house. Jean was conditioned, but not without a spark of intelligence. She knew that Wisteria would simply take away anything that pleased her, as she had done with even fragments of dolls found in the street. Wisteria brooked no distractions; hers was a police state where information was controlled and outsiders distrusted. She didn't want anyone giving Jean ideas. Jean stood at the bottom of the stairs, reluctant to take another step towards her punishment. But Wisteria was in no hurry to give it.

'Take the bunting down,' she sneered over her shoulder as she turned away. 'The bastard's back.'

She slouched into the flat and kicked the door shut with a slippered foot. It would be opened again, after dinner was gone, after Jean had already had to pee in the vegetable patch and drink from the old birdbath. Crouched down among the turnips and leeks, she fired an imaginary slingshot up at the window and smiled. 'I've got Gloria and you've only got me,' she thought. 'Who's funny now?'

Later that night, Jean would have one eye beaten shut for her lateness, but the next day Gloria just turned her into a pirate — after she had given Jean's eyelid a kiss to heal it. Jean nearly expired from happiness; she had never felt anything so soft against her skin.

From then on they were bound. Jean found respite from brutality, and Gloria made her fantasies of salvation flesh. The hours and minutes of Jean's life were jealously guarded by Wisteria, who had uses for them all. But Jean could wrap a year's abuse in a minute's kindness, so Gloria was enough for her.

The friends entered womanhood at the age of fourteen, within two months of each other. Jean had staved it off the longer of the two, her body perhaps knowing that Gloria would have to get there first, as no one else would be waiting for her with cups of tea and soothing words. Armed with a parcel of clean rags and some new and shocking information, she returned home. Her mother and grandmother were having tea by the fire — her grandmother took hers in a baby's bottle by then; Wisteria had no patience with people breaking cups. Jean told her the school nurse had provided the rags. 'Just gets worse, doesn't it?' Wisteria jeered. ''Bout time you got a bloody job if you think you're that grown up.'

Jean left school and childhood behind the next day. Wisteria sent her to work without expectations of anything more than Jean repaying her debt. On her first day at the cardboard factory, Wisteria walked her to the door. 'Listen hard and do what you're told,' she said. 'No one's going to forgive you anything.'

6

As the country advanced out of depression and again towards war, Jean expanded in a well-measured arc from lumpen child to sprawling adult, her forehead permanently discoloured from bruising run-ins with beams and bus roofs. Her large, liquid eyes conspired with her large, solid frame to put some people in mind of a cow; the fact that she moved and smiled with near bovine shyness reinforced the image. Gloria, meanwhile, soared from plump adorability to voluptuous sweetness, a twist of mallow from one of her father's own shelves. Her romantic nature had developed in tandem with her bustline; both were full to bursting. Everywhere Gloria went, she went to fall in love.

Gloria left school the year after Jean and went to work in her father's shop. Going to and from the factory allowed Jean to pass by every day, and stop in for hot tea and gentle words. And so they continued. Too old for outdoor games, they mastered the interior. Secrets are the currency with which women secure their friendships, and by telling hers to Jean, Gloria might as well have buried them in an oak. On snatched afternoons, she showed Jean the wedding dress she would wear, the baby carriage she would push, the flat she would live in, above a shop just like her father's. The man she would marry was cobbled together from film-fan magazines, eyes from one, the chin of another. She had only to wait until she was eighteen, and it would all be hers. Jean hoped he might be wealthy enough to employ her as a servant, freeing her from the less pleasant servitude of her mother's house. Together they imagined this enchanted life, which seemed Gloria's due. She was too lovely to imagine in any other scenario.

Since starting work in her father's shop, Gloria had been besieged by hordes of spotty youths, whose skin never improved thanks to the amounts of whipped, beaten and crystallised sugars they were obliged to consume. A steady stream of hopefuls sacrificed skin and dentine at the altar of Gloria, loitering in the shop, watching her measure out quarters of sherbet until their heads ached from the sugary air. Aware that the long Saturday night of a father's life had begun, Gloria's gave his sixteen-year-old daughter permission to start walking out. He also made a condition; if she was to walk into the darkness and the anxious, ambulatory arms of the young men of the district, Jean would go too.

Wisteria was still unaware of Gloria. A story had to be invented; one that left Jean innocent of having kept anything as prohibited as a friend from her mother. A chance meeting was decided on; old school fellows whose paths had crossed at the factory gates. Wisteria accepted the meeting, but was unconvinced of the outcome.

'Why's she wanting to saddle herself with you? Is she simple or something? I'm not having you gallivanting about with some tart, getting up to all sorts while I'm stuck here with your gran running myself ragged. I know what you want, you little whore, and you're not getting it.'

This was not unexpected. Jean had then proffered the enormous box of chocolates sacrificed to the mission, the sight of which caused Wisteria to drool a little, and began her speech.

'Mr Smith says to thank you for considering letting me chaperone his daughter. He's sure . . . he's sure that she won't be bothered with me alongside her. Boys being what they are, he sees no harm coming to me, or her.' They thought this would appeal to Wisteria's sense of her daughter's prospects. 'He wonders if you won't be offended if he makes up for the time lost with this gift.' Jean showed Wisteria the price tag, which made her drool even more. As an offering, it cost Gloria's father little, but it was the only ransom anyone would ever pay for Jean, and it had to be enough.

'You've got sheets to iron, and the fires to set.'

'They'll all be done before I go, Mum.'

Wisteria snatched the box from her daughter's grasp. Even with her canny management of Jean's pay and her husband's pension, this was a luxury she could rarely afford.

'Once a week till she's sick of you, with the same every week for me. No less. Pictures and back, no talking to men, no dances.' Wisteria forced three chocolates at once into her gummy maw and sighed with undisguised pleasure. 'Go on then, Cinderella, fuck off.'

Her instinctive response would have been to deny Jean the simple pleasure of a companion.

50

To be taken an interest in or even shown something like kindness could corrupt her, fill her full of expectation that Wisteria would then have to beat out of her. But Jean earned her nothing sitting at home, she reasoned.

If her daughter had been prettier she would probably have prostituted her outright, but Wisteria was at least sincere in her belief that none but the wholly perverted would have anything to do with the likes of Jean, and would no doubt pay less than the cardboard factory for the pleasure. She was satisfied with expensive confectionery and the promise that Jean would be returned with her ignorance and virtue intact. Wisteria had a very small yet very real fear of losing her daughter. Despite the certainty she felt in Jean's mismatch with the world, she knew that if anything happened to her, she would never be able to afford a servant to replace her. She also couldn't hate a servant as much. And hating was what Wisteria loved. Letting Jean out would put her in the way of possibility, but would also show her what it was to be in the world, what it took to be accepted by it. Jean would quickly learn that she had no place there, that there would be no fairy-tale release from bondage for her as no one but Wisteria would give her house room. She was lucky, she'd see, to have somewhere to hide away, somewhere her aberrant nature was tolerated if not excused. And so Jean was allowed to accompany Gloria out into the world.

7

Gloria turned eighteen unwed and unimpressed. By the time of her last peacetime date, a cold war was being waged against her. She had first appeared both pure and approachable, particularly in her father's shop, when sherbet crystals were embedded in her cuticles. She was on display for seven hours each day and was frequently called upon to stretch in any one of perhaps seven directions in order to locate the precise brand of confectionery requested. Once Gloria had been discovered, there didn't seem any point in looking for anyone else; all that remained was the matter of who would actually win her. As if they had a say in it. They didn't know what she was waiting for, nor the extent of her patience.

Her creation was as real to her as anything; she was waiting for it to be flesh. As Gloria tried and rejected each new suitor, the tide turned. Her beauty became a reproach. Her devotion to Jean, always seen as strange, was now suspect. A new note was being sounded in the shop's calorific air. The boys that came were no longer enthralled, silent and blushing. They seemed aroused to vulgarity, smirking and suggestive. She had been unobtainable too long. Gloria began to sense that although she was still desired, she was no longer liked. It seemed that unless it was to cross actual frozen wastes,

Englishmen didn't much like a challenge after all.

Jean faithfully accompanied Gloria on every date, earning the nickname 'The Shadow'. Then one wag noticed her thick dark hair and the ghost of a moustache on her pale upper lip, and she was dubbed the 'Five O'Clock Shadow'. She expected nothing for herself from the search, knowing it to be a fact that she was unmatchable within the laws of man and nature; her mother had seen to it. Wisteria may have known little about men — she sought compensation, not experience, from life — but she knew that the loneliest fringe could be home to more than one. Jean once went out with a paper flower clipped into her hair; Gloria had told her it would make her look pretty. Wisteria told her she might as well cast a ribbon onto a dung heap but tore it out anyway, saying: 'You may be a big dumb animal, but there's them that'll worry a cow in a field.' Jean was an aberration, and the only thing worse than that was someone who had a fancy for one; that was a sickness. Jean didn't doubt it. Her size threw men into confusion, like birds during an eclipse. Most could not bring themselves to walk alongside her in plain sight and, having been trapped into the role of Jean-wrangler for the evening, allowing their friend who was better looking, older or more skilled at coin toss to accompany Gloria, would wander vaguely behind her like an embarrassed concubine, eventually disappearing into the past or a concealed ditch. Sometimes Jean longed for these nights to end, but that would only happen when Gloria had found her ideal, and then Jean would be lost for ever.

The Friday before the war, not quite forty-nine days before the dissolution of the house, Jean was waiting for Gloria to arrive. Her day had been spent at work as usual, her evening cooking, cleaning, and then reading aloud to her soured mother and ancient, rotting grandmother. Wisteria liked historical romances in which women were stretched on the rack or by childbirth and died in tightly corseted misery. Crime novels were also tolerated. Thanks to a misdirected order from a reading club, Jean was presently engaged with a book in which the goodness of a young governess triumphed over more obvious physical charms to win the heart of her troubled master. Wisteria found it a wicked black comedy in which a dullard was duped into becoming handmaiden to a cripple. 'I'd have more sense,' she sniffed. Jean read from it again that evening, and on reaching a particularly impassioned speech from the heroine — in which she argued that poverty and plainness was no barrier to soulful feeling — had to pause while her mother recovered from a bout of hilarity. Wisteria's smoky laugh started like a cold engine and rolled from the back of her throat. Jean placed her finger on the book and waited for the laughter to turn into a coughing fit and be spat out.

'Silly bitch,' Wisteria chuckled. 'Doesn't she get on your nerves? No wonder he only wants her once the house has fallen on him. Wouldn't look twice otherwise.'

Wisteria had conveniently forgotten her deliberate targeting of her weakened husband. The story was that he had begged her to marry him before the war and she had been kind enough to overlook the fact that he was no longer fit. She flicked her eyes at Jean, who was sat on a cushion on the floor, saving the furniture. She had been saving the furniture since she was nine and had gone through a very old chair.

'Shame we can't do that for you, eh, lumpy? Get you a nice cripple boy who won't mind so much.'

It was routine for Wisteria to snap on the psychic shackles prior to letting her daughter stray into the path of humanity which, with its deviancy and vice, could contain a threat to her rule. Gloria had negotiated a double bill at the cinema, and so four hours of freedom had to be weighted with terror and disappointment before Jean was let loose. The purloined book suited this purpose of Wisteria's very well. The long laugh petered out into a wet cough, then Wisteria cleared her throat and spat into the fire. Jean marvelled at the amount of her mother's insides that got expelled each day and imagined the disgusted fire spitting back.

'That's what you need,' Wisteria chuckled, 'someone who's generous to a fault, or two. Bring the house down, you would, just leaning on a beam. Pure poison. Still, soon there'll be nothing left but the lazy, the lame and the mad,' she continued. 'Have your pick then. Though I don't know why they bother sending all the shiny new ones off, if it comes to it, should just send the dregs from the last war.'

Jean nodded as if she were appreciating the cleverness of the remark while she imagined the walls tumbling down around them. Lucky bloody orphan, she thought, clutching the book. She glanced at the clock. Gloria would be another ten minutes at least.

'Make some tea before you go, and wash the cups properly this time. I could taste last night's pie in the last lot.'

Probably still had some stuck in your teeth, thought Jean. She picked herself up and placed the governess and her hard-won lover back on the shelf.

'What about Gran?'

Wisteria glanced at her mother in the corner, deeply involved in chewing some imaginary piece of food. She shook her head. 'She's had three cups today, don't want her leaking it.' She lit a cigarette. 'Put her on the pot before you put her in the bed.' She flicked the match into the grate and inhaled deeply; Jean could see the anticipated pleasure of being alone with her bribe from Mr Smith was building: she was practically smiling.

The unpleasant job done, Jean rinsed her hands and then filled the kettle. Her strapping, inescapable self filled the low kitchen window. She had passed through the window in stages. First, only the top of her head was visible; the window's gaze now rested square on her chest and her head was to be imagined somewhere above it. Jean closed her eyes and waggled her fingers in the cooling, greasy dishwater. Since Gloria had introduced her to play, she often tried on her own to transport herself to the other worlds glimpsed in her friend's company. Gloria created husbands and children from air and built them houses to live in, spun them clothes to wear and sometimes even killed them tragically so that she could mourn them beautifully. But without Gloria, Jean was immovable; each day brought the impossibility of change. She had enormous form but as yet no function.

'Just what *are* you for?' she asked her reflection. The shockheaded ghost said nothing; they were no longer alone.

'Talking to yourself? Fit for the loony bin, you are.'

Wisteria was in the doorway; she had waited too long for her tea.

'That'll get you off my hands, won't it, get you put away in the nuthouse. I should've thought of it before. Get the doctor round in the morning shall I, sign the papers?'

As Jean grew, Wisteria realised that she had little physical control of her monstrous child. To hold her fully, Wisteria would need to turn her from the inside out. Only for the very rich and very poor is madness a refuge; the destitute can ramble from shop doorways, and the moneyed have vast houses to wander round in with their hair on fire. But be just poor enough and just unloved enough and just useless enough, and they could take you. The bleakest, filthiest room in the asylum awaited Jean. She would become even stranger, her legs would twist and so would her brain. The pain of it would make her present life seem like a kiss.

Wisteria kept her daughter near with the threat of that dark room; she let Jean know that if anyone found out how she really was, how she shamed her father into an early grave, gave her grandmother a stroke and nearly finished off her mother, they'd take her away in a second. While she was under that rotten roof, with a mother to vouch for her, she could pass for normal at least. Jean hugged her arms, feeling the sane straightness of her limbs; the one thing she doubted less than them was her mother's ability to take her out of the light. As long as she could remember it, it had been prophecy. She slipped her hands back into the water.

'I was just going over the words to some songs, for the singalong before the picture.'

'Oh, really? Didn't sound like that to me. The doctors'll have a field day with you,' her mother sneered. 'Hope they've got a jar big enough for all the bits when they've finished.'

Jean broke the handle of the cup under the water. Her hands were shaking. She would have to hide it and glue it later.

'Do you still want that tea, Mum?'

'Unless I have to get it myself on top of everything else. Be quick about it, Little Miss Tits is here.'

8

Gloria never lingered at Jean's. On her first visit, she had found it very much as she had pictured, but too real, too full of menace. It dampened her imagination even as it strengthened her resolve. There was so much to rescue Jean from it might never be done. Wisteria had looked her up and down, sneering as she did so. She let her eyes linger on Gloria's lipstick, hair ribbons and newly shined shoes, coming close enough for Gloria to smell her breath. 'Pah!' was all she had said, the force of the word hitting Gloria square in the face. She felt her eyes water from humiliation as well as Wisteria's halitosis, but still returned the next week, armed with soft toffees and inexhaustible Christian charity.

The exchange that night was swift; Jean for sweets. The double bill was the cover for a dance, and they took their time walking to the hall, savouring the opportunity to smoke cigarettes and laugh at Wisteria, who became pathetic once out of striking distance. They were both a little nervous. It was more than what was to come, it was what might never arrive.

Paul Bradshaw would be the end. An apprentice mechanic and enthusiastic torturer of cats, he was unknown to Gloria until he passed the sweet shop and happened to look in when she was up a ladder reaching for some dusty jar. Her father had put the foulest sweets up high in a bid to keep her on the ground and was, in a small way, responsible for their continued production long after they had fallen out of favour elsewhere. Having not attended their school, Paul was a mystery to Gloria and Jean. In a town such as theirs, gossip often bred and died within just a few streets. Though people could be suffocated by the weight of words exchanged, to escape from under them sometimes required a journey of just a mile or two. Gloria and Jean had never heard of him, but he was well known to others.

He was at least bringing a friend, this was a condition. A cousin. Leonard. Cousin Leonard came down from town for two weeks each year. He had been raised by his parents so as to guarantee that not only would he never come to live in a declining seaside town but that he would be entirely unable to carry out a civil conversation with anyone from one. Their aim had been achieved through a combination of neglect and expensive schooling.

Faced with fourteen days of uninterrupted tedium, Leonard, a studious milk of seventeen, had taken the precaution of bringing thirty-two paperback novels with him. When his aunt helped him settle his things into the half of his cousin's room that was to be his for the fortnight, and saw the great stack of books, she exclaimed: 'You won't need all those, silly. It can't rain every day.' He withered her with a glance.

Cousin Leonard was a reluctant participant in the evening. He had learned his fate at supper.

His aunt, who was in the know, could barely contain herself, and a saucy, conspiratorial look roamed about her face like a cat under a blanket.

'Going out courting, are we?' she spluttered, with a wink that pierced Leonard's soul.

But as his choice lay between the date or staying at home with his aunt and uncle and only a wireless between them and the possibility of conversation, Leonard had acquiesced. Ten minutes after the last mouthful of liver had been coaxed down his protesting throat, he was marching miserably towards his fate, trying not to suffocate in the exhaust plume of toilet water, hair oil and cheap cigarettes that trailed from his cousin. Leonard's mood was black. Having heard Paul's description of Jean, he imagined himself grappling with a bearded lady, while his cousin charmed his way under the shirt of her luscious friend, as he had promised Leonard he would do. Before leaving, Leonard had filled every available pocket with a paperback novel. If he could not persuade the creature to let him alone to read, he was at least sufficiently weighted to throw himself into the sea and drown.

Usually, Jean had consciously to slow her steps to allow Gloria to keep pace, but on the way to social events they were effortlessly abreast. When they arrived, it was still early, but the atmosphere in the church hall was that of the last fifteen minutes of a marathon dance. Crêpe streamers already sagged down over the empty floor. A tired trio of local ladies sawed out some half-familiar tunes on borrowed instruments. A trestle table, bowed from the weight of tea urns and orange squash, was positioned in front of a low stage. The stage was masked with thick dusty curtains behind which couples attempted to disappear, but were beaten out like moths by the chaperones — flinty-eyed knitters armed with disapproval and rolledup newspapers.

Paul Bradshaw was waiting by the refreshment stand holding a cup of spiked orange and few good intentions. Cousin Leonard stood next to him, sipping an unadulterated cup of tea. Jean and Gloria lingered at the doors, scanning the room. A spotlight illuminated them and made Gloria's hair shine like polished metal. She had a knack for seeking out a flattering aspect. Jean noticed that the attention of almost everyone in the room was directed to the left of her; she turned and looked too. Gloria really was lovely. Her blonde hair fell in perfect waves, while her heart-shaped face was the signifier of her sweet nature. Her eyes were limpid pools, her mouth a rosebud, her ears shells and her teeth pearls. An artist could have captured her, but any child could have invented her. She was not a challenge, she was obvious and undisguised in her loveliness. Jean felt she had been thrown into sharp relief; requiring, on the other hand, more than a little imagination. They stepped out of the light, and one or two boys audibly sighed.

Paul drove his elbow into his cousin's side, causing him to spill his tea.

'The blonde one's mine,' he said, squeezing the words out of a very small gap at the corner of his mouth.

There was no need for him to stake his claim; Jean and Leonard recognised each other immediately. To her, he looked like an armchair that was losing its stuffing. His jacket struggled to contain the paperbacks that were sprouting from his pockets; he bulged at the hips and chest and seemed in dire need of some parcel string. To him, she looked like a sight gag, and he almost laughed when he saw her; the bashful, burly best friend being led by the petite little maid. He imagined her in a silent comedy, under a wide brim hat with a pouffy crown, holding a fringed purse and making cow eyes at a hapless Milquetoast who would then run up a finely balanced plank to escape her. The urge to laugh deserted him when he remembered what part he had been assigned.

Leonard patted the paperback-stuffed pocket and felt soothed. He would sit out this ridiculous mating dance and appear very severe and intellectual as he read. Some local beauty would probably want to strike up a conversation with him, so remote and fascinating would he seem — although he did fear being snared entirely by some pretty suburban sexpot, who might cause him to be dashed on the rocks of middle-class respectability. He wondered if the lady navvy could read.

Paul thought he had the measure of Gloria from their encounter in the sweet shop. Over-appreciated. She had taken his gift of chocolates as if she got chocolates every day of her life. Which she did. Gloria had tried to seem enthused. If she worked in an ironmonger's, she wondered, would they just buy the first bag of nails they saw on entering the shop and present them to her with such self-satisfaction? He had leaned right across the counter, and for a second she had been concerned for the till. Her father had rigged up a pull that led to a bell in the back, and she had hooked her finger lightly round the cord, not fully letting go until the door had closed behind him. Still, she told herself, he's not bad looking.

Paul offered Gloria a cup of orange, into which he had poured some more of the gin that he had swiped from his mother. She just needed loosening up, he told himself. It would do her good to let her foot slip off the pedestal. He was feeling thick-lipped and randy from the gin. Gloria turned her nose up at the orange.

'Tastes funny,' she said, grimacing. 'Here, Jean, you taste it.'

Jean drained the rest of the cup and shrugged. 'Seems all right,' she said, as a net of butterflies was turned loose in her head.

Paul smirked and offered her his cup. 'Here, have another. Plenty more where that came from.' He had lined up three more cups. 'Shall we dance, Gloria? Work up a thirst.'

'All right, Jean?'

'You go ahead.'

Paul grabbed Gloria's hand and spun her round before pulling her close to him. They danced away from Jean and Cousin Leonard, who immediately opened a book.

'Shall we sit down?' Jean asked, gesturing at the wall. She felt a little hot and swallowed another spiked orange drink. 'I think I'd like to sit down.'

Leonard shut his book with a sigh; he would have liked a hardback to make a dismissive noise with, but had to make do with the flap of a paper cover to convey his annoyance.

'Let us get some things straight between us. I am here only because the alternative is much, much worse, if you can believe such a thing.'

Another one that means to punish me, Jean thought. 'I hardly can,' she said as agreeably as she could. 'But, um, we could get clear of the middle of things?'

Leonard's affected manner had attracted few admiring glances since his arrival; paired with Jean, he was a magnet for derision. He seemed unaware of this as he preened in his cubist jacket and overlong hair. But Jean could feel the wash of ill-feeling lapping at their feet. She took a step towards the wall, where, between the bright spots cast by paper lanterns, welcoming pockets of darkness offered respite to the odd.

'My feet are really killing me,' Jean lied. 'I could really do with a sit down.'

'Very well,' Leonard assented, ungraciously. 'But we shall sit with one empty chair between us. I have already dealt with much unpleasantness tonight; to force more upon me would be a mistake.'

Jean gratefully made for the safety of the chairs and settled herself into the semi-darkness. She breathed a sigh of relief and leaned back, ready to make the best of a hideous night in relative comfort. Though the glare of attention was off her, she still felt a little warm, particularly in her face. Should have had another orange, she thought. Leonard sat down, directly under a lantern. He wanted to be seen not enjoying himself, passing judgement on the entire enterprise, and the lantern would serve as a reading lamp. He took the books from his pockets and tucked all but one of the precious paperbacks under his chair.

Leonard's taste in literature tended towards the controversial. Through business contacts in New York and Paris, Leonard's father furnished his son with the obscene works of the day. Leonard thought of himself as a pioneer, a renegade, an anarchist, even, in his proclaimed search for truth but — in truth — he asked for the books only to outrage his parents. These daring works distanced him from the bourgeoisie — which he considered his parents paid-up members of — and enhanced his view of himself as something of a radical. The fact that they left him baffled and/or queasy was neither here nor there.

He noticed Jean watching him attend to his little mobile library.

'I always carry at least one book,' he informed her. 'One never knows when one might need not to talk to people.'

'Oh right, very clever.' Jean had not realised that, on this occasion, she was people. 'Very prepared.'

The warm glow in her face had spread down to her neck, making it feel loose and long. She looked around at the couples now dancing, some

66

of them pointing at Leonard and whispering to each other. She was quite pleased to be only the second most ridiculous person in the room and felt well-disposed to him because of it. She didn't realise she was smiling at him. It irritated Leonard like a burr in his sock.

'So are you down from town for the summer? We get quite a lot of people from town, you know. Gloria serves them in the shop. I've never met any of them though, you're my first — '

Leonard cut Jean off by suddenly diving for the floor, as swift and pointed as a heron after a fish. He surfaced with a book, its cover obscured with brown paper, and leaned into the space between them.

'Do you read?' He seemed to have found a smile on the floor and was wearing it, despite it being tight and ill-fitting. He seemed less to speak the words than to sieve them through his teeth. Jean wished her jaw was as rigid; it felt loose.

'Oh, well, yes. I like to read, actually.' She waved her hand around, it too felt insecurely attached. 'Um, you know, books. Different books. I read to my mother, and grandmother. But she's had a stroke so I don't know if she hears anything. We haven't got many books though, not like you.'

'Perhaps you'd like to borrow this one?' Leonard interrupted. 'It's *very* different.'

He handed her the disguised book, and Jean took it, noticing a queer glint in his eye as if he had managed to buy a cow from her for a handful of dirt. The book he had given her was a particular favourite of the boys at school, and its ownership had spared him several thrashings, though it hadn't exactly made him popular. It was translated from the original French. Leonard had decided to make what little he could from the evening and amuse himself at Jean's expense. He had slipped her a literary mickey. The scene played out in his mind: her shock, consternation, her tiny mind convulsing at the dangerous words. If he could have wriggled and trilled 'delicious' without fear of a beating, he would have done so.

She took the book and leaned slightly towards the circle of light surrounding Leonard in order to see the words. Both their heads were now bowed in silent contemplation, as if parodying a medieval portrait of pious scholarship. Jean began to read.

On the dance floor, Gloria wrestled with the inebriated Paul. His hands were fast and profane, and his oil-stained shoes left smears on her summer sandals as he stumbled over her feet. Gloria tried for anger when it was fear she felt, fear this was all that was due to her.

'Stand up straight, what's the matter with you?'

'Whassa matter with you?' His eyes were glassy and unfocused. He buried his head in her neck and began to whine. 'Don't you like me?'

The dance floor had filled, bodies were packed in tightly around them. There were two lines of couples moving to the music, a wheel within a wheel; through occasional gaps in this slow-moving zoetrope Gloria could make out Jean, sitting by the wall. Reading. Gloria wrenched her arm free and waved at Jean, calling to her over the tuneless din of the band, but she didn't hear. Paul rubbed against Gloria as if she were a towel on which he was trying to dry himself. She felt his teeth at her neck and jerked her head away.

'Stop that! Leave me alone!'

He raised his head and looked down at her, running his tongue along his teeth.

'Mmmm, treacle *tart*; my favourite.'

Gloria gasped and tried to pull away. He held her by the wrists and swung her around, giggling. None of the other dancers seemed willing to notice her distress. The collective decision had been made; Gloria's time had come.

Cousin Leonard, meanwhile, could not work out what was going wrong. There had been no reaction, no screams, no embarrassment, no vomiting. He had chosen a book that went straight off, with no messing about; it must have had an effect by now. He was beginning to get impatient. He wondered if the idiot girl actually understood anything that she was reading. It was clear enough, although if she needed diagrams they were there too in the form of wickedly detailed illustrations. Jean read on, glad of the plain brown cover. The book concerned a young girl's sexual awakening at the hands of some dirty old man, its style a mixture of Victorian-lady allusion and butcher's window graphic. Jean was fascinated. Though some of the euphemisms left her confused as to whether she was reading about anatomy or horticulture, the occasionally explicit exploration of the human body was something altogether new to her, as was the concept of pleasure taken in a body and from one. Her head felt light from a mixture of gin and heresy. Could this really be happening somewhere? Was it possible for anyone, or just French girls with wicked old men? It seemed too large a leap to make between what was on the page and her expansive form. But no one she knew could jump higher.

Having invested some time and effort, Cousin Leonard felt cheated; this wasn't fun at all. She wasn't shocked, she wasn't sickened, she wasn't appalled. He had hoped for a lower-class explosion of 'ooh's' and 'well I nevers', followed by a theatrical exit. He would have chortled at her narrow-minded predictability and told the chaps about it. The dirty mare was simply drooling over the stuff. Leonard cheered himself with the thought of telling the chaps at school his version anyway. He restocked his pockets and buttoned his misshapen coat. Jean was still deeply immersed in the fleshpots of Paris; having reached a particularly tricky passage, she was flipping forward in search of clues when the book was snatched from her hand. She looked up to find Leonard bent down close to her, his breath hot on her ear.

'Slut,' he hissed.

Jean was bewildered. 'What?'

'Slut,' he repeated. 'Dirty slut.' Jean looked around in embarrassment and confusion.

'I didn't mean to. You gave me it, I didn't know.'

Leonard sneered, enjoying the small surge of power her distress gave him. Not what he had expected, but enough to be going on with.

'Your friend, the smaller slut, has gone off with my cousin. Not part of the deal, dearie, I'm not sitting here with you while he's away having it away. Ta ta to you.'

Cousin Leonard turned on his heel, a manoeuvre rendered less elegant than hoped by the fact he came loose in a pool of orange squash. Jean left him sliding in it, his balance compromised by the forest of paperbacks sprouting from his every pocket.

She headed for the middle of the dance floor; where was Gloria? Her forehead was suddenly slick with sweat, and she felt sick. The dance floor was a jumble; hands, knees and bumps-a-daisy. A side door had been opened to alleviate the heat; she looked just in time to see Paul push Gloria through it. Jean squeezed her way through the crowd, drawing curses from men and their partners as she threw them off their step. She lumbered through the door, knocking away the brick that was holding it open. The door swung back slowly, and before the light disappeared she saw Paul with his hands on a terrified Gloria — and he saw Jean, enormous against the narrow doorway. The orange glow that escaped from the hall gave her a dreadful outline; her hair looked aflame. The heat and nausea left her body; she trembled with rage and the certainty of her strength. A roar began deep in her; she felt it in her ankles, then behind her knees, coursing upwards with her blood to her thighs, buttocks,

71

the small of her back. It ran up her spine into her arms, filling her lungs to bursting before it gushed out of her mouth; a deafening tsunami of sound that became an anguished scream. Paul's jaw slackened; he looked at Jean as if she had appeared from the mouth of hell.

'God help me,' he gasped, throwing Gloria down and holding up his hands.

Jean did not want surrender; it wasn't enough. Rapid currents were reversing; the warming force of lust was giving way to the burning, propelling fuel of anger. Jean looked at Gloria on the grass, small and crushed, her blouse open and her lipstick smeared, and she knew what she wanted. Jean was more than furious; she was wounded. She was going to let herself hurt something.

A fresh wave of rage tore through her when she saw how afraid he was, how spineless. Jean opened her arms wide and let another roar roll out like a spiked tongue from her mouth. She heard the patter of urine dancing on shoe leather. He thought he could do what he had tried to do to Gloria because she was smaller and weaker than he was. Jean would teach him something about the responsibility of size.

She gave him a second to make his peace before she advanced. He quivered then ran like a rabbit, showing a flash of pale ankle instead of a tail as he bolted into the darkness. Jean roared again at the sudden removal of him — she had been denied.

'No!'

Jean jumped from the step; she thought she

felt the ground buckle from the impact of her, and her confidence surged. Paul had taken off into a thick line of trees, a remnant of some ancient forest where witches took the children they would devour. She followed him in. It was dark, and Jean's footsteps were heavy; but she wasn't trying to hide; she wanted him to hear her coming, to hear the weight and power of her stride. She could hear his scrambling as he darted between trees; she thought of a rat being chased by a ferret, then corrected herself — no, not by a ferret, by a great hound. 'Here I come,' she whispered. 'Here I come.' A fence ran around the edge of the trees; Jean heard the twang of it as Paul's face made contact; the sound throbbed in both directions, throwing Jean off. She ran with her hands out in front of her, taking slow, lengthy strides so she could find the trees without breaking her wrists. She had spent her life moving as if she were in a box of swords; running in the dark just required a modification. It was lucky that he stank like a patch of dirt where a bottle of gin had been dropped over a bottle of hair oil. A flash of shirt-tail broke from behind a tree, and she lunged to head him off.

Caught between the fence and a thick circle of broken trees, Paul shimmered. His white shirt trembled in front of her like a sheet on a wire. He was sweating and sickened; his head was spinning, he was running from a girl, and he thought he might have lost his testicles somewhere up inside his body. Panic had sped the passage of the gin, and his brain swam; he wished for a length of wood, a bag of nails. He cast about miserably; there was only crushed grass beneath him. As Jean focused on the stinking flicker in front of her, he began to take shape: the pale ankle through torn trouser cuffs, a greasy strip of skin under his dark hair; he looked like a lick of fat streaking across a dark window. Jean forged strides and ran as she had dreamed of running; the pursuit was almost secondary. Jean smiled, and her teeth caught a piece of moonlight.

Paul watched her approach, violent fate in a thin dress and brogues. He tried to summon the old feelings, the urge to maim, the joy in it. But couldn't. He didn't know himself. Jean was close enough to touch him now; her fingers tingled with the anticipation of harm. She had never told anyone anything; Jean was a receiver, a receptacle. But all the lessons in hurt and punishment she had absorbed over the years suddenly became viral, and she had to pass them on.

'You'll learn,' she assured him. 'And you won't forget.'

Tears licked at the inside of his nose with bristling, ticklish tongues and pricked the backs of his eyes with nimble fingers. His humiliation was unmissable, it felt like a port-wine stain spreading across his face. He looked at her, the ridiculous bitch that had run him to ground. He wanted to smile, to spit in her eye. To grab her breasts and twist. He couldn't stand knowing he was more likely to vomit than do any of those things. One last gasp, he promised himself. He was drunk, sick, piss-stained and cornered, but he swore he'd take something. Then he saw the branch in her hand.

'Fucking bitch!'

He screamed and disappeared into a pool of darkness as if off a cliff. Jean hurled the fallen limb at the air he had taken up, but he was flying away from her, a lucky little monkey again. Paul saw the branch sail past his heels and let out a bark of triumph that was cut short by the sudden meeting of his face with the trunk of a tree. Jean heard the crunch of cartilage on wood, followed by the soft whump of a body falling onto grass. She pulled up like a horse that has thrown its rider, her rage unseated.

'Bugger,' Jean whispered, and felt everything loosen.

9

She'd killed him. That was her only thought, the only possibility. She closed her eyes, not wanting to see what she had done. Her breath sounded like cloth tearing; it was all around her as if she were shredding the night. Her heart was punching at her breast. Jean silently begged for two minutes back; in eighteen years her life had not quite begun, and yet she had managed to end it in two minutes. Even she did not think that was fair.

Jean slowed her breathing before it could deafen her; she placed her hand over her heart and pushed down hard. It protested against her palm. She felt again the breeze on her face, making her suddenly aware of the oblivion of her panic; her eyes opened and the dark took shape. Jean looked down. Her shins were glossy in the darkness, wet from the dew kicked up running, her heavy leather shoes, some dead man's, flattening the grass. She was glad of them suddenly: 'They'll think a man was here,' she told herself. No one would think a girl capable. She could attract attention without real notice; big, they would say. A big girl. Tall as a house. Not many people had ever bothered to learn her name. Would big be enough, she wondered. Yes, she told herself, it would be enough. She wondered if she could bury him. God gives you hands like shovels, the least you can do is dig.

She couldn't see as much as a trouser leg from where she stood. The dark was immobile and surrendered nothing, everything stilled when he fell. Jean lowered herself to the ground, swiping the grass gently as if looking for a lost house key, her trembling fingers lightly skimming the blades hoping for and dreading contact with a lifeless foot. She would find him, then she would think about what to do with him.

★ ★ ★

A bewildered Gloria held her compact up to her face; in the small round mirror she saw a new self. Foolish. Worthless. Vain. Beaten. Her face belonged suddenly to a victim, not to her. She wondered how such a creature had crawled into the glass. The pretty blonde who dished out lemon drops and whose smile was firmly fixed in self-belief was now a wrung-out dishrag of a girl sat outside a dance with no longer any right to go in. It seemed very common and public. And sudden. Her eyes glinted; there was a thorn of knowledge in there now. She closed the compact on this new girl and began to whistle, thinly. With reedy, wayward tones, Gloria pushed the dark back a little and tried to summon Jean from the wood.

★ ★ ★

Where was the body? Jean entertained the half-hope that she was insane rather than guilty, that she had been chasing a phantom of her own anger. She abandoned the thought when her hand swept through grass that was warmer and heavier than the rest. She drew her hand to her face and sniffed; the tuppence smell of blood was on her fingers. Crawling backwards, Jean wiped her hand on a clean bit of grass and hitched the bottom of her dress into the waistband of her knickers. With thighs exposed, skin and knickers glowing white, she backed away from the flattened patch where he had lain and bled, careful not to mark herself with the evidence of her crime. The desire to hurt was melting into the desire to pity herself; her knees were weak and her bladder insistent. She felt cut from the same cloth as Paul, her vengeance as ridiculous as her position. She couldn't bury him, she couldn't tell anyone what she had done, she couldn't even find him. She was lost.

★   ★   ★

The small scrub of wood at last gave Jean up; she staggered out damp and defeated. Gloria lifted her head from her knees, her collapsed face pulling itself together with the speed of indignation.

'You've been bloody ages!'

Jean could only stare at her. In the few minutes she had been gone, Gloria had deteriorated. She looked as if she had been chewed. Grief was like a stitch in Jean's side; she had proved utterly useless.

'What have I done?' she whispered.

'Killed him, I hope,' Gloria gulped.

Jean crouched down and tenderly brushed the tears from her friend's face; she noticed that the tops of her arms were spotted with finger marks. Gloria smacked Jean's hand away. She needed to hurt someone. And there was only ever Jean.

'He's gone now,' she soothed. 'I won't let him come near you ever again. I'll . . . make sure.'

Jean put her arms around Gloria and held her while she sobbed, absorbing the blows Gloria needed to strike and stroking her matted hair when she was exhausted and couldn't rage any more. Jean held her friend as if she were her child, with a care that came not from memory but from simply knowing. After a few minutes, Gloria's sobs slid towards hiccups and she struggled out of Jean's arms and wiped her eyes.

'What are we going to do?'

Jean didn't know. How would she know what to do after this? So she smiled and touched Gloria's hot cheek. 'Go home.'

Gloria nodded. Her head swung limply; she was fading fast. Jean scooped her up and carried her to the path. She could do this at least.

'Jean.' Jean looked down to see Gloria staring at her with changed eyes, as if an older girl were looking out from behind them. 'It wasn't your fault. You didn't hear me the first time, but you came. You knew.'

Gloria held her gaze and then leant her head back against Jean's chest and closed her eyes. It was done, and she was saying it had to be done. Jean saw how brave Gloria was, how fearless. It takes courage to love a freak. Jean bucked her up and Gloria tightened her grip around Jean's neck, her hair trailing over Jean's shoulder and clinging to the fabric of the dress Jean had yet to untuck from her knickers.

★ ★ ★

The photograph-covered walls were Jean's favourite part of the flat above the sweet shop. Gloria's evolution from dimpled babe to luscious young woman had been painstakingly catalogued by her proud parents. They had been unable to have more than one child and so made a family of their sole daughter, populating their home with dozens of babies, girls and young women. The care with which the Smiths documented Gloria spoke to Jean of love, the need to fix the fast-disappearing days of childhood onto paper so not a minute of her would be lost. Jean appeared in a couple of the photos herself, usually a large blur as she tried to lumber out of the way, a meaty hand making to cover her face. (There was no photographic trace of an earlier life for Jean. Wisteria carried Jean's childhood in her vein-ridden legs, her stitched gait and her venomous disposition. In the house they inhabited, the days were thrown out with the rubbish and brought in with the milk and could not be made memorable even with a photograph. Mournful dogs and depressed wheatfields spattered Wisteria's walls.) Jean studied Gloria the fat, white-haired baby as the adult version was fussed over by her mother who had arnica and bandages at the ready.

'But, Gloria, love, how did you fall down a

bank? What bit do you mean?'

'I don't know, I think we took a wrong turn in the dark.'

Her mother gave Jean an exasperated look. 'Weren't you there, Jean?' She had a touching faith in Jean's ability to prevent harm coming to her daughter, believing, correctly, that the girl would lie down in front of a runaway tram if need be. Jean gave an apologetic shrug.

'I got caught in some brambles.' The tears on her legs bore her out; she was just beginning to notice their angry itching.

They had worked it out on the way home. Gloria knew she wouldn't be allowed out again in just Jean's company if her parents thought her in any danger. And Jean was relieved they would never discover how she had abandoned their beautiful child. So together they made a lie. Jean hugged the warm debt of it to herself when she walked home through the cooling night. If the police came for Gloria, she would only have to admit the attack. But when they came for Jean, she would tell them that Gloria had no knowledge of her crime. She would at last be able to do something for her friend. Gloria was put to bed and was careful to weep quietly.

After her sole childhood visit to the circus, Jean had begun to dream herself bigger. She dreamed that she was transformed by darkness and became a giant night creature, pale and terrible in the moonlight. She lived in the sea during the day and would emerge when the sun went down, the wetness clinging to her body like oil. She would roam about the town, peeling the tops from houses to get a look at the people inside, fascinated by the atoms of their lives. They would stir under her gaze, perhaps throwing off their bed covers, which she would gently replace, lifting a corner with a silver-green fingernail as long and curved as a scythe. She would watch over them, her little neighbours, entranced by their funny little ways. Then she would sit on a hill as if it were a footstool and comb her hair with a telegraph pole, enjoying the moon on her skin as if it were the midday sun. Before the sun rose she would return to the sea, existing only as the last dream a person remembered before waking.

On the night Jean ran Paul Bradshaw into a tree, it could have been true. Gloria's parents let her off with only a light grilling; they knew she faced much worse at home. Once she was a safe distance from the flat, Jean took off her shoes and felt the cold pavement absorb the warmth spilling from her feet. The moon was now strong enough to cast her shadow, and she walked with her night-creature self towards home. The dark entered her with every breath; she sucked down stars and the sound of the sea dozily rolling on the beach; the gossipy rustle of branches and the books-sliding-in-a-trunk sound the milk and coal trains made as they slowly sashayed in and out of town. She felt less imprisoned after dark, it seemed a more democratic time; the smallest sounds, ignored during the day, were magnified by the stillness; she felt she was able to unfold, to lengthen her limbs in this expanded world. The streets were empty. All the people were inside, making preparations, saying prayers, waiting for news. She imagined them huddled together with her looking down on them, unable to share their concerns but sympathetic to them.

Jean stretched up on tiptoe and measured herself against the heavens. She felt there was still possibility here. In the morning they would come for her, but for now she could let herself reach into the dark and pull herself up, free of the ground. She would be shut up in a box tomorrow, but tonight she was as big as the sky.

Jean hesitated at the door to her house. For the first time, she considered sedition. She at last had a crime to go on the run from, a reason outside of these walls, outside of Wisteria's control. But then they would come for Gloria; she was sure of it. Jean crept up the stairs, shoes in hand, and gently pushed open the bathroom door. Her feet and legs were filthy, and she had cobwebs in her hair. She wanted to wash it all away and no longer know anything she had learned that night. She wanted a bath.

The bathroom was a dense forest of stockings, vests and socks, suspended from the moist ceiling by criss-crossed lines of string. There'd be an argument over the coal, as it wasn't the Clockers' night for washing, but Jean couldn't rest until everything was rinsed away. She stood naked and shivering, waiting for the tub to fill. There was only a small, rusty-edged mirror in there, and Jean usually avoided it; she didn't like to be caught in anything so small. She took the mirror off the wall and angled it towards her blackened feet and dirty shins, moving it along her body, past her knees, thighs, hips, and breasts, stopping before she reached her face. 'So this is what all the fuss is about?' she thought and put the mirror down.

When the tub was full, Jean clambered in carefully and then curled up and rolled slowly under the surface in an attempt to baste every inch of her in the scalding water. She rubbed her feet and legs clean and then hung them out over the side of her tub so she could dunk her hair. She surfaced in the now-greying water and wasn't sure if she felt less soiled. Paul and Leonard were beginning to sink into her skin. She hadn't understood anything about that night, but then, all her information came from Gloria or Wisteria — extremists both. Between men and women, Wisteria saw only traps, transactions and the certainty of ruin. Gloria not only believed in love but believed it to be a birthright, a pure essence no one could live without. Jean only hoped that she could, as she would probably have to. She winced as she thought of Gloria, of all that had been destroyed for her that night. Jean studied her body in the blue light filtering thought the window. Her legs were still lewdly splayed out on either side of the tub; feeling suddenly abandoned and open, she drew them back into the water. Her belly was cut off from the rest of her torso; an island in the grey water. She rubbed her hand over it, trying to warm the exposed skin.

Despite her mother's warnings about cow-worriers, her body so far had proved unassailable. Jean thought about the face of the boy who had attacked Gloria, contorted by a violent stew of emotions. Hatred, she thought, arrogance, fear. She didn't see desire, she didn't see love. What she saw frightened her; he wasn't looking at Gloria, he was looking at something in and beyond her that he wanted to destroy. Something that Gloria believed about herself. And there was something that Jean had wanted to tear from him; something she knew she'd had her fingers around when he lost control of himself. But he had got away from her. She dunked her head under again, trying to sluice him from her memory. She had so much to think about this one night, her last night, as she believed it to be. She scooped water up her arms and over her chest letting her nails stroke the skin; it bristled in response.

Jean thought back to the book the cousin had given her, how his lip curled when he said 'Slut', the 't' so sharply enunciated it sounded like a pencil jabbing through taut paper. Was that what she was? She certainly hadn't recognised her body in that dirty book, the parts laid out as if on a slab with strange names and stranger uses. But she knew somehow it was her body, in an abstract way, as a language to be learned. She felt guilty thinking about it, the shame of having been reading about that when the boy was trying something like it with Gloria; perhaps he had read the book, and it had driven him mad with lust. She hadn't felt angry, or hateful like him, though. Only intrigued. Her legs were beginning to ache. She stretched again, careful to keep them together this time.

Jean tried to see her body as the girl's in the book. Her curiously described mounds and valleys, mossy glades and forbidden . . . what was it? Orchards? She shrugged and closed her eyes, dragging her fingers up and down the outside of her right thigh, feeling the soft hair lift from the skin. It was a strange sensation, being touched, without urgency or malice. The word aberrant formed in her mind; shivering, she plunged her hands under the water and the heat made her fingertips hum.

Wisteria's voice cut the silence like flying glass.

'You marrying that bath? No? Then why's it wearing your ring?'

Jean slopped down in the tub, water rushing up her nose. She surfaced spluttering and blind, quickly doubling over to hide herself. The dirt had settled around the tub in a silty stripe.

Wisteria stood in the doorway, wisps of steam curling around her like dragon's breath. Jean hadn't even heard the door open. Panic whited out her mind. She had no idea how long her mother had been there or what she'd seen, or if there had been anything to see. Jean felt confused by the heat, suddenly heavy and stupid again, the bath snug around her hips.

Wisteria kept her distance, her arms folded tight across her bony chest. Her head glinted in the dark, with its rows of metal pins. Jean played for time, continuing to wipe her eyes, stealing glances at the door. Wisteria gave nothing away, she was looking her usual disgusted self. Jean hugged her knees and paid the floor close attention.

'Gloria fell down a bank. I climbed down to get her; I didn't want to get the sheets muddy.'

'Idiot bitch. I'll need extra for the coal, you know that. It's not your night, they'll only come and ask me.'

Jean nodded but made no move to get out. She wanted to wait until her mother had gone, worried that her body would be changed by the way she had looked at it, considered it. There might be signs. Wisteria saw how she cowered and shielded herself, protecting her middle. It ignited a fear.

'You great whore!'

The words exploded out of Wisteria, and before Jean knew it, she was at her, scrabbling at her arms trying to get a grip on the cold, damp skin, then pulling her backwards, exposing her body and causing her to slip under the surface of the water. Wisteria pushed up her sleeves and plunged her hands in, grabbing at Jean's breasts and belly. Jean's face was half-submerged, the water around her nostrils churned as she snorted in panic; Wisteria's hands were thin and knobbly, the bones pressed into Jean's flesh as she squeezed her belly hard enough to push splinters out.

Satisfied after a few hard punches, her mother let go, and Jean threw herself at the side of the tub, hugging the cool hardness to her sore body. She was sobbing, her mother hadn't been able to extract that from her for a long time.

'Wh . . . Why?'

Wisteria was shaking as much as her daughter. 'You will not bring a bloody little bastard into this house, hear me? You listen to me now because I won't tell you again. I know what's going to happen, don't you think I haven't seen it before. I won't have you bringing more misery down on me. And you're not to see that tart again. She can find you trouble but she won't get you of it, you can rely on that. Now get out of that bath, and clean up after yourself!'

She wiped her hands on a neighbour's towel before leaving. Jean bit down on her lip and pressed harder against the enamel bath, trying to flatten out her body, make it smooth and sexless. Her tears ran over her arms and down the side of the tub, joining the dirty water pooling on the floor. She couldn't, didn't want to, move. If she stayed in the water long enough, she might shrink; her fingers were already shrivelling. If she stayed in all night she might be normal by the morning. They wouldn't find her then; Jean would have gone away and something small would be in her place.

It was over. She knew that. It was all over for her now.

10

The next morning, Jean put on her coat at eight o'clock and waited on the stairs. At noon she went back up to make her mother's lunch and feed her grandmother. She returned at half twelve and waited again until five. At a quarter to six she was back and sat until ten, with breaks for Wisteria's tea and biscuits. No one came. Jean didn't understand. An aberrant nature will always out. Hers had. The punishment was to follow swiftly. At eleven o'clock, she hung up her coat.

'Thought the gypsies were coming back for you?' Wisteria asked, with a customary sneer. Jean went to bed without replying and got an ashtray flung at the back of her head for her insolence.

No one came. Bad things could go unpunished. *She* could go unpunished. That night Jean lay in her undersized bed and marvelled at her first action without apparent consequence. She had broken her bonds, and her anger had been catastrophic without being final.

Jean had feared herself since childhood. She had been made to see only how her size could harm; now she could see how it could punish. How *she* could punish. Raised without a moral compass, she found herself lacking a true north; in her head needles were spinning. What was she capable of? And should she allow it? Something in her had stirred, a worm in her core. It was similar to whatever in her delighted in walking alone at night, to when she felt a yen for the fairground booth. It was a giddy, anxious feeling, brushing up against her ribs and trampling on her stomach. She could perhaps choose.

Jean had no real possessions. She took the few things she had learned and wrapped them and buried them deep in her brain where they could not fade or wear. Among those few wisps of knowledge she placed this new piece of information, like a shiny piece of costume jewellery, still too bright to wear.

War was declared the next day.

★ ★ ★

Of Jean's family, Jean's grandmother was technically the first victim of the new conflict, dying at some point during the broadcast announcing it. The death was discovered when Wisteria learned forward and poked her with the fire iron, which garnered no response. Wisteria claimed the shock of it — the declaration, not the fire iron — had finished her off and wondered if there would be compensation.

Having had the similarities between the back of her hand and an ashtray demonstrated with Wisteria's lit cigarette, Jean was deemed to have been sufficiently punished for her late-night bath. There was not much else her mother could do; she needed her daughter fit to work. The violence left in Jean from that night had drained quickly away, and she was in no hurry to

90

summon it. It frightened her, being untrained and unpredictable. Though it seemed she had got away with it, from the back of her mind she heard a knocking; the fact that she might have taken a life hunkered down and waited for admittance. Jean was sent out early that Sunday morning for coal; Wisteria had it in mind to be a hoarder, or a black-marketeer if she could accumulate enough, and had instructed Jean to filch what she could from the train sheds. Jean buried her haul in the garden, while the rest of the house — the rest of the world it felt like — huddled round the wireless. The churches had been full, too, Jean had noticed coming back from the sheds, and she had slowed when passing their doors. Hymns poured from the buildings, sounding hopeful and defiant, though she couldn't make out the words.

After the broadcast, doors and windows opened, and great floods of noise spilled out as neighbours called to each other. They ran into the streets, shouting, and a flock of chatter took to the skies and circled above Jean; she knew that it was starting then. She ran upstairs to find her mother standing over her grandmother, the fire iron in her hand. Murder was her first thought: Wisteria had threatened often enough.

'Mum? What have you done?'

Wisteria whirled round, the fury not quite covering the satisfaction in her face. There was, after all, one less mouth to feed now.

'What the fuck do you mean, what have I done? I've done nothing, it's you, you great ox. She couldn't stand another minute, could she,

91

you galumping all over the place, frightening her to death. Well, now you've done it, haven't you? She's gone.'

And Wisteria stepped aside so Jean could see her handiwork, the waxen figure of her grandmother, slumped to one side in her chair. Her jaw had slackened beyond retraction, and her eyes were unnaturally fixed. It was as though someone had drawn a face on a sack.

'We'll lay her out in your room till the doctor can come. He'll ask for more, coming on a Sunday. You'll get him in the morning.' Then she sniffed the air like a rat. 'Ugh, it would have to be warm today.'

Jean looked at her mother's face, searching for a trace of sorrow or compassion. She thought of when her father had died, and how Wisteria had made a fuss with the veterans' association until they came and carted him away for burial. She assumed Wisteria would have put him out with the rubbish otherwise, and wondered who the old woman would be palmed off on; perhaps Wisteria would order her buried in the garden, next to the stolen coal. Then Jean's questions were answered. From inside the folds of the ancient shawl draped around her mouldering antecedent, Wisteria extracted a gold watch and chain that Jean had never seen, never even heard tick.

'That's for the funeral. You can take it in after the doctor's. And get a good price, or you'll make up the rest.'

Mother and daughter stripped the body for washing. They could have left it for the undertakers, but Wisteria didn't like the idea of strangers doing this part of it. Jean thought there might have been some tenderness behind that, but Wisteria insisted it was because there were odd people in the world and she didn't want any of them getting hold of her own mother. Jean realised then it was likely they charged more for the service. She was surprised that her grandmother had a body like her own; to Jean she had become little more than a head that topped a swirl of shawls and blankets like a moth-eaten cherry. But here she was whole: the same sex — the same parts in the same order — as Jean; although her body seemed to be even more at odds with itself than Jean's, not enough height with too much skin, and knots and kinks belonging more to branches. But still a woman's body, a body that had given birth to Jean's mother and had once been as firm and smooth as Jean's. Jean saw herself lying on the bed, wearing her grandmother's wrinkled skin like a suit, her mind trying to stretch it over her young healthy bones with no great success.

They worked down the body, from opposite sides of the bed, lifting the old woman's stiffening arms to clean her hands and fingernails and her head to clean around her neck and ears. Her hair was sparse but still long; Wisteria snipped it off and dropped it into a paper bag.

'Might still be worth something to us.' Jean didn't think there could be much call for wigs in lardy grey but kept quiet.

When they were done washing, they rolled stockings up over her bowed legs, put fresh

93

drawers on her and even laced up her stays under her dress so she looked as proper and unforgiving as she had in life.

'What do we do now?'

Jean turned to her mother for guidance. The familiar malice sauntered into Wisteria's expression as the crowning glory occurred to her.

'Well, you'll sit vigil, of course. It's only proper.'

*   *   *

The smell was cabbagey and rotten. Jean had to stick her head out of the attic window and smoke all her precious cigarette allowance. Over the rooftops drifted the sound of a nation newly at war. Jean could hear snatches of arguments over politics, the puffed-up bragging of men spoiling for a fight, the tearful wails of children, some laughter even, some songs. In the bed — Jean's bed — her grandmother rumbled. Jean was not familiar with the noxious business of a body after death, and the first emanation had left her gasping. Wisteria had laughed — 'There'll be plenty more of that' — and left Jean to it. She went to listen to the wireless, a programme of stirring, patriotic tunes, and complain at it about her usual choices being taken off because of the war. 'Pain in the arse already,' she pronounced the conflict. Jean desperately inhaled smoke and clean air and wondered what this war could mean. If she were a man, they'd call her up and Wisteria would have no say in the matter; they could send her abroad, and she might never come back. If she were a man. Jean wondered if she could disguise herself. But she had seen a bit of an army physical on a newsreel and knew she would have to go down to at least her vest. They would discover her, and call her mother, and then Wisteria would have her committed to the asylum. Best to stay put for now.

★　★　★

By eight o'clock the next morning, the streets were crowded with people. Driven by the need to be with others during a crisis, they were chattering in groups, forming battalions ready to march down to the recruiting office, or simply scurrying in a panic from one shop to another. One woman staggered past Jean dragging a sled laden down with tins of peas, the wooden runners protesting at the dry pavement.

Jean could not be sure for how long she had slept; it felt like only a minute or two. Her grandmother had quietened down, but the stench had been restless and circled her all night, along with the fear that the old woman would rise up. The vigil had been among the worst of her mother's punishments. Jean would rather have taken a beating. She waded through the crowds, uninfected by the excitement. Wishing she could cry, she blinked furiously, but her eyes wouldn't moisten, which seemed very bad. She must be very bad, feeling nothing but fear and revulsion while in that room all night.

At home, Wisteria cleaned. She expunged. Her house was often dirty, but she was removing more than dirt. Her mother lay dead in the attic while Wisteria whistled and poured black water down the drain.

To Jean, it seemed frighteningly easy to disappear from your own house, even disappear in it; her own father had slowly evaporated over the years. Jean broke into a run, the heavy thud of her shoes on the pavement reassuring her she was still there. That would be her spot in the corner now, the nicotine and grease stains painting her outline onto the wall. She could disappear next, and no one would come to look for her, not even for what she had done to Paul Bradshaw. And Gloria would have to give up eventually.

The doctor's waiting room was crowded already: hysterics fractured by the news of war, injuries sustained after the pub had shut while demonstrating exactly what they were going to get if they tried invading here. Jean reached the little window behind which they kept the receptionist; it slid open and the caged woman asked 'Yes?' Jean hiccuped twice and was sick, the receptionist unable to pull the window shut in time.

★ ★ ★

The funeral was short and ill-attended. Gloria had sent word that she would like to be there, but her note was put back out on the mat. Wisteria and Jean stood at the graveside for as brief a time as was decent, and then Wisteria took hold of Jean's arm with a cold, gloved hand

and steered her away. During the brief service, Jean had been shocked to find out that her grandmother's name was Eugenia. She had been named for her. Probably one of her mother's jokes. Jean felt icy footsteps on her spine when the name was read out, and thought it could only be the worst luck to hear your own name at a funeral.

Her mother hung heavily on her arm, slowing Jean's pace and forcing her to shorten her lengthy stride. Jean knew she was going to get a talking to and wanted to run. Wisteria could feel the impulse to bolt form in her daughter and dug her fingers into the soft flesh behind Jean's elbow. At the edge of the churchyard she halted her with a pinch. Cold seemed to spread from Wisteria's grip, like a heart attack. Wisteria looked up at her daughter, her face filled with neither grief nor hatred, anger nor sadness. She looked determined and somehow honest.

'I did the right thing by her, Jean. I buried her right. I'll ask the same of you one day, and you'll be there to do it. You'll never leave me. Do you understand? I'm telling you, you're not going anywhere. You've spent your life under my roof. No one made me do that, I could have given you to the Christians or left you in a ditch, but I took you home and I gave you a life. So it belongs to me. I never left her, Jean. And you'll never leave me.'

Wisteria searched her daughter's face for some sign of understanding. Seeing horror, she gave a grunt of satisfaction and let go of Jean's arm. 'Go on, get the flowers before someone nicks them; see if you can get something for them at the market.'

Wisteria walked on to the gate without looking back, then turned towards home. Jean stood in the graveyard watching her mother leave, her good coat drawn tight around her, greasy hair screwed down into her scalp, everything close and tight and impenetrable. The fear that had seeped in unnoticed for years caused Jean suddenly to crumble. She had always known she was unwanted; she had assumed it meant that she would not be kept; that at some point she would be abandoned to the world. In time, she hoped to find Gloria again. But Wisteria's grip would never be loosened. Jean saw that she had been prepared for this for years; she had been born into it and with each miserable inch she added onto herself she had confirmed it. She was built only to serve and withstand. Jean sat down behind a gravestone and cried onto the wet grass, where it made not a bit of difference.

Gloria watched Wisteria leave the churchyard and decided to stay in the bus shelter for a few minutes more, just in case. She could see the top of Jean's head wobbling behind a stone angel. The angel faced the other way and looked very callous, her white stone eyes fixed on the sky as if she were rolling them sarcastically to heaven. Gloria looked back at Wisteria; her matchstick legs with the knobbly anklebones sticking out as though she had golf balls down her stockings. She took mean, fast little steps. 'Careful you don't rub those little twig legs together,' thought Gloria. 'You'll catch fire.'

It didn't take Wisteria long to reach the top of the road, wheezing all the way. Gloria stepped out of the shadows, very pleased with herself for not having been seen, and skipped over to the churchyard. Skirting round the areas she thought might be directly over a body, and pausing to sigh at the graves of children, she trod so softly Jean didn't hear her approach. A devilish notion seized her. Gloria crept up onto the angel's plinth and hid behind her flowing stone robes.

'Jean . . . Jeeeaaaannnn . . . Can you hear me, child?' she warbled.

Jean looked up and around her; she wiped her raw stinging eyes but still couldn't see anyone.

'Up 'ere . . . *here*, my child. Look up here to me, *behind* you. It is I, the angel of the graveyard, here to help you. Perhaps by sending a thunderbolt up your old mum's bum?'

Jean's screams were heard inside the church and halfway down the hill. Gloria jumped from the statue and flung herself on Jean, hugging her tightly about the neck.

'Jean! It's me! It's me! I was making it up! I was just doing a voice!'

Jean toppled sideways with Gloria on top of her, holding on fast, her tenacity a surprise to them both.

'It's me! Calm down, would you? My dress is getting ruined!'

At that, Jean knew it really was Gloria and relaxed. Gloria slid from her friend's back and stood up, brushing herself off. Jean remained on the ground; her clothes were muddied and her hair looked like an abandoned nest.

'What the bloody hell did you do that for?'

Gloria adjusted her underwear. 'To cheer you up,' she replied, indignantly.

★ ★ ★

Gloria had, as ever, plundered the shop's stock and they shared a box of chocolates while sitting on one of the oldest tombs. The pair swapped soft centres and stories; they had been apart for days during which time the nation had gone to war, but it would be an hour before they got round to it.

'You saw him?'

'He was a bit hard to miss. Flattened nose, two black eyes and his front teeth missing. He was marching a bit faster than the others as well, I reckon. Couldn't wait to get away. What did you do to him?'

'I thought I'd killed him.'

'Couldn't've. Someone would have said. That's what I thought anyway. I even went back to look.' Gloria took Jean's hand and turned it palm upwards. Onto the scored skin she dropped two enamel chips that emitted a faint aroma of tobacco and bark.

'Are these . . . ?'

'I dug them out the tree.'

Jean stared at the teeth in her hand. They were short and mean.

'You're a cold-blooded one.'

'You can talk. You thought you'd killed him and you just went home.'

Jean turned her palm in the light, but the teeth

were dull and reflected nothing.

'What shall I do with these?'

'I don't know. String them onto a necklace?'

'That's disgusting.'

'Throw them away, then. I just wanted you to see them. You taught him a lesson. One he won't forget.'

★ ★ ★

Paul Bradshaw did forget, though. He forgot everything. The war marked his card as quickly as it would Jean's. While attempting to desert, he snuck past an unmanned gate and scaled a half-finished fence from the top of which he fell onto a wooden post, which smacked him square in the temple. The fence continued only for another fifty yards and then consisted of open spaces between markers, the wire having not yet arrived. The incident left him irreparably benign. Despite the discovery that Paul had lined his trousers with petrol coupons, and the inanity of his chosen method of absconding, he was dealt with lightly by the authorities. There was little left to deal with, as he had no understanding of where he was or what had happened to him. Gloria went to visit his parents, not to gloat or scold, but to see.

He was lolling in the corner, sporting a forehead like a rugby player's kneecap. Gloria gave a little squeak when she saw him but soon recovered. Paul's mother showed her to a chair, and Paul gave her a gummy grin; he'd lost most of the teeth that Jean had left him with on the fence, and the rest had been removed for the sake of convenience. His mother told Gloria how nice she was to have come to see him, how happy it had made him.

'See? You can tell. His eyes just light up.'

Gloria looked at the gurning clown in the corner. He did look genuinely pleased to see her.

'Must be a relief to have him home. However he . . . '

She faltered and retreated behind a smile. Paul's mother was allowed the words Gloria couldn't claim.

'Yes. However they come home, in a war you're just glad they do. Course he's a baby for life, now. But I don't mind, better alive and, you know, than dead from a bomb or a bullet.'

Gloria nodded, unable to draw her eyes away from Paul. She had never seen anyone made so happy by a metal rule. He was using it to scratch his gums in between wide-mouthed gurgles of joy.

'You know, sometimes you can't help it. You do want your baby back,' his mother said so softly Gloria wasn't sure if she knew she was speaking out loud.

'He's more like the baby I wanted now than he ever was. Never slept, always howling. His teeth came in early, you know, so I took him off. He didn't like that. Started to bite. Went on from there. Meek as a lamb now, though. God forgive me, if it isn't better. No one can hurt him now.'

She took a teacloth and wiped some spittle from the corners of Paul's mouth and ruffled the patches of hair that hadn't been shaved off. Her son squirmed with delight under his mother's hand, pushing his nose into her palm. Gloria set down her tea and made her excuses; she left them together, happy in reinvention. She would see Paul from time to time, being pulled along in a wagon by his father or helping his mother with her shopping. She would look at him, smiling and playful, his uncoordinated legs taking mismatched strides, and try to see him as a highly coloured illustration of some parable. But she could not decide if he had been redeemed or merely neutered. Gloria told Jean that he was harmless and they should forget him, but she never quite managed to push him out of her mind. Or wonder exactly what had been knocked out of him by a fence post.

★ ★ ★

'What are you going to do now?'

They had finished the box. Jean looked at the empty paper shells sadly, suddenly realising that she could not recall the exact taste of each individual chocolate. And they would be her last. She wondered what Gloria would do if she told her she was banned from ever seeing her again, whether she realised that nothing she did could make any difference to Wisteria. It had all been decided. Gloria sucked the sticky residue of a strawberry cream from her molars as she considered her future.

'Oh, I don't know. Train as a nurse, I should think. They have such lovely uniforms, a little covering, but very impressive. They'll need plenty, and there's two big hospitals here. I may even get to go up to town. I'll bet there are some really nice places just for officers where they're all dying of love for the nurses. Maybe they went to war without sweethearts. Probably just as well I didn't settle for anyone yet; be awful not to be free with all those handsome soldiers around. What about you?'

The same, she thought. From now on and for ever, the same. Apart from you. She supposed the factory would go on and she with it. Jean had already been informed that she was not to join any of the women's services. They didn't do uniforms in 'lump', and she was needed at home.

'Not sure. I'm not sure yet what I'll be good at.'

'Oh, tons of things, I should imagine. Why don't you be a nurse too, with me; one that lifts people in and out of bed. Then I can do all the other stuff, bandaging and pillows an' that.'

'P'raps.' Jean eased herself off the tomb and brushed the powdery green lichen off her clothes. It was time she went home.

'Are you coming out at the weekend? There's so many dances, all farewell ones. I'll say we're going to the pictures.'

'I can't come out for a while. Mum says; because of Gran.'

'All right.' Gloria jumped to the ground and checked her coat and stockings for marks. 'When she's ready to let you out the dungeon, I'll be waiting. Wouldn't leave it too long, though, they can't have a goodbye dance every weekend for

104

ever; they'll run out of people to say goodbye to after a while.' Jean smiled and leaned down to hug her friend; Gloria's blonde hair was cold and slippery against her neck. And then she had run out of people to say goodbye to. The only thing to do was to go back home and let Wisteria wall her up alive. Jean used her irrelevant strength to gently, yet firmly, push Gloria away.

She would have ended there, but for the bomb.

Part Two

DELIVERANCE

11

There was no siren, no warning. The bomb that buried Jean and divorced her mother from the misery of existence burst out of the sky unannounced, an ill-mannered thing. It was their own side; someone only just learning to kill, the technology for it still beyond them.

The living inhabitants of Jean's street crept quietly from under their beds and tables. The sound of slippers shuffling filled the stranded night, tempting others to follow, like drumming on the earth for worms. Soft, round figures spilled from the neat, uniform houses, puffy from interrupted sleep, hidden deep inside quilted housecoats.

The dust coated them all, as if they were all survivors from the heart of it, their dazed expressions those of people who have brushed past death too quickly for understanding. Everyone was silent; the silence itself became a spell that, broken, meant certain death for those inside the jagged little peak. Hands were clasped, lips were bitten. Someone would start forward only to feel a gentle pressure on the elbow; stay back, stay back from the unknown. The house settled a little, and a groan of brick skittered down the heap. Then the engine sirens began — rescue, comforting authority on the way — and all heads turned towards the sound and began to hope.

Officials with loudhailers quelled the panic before it could spread, before the whisper of 'invasion' could become a hysterical scream. A van from the gas board would later park by the site, designated the result of a freak mains eruption; the gas was cut off for three days to lend credibility to the story. It had been a terrible, unique disaster rather than the beginning of the end.

They worked slowly, by moonlight, using touch rather than sight. The firemen organised rescue chains, and small satellite piles of rubble began to form. Once bodies were occupied, voices were raised — relaying orders, shouting cautions — amplified by the relief of being given something to do. At the centre of it all was the house; and at the centre of that was Jean.

'If I am dead,' Jean thought, 'I am not in heaven.' Contained within an upturned bathtub, her body screamed. She was folded almost in half, her legs tucked up into her chest, while one arm reached down between her legs. She could cup the soles of her feet with her fingers, if they moved. The other arm was lost behind her in the rubble, buried deeper that the rest of her; a floorboard ran through the crook of her elbow and along her back. It twisted her torso and kept her lungs open. One side of her face was pressed into dirt and splinters, the other close enough to the enamel of the bath to feel the coolness coming off it. Strange sounds trickled down through the gaps in the fresh-made hill. It was the scrabbling in walls that you try not to listen to at night. But she was in the walls now, pieces of them were all around her.

The manic jump and jive of the disintegration gave way to a shifting, lecherous slow dance with Jean at the centre of it. The house began to breathe under her; she could feel it rise and fall; the bed of brick that she lay on moved around her body, digging into her spine with kneading fingers. Above her, the bath flexed and groaned as the house bore down on it. Freed from its larger self, it was as if every brick and splinter was alive and ambulant, intent on reaching Jean and taking a piece of her, a souvenir of the last living human. Oily water wound round her neck and trickled between her breasts, a cockroach shifting off its back set off a slide of rubble that crept under the tub and nestled between her legs, pushing at her, trying to find a way in. Her breath was short, her lungs filled with a slurry of mucus and dust, her eyes were swelling shut. The fleas and mites, the spiders, the silverfish out of the hall carpet and the rats from the yard all shook the dust out of what eyes they had and began to look for a suitable place to relocate. Some made for her, sensing her warmth; others made for their preferred dead meat. Something crawled up her thigh, seemingly enjoying the long walk on soft, bloody flesh, it stopped often but kept on course, moving ever upwards. She forced herself to piss it away and it slid off her thigh in a warm, stinging torrent. She allowed herself a sigh of relief; her chest flexed painfully, and her shoulder burned.

Though she could barely move an inch, Jean — like the house itself — was in constant motion; she flinched, oozed, spread, clenched and ground. She tried to pull her limbs closer and rotated in the tiniest circles; pushed bricks away from her face with her tongue; tried to gouge a breathing space from the gathering dust. As far as she knew, the world had ended, and where she was, was all there was. She wondered if she was somewhere Gloria could reach.

She tried to focus her mind on the familiar, the physical. She had to deny her body the range it craved and control its impulses. Skilled since childhood in suppression, she set about communicating with every wayward inch of her body; she would manage her every breath and try to still the groping chaos around her. She would not think, she would not regret, she would not fear. She let her body become her world. Her brain felt hot inside her skull, its temperature rising as her limbs cooled. Above her, they began to remove the bodies. The children were carried so delicately it seemed that the rescuers were afraid to wake them, and would only deliver them back into the soft beds they had been shaken out of. The onlookers gasped when they were placed on stretchers and sheets were drawn over their heads.

Underneath this, Jean's brain conjured pictures in the thin air. The pain overwhelmed her every few minutes and she would fade, her eyes rolling behind their swollen lids until some new, urgent hurt seared her again and she came to. Cramps burned in her legs and arms, her neck muscles stood out like cords, pulling her mouth down into a rictus. Dirt poured into her wounds and began to swim in her body as fancies swam in her mind. The pain boiled in her until it flooded the space around her. She floated in it, an acid bath. Her eyes were directed inwards and saw only her fevered dreams. She began to lose the idea of herself; she could no longer distinguish her arms from her legs. She felt herself melt into the rubble. She was letting go. Her heavy head pressed deeper into it, dirt began to clog one nostril, and her dry, sticky mouth let only the tiniest bubble of air escape. It had been a long time.

The hours passed quickly up top; the edges of the night brightened and the street started to look inside out. Furniture crowded the pavement so diggers could take a rest on a chair at a table. Tea was brewed and sandwiches prepared; the residents sat squarely outside the boundaries of their own homes as if surrounded by invisible walls. Sounds began to filter through the darkness of the house, hands clawing at the surface, tapping, waiting for a response then moving on the next few inches of ruin. But all Jean heard was the sway of branches, scraping at a window. Her mind wandered away from where a stinking, piss- and blood-stained girl lay and tried to find somewhere safe to rest. She found a forest coloured with brilliant greens and velvety black shadows. The sun couldn't penetrate the thick branches that spread over the glade, but its warmth reached down to the tangled floor where a broken girl lay in a glass casket. Stars glittered overhead as blood vessels burst behind her eyes. Jean felt the wet coolness of her own gore spread around her turn into a bed of silk ribbons. The weight of the house lifted from her, and she felt her limbs extend and her chest rise. 'I have been enchanted,' she thought. 'I will sleep for a hundred years.'

As Jean slowly died, two thirteen-year-old boys were making their contribution to the rescue effort by hauling bricks from the rapidly diminishing heap that covered her. Their imaginations fuelled by a comic strip, they had come to believe that bombs merely blew beautiful women's brassieres off, and had become tireless would-be rescuers, patrolling their own street and those surrounding it in search of nubile blondes wearing only panties and a dazed expression. This was the most exciting night of the war, which they thought had been pretty dull so far. They sang as they dug, hoping for a live, unclothed woman (though admitting privately that an actual exploded body, male or female, would be all right too). 'Hi ho, hi ho, it's off to work we go, with a bucket and spade and a hand grenade . . . ' Their voices reached through the cracks and found Jean, their childish song pushing her deeper into the forest. Jean heard the little men coming for her, the seven of them with their lanterns aglow and their pockets stuffed with gems as bright as cubes of strawberry jelly . . . 'With a smile and a song and an old Mills bomb, hi ho, hi ho, hi ho, hi ho . . . '

'They've come for me,' she fancied, her lips splitting into a smile; they would soon have her out and put her into a little cart and trundle her away. The sound of feet on rubble was like the noise inside of a giant mouth, chewing. They were overhead. The pressure on her increased as the men added their weight to her burden. She tried to cry but couldn't remember how.

One of the boys screamed as his foot broke though a thin panel of wood covering a deep channel; his leg disappeared to the shin and his foot landed on Jean's buried hand. Pulling his foot out tore at the flesh of his shin, and he screamed again from pain and panic. He looked down the hole he had made and saw Jean's fingers twitching. 'There's one alive!' she heard, as the forest crunched around her from the many pairs of feet now trampling through it. The bathtub started to move as, above Jean, four firemen carefully scraped the detritus from its edges and removed the beams and frames that held it down. 'Poor little things,' she thought, underneath it all, 'such a heavy casket, their rosy cheeks will be all puffed out from the strain, and the stupid one pushing down when everyone else is pulling up.'

The end of the tub suddenly lifted up, and hands poured down into the dark, looking for something to latch on to. The first hand made contact, brushing Jean's neck and then grabbing at her shoulder, mixing a handful of skin with the remains of her nightshirt, reduced to a clownish frill around her neck. The bath was flipped onto its back and other hands found her body, took hold and began to pull. A splinter of glass licked her back as she slid towards the air. Another grinding effort, and her face was free. One of the rescuers took a canteen and poured water over her, using his finger to swab out the dust from her gums and under her tongue. They held her as she vomited out as much of the dirt and dust as she could, her legs still lying uselessly in the hole she had made.

Jean opened her eyes a fraction, the morning light hurting like pins. She squinted into the face of one of the men who held her; a bearded, smiling face, framed by dust-whitened hair, like clouds around the moon. She spoke her first words for a hundred years.

'Happy,' she said. 'Happy.'

'So you should be, love,' he replied, his voice cracking with dirt and grief. 'Every other bugger's dead.'

And with a final pull they delivered her from the house, slimy and leggy as a calf.

12

The gnarled hand of a giant tore off the roof and threw it into the sky; bricks jumped up to dance then fell like dead birds, leaping up again to a soundtrack of manic laughter. Somewhere a swing band was playing, faster and faster, making the debris jive to its tune; knives and forks left their trays and marched across the sky, then rained down, piercing Jean's flesh as she lay in bed. Madness hung in the air for her to see; gales tore through her head, spewing out of her eyes and ears in dusty trails. And all around the hurricane encircled them; it was made of air and heat and laughter and pain. Strapped down as the frames whirled in the air, Jean and her mother flew in their beds. The remaining walls of their house seemed to be pure, rushing liquid; great fountains of dirty water gushed from every crack. Jean screamed and water flooded her throat and turned her screams into gargles, her hands bound by the sodden sheets.

Wisteria's face was crazy-paved where the plaster had caught in her cold cream, Jean's hair was writhing with snakes. The hand scooped up the bricks and threw them down into the roaring funnel of water. They dropped harmlessly around Jean, but Wisteria was crushed, her skull dented as an old bucket. 'What the fuck have you done to me now, lumpy?' she screamed as her brains came spilling down her face. Jean pulled at the sheets with her teeth, they were as tough as canvas sails. 'You prayed for this!' Wisteria's voice lanced Jean's ear, running through to her brain. 'You wanted me dead, you did!' Jean's teeth broke and she spat blood and enamel. Wisteria's wails seemed to come from another world already. Her brains had dribbled away and she had just an empty little doll head now, nodding on the tide, rolling white marble eyes, a grey tongue lolling inside a blackened mouth — but still Jean could hear her. 'You did it! You did it! You!' Jean was shaking her head as she tried to push her nails through the sheets. 'It wasn't me, it wasn't me!' she screamed. 'Well, who's that escaped from the circus then?!' Wisteria demanded as Jean looked up and saw herself, as big as the sky, raining down death with savage glee, bricks in her huge hands, the joy of destruction writ across her face. She opened her mouth to scream and let the water rush in, filling her up and pulling her down. The pair dropped through the house, through the earth and kept going. The roots of great trees clawed Jean as she fell past, but when she tried to grab them, the earth gave them up easier than baby teeth; nothing would stop her from reaching the bottom. They were going down into the dark together; she would never leave her mother, never. Jean opened her mouth in one last scream and felt her lips split and the blood spill over her hot dry face. She was awake.

A nurse came with cold wet flannels and pressed them down over Jean's mouth, she sucked at the cloth and let it rinse away some of the dust that still lingered in her throat. A cool hand passed over her forehead, Jean strained to, but couldn't, open her eyelids. The eyes behind them felt mushy and weak.

'Am I alive?' she whispered, tiny blood bubbles bursting on her lips.

'Yes.' It was a woman's voice, low but clear, with years of practised night soothing in it. 'You've surprised us all, young lady. By rights you should have been dead.'

Jean nodded. 'Was always meant to be,' she tried to explain, and then went back to the dark, watery place where she had left her mother.

* * *

A day passed before Jean regained conscious-ness. The pain shimmered in a haze around her; she burned like the horizon and there was only red behind her eyes. She could feel a vague outline of her body against the sweat-soaked sheets, it was unclear what of her was left. She thought she was in hell. She begged to be released, or even acknowledged. When the doctor came, she was on her hundredth 'please'. He placed his hand on her arm. 'Stop that crying now, it won't help you here.' She screamed and split her lips again; they had to put fresh stitches in.

She was on her back, her crooked arms and legs forced out from her body. She looked electrified, caught in mid-jolt. Both legs were bound to splints, as was one arm and both hands. Her eyes were open but tender, bordered by bandages over her nose and across her forehead, her torso was thickly wrapped and her feet were in bags of salve — they alone had been burned; the rest was done by glass, brick and wood. It was night and she was alone in the ward. In the morning, a doctor and six students would explain to each other why Jean was interesting, why they were lucky to have her and what they could learn from her flayed skin and chipped bones. Then nurses would come and peel away some of the bandages before they could sink into her healing skin, while she tried not to scream, and replace them with fresh ones.

Fractures laced her cheekbones and nose, but she would look like herself again. Her face wasn't an impossible puzzle, it had been left mainly where it had been found by the debris. The girl used to retracting herself around people had managed to pull herself in. It might have been her shyness that saved her from being splintered when the house she slept in folded in on itself. She curled as she tumbled down and down, tucking in her loose limbs even after she no longer felt the sharp cracks and tears as she struck edges. She shied gently away from death as she had done so politely with its dance partner, life.

★   ★   ★

At first, Jean took consciousness a few hours at a time. It is at its most manageable in such small doses, and the timing of her medication left little argument. When Jean properly came to, she saw

120

the white uniforms pass by her, felt the cold of their instruments on and inside her and knew where she was. She saw that the room was empty apart from her and knew she was alone. A cold fact pooled at the base of her brain, the knowledge that everyone had been killed but her. And she felt the wings of something scrape against the inside of her skull, something desperate to be let go. Relief. Freedom. Joy.

Some things are too dangerous to be thought about in the day, they can turn the skull transparent and everyone can see into the filthy little crevasses from which such things are born. Jean lay in a daytime pretence of peaceful desolation. It seemed the only right thing to do. At night she admitted the thoughts, memories and things learned; the dark covered her mind as she had always relied upon it to do for her body. Jean would try not to think that the bomb had set her free. But with her first breath out of the rubble, she knew it.

She knew it because she was terrified. She tried to remember the fear of being buried and compare it to this new fear that had been left in her along with the catgut, the pins, the dirt and germs. It was a fear born of a new certainty: that she was not dead, that she would not die soon. It can be a terrible thing to realise how precious life is, and be simultaneously certain your own has been mostly wasted. It has an appetite, an expectation. Jean could feel its hunger, every scratch on her generated more.

Of this bomb, from this chaos, she was born for the second time, with hardly more of a clue of what to do next than the first. There were no excuses, no reasons. She lay awake at night with joy and terror in her blood and wondered how to live up to life.

★ ★ ★

After a few weeks she found she could walk. Jean refused the wheeled chair and staggered about, bandy and drunk-looking, after that. The nurses called her Wishbone. She was the least complaining adult they had come across. Even when her exercises pushed her to the edge of consciousness, she gritted her teeth and continued. She was in something's debt. They told her she had been lucky to see such good doctors, but privately said that it was her own will that healed her legs straight and knitted her poor skin together. It had been a fierce recovery from a meek life.

When Jean was released, she waited for Gloria on the side steps of the hospital kitted out in a sorry ensemble culled from the clothing drive for victims of the air raids to come. Jean was the first recipient, a special case. An Edwardian-style ladies' silk blouse, tropically striped, billowed about her chest before being cinched into a pair of high-waisted tuxedo trousers (given by the wife of a young man of generous height and hips when she discovered her husband hadn't enlisted at all but set himself up in the city as a black-marketeer and pimp). A heavy purple cape hung off one shoulder down to below her knees, while her feet were protected from the cold with a pair of heavy knit socks strapped into place by men's sandals. A deep nick above her ear had reopened and then been slow to close, so her head was still extravagantly bandaged. She looked like the doorman to some fashionably exotic West End nightclub; visitors hesitated to pass, perhaps waiting for her to beat a gong in welcome. Alone and badly dressed, Jean felt herself growing taller; she pulled the cape tighter around her and lowered herself down on the steps. Her legs had mended beautifully, but they ached in the cold and were not used to carrying the full burden of her yet. A big top after the circus had left town, the voluminous cape drooped around her, making a saggy circle, with only Jean's feet and bandaged head poking out into the gloomy air.

'Blimey, Mustafa, where'd you park your camel?'

Jean looked up to see Gloria standing over her, neatly dressed and flushed with the cold. She carried flowers and had a heavy wool coat over her arm. Jean made a solemn gesture with her head towards the municipal baths.

'In the valley of the Blue Nile, many moons' travel from here.'

'Better get the bus back, then.' Gloria grinned, but was unable to put much into it. She wanted Jean to look like herself again. After the splints, blood and bandages, this was barely a turn for the better; Gloria hoped the outfit didn't signal some mental deterioration. 'You all right, then?'

Jean had been born again into an entirely new world. She had been through weeks of agony that

123

she hadn't the words to describe, tortured by thoughts she could barely admit. She looked at Gloria's eager, clear eyes.

'Yeah,' she said. 'Not bad.'

'Good.' Gloria advanced, waving the asphyxiated stems that she had gripped too tightly. 'Brought you these.' She placed them on the step in an odd gesture, as if in front of the Cenotaph. Jean reached out and touched the flowers with an ungloved hand. The petals were cool and unlined, like the inside of an arm. She marvelled that she could still feel something as thin as her own skin. Gloria looked at Jean's yellowing face, the bruising all but faded, a few livid scars remaining.

'You look so much better. You've really come on.'

Gloria regretted casting Jean as so many tragic heroes and disposable villains in their adolescence; together they had rehearsed her death a hundred times in a hundred gruesome ways. The battered Jean looked very different from one of Gloria's bloodless fantasies. Gloria promised herself she would never again think of death and horrifying injury as romantic and beautiful while simultaneously picturing herself in a flattering nurse's outfit standing over a handsome soldier with one perfect scar interrupting his silken cheek. She smiled at Jean and proffered the coat, an old one of her dad's.

'Shall we go home, then?'

★   ★   ★

An hour later, one whole week's worth of hot water brimmed over the Smiths' tub. Five different kinds of salts had been mixed in, leaving the water gritty and overpowering with the fragrance of flowers. Gloria and her mother, silent as handmaidens, unwrapped Jean's head and body and held her arms as she stepped into the bath and lowered herself into the water. Anyone watching would not have been able to tell if she was being prepared for marriage or sacrifice, so closely was the girl with tortured flesh being attended to. Gloria and Mrs Smith stretched out Jean's arms and drew the sponges along their length; then did the same with her legs, extending each as far and as straight as it would go; then finally stood her up to rinse her back before lowering her again into the water. When she was clean, Gloria's mother let a little of the water out and went to fetch some more for a soak. Jean leaned forward and rested her head on her knees; the heat and the extraordinarily pleasant sensation of being cared for had left her feeling weak, and she worried she might cry. She closed her eyes against the possibility. Gloria sat on a little footstool by the bath and absently dabbed Jean's back with a sponge.

'Isn't it better to be out of those clothes and all nice and clean?'

Jean nodded, and wondered what she would wear now. She wasn't aware of owning anything. At that moment, it hardly mattered. 'Tell me about the funeral,' she murmured.

'I told you ages ago. Don't you remember?'

'No.'

'It was right after you woke up. I came straight away, as soon as they'd let me.'

'I know. I know you were there, I just don't remember.'

'Well, anyway, there wasn't many of us there. Me, Mum, Dad, the vicar. It was very cold, that day — might have been a bit of rain — not turnout weather. We didn't know what to do after, but we thought we should have a cup of tea at least so we went to Simpsons on the front. We could have done it at home but then it would have been just us having tea, so we thought we'd have it out, then it would count.'

'That was nice. Someone was there at least.'

'The gas people sent a wreath, isn't that nice? Seems a pipe under your house blew up, they don't know why yet, even after all this time. Just one of those things. We all thought it had started. Next door went into their shelter and didn't come out till the next morning. I saw her brought out you know, your mum. And you. She was under a sheet but you they carried out in a blanket. There was a bit of fuss at first.' Gloria leant closer to Jean's ear. 'I don't think you had anything on.' She giggled. Jean waited for a flush of shame to creep over her wet skin, but it remained only steam-heated. Like women who have given birth to wanted children, she could no longer be embarrassed about a body that had served her so well. It had managed to keep life inside it. Gloria playfully squeezed the sponge over her ear, and Jean obligingly shook her head and laughed.

'I was waiting for hours, night and day for

126

you,' Gloria elaborated, clearly lost in a moving picture of her own making. 'You looked so happy to be alive, everyone was crying, and you were smiling. They'd all but given up hope.'

Jean vaguely remembered smiling and waving as she was carried down to the ambulance, which she'd fancied a carriage waiting to return her to the palace she'd been stolen from. She shuddered with the shame of having been borne away from death grinning with life. Gloria took the movement as a sign Jean was getting cold and squeezed more hot water onto her back.

'You didn't tell me that before.'

'Well, I didn't want to in there. Everyone listening in. And the ward sister! Mum and Dad tried to come with me once, and she wouldn't let them both in. Two visitors, twice a week, that's the rules, she said. Cow. She used to give me evils and she put her paws all over the confectionery, as if I was smuggling in a saw or something.'

'I'm glad you came, though.'

'Well, I wasn't going to leave you, was I?'

Jean had tried not to cry every time Gloria left her. When her visits went down from twice to once a week, Jean at least knew she was getting better. Gloria dabbed at a small scar on Jean's forehead that she had received some years ago by way of an airborne breadbin.

'She was a right old bugger, your mum, wasn't she?'

Gloria felt Jean's head nod in agreement under her fingertips.

'I mean, you shouldn't speak ill of the dead,

but sometimes you're just better off, aren't you?'

'She wasn't happy.'

'No, she wasn't, Jean. Indeed she was not. Perhaps she is now, eh? That's a better way to look at it. She's happy and at peace now.'

'Who is?' Gloria's mum was on her way in with a steaming jug of illicit water.

'Mrs Clocker. I was just saying, she's on her way to heaven now, isn't she? So she'll be happy and at peace.'

Gloria's mother raised an eyebrow and set the jug down. She turned again at the door to give Gloria the eyebrow again and then left them alone. Gloria turned her attention to a spot on Jean's back to cover her guilty grin while Jean rested her chin on her knees and imagined her mother at the pearly gates with all the other hundreds that died that night, a lot of them foreign to boot. No heavenly choir, just a queue as long as the butcher's with her mother trying to get anyone who would listen to acknowledge her special status as the repository of all earthly woes, pushing to the front and demanding to see who was in charge and then spending eternity in righteous indignation at the lack of recognition of her martyrdom.

'Yes,' agreed Jean. 'She's happy now.'

★ ★ ★

A spare bunk was being brought round the next day, but for that first night they would sleep in Gloria's bed. It wasn't wide enough, and Gloria clung like a baby monkey to Jean's back. After

128

her bath, Jean had been dressed in Mr Smith's pyjamas, then given cocoa and buttered toast and a kiss from Gloria's mother that was full of powder and perfume. 'Goodnight,' she said at the door. 'God bless.' Jean had trouble keeping her toast down when the thought crossed her mind that if she'd known all this was waiting, she might have killed her mother herself. Gloria's body was pressed tight up against her and the unfamiliar warmth was intoxicating. She could feel her eyelids being dragged down by sleep but resisted so she could enjoy one, three, five more minutes of this closeness. Gloria had tied a scarf round her head to set her curls, and one around Jean's to keep the silverfish out of her ears. She sometimes felt the memory of them crawling in there, and missed her bandages.

'Can you hear me?' Gloria whispered. Jean nodded and squeezed her hand in confirmation.

'What did you think about, Jean? Did you think you were going to die?'

Jean tried to think back to the house, to everything that had ended there that night. She couldn't remember. She couldn't remember if she had thought about death, or life, or anything more than not making it worse. Which she did a lot of anyway. She wondered if she had squandered yet another opportunity. But Gloria required an answer.

'I think I thought I was dead. For a while. And then I thought I wasn't there at all. I don't know if I thought actually about anything. There wasn't much to think about in there. It was very dark.'

She felt pained at the inadequate answer and contracted slightly in embarrassment. Gloria took a handful of pyjama top to steady herself.

'But didn't you wish for anything, Jean? I would have wished I had been in love. It would be terrible to die without having been in love first, don't you think?'

Jean stared into the darkness. If the house had not been exploded, she would have continued to live without love and only on her death would anyone have thought it terrible. Death would have made it so; life made her merely pathetic. She understood now; it had not been terrible before because she had not been considered living, only waiting to live; waiting for the romance that would animate her, put blood in her veins and breath in her lungs. She had not yet been born, despite having been delivered twice.

But she hadn't wished. Even in the hospital, when her brain wrestled with her new state and possibilities, she didn't wish for love. Could she tell Gloria that? Jean took Gloria's hand from her back and held it.

'Terrible,' she whispered.

Gloria squeezed her hand and then pulled away from her grasp. She drew the eiderdown up over Jean's stomach and held it in place, her fist tucked under Jean's chin.

'It's the only thing in the world that matters,' Gloria breathed in her ear. 'That must be why you didn't die. You were spared because you have to live and find love and get married.' Jean heard the voice of the eleven-year-old Gloria in her head, a lisping undercurrent to the breathy whisper of the young woman next to her. 'Every day from now on is a day on which you could fall in love. You have to be aware of that now. You have to believe it, and it will come true.' Jean closed her eyes, too tired to resist any longer. She could sense Gloria's excitement for herself as well as for Jean; the war had decided it. Gloria had recovered from her disappointment and fallen back in love with love: the romance of uniforms, forced partings and well-dressed torment. Jean could feel Gloria's ideal of love surrounding her, nudging its way into her, tickling her chin so she would open her mouth and take the medicine.

Jean had once made the mistake of telling her mother that she was going with Gloria to watch a romance at the pictures. This amused Wisteria, never a good sign.

'Off to dream, are you, dream of love? Think it'll happen, do you? Think you'll find some young man, get yourself married and out your old mum's house?'

'I hadn't thought, Mum.'

Wisteria took a drag and narrowed her eyes, their gleam piercing the smoke that wreathed her face. She pointed at Jean, the cigarette glowing between her fingers.

'There's no other place for you in this world. Just the one you have here, the one you tore out of me. Where else do you think you're going to rest that great body of yours, that big head, those moony eyes? Some things don't fit, and you are one of them.'

She was leaning forward in her chair, tensed, as if she was about to be shot out of it into a net. Jean felt herself adrift in dangerous waters, but somehow she started talking.

'Gloria says that everyone falls in love, everywhere, all over the world. She says that love and marriage are what we're made for.'

Wisteria smiled. 'Do you really think that's what *you're* made for?'

The course of Jean's life had been set by her body; she realised that was what she was being told. It's a cold and leaden feeling to know you will never be loved as much as you want or need to be, or at all. To look at your face and know that it is not a face to inspire passion of any kind, that the most you can hope for is tolerance. To know that you have reserves of love that will never need to be drawn on, that will dry inside you. To feel the waste of your life as you carry it from day to day. Suddenly, Jean could not remember a time when she had not known this. Wisteria saw the realisation dawn in her offspring and, satisfied, settled back into her chair.

What Wisteria had said had felt like truth; something in Jean had accepted it readily. But Gloria's words felt like a kind of truth too. The kind that is dangerously close to hope.

Gloria had fallen asleep, the words that had poured out of her like a spell nestled in Jean's ear. Jean held on to her friend's arm as she moved from under it, Gloria stirred but didn't wake, and Jean slipped out of bed. She stood in front of the mirror in the cold bathroom, barefoot on the lino. The course that her body had set had been changed. She was still herself, and yet she was now things that she should never have been. Free. Alone. Alive. Perhaps not everything she had been told was truth. Your life belongs to me, her mother had once said. It is not yours to give to someone else, even if they wanted it. It's my compensation. Who did she belong to now?

Jean studied her face, daring herself to like something about it. Dark brows and thick lashes framed her brown eyes; her mouth was full, the lips more brown than pink. Her nose had been broken and was now a little wider at the bridge, but it had been set straight and was not too long. Her complexion was clear, apart from the scars. Her face had been lightly scored, two sets of parallel lines cut into the apple of each cheek. She looked at the pinkness of them against her creamy skin; the delicacy of the lines and the weird symmetry of the markings, just a few millimetres deep. Here was something; they were beautiful. 'Hottentot,' she whispered and pressed her lips against the cold glass.

As she withdrew she thought she saw a lick of ashy hair and caught the aspic glitter of a lifeless eye, a shadow trapped between layers of glass.

'Mum. So . . . so you're haunting me, then?'

The thin, shadowy Wisteria smiled. It seemed there were no dentists in the afterlife. As clear as day, Jean heard the reply.

'Why stop now I'm dead?'

133

13

A country whose dictator has recently been toppled can take a while to settle. Wild swings are common, euphoria and depression follow each other as with champagne and a sick headache. The desire to loot and burn is often strong. The land Jean had inhabited was gone; she had nothing to work on but herself. She felt horribly chosen.

What she *was*, had always been known. Passing her pram, women in the street would stop to ask Wisteria what she had eaten to produce such a large baby. 'Smaller babies,' she replied once. No one had yet been able to pinpoint what Jean was actually *for*, however. After the bomb, she felt she had to decide; she had been called.

★   ★   ★

The problem was in knowing what to embrace first. Jean found it hard to concentrate, as everything commanded her attention equally; she felt as if she were in a room full of barking dogs.

'So, what next?' Gloria had asked her.

'Everything,' Jean would have said, had she dared. She heard the word in her head but it hid from her lips.

It was decided that the first thing to do after

the revolution was erase the images of the old guard. They would build Jean again from the ground up, but she would be different, an altogether softer model. Under the new regime, she began to expand freely.

When people are denied love, they don't eat. When they're denying love, they don't feed. Jean's proportions were all the more miraculous for having been achieved on such a small amount of bad food. Resident with Gloria's family, she quickly became truly splendid. Her body had always made the best of what fuel it was given, but her muscular, almost androgynous form was transformed by her stay with the Smiths, who rejected rationing of all kinds. Mrs Smith believed that Jean's wounds would be less deep if she herself expanded to fill them. The new regime was based around bread, potatoes and custard. Supplemented by chocolate. Rounded out by stew and dumplings. Jean quickly became voluptuous, on a grand scale. Before, her body had been unavoidable; now it was compelling. Her breasts swelled and became heavy, her hips and backside rounded. The gravity of youth supported this expansion and she became a fabulous terrace of fleshy levels, swooping in and out like tides. Things did hurt less, there was more between her and the world with its sharp edges and door frames. Jean enjoyed the swing of her new-found prosperity; she wore her flesh like a new dress.

In the months it had taken her to heal, the world had changed. It had become both more and less real. In her hospital bed, time was dished out to her. Hours for sleeping, hours for sitting up like a good girl, hours for walking, half-hours for eating and quarter-hours for washing. Weekdays and weekends leaned against one another until they merged; visiting hours shrank to minutes as her miraculous survival became more boring with each passing day. Christmas was paper streamers and a tree in the courtyard, New Year was a drunk nurse blowing a cardboard trumpet at midnight. Now the seasons mattered less than waking up each morning; each night people were told to turn out their lights as if they had no memory from day to day; the confusing ideals of live for today and conserve for tomorrow were bandied about. Everything was stop-go.

Jean had heard it clearly: 'Everything'. Everything is to come. As soon as war was declared, some women had flown out of the gate to find that the race hadn't yet started, their haste indecent, their celebration of life in the face of death not yet appropriate. In Jean's world people saved for funerals rather than holidays and worried more about surviving in debt and shame than being killed intact and in credit. There was not enough death around yet to justify going mad about it. Gloria had been made all sorts of indecent offers by lads on their way to war.

'I might be dead tomorrow, that's what they all say,' Gloria recounted during one of her hospital visits. 'I said you maybe, but what if I'm not? Leaves me nowhere, that does.'

Jean considered what Gloria had told her about what everyone on their way to war had on their minds and wondered if it should be on hers too. Wisteria had deliberately left her daughter in a state of neglectful naivety, and Jean had been in no danger of revelations delivered by her educators. Cousin Leonard had done more for her with his contraband book than he would ever physically manage for another woman, but that was still very little. Jean decided that she would simply reject nothing.

The rebuilt Jean was to be launched at yet another mixer, a dance designed to peel those such as her from the wall and abandon them in the trembling arms of someone as socially maladroit. She had once hoped the war would bring an end to these, but it seemed that there were just enough men to keep them going — and always more than enough women.

On the night of the dance, Jean sat on her narrow bed and stared at herself in Gloria's nearly-full-length mirror. She had to slump to fit in it. She was in her underwear, a sturdy bra of white cotton teamed with knickers the size of football shorts. Her bath after the last peacetime dance had been the first time she had ever looked at her body for any length of time, and now it had gone and changed. The puckered and seamed version before her was going to take some getting used to. The pain had taken so long to ease, it surprised her how empty her scars were, little pink trenches all filled in.

Jean hooked a chair under the door handle and slipped out of her underwear; Gloria was still in the bath and should take another ten minutes at least. She just wanted a quick look.

She pushed the mirror against the wall and walked as far away from it as possible until she could see everything but her feet and ankles. She took a deep breath and stood up straight.

She was bewitched. In the half-light cast by the feeble lamp, her maturing scars swirled over her like smoke, darkness filling and softening them; the stretches of smooth, unblemished skin made all the more perfect in contrast. She turned to see her body in profile, the rise and fall of her, the firmness of muscle supporting the soft swells of flesh. Her body was a changing landscape, furrowed, scorched and renewed. She raised her arm and traced the line of her underarm down to the small of her back, a path flecked with ridges where she had skated across glass. All the intrusions made were marked on her body: entrance and exit wounds, the marks of reconstruction. She looked like a statue, pitted with decay; a suggestion of beauty ruined supplanting unblemished mediocrity.

The shifting textures of her skin invited touch, but her fingers felt too heavy and clumsy; Jean worried she might crumble away. This delicacy was foreign and not altogether pleasant; vulnerability was not her natural state. Jean held her hand over her heart, hovering a tongue's width above the skin; her palm began to throb as waves of heat broke against it and rolled back into her breast; she felt the air move with her heartbeat. With her eyes closed, she inhaled deeply and forgot her skin; there was only the blood in her veins and the heat pulsing between her palm and her heart. It flowed over her, dissolving the surface to reveal the nerves. Her body was alive. Why did she have to nearly die to know this, to know its beauty? Why had she tried to control it always, punish it? Her breathing grew deeper; she felt as if she could put her hand inside her chest and hold her heart.

When Gloria knocked on the door Jean nearly screamed. She hunched over and gathered herself up, grabbing breasts and belly with trembling hands. The mirror reflected a mortal again; bunched with the fear of discovery, she looked like a shopper trying to stop a collection of stitched parcels from sliding to the floor. Jean smiled sheepishly at the reflection of her knees and hooked her knickers with her big toe; she was almost glad of the opportunity to retreat.

★   ★   ★

The Palace Ballroom appeared to have been decorated by a patriotic tornado: strings of Union Jacks hung from every tier of the auditorium, and the central chandelier wore a ragged skirt of red, white and blue streamers. There were bowls of punch dyed to match, and many of the dancers wore their country's colours on their upper lip. Everyone danced and drank too fast. Jean hadn't seen such speed of consumption before, the prewar world seemed under-cranked by comparison.

The full mania of a country at war had so far passed her by, but Jean was beginning to catch up. She stared while Gloria grumbled about the exorbitant cost of a night out: first the entrance fee, then the relief-fund tins came out, then the cloakroom.

'All done. Now, I'll get us each a drink, but then you should try and get someone else to get yours. We won't get many nights out at this price, and there's no telling what this one'll turn up.' She had an instinctive grasp of the economics of romance.

'Rule Britannia Red or Bulldog Blue? The white one just looks like milk with — ugh — lemonade in it. Makes no sense to me.'

'Red, please.'

Gloria disappeared into the scrum surrounding the bar and quickly returned with two cups of alarming crimson liquid that coated the inside of the clear cups as it sloshed around. 'Cherry brandy with cherryade,' she announced, her top lip bearing a slight stain. 'Not too bad.'

They clinked, careful not to spill any of the viscous liquid, and drank, their painted lips curled back like horses' at the trough. Khaki uniforms dotted the crowd, the new boots making once-familiar dance steps alien again, the pained expression of many of the young girls telling of crushed toes and torn nails.

'What a racket!' Gloria bellowed over the din. 'There's a million people here — haven't seen half of them before. Do you think they're local?'

'Can't tell, everyone looks so different.'

'That's the uniform,' Gloria said knowledgeably. 'It changes a man, gives them character.'

Gives them an itch, thought Jean, watching some squaddies squirm under the unfamiliar weight and coarseness. Her chest felt tight;

excitement glittered in the air like frost; she could feel the current generated by this vast machine of people. It did seem different; it was as if the outside world had come crashing through in a hundred ways. Everything was larger, louder and wilder. She felt less out of place in the chaos; there was no time to worry about that sort of thing now. She grinned at Gloria, who winked back, satisfied that she had done the right thing bringing Jean here.

'To new beginnings,' she toasted.

Jean clinked her cup again. 'Here's hoping.'

Gloria had insisted Jean make a list; they were hoping to knock a few items off the top tonight: she would try out alcohol, dancing and attracting the attention of the opposite sex. Gloria had suggested alcohol first and dancing last for Jean; her own ranking was flexible. A towheaded youth with lashes as blond as a pig's approached Gloria, wringing his cap between his hands. His cheeks were flushed dark red, which, teamed with his blue mouth, made him look clownish and innocent. He brought his cap to his forehead in salute, the insignia making a dull cracking sound as it hit his brow. He pretended not to notice and Jean and Gloria, being polite, pretended as well.

'May I have the next dance, if you're not engaged, that is?'

Gloria looked at her ring finger and held it up to his face.

'Don't seem to be.'

She laughed at her own joke and handed her drink to Jean.

'Do you mind?'

Gloria was smiling but her face was tense. Jean remembered that this was a night of firsts for her too, the first time she had been out since Paul Bradshaw's clumsy shredding of her ideals.

'I'll watch you,' Jean promised.

Gloria hugged her and with sweet cherry breath whispered, 'That's all over with, isn't it. New beginnings.'

The soldier was not sure how well his suit was going.

'So, are you going to dance with me, then?'

Gloria turned to him and held out her hand.

★   ★   ★

Jean haunted the back of the room; every so often she saw Gloria's shoes or her hair spin past her partner's head. They had practised the dances together, Jean throwing her feather-light friend high into the air — but she knew she was unlikely to find a partner who was able to take her for a turn without some kind of pulley system being involved. She watched Gloria leave the ground again and again, fearless in her enjoyment. Gloria seemed able to shake everything off, believing no one could seriously mean her harm. The greasy boy with the oil-stained nails had been an anomaly, as well defined as the enemy in war.

Jean scanned the room for familiar faces but could find none, and was content, as ever, to watch. The atmosphere was bright to the point of manic; there was more screaming than on the rides at the seafront as girls were chased and pints downed in wagers. Jean felt alive to detail; the low, brassy buzz of the band made her insides feel as if they were being squeezed like an accordion; a mirrored ball scattered light over everyone's heads; she extended her arm and captured discs of it in her hand. 'Everywhere something is happening,' she thought. Jean felt pleasantly part of it all, the ballroom, the crowd, the whole business. She took a sip of her drink and left a cherry brandy smile curling at the edges of her mouth.

From a dark corner, a young soldier watched her. He was sweating under the heavy uniform, but his head felt cool, the regulation haircut having exposed a fair bit of his scalp. He kept patting the bald patches, as if hoping to find them magically regrown. He was rattish in the face, with a long, sharp nose and protruding teeth, but his features were softened by his eyes, which were beautiful and held the possibility of kindness in them. For ten minutes he had watched the big girl as she surveyed the room, liking her curiosity and the fact that she was enormous, indestructible-looking.

He didn't expect to live; he suspected he had no talent for it and would probably be shot straight away. He hadn't done very well in training and had been bawled at by massive sergeants who assured him his chances of survival were less than nil. He had found himself agreeing. He wished he could climb inside the enormous girl and wait out the war safe in her.

Glasses of punch were passed backwards from the bar, baptising everyone in their path with splashes of sticky colour. Dismissing the likelihood of being bought a drink, Jean joined the queue. A large group of soldiers ordered drinks for an even larger group of girls, cannily increasing their chances. One turned from the bar, each hand occupied with brimming cups of Bulldog Blue, to find himself face to chest with Jean.

'Christ!' he exclaimed, looking up. 'A tank in a dress, nothing less. I hope you're on our side, darlin'.' And then he went on tiptoe to kiss her brandy-stained lips, earning cheers from his mates. Jean blushed, unsure whether the kiss was part of the joke. He handed her a drink and clinked their glasses together. 'Chin chin!'

They were all looking at her now, a dozen or more scrubbed young faces poking out of ill-fitting uniforms. She raised her glass, unused to being the centre of so much attention.

'Would you look at that!' A harsh city accent came out the crowd, its owner lost. He sounded small, and bullish because of it.

'She's a one of a kind,' said a redheaded boy, so flushed with drink the start of his hair and the finish of his face had merged. 'That's got to be good luck!' He jumped forward onto his mate's back and planted a kiss on Jean's chin. He had started a riot; the rest crowded forward, eager to touch the sainted freak. Jean found herself being grabbed and kissed more times by each individual than the total she had received in her life. She was pulled down by the ears so the smaller ones didn't have to jump up or hang from her neck; men climbed over each other and balanced drunkenly with a foot cupped in a mate's hand. They cheered and insisted she drink with them; the girls they were with were applauding too. Jean downed three drinks in quick succession, each one striking her brain and sending a shower of sparks into her eyes. She felt wonderful and hot and sick and wonderful again. Something *had* changed.

'What shall we do next?' The initiator was looking around for the next jape. He jumped to kiss her on the cheek, and then, without malice, smacked her on the rump. He held up his hand as if it had inspired him.

'Let's go find a hunchback and rub its hump!'

The group roared their approval as they swept past Jean, heading for the street. She was alone again. Jean felt stripped, a thing uncovered by the tide of laughter that had gone out. She was a lucky freak, something so anomalous as to signify good fortune for others, a collision of stars or fates. Jean felt herself get taller; her head hit the gilded ceiling, bobbing among the balloons, as empty and silly as they. She was ridiculous and huge and wanted nothing more than to be invisible. The rat-faced soldier saw his chance.

'Come with me.'

Jean looked down to see a man offering her his hand; she took it and he pulled her from the room. For all her bulk, she seemed not to have the power to move herself.

'Where are we going?'

He didn't answer her, but kept hold of her hand and kept them both moving. The sounds of the ballroom faded away as they passed through the heavy curtains to the foyer; she could hear his uniform against his skin. The interior sign for the side exit was illuminated, casting a sickly yellow pool onto the carpet, but, when he opened the door, the outside was completely, invisibly black. He stopped, and turned to look at her. Jean couldn't read what was in his face, whether this was an escape or an abduction, but she couldn't see anything to fear. He bowed slightly when opening the door, and when he swept his hand over the threshold, it disappeared into the darkness. No one had wasted mystery on her before.

★ ★ ★

The alley behind the dance hall was slick with rain and rubbish. Jean picked her way through the rot. His boots sucked the ground behind her, urging her on. A vent above their heads poured warm, sickly sweet air down over them. She moved away from it, searching for crisp, sobering cold. He caught her arm and with gentle but insistent pressure pushed her against the wall.

'This your first time?' he asked.

'What, in an alley?' Jean tutted as if he was an idiot, and he smiled at her confusion.

'Don't worry,' he said. 'This'll be nice. You'll like it.'

It seemed like a promise, so she accepted it as one. She was not sure what was coming, but she knew it had something to do with her being more than a child, with taking this new freedom and doing what was expected with it. Jean's usual wants were food, sleep, respite. Romance was nothing to a day without being walloped, spat on or just exhausted by the demands of others. But kindness surrounded her now; she was plump with food and affection, and starting to feel a different sort of hunger. She was getting the idea that it could be a nice thing, to be kissed.

The vent carried the sounds of the ballroom on the sweet air it exhaled; the dances often called for a collective something-or-other, shriek, slap or kick, to punctuate them. A communal gasp, reduced by distance to a sigh, floated down. He opened her dress quickly and pressed the flesh of her stomach hard until he could feel her pulse beat through the skin. She was just pieces in the dark; where the air raised bumps on her flesh, where the warmth of her dress was receding — small islands in black water. Her body raised a ruckus talking to itself; messages darted, sparking confusing chains of sensations far removed from the site of activity. She was abstract, cartoon squiggles set to music. It was more interesting than fun, more striking than harmonious.

The darkness was whole; Jean felt as if she were back in the rubble of the house. There was a strange pressure on her skin, an all-over insistence, like the vacuum of the tub. She felt surrounded, her body again being explored with dispassion. She sensed he had no more feeling for her than did the creatures that had crawled inside her looking for warmth. He also was looking for life.

Jean leaned her head back against the wall and tried to make sense of what was happening. He was her first project; he would tell her something about herself, something she could use. Her nerves tingled with the excitement of impending enlightenment; part of her problem, she knew, was that she didn't know anything. She was an innocent without a map or a feel for the landscape. He was going to show her the way. She winced at the feel of cotton suddenly inside her; he seemed to be taking a roundabout route.

'What're you doing?'

'Be quiet. Just keep still.'

Jean had once seen a street magician use two fingers to wad an entire handkerchief into his closed palm. She wondered if the boy was trying to do that to her, with her own underwear. She gasped at the sudden awareness of her insides and at the pain caused by his endeavour. She found it hard to control her flinching. After a minute or two, he withdrew his fingers and applied them instead to the waistband of her knickers. Jean was so glad to have them pulled clear of her that, for a moment, she forgot to be concerned at the serious turn events were taking. Raised in the damp dark of ignorance, she may have had no more than a mushroom's idea when it came to sex, but she knew that underwear was more than fabric and stitches; it was the shield that stood between a woman and ruin, between the parlour and the gutter. And hers was somewhere around her knees.

Fear nibbled at the edges of her excitement. She feared not for her physical self, but for something she couldn't name. Her moral self, perhaps — though she hadn't one as far as she knew. She was as a child, a list of prohibited and permitted. So far, he had done nothing that she could identify, nor place in either column. What it was didn't feel quite right, but it did not feel unnatural. He was pulling at his own clothes now, the scratchy army khaki was irritating her skin; she squirmed against it, which made him push at her harder while he rummaged inside his trousers. He grabbed at her shoulders with shaking hands and tried to hoist himself up onto her like an acrobat in a formation team. But fastening onto her, he jittered up and down like an excited whippet. With a shod foot he tried to prise her knees apart but she resisted, though his heel scraped painfully against her skin. When it was clear she was not going to give in, he gave up and wrapped himself instead around her, her insides losing their appeal as her exterior apparently served as well.

Jean wondered if this was supposed to be pleasurable, or would perhaps become so later on; or if there would be a kiss at the end. She bore it the only way she knew how, lifting her head above the unpleasantness and counting until it stopped. Which it did, at thirty-seven. At forty it started again. At eighty-three it slowed, until at one hundred and nine it stopped. At one hundred and thirty she was confident it had stopped for good, though he still hung about her, seemingly unable to get down. With her eyes raised to heaven, she sighed and shucked him off. He slid to the floor like a rain-sodden overcoat.

Suddenly concerned for her new dress, she ran a hand up and down the fabric. There were no rips or tears, and it was dry. For his sake, she was glad; the urge to thump had flared fast and brilliant. Her back was a little damp from the wall; she hoped it hadn't stained. Jean buttoned herself up; the soldier was still on the floor and had made no move to rearrange his clothes.

'Was that it? You said I'd like it.'

The crumpled figure began to cry. Jean pursed her lips in annoyance; she hadn't discovered anything worth this strange feeling she had been left with, a sense of compromise, of exposure. Of being cheated. She had discovered nothing but that her underwear could be wadded up. A bike ride on a loose saddle could have told her that much.

'Was that all?' Jean persisted.

The boy's sobs became more guttural as he tried to mix words in with them.

'I just . . . I ju . . . I d . . . don't want to die.'

This finished him and he curled up in a ball, shoulders heaving. Jean felt her foot catch his side as she stepped over him.

'Well, I don't see how that's going to help,' she snapped, and groped her way towards the exit door. She went looking for Gloria but was instead found by her, hours later, in the ladies' lounge, asleep under her coat.

14

Jean hadn't counted on being so swiftly abandoned, but, after waiting so patiently for her friend to be uncovered, Gloria went and buried herself.

Jean had been wrong about Gloria; Paul Bradshaw had scarred her. She hadn't shaken off a thing, not the feeling of inadequacy when he had overpowered her, nor the knowledge of his contempt for everything that she was. She had been grateful for the excuse of Jean's injuries, which had allowed her to withdraw and mourn her lost sense of self. Her appearance at the Palace Ballroom had been an act of recovery; she had wanted to find that she was again the girl of someone's dreams. It hadn't really mattered whose.

She hadn't even remembered the boy in the morning, waking only with the sense that she was admired again: whole. When he, her fiancé, turned up on her doorstep, the full horror of what had occurred dropped on Gloria like boots out of a window. Her mother took her into the kitchen, smacked her backside and then went out to welcome the young man into her home.

A bewildered Jean was sent to church and sat through three rousing services in which God allied himself firmly with the English. Church-going had not been a component of her life up until then, Wisteria having told her daughter it was her birth that was the proof against God.

Sitting on the bone-hard pews, Jean came to see the religious quality of her mother's rantings, full of dark warnings about penance, retribution and divine will. Hers. Jean felt oddly at home and settled in, being under strict instructions from Mr Smith not to return home until six. The vicar was enjoying himself and felt renewed passion in the same old tenets; these would be his glory days. Threatened with death and chaos, believers crowded the pews, seeking the comforting, familiar words designed to quiet their fear of the random and the inexplicable.

Gloria, married. Jean could not see it. The night before, she had not been in love; the morning after, she had a fiancé. Something terrible or wonderful had happened in the hours they had been separated. Something that, either way, didn't include Jean. Her legs began to ache from the sitting, and she longed to be in motion again. She comforted herself with the thought that Gloria's husband-to-be was a soldier, and might be killed before he could return for the wedding. She scanned the walls of the church for interest and alighted on a tapestry rendering of the ten commandments, not seen or thought of since schooldays, when they made not a bit of sense to her. With a little more understanding behind her, Jean realised she was already past perfection.

★　★　★

Gloria had always been keenly aware of her reflection, in mirrors or in the eyes of others; the

152

image returned to her was beautiful and sweet, constant. In recent months, however, she felt as if she were looking at the back of a spoon. Unfair distortions of her looked back, curled in the heat of rejection. Perhaps the boy was supposed to cure that. She couldn't remember. She only wanted him to stop looking at her now; she was not the angel he was seeing. She could feel his pale gaze, like clammy fingers, wandering over her face, and wanted to wrench her head away; she couldn't bring herself to meet those blond-fringed eyes. She had finally settled, and for so little.

Slivers of the previous evening pierced her conscience. Her own voice rang in her head. 'Yes. Yes, you brave boy, I will marry you.' Brave boy. It sounded like her. The brave boy was called Harry; he introduced himself to Gloria's parents, as she was unable to. Mrs Smith had produced a cake that sat uneaten on the table. Harry at least acknowledged it, but no one had any appetite.

'That's a lovely cake, Mrs Smith. I'm sure I won't see anything as good as that for a while.'

'Shall I wrap it for you? We've hardly touched it. In all the excitement.'

'Oh, I . . . I'm not sure. I don't think it'll go in my kit. I don't have a tin.'

'Oh, I don't think I've got a spare one either. Never mind, have another piece now?'

The first slice lay sweating on his plate, made warm and flabby by an hour of neglect. Mrs Smith wished he would eat it and take another, knowing he would never have Gloria. His fiancée kept her eyes on the floor; sweats and chills raced up and down her back and she hoped she would not vomit. It was as much the guilt as the cherry brandy; she knew she had made a horrible mistake and she had no idea how to undo it without being what everyone said she was: Gloria the tease, Gloria the bitch, Gloria the stuck-up, heartless cow. Could she really do this just to be thought of as good and nice?

'And your family has a farm, Harry?'

'Dairy farm, Mrs Smith. Just on the county border, not far at all. The next village'll be getting a bus service in six months, or a year. If we're married on next leave, Gloria can still come and visit regular.'

'That's very thoughtful, dear.'

Gloria swallowed bile and prayed for the sky to fall.

★   ★   ★

It went on for two hours: Harry's bright optimism, Gloria's cold silence. He wouldn't give in; he would take the possibility of her with him. The information he gave about himself was as much for Gloria's benefit as for her parents. He could tell on the doorstep she hadn't remembered him; he could have tried to sell her a magazine subscription and she would have been none the wiser. He looked at her red-rimmed eyes and told himself it was for him and his precarious future she had been crying. He knew it was a lie but why should he be fair? And he had meant it, he did want to marry her.

He had thought that as soon as he had seen her. She had listened to him talk about the farm and pronounced it wonderful; she had touched his arm and looked into his eyes, she had let him kiss her after he said it would bring him luck in battle, her eyes growing huge and watery when he said he would die happy after kissing such a pretty girl. But he knew.

Gloria was made to see him out. They lingered at the door, Gloria waiting for the courage to tell him never to come back, Harry hoping for a kiss. He had so little time to impress her, and wanted so much for her to like him.

'Will you write to me?'

'Of course. When I can. When there's something to write about.' She shrugged, preparing the stony ground onto which his hopes would fall.

'I won't care what it is. If it's from you, it'll be the best letter ever.'

At this, tears welled in Gloria's eyes again. He at least thought she was good and kind and worthy. So she told herself some lies. She told herself she could be his fiancée just until the end of the war and then break it off, that it wouldn't be fair to send him into battle thinking no one cared for him. Or that although they weren't in love now, they could be later, through the exchange of horribly romantic letters, smeared with the mud of the trenches. Gloria made up her mind, she would not welsh. She would sacrifice herself for the greater good. Thinking of it like that made her feel a little better. But not much. She managed a smile and directed it at the boy in a soldier's costume.

'Take care of yourself, won't you?'

If it had been a solemn vow, he could not have been happier to hear it; he flung his arms around her and kissed her; the tears running down her cheeks crept into the kiss and wet their lips. Gloria put her arms around his neck in an approximation of passion. She had practised feelings her whole life and knew the appropriate gestures at least. If her arms felt a little slack and her mouth a little tight, he didn't let on. After a few seconds, she began to tire and pushed him away. He had no ring to give her, and so Gloria was left instead with a locket containing youthful pictures of his parents. She covered their faces with red paper. Jean returned later that night to a different house.

Acts of conversion were taking place all over town. The cardboard factory was turned into a munitions plant; flower beds were victory gardens; Gloria had become hopeless. When Harry's first letter arrived, she retired to her room and plumped her face with tears. She emerged an hour later, desperate with grief.

'He's always going to love me,' she moaned, and sank into a chair.

Jean could do little more than shrug helplessly. She and Gloria were out of their depth. Their futures were both unexpected, Jean's little short of miraculous in its existence, Gloria's total in its disappointment. What the night had made romance, the day revealed as fear. Now her war was over, and her god had abandoned her.

15

As the war took hold, the town's young male population gradually bled out. After the first waves of enthusiasm, the departures were not as noticeable; there were fewer grand send-offs and more quiet disappearances, as if the men were stolen in the night like princesses. Then only the old and the lame were left behind.

A creeping feminisation of the town followed. Like strange new species emerging from under their protective rocks, more and more women appeared. Spinsters emerged, blinking, into the present; young slatterns took the street corners vacated by young louts. There were some like her, once conspicuous in their aloneness, now liberated by others' isolation. Like a drop of wine on a dark skirt, they didn't show. They were free to move around and take in their surroundings unseen and unselfconscious. Jean no longer had to find a mate to hide her from the world, to try to cover her freakishness with respectability. She had been released from the round of rejection and anticipation before it had a chance to curdle her. She felt she might join the world.

Gloria, meanwhile, was in retreat. She saw her other dreams slide in sympathy with the romantic imaginings that had turned to congealed reality. She vomited and passed out during her induction at the hospital. It was not always an automatic disqualifier, but the sister saw something in Gloria that was at odds with the ideals she intended to foster in her girls, something romantic and immovable. She would be trouble. So Gloria now would not spend her war nursing photogenically wounded officers, and they would not spend the war nursing crushes on her. Her father had expanded the range of their business, seeing shortages in the future, and now she bagged potatoes and cabbage as well as fruity gums and crystals. Gloria insisted the smell of cabbage had worked its way into her hands like acid; in the evenings, she would slump in an armchair, sniffing at her fingers. Beauty was rewarded, this was the central tenet of her faith, and it been exposed as a lie.

Mrs Smith told her to break the engagement off, but Gloria refused. 'If I took away his reason to live, I'd be good as killing him, wouldn't I?' She still thought love had some control over the universe, though the pursuit of it had set hers spinning. When the first telegrams began to arrive, Gloria realised fully what the war could do. She saw a neighbour collapse on her own front step, her children wailing at the sight of her, women rushing to pull her indoors. In her hand was a rectangle of yellow paper. Gloria told herself she was no more miserable than girls with genuine sweethearts, who carried the fear of losing them day to day. But she had thought there would be a great, shattering love in her life. Instead, its place had been filled by Harry. Sweet, unloved Harry.

Until the explosion, Jean had survived:

proficiently but also merely. Afterwards, she was faced with the problem of finding what use she could be. She sought purpose, just as Gloria was losing hers, and it put miles between them.

The shop was too small to employ both of them, though Gloria's father sometimes wished it was Jean he could keep on. Drifting through intangible misery, Gloria moved with the put-upon grace of a model in an extremely heavy hat. At each request for goods, she would pause and sigh as fate's hands pressed on her shoulders, then she would shrug and move out of reach, turning to the shelves for the tin of paste or jar of gherkins.

As Gloria would not now be marrying the rich man who might have employed her lumpen friend as a maid, Jean realised that if there was to be a place for her in this new world, she had to earn it — she had to be allowed to. She had no expectations, only hopes. So when the letter arrived telling her to report for assessment, it felt like being given a passport. The war was not only happening around her, it was going to happen to her.

A more enlightened military would have posted her to the front immediately, if only as a deterrent against invasion, but she was rejected by all branches as being insufficient: insufficiently educated, insufficiently responsive (still the old fear of sudden movements at close quarters, the parade ground was no more than a bowling alley to her) and insufficiently feminine (no uniform or shoe would fit her). She would not convert. So she continued as she had been, and went into demolition. The women of the crews would come to be known as Amazons.

War saps individuality, and Jean was happy to give a little of hers up. The overalls she was issued with were exactly the same as everyone else's — a point of great pride — just in a man's size. She loved the length of stride they afforded her. (Despite their practicality, Jean had been denied trousers until the war, her mother finding something immoral in covering the legs separately.) She now discovered that she could kick as high as her own head and enjoyed finding obstructions to jump over. The overalls were cinched at the waist with an old belt of Gloria's father's; the cuffs hovering above Jean's ankles revealed a donated pair of brown brogues — more comfortable than the pair she lost in the house — worn with clean white socks; she pushed her sleeves up to hide the fact they didn't meet her wrists. A red hanky struggled to contain her hair. Jean had an identity, an occupation. She was Women's Civil Defence. They set about the bombsites after the wounded and dead had been taken away, sorting the reusable from the unrecognisable. Though she could never bring herself to enter a cellar, and would one day write a will that specified pins be jabbed in her arms before the coffin was sealed, the sight of a bombed house caused Jean no pain or fear. She enjoyed her work with no pangs of recognition or regret; she was involved in salvage now, and it seemed appropriate. As seamed by scars as any veteran, on some days she felt them sing as if they were power lines that carried electricity through her. She wondered if others could hear the lifesong they transmitted; it must seem an obscene ditty to some, she thought. Those who had lost instead of gained. Like Gloria.

Jean didn't know how to comfort her. Gloria had been expert at distracting Jean from the realities of her life; the thought that she ever would have needed the same was too foreign to take in. Instead, Jean surrendered to the pull of the war.

It amazed Jean to emerge every morning to a landscape different from the one she went to bed against: trees uprooted, houses spirited away, great yawning mouths in the middle of roads. There was so much invention. She worried that if she did not make herself new, this renewing world would leave her behind. But there was no time to think, only to be. The war consumed her interest and all the hours she could give it, its hunger making her feel wanted. She followed the radio reports, collected scrap in her spare time as well as at work and accompanied Gloria's father on fire-watching duty, a huge thermos strapped to her back, warming it nicely, leaving his hands free to hold the binoculars and metal whistle. Though she was terrified, though she grieved with every hit, every loss, part of her spent those nights on the roof looking for the edge of the war, its end, hoping she would not find it.

Death came often to the seaside. Jean grew strong shifting tons of rubble left over from lives taken, and the survivors added their own lifesongs to the din around them. The air crackled with the static of people.

It could go in any direction, the static, numbing life or making it a fierce itch that can never be quelled. Jean let hers sing through her arms and legs as she worked; she didn't want to stop at the end of each day because then she would be deafened by the excess of life within her and reminded that what she was, was not enough. Not yet. If she could have opened a vein to let it out, she would have. But it was more than blood, it was something that had entered her with the bomb, and it was multiplying. As were her secrets. Sometimes she would come home so alive with the possible that she would have to bite her own tongue. She couldn't tell, there was too much to lose. How could she tell poor, disappointed Gloria how much she loved it all? She could barely stand to admit it to herself.

Jean's favourite day was bloodless and strange. A plane had crashed but not exploded; the roof of an ordinary suburban house wore it at a jaunty angle, like a pin through a hat. The owners had been in their shelter, and no one had been hurt; even the pilot wasn't badly injured and was hauled off by the police, who hadn't a clue what to do with his craft. For a few days it was quite the tourist attraction, crowds gathering to gaze at the accidental wonder. Then the ministry declared it a hazard, and its removal was ordered. Jean had walked past the plane every morning since it had hit and had crept out to see it once at night. It was the most magical thing.

This was her shame; she loved the chaos of war. It wasn't a theatre, it was a circus, and it had finally come for her. It could be something other than brutal and nonsensical, and these rare moments had to be savoured, enjoyed like English sunshine. Jean had seen the storm of limbs, the juggling of arms, heads, teeth — the moment when even the plainest human realises their extraordinary beauty before it is scoured off them by fire and raked by shrapnel. She now secretly suspected there had never been anything so perfect as her back before the bomb; as broad as a double bass and as sensuously curved, it had been unblemished. One of the scars even looked like a sound hole, carved beside the strings of her spine; an adornment rather than a wound. She added this to her pile of secrets, fearing that she was the only one who could see it this way; that she alone could love plainness with the fierceness of one who almost died before living.

On the day of demolition, Jean slowly made her way to the house. Her feet dragged when usually they leapt. She ached at the thought of having to tear the beautiful joke apart. It seemed a cousin to her, and she should respect its right to exist. A small crowd awaited the spectacle of the aircraft's removal, which went against the wishes of the owner; he believed it was the only thing holding his house up. He was arguing with the firemen even as they manoeuvred the winches into position. Jean waded through the crowd to join her crew, who were holding people back with a barrier of swearing and cigarette smoke. Two children considering a push for the front changed their minds immediately. Ringside, Frankie — a redhead with a dirty laugh born of sweet experience — felt someone move behind her and used an elbow to reinforce the message of the cordon. It sank harmlessly into Jean.

'It's me. Am I late?'

Frankie looked up and gave Jean a crooked, welcoming smile; the gap between her two front teeth had inspired her husband to propose after just two weeks. The night before he left, he gently pressed a fingernail into the gap, measuring it for remembrance, crying as he did so. Frankie had enjoyed three lovers since he had joined up, all of them similarly beguiled. 'It makes them think,' she told Jean, 'what else can't she quite keep together?'

Frankie slipped an arm through Jean's, transferring her weight to her by way of a greeting. Frankie was another secret. Where there was no longer understanding between her and Gloria, where Jean was afraid to tell the truth, Frankie entered. It was so harmless, but Jean felt the guilt of infidelity — she had yet to realise that to reach out for one thing did not always mean relinquishing your hold on another. And Jean needed Frankie. She had begun to tell Jean things she wanted to know.

They tied handkerchiefs over their noses and mouths to keep out the dust. Frankie lifted hers and spat. She was smaller than Jean — they all were — and skinny, but strong in her way. The two had become friends after competing over a slab of lead roofing that was too heavy for any of the others to lift. Frankie had sat on it to stop Jean stealing the salvaging glory, and in a moment of frustration — she hated anything that came between her and her calling — and perhaps exhibition, Jean had lifted them both, holding lead and Amazon above the ground for a few still moments before depositing them in a wheelbarrow. Frankie reclined as if in a chauffeured car and made Jean wheel her round the site while she waved with regal distaste at the rest of the crew. On their next break, Frankie slipped Jean some gin from a flask, and even Jean recognised this as an overture of friendship. They were both intent on proving something, on putting themselves to use.

'Can you believe it?' Frankie tutted. 'I promised my eldest I'd take them to see it at the weekend.'

Jean shook out her clean hankie and began to tie it behind her head. 'Do you think it's going to go?'

'It won't unless that herbert gets out the way. Says he's been there since six.'

The middle-aged owner of the house was lying down in front of the gate. He was red-faced and angry and kept repeating, 'Home and castle, mate. Home and castle.'

'Bloody old fool,' Frankie muttered, 'just get on with it.'

Two policeman were now trying to haul the corpulent, cantankerous objector up. He had the toddler's trick of making himself completely rigid, and they were able only to roll him about the pavement as if he were on fire but refusing to accept the fact. The attendant police and fire officers were clearly ready to kick the man into the gutter when a quick-thinking member of the ambulance volunteers shoved a stretcher under him mid-roll, and before the man could object further, he was hoisted up into the air and then into the back of the ambulance, accompanied by the cheers of the crowd.

''Bout bleedin' time!' Frankie shouted, drawing another chorus of approval. The police and Amazons moved the crowd to the end of the street, and the extraction began. It lasted all of a minute and a half; it seemed that as soon as the crane got a hook on the tail section of the plane, the house knew its glory days were over and the entire thing collapsed showily. In the ensuing squall of rubble, one policeman suffered a broken wrist and another a broken nose from the owner, who had managed to get out of the ambulance. Frankie, Jean and the others surveyed the perfect puffball of dust that rose in place of the house, the plane just visible swinging from the crane on its metal noose. Dismay settled on them along with the fine powder of old plaster.

'Ugh!' Frankie pressed the handkerchief against her nose and lips. 'What a bloody mess.'

Jean sighed and turned away, blinking the grit out of her eyes. It was all usual again, and ugly.

The Amazons' leader was a stout woman of forty-five who attacked piles of rubble with a furious indignation, as if they were obscuring her hall carpet. She was keen to get going and blew the whistle signifying the crew's advance to the settling mass.

'Shame, though. Isn't it?' Frankie said absently as they walked.

'Oh yes,' Jean agreed. 'Lovely house.'

'No, I mean the thing of it.' Frankie went on, looking down at her legs, shaking out the material loosely gathered around them. 'Shame it had to go. It was funny, really. The plane going in like that. Like a stray dart at the pub. I really wanted the kids to see it.'

She strode off without waiting for a reply. There was something about being behind masks that made them say what they felt. They were never quite as honest when they had their faces uncovered, even in the pub after work; sordid details were shared easily, but real truths were harder to come by. Jean allowed herself a smile once Frankie's back was to her. She wasn't the only one to see it — there *was* wonder here as well as horror.

16

During a raid, Jean would sit under the Smiths'
kitchen table and listen to the bombs drop,
shaking with the impact. Each hit seemed to be
saying, 'do something', 'do something', 'do
something'. Sometimes she wanted to run out
and shout at them, 'What? What do you want?'
She had thrown herself into the war, fulfilled
every one of its requirements save dying, and
still she could feel something telling her: 'do
something', 'do more'.

Frankie thought she knew. 'That's your
knickers talking, Jeanie-Bean,' she said. Jean had
not really understood what she meant, but
smiled and wriggled as if someone had poked a
finger in her side and she had found herself to
be ticklish. Frankie had given her a nickname;
Jean's first kind one.

Frankie had an instinct for pleasure; she knew
the simplest hundred ways to give it. For Jean, it
was a name, something small and sweet that
could belong to the child she never was. It had
been bestowed in the pub, after a long shift. Jean
spent more and more time with her crew and
less at the Smiths' cosy flat. There was often too
much to hide from them, and she needed an
hour or so after work to tuck it all away before
she went back for her tea. That's when she and
Frankie would talk, and she told her, as she had
told no one, of the feeling she got sometimes,

168

like a pounding on a door. In the dark of an alley behind the Palace Ballroom, Jean had tried to understand something about life: the response that it requires from the living. She had begun to see, to fear, that it was more than mechanical, it was more than the airy creaking of her lungs, the thick liquid in her veins, the penetration of her body. Wisteria told her daughter all the ways she was wrong; Gloria told her friend of all the wonderful things to be had; neither of them could tell her what she was *for*. Then Frankie told her about the strange notion of pleasure.

It had been a revelation, fleshing out the suggestion contained within Cousin Leonard's dirty book. It came from a confession. Frankie had to tell someone, and there was no one else who wouldn't tell her husband, who wouldn't think of her as betraying him. Jean had no desire to hurt, no experience by which to judge and no talent for censure. Frankie would never admit she was asking for absolution, but she did feel absolved by Jean, comforted beyond reason.

Her first affair was after a bad night in the shelter with her two children; the fear of them dying had been like acid inside her. Frankie emerged in the morning feeling charred from the back of her teeth down to the pit of her stomach. Tea was dishwater, food was ash; she pulled her children to her and inhaled the fragrance of their hair and skin, the white-bread and milk smell of the youngest, the elder's sharper, grassy tang. It filled the empty core of her for a while, until the fading scent scared her as much as the scream of the raids. She wanted to take pieces of her children and preserve them so they would keep their smell and their softness for ever. She cut locks from their hair and stood poised over them, with open scissors, for a second too long. Ordering them outside, Frankie sat in her kitchen and told herself she was going mad. She took the children to her mother's and went out, resolving to stay out until she could taste something other than the death of her babies. She found him in a pub; he bought her a drink and stared at the gap between her teeth, wondering how much of his tongue he could push through it. For a night she felt her body ache with something other than anticipated loss; how could she not want it again?

'If Bill was here, it would be different,' she explained. 'It wasn't another man, so much as the way it just is with a man. I didn't even know I was going to do it until I saw him in the pub. I want to die warm. Or at least only just cooling off.'

The remark had floated on silence while Jean turned it over in her mind. This was Frankie's first test of her, of her own suspicion that the dark, heavy girl could hold mystery in her till it suffocated.

'Have I shocked you?'

Jean had shaken her head. 'I'd like to feel like that,' she admitted. 'If not warm then just cooling off.'

'Well, you just need to find someone that does it for you, then. Not everyone will. Not even the ones you like, sometimes. You've got to have a bit of patience.'

Frankie seemed to think that Jean was not automatically disqualified; pleasure could be hers, under the right conditions. Though Jean found that war had raised her stock slightly, she attracted only a particular type of man, a sort of incubus, hollow-eyed and deadened like the boy in the alley, trying to avoid death by stealing life. War often removed aesthetic objections to her, the threat of death a more effective beautifier than five successive pints. Anybody, any warm body, could do in a pinch. But the feeling still was that you had to be pretty far down some crooked path to attempt something of her ilk.

Her curiosity had allowed a couple of expeditionary gropings, a brush past in the blackout turning into something more intent when not immediately repelled, but her disappointment in them had turned to disaffection. The racing excitement of approach was not followed up on landing. One of her night creepers actually kissed her, pushing his tongue so far into her mouth that she worried she might gag. He moved her head with his hands. She saw herself reflected in a window, ill met by moonlight. She looked like a horse trying to work the bit out of its mouth. Jean started to avoid alleys and cloakrooms, as this seemed to be where they loitered, waiting for something unnatural and shadowy to join them, and carried a half brick in a strong sock. Meanwhile she and Gloria lived as closely and sexlessly as a husband and wife, when shared bathrooms and bedrooms cause only inconvenience rather than intimacy. Though Jean's knowledge increased, her body remained a vast mystery, something more half-awake than alive. The conditions were not yet right.

While they dismantled the art of the hat-pinned house, Frankie took the opportunity to relate her latest adventure, which took the form of a sailor from Nottingham. She finished the confession and, having been rewarded with a conspiratorial giggle, felt again clean and whole. Although they helped her to live, she worried the men were erasing some part of her. Some part that was supposed to withstand. It was different for Jean; there was no one counting on her remaining whole.

'So what about you and that friend of yours? Found anyone for my Jeanie-Bean?'

Jean shook her head. She and Gloria didn't go out looking anymore. Gloria would wait for her to return home from work, catch the scent of port and cigarettes on her and know Jean had been with people she called friends, that she now had that option. Gloria never bothered to keep the wounded look from her face. Jean brought home the smell of company, and Gloria was alone.

'I could find you someone,' Frankie continued. 'You should come out with me; places I go are always packed with soldiers and randy reserves. Bound to be some young thing looking for a challenge. You can't meet anyone stuck at home. It'd be a shame, Bean, to see a body like yours go to waste.'

'I'm not sure. I've got to keep Gloria company.'

'Come on now, don't you get lonely?'

172

Jean shrugged. She had a pit of loneliness in her so deep that she feared nothing would ever fill it. Her mother had sunk it, and then the years of her unloved existence had dredged it. Gloria's friendship, and now Frankie's, had at least sent stones to the bottom.

'Little bit.'

Frankie rolled her eyes. 'Little bit? You can't be a little bit lonely any more than you can be a little bit pregnant. Once the rabbit dies, that's it. Come out with me, Bean. You want to get warmed up, remember?'

'I'll see,' Jean promised.

Gloria had tried to find her romance, which seemed a doomed enterprise. Frankie was offering something much more tangible: experience. While Jean's body had become exciting to some disturbing, if not disturbed, individuals, it resolutely refused to throw up its secrets to her. Confusing flashes, like distress signals from circling boats, crackled through her, directing her where she wasn't sure she could follow.

What she had allowed felt like the beginning of a path that led somewhere dark and unacknowledged. She didn't want to be led that way, by them. It was not where she belonged. Nor was she meant for Gloria's world, where the worship of love held sway. Love seemed to Jean to be a cheapening thing; if it is all that matters, then whatever else you have, you have nothing. She wanted what she had, what she was, to be more than nothing. Jean was fed up of being told that the one thing that would make her happy was the one thing she didn't have a hope of possessing. She was happy to be of use, of that much she was sure. And as for the hum in her blood that hard work and sleep couldn't quieten, that drink couldn't deaden — she had ignored far worse for far longer.

'I just want you to enjoy yourself.' Frankie was ending the conversation; there was nothing more to say. 'Don't sit at home because you feel you have to. You want to be able to notice the difference between alive and dead when it happens. Ask your friend to come too.'

'I'll ask,' Jean said without much hope. 'Can't hurt to ask.'

★ ★ ★

But before she could, Harry came back on leave. When others tumbled into rented beds, ate extravagant lunches scraped together from a week's worth of coupons, got drunk enough to fall down or just sat in a favourite chair and memorised the pattern of the wallpaper, Harry and Gloria sat in a wooden shelter facing a slate-grey sea while chip fat soaked newsprint onto their hands. He had hoped for a meal in the cosy flat, with its Gloria-covered walls and the smell of sugar that had seeped into every fabric and made his head ache in a delicious way; her mother, generous with the food, a pleasingly soft and round vision of what Gloria would become; the strange friend that reminded him of his slow brother who took too long being born and had taken his time over everything else since. It seemed like home to him, which was why Gloria couldn't stand having him in the house.

He had five hours. Harry had worried that the time would pass so quickly that he would barely notice it, but it hobbled by in lead boots. The seaside off-season can embalm a single minute and make it last for ever. He would have been glad of it had he been able to look at Gloria properly, but she looked only at the sea and wouldn't meet his gaze. Every ten minutes, she asked him how were the chips. It was a horrible, dead time. When it got too cold to sit out anymore, they warmed their hands around cups of tea in the station waiting room. Gloria felt the failure of her imagination as she saw only the boy in front of her: no future husband, no children, no happy ending.

'I did try,' she assured him. 'I really did.'

He held her hand as if she were dangling off the side of a cliff; her fingers ached under the pressure. At the carriage door, he reluctantly let go, and she fell away from him, her face receding into darkness at astonishing speed.

Gloria returned home after dark, her hands stiff with cold. Jean had to help her unknot her scarf, and noted the locket's absence when she eased the coat off Gloria's shoulders. Gloria pushed her hands into Jean's, and leaned against her. They stood like that until Jean could feel her warmth flowing into Gloria, and then delivered her friend into the arms of her mother, where she stayed and cried for another hour or so while Mrs Smith stroked her hair and whispered, 'I know,' over and over.

Gloria had not often failed to live up to her

own expectations. To find herself bad, lacking, unworthy, was as unusual as it was unpleasant. That night, Jean pretended to be asleep while she listened to the soft whisperings of Gloria's mother, perched on the side of her daughter's narrow bed.

'There's enough suffering without making more.' A soft rasp underscored every word as the dry skin of her palms skimmed over Gloria's thick gold hair.

'Enough mothers have given up sons to this; do we have to give our daughters too? I know you're lonely, I know you're scared. But you can be lonely and scared in a bed for two. Just as easily. You can't change what will happen by marrying him.' Gloria began to sob, quietly, into her pillow. 'You did your best but you couldn't go through with it. It's all for the best, you'll see.'

When Mrs Smith left, Jean leaned over and tapped Gloria's arm. It took three goes before Gloria would acknowledge her. There had been no time recently to examine the distance between them, as it was filled with the war. Sitting across from one another in their small beds, Jean and Gloria experienced the deafening awkwardness of two friends in a room, breathing and not speaking. The air seemed to become dense with exhalations, begging to be cut through with words, but neither girl had any at her disposal. Jean supposed she should say sorry that Harry was gone, Gloria wished she would not, and somehow the words were kept down. Gloria tried to run a hand through her hair, and it snagged.

'Ouch,' she said, quietly.

'You all right?' Jean's voice was soft and solicitous, halfway to making an apology for something she had no knowledge of doing.

'My hair's tangled.' Gloria sounded sulky and petulant.

'Let me,' Jean said, and eased herself out of bed.

As Jean carefully worked the knots from Gloria's hair, she could feel her friend relax a little under the rhythmic pressure of the brush.

'Do you want to go to the pictures tomorrow?' Jean asked.

'I fancied going last week, but you were busy.'

Jean blushed, thinking of how wonderfully occupied she had been in the past months, too full of purpose even to comfort her first and, until Frankie, only friend. Gloria sighed and slumped a little lower.

'You left me.'

Jean hadn't yet, but she had been intending to, if only for a time, a night, in knowledge and, perhaps, experience. It suddenly seemed an awful betrayal. She had become a selfish thing, interested in notions of pleasure that were never meant to reach her. A life had begun in Jean's mind, one where she found more uses for her startling form, uses that caused the internal tirade to quiet, for a while. Where had Gloria been in that life?

'I'm sorry,' Jean whispered. 'It's just, with the war and everything . . . I got so carried away.'

'Away from me,' Gloria sniffed. 'I'm all alone in the shop. None of the girls from school come to talk to me. You'd think I was a flamin' leper.'

'I'm sorry. I thought, what with you getting married . . . ' Jean didn't mean to rub salt in the wound, but managed anyway. Gloria stiffened.

'I wasn't married yet.' Gloria took the hairbrush from Jean's hand and began to pin her curls. 'So what is it, you got a fella or something?'

'No.'

'Didn't think so.' Gloria's fingers got tangled in a curl and she threw the pin down in frustration, then covered her face with her hands. 'It's just all happening at once, Jean. You never here, no fun, no nothing. Everything's just disappeared. I hate this bloody war.'

Jean took the hairbrush and, for want of something better to do, began to pull Gloria's hair from it.

'I could come straight home,' Jean said, winding the golden strands around her fingers. 'You wouldn't be alone. It's just that a couple of the girls like a drink after work. I'd rather be here, but you know how it is. I'll stop it, though, just say: 'No thanks.'' She hoped she made it sound easy.

There had just been so much to reach for, suddenly. She had not meant to let Gloria go; there had to be a way to fill both hands with life.

'So, pictures tomorrow, then?' she asked, pulling the skein of hair from her fingers.

Gloria straightened her back, trying to catch her reflection in the long mirror. 'Suppose. Am I pretty, still?'

Jean fell into the familiar pattern of praise and

reassurance. It meant that if she was not yet forgiven, she could be.

'Yes.'

'What if people say things about me, because of Harry? What if they come in the shop and say them?'

'I'll look after you.'

Gloria sighed again.

'Do you mean it? Am I your best and only friend?'

She was still a disappointment to herself, but Jean would find her worth defending; Gloria relied upon it. And for Jean, to be needed would be enough; it seemed to her more real than to need. She had almost disappeared from view, inside her mother's house, with no one to so much as remark on it. Gloria had smuggled her out, trading confectionery for time; then waited for her when she was buried; and after that until her bones knitted together and her wounds closed. She hadn't disappeared; they would keep hold of each other from now on.

There were only so many beginnings for Jean; Frankie would not be one. Jean had never rejected anyone before; ingratitude was not part of her make-up. The first day was the easiest. Gloria was a fresh excuse, thanks to Harry.

'I'll take you to the Arms.' Frankie was outlining their proposed expedition as they tackled what remained of a school playground. Shards of the hard surface curled back from the bomb craters like stiff petals, and had to be hacked away. 'It's nearest the camp, and they get passes on different nights so there's always someone in there. Be good to have someone to go with, can't go down there too many times on my own, I'll get a name for m'self.'

'Better not,' Jean replied. 'Gloria's just broken it off with her soldier. She needs a bit of company.'

'Oh right,' Frankie was only a little put out. 'Fair enough. Another time, though?'

Jean smiled and nodded, hoping it would feel less of a lie without words. Frankie gave her a week before asking again, a week Jean gratefully drank in as if it were the last of a hot summer. But when the moment came, she denied Frankie again, her refusal seeming like judgement to the redhead, who felt suddenly stripped down to her secrets, naked in the street.

'Suit yourself,' she snapped. If only, thought Jean.

Frankie soon caught on; there would be no adventures in the company of this girl. If they were walking near her house, she no longer invited Jean in for a cup of tea. Her breaks were spent in the company of other women, who talked children and men to her, but never sex or chaos. The confessions stopped. Frankie became bloated with secrets, and Jean thin with ignorance. They couldn't go back to not knowing who the other was, to being content with talk.

As the defaulter, Jean was the one to leave. When half of the next district's crew was killed in a building collapse, she volunteered to make up the numbers. Her crew made her a cardboard cake, put a real scone on the plate under it, and took an extra fifteen minutes at break to say their goodbyes. As they all shook hands, Jean held Frankie's gaze longer than the rest, long enough, she hoped, for meaning to soak through their palms, for Frankie to understand that Jean wanted everything she was offering and more time to take it. Frankie extracted her hand, grimaced, and wiped it on her overalls.

'Aren't you a sweaty Betty. My hand's wringing.'

Jean pushed her dinner-plate palms into her pockets and shrugged.

'Sorry.'

She at least got to say that. Frankie turned away and then remembered herself, what she was good at. She turned back to Jean, went as high up on her toes as she could and placed her lips on Jean's chin, keeping her eyes from hers. Jean had hoped she might return one day to the offer of adventure, but with that understood it had been withdrawn. She couldn't blame Frankie.

'You'd have had more fun with me, you know.'

Jean blushed. 'I'm needed over the way. They don't have enough hands.'

She had turned out to be such a disappointment, and Frankie couldn't disguise it. 'You could be dead tomorrow, Jeanie-Bean.'

Jean tried a laugh. 'Never am though, am I?'

Frankie misunderstood it as arrogance, and that's how it was left. The last thing between them. Jean's new crew were uniformly unsettled by her, it perhaps being too soon after they'd seen colleagues flattened by an unstoppable force. They shared little more than tea and instructions with her, and she went straight home each night, as promised. In the little flat above the Smiths' shop, Gloria and Jean waited out the evenings together, the wireless filling in the silence between them, the air tight with guilt. And then death came again, with its way of changing the weather.

Harry went first. He didn't take his own life, he didn't stop wanting to be alive, he didn't blunder around in a stupor of Gloria-induced grief. He was just killed. When his name appeared in the paper, Gloria cut it out, intending to paste it into her diary. But she couldn't manage it. She couldn't then put it in the bin or on the fire as it seemed like dismissing him all over again, and this time when dead and defenceless. This sent her into a fit of distraction, wandering about the flat with his name hanging off her fingers. Mrs Smith finally halted Gloria, peeled the sliver of newspaper from her hand and rolled it into a speck between her fingers. 'There's a limit, Gloria,' she said, and her daughter nodded and sat down. They had been through it all before, and Mrs Smith decided there was to be an end; the pretending had gone on too long. Gloria realised with a shock that that left her with nothing at all. She caught herself wishing she still had the locket, some token of what she had meant to him, some proof she had meant that to anyone.

Frankie died in a raid three months after she had been sacrificed by Jean. The names of fallen Amazons were read out to every crew, 'Rest in Peace' murmured after each one. At Frankie's name, Jean's lips gummed together and her mouth drained of spit; a warm patch flared on her chin where a kiss had been. Frankie had tried to tell her so many times; make use of me, make use of me before this is gone. 'If I was different,' Jean thought, 'it would have been different.'

The old outhouse was the only place she could go. There she cried until she thought her throat would tear. She cried for all the things she wouldn't now know, for the kindness that had been cut short. For getting it all so wrong. Jean leaned against the rotting planks, barking out her grief in sharp bursts. From the back of the shop, Gloria could see Jean's hair, quivering above the door. She pulled the window shut, trying to keep out the sound of her friend's grief. For her it was like watching a parent cry, seeing someone you trust to be always strong come spectacularly apart. A terrifying, changing thing. Gloria began to suspect that there were things about Jean that she didn't know, and she wasn't sure if she liked that. Gloria didn't like mystery that wasn't of her own creation.

17

The distance between Jean and Gloria would grow over, as will a shattered bone. They held on tight to each other again, feeling the times pull on them.

After Harry died, Jean wanted to tell Gloria that she knew, that she knew all about how good and terrible it felt to be free because of a wrong done to someone, how just going on felt like collusion with something bad inside of you, but she was wary of sharing knowledge now. She saw what it brought and how little it mattered; what would Gloria gain from knowing she was like her friend? So Jean damped everything down though the lifesong in her had built up to a scream, and she had to strain to hear the world over it. She couldn't hear Gloria plotting, though she could feel the tension in her. So they went on, pretending, almost feeling, things were as they had been before.

The war had become life and life had become war; neither of them could properly remember a time without it, without that memory seeming like a fiction. It unnerved Gloria that it had been made normal for her to be as she was — unremarkable in her situation and prospects. She was not having the war she deserved, she felt. She embarked on penance for Harry as best she could, doling out tea at the station, rolling bandages for the hospital, serving in the shop and knitting though the evening until a lonely bedtime. Dances were no longer graced with her presence, and you could paper a small wall with the war bonds she purchased. But she was plotting, nevertheless.

Gloria had come to believe that her future lay not only outside of the ordinary but outside of the country. She had made a terrible mess of things in it. So few people knew about the engagement that its demise caused little scandal or reproach. But round her neck, she still felt the cool metal of the locket; it became like a rash that rose at times of anxiety. A blond boy in uniform had triggered it once, passing her on the promenade and giving her a shy, hopeful smile. She had turned away to hide her shame and found herself looking at Paul Bradshaw, being pulled in a wagon by his father, a paper windmill in his hand spinning as crazily as his eyes. She had to clap a hand to her mouth to stop the scream.

The invasion was her only hope. It had been promised for months, and she tracked its coming night after night, drinking in the newsreels as if they were a pledge made only to her: 'Soon.' Jean assumed Gloria was hoping for an end to it all, and wished she could be as keen. After Frankie, she found less joy in her work, but still the same exquisite purpose. She searched the newsreels too, for the time when it would be over and she would never be understood, or of use, again. Jean had wrung two years from the war by the time they arrived, and wondered if that now would be all.

When the Americans did come, they came down like rain over a parched land. Watching the troops pour from ships like handsome rats, Gloria felt as if the tide were rushing in, up to her throat. The slow drain she had felt since abandoning Harry stopped. The familiar feeling of certainty returned. She tried hard not to show fevered anticipation, but internally she felt herself approach the fulfilment of her promise — she had been freed for a purpose, not to feel shame and guilt. The flickering images of the newsreel confirmed it; with white teeth and broad shoulders they arrived, with no knowledge of nor respect for tradition they arrived, with possibilities they arrived.

'Americans, Jean.' Gloria gripped her friend's arm, her face lit up by the first genuine, hopeful smile Jean had seen in months. 'They're our best bet.' It would be six more weeks before they were delivered unto her.

★ ★ ★

The women had been laying siege to the picture house for years, but with the coming of the war, it had fallen entirely into their hands. The last remaining men had been seen off by the fierce and highly vocal debates — concerning the male stars' projected sexual prowess and the female leads' masking of congenital deformities with panstick and foundation garments — that were carried on from the balcony to the stalls, and often between the two, as opposing factions would form and regroup each evening.

A jungle picture, unaware of its own irrelevance to proceedings, was occasionally to be heard over the chatter. Gloria and Jean were sitting in the balcony; Gloria, slumped deep inside a bad mood, was picking around in a bag of sweets for the good ones. Unable to locate a preferred flavour, she passed it to Jean. The cinema for Gloria had been a rich repository of material, she regularly restocked her fantasies there, but the jungle one was old and didn't interest her. She didn't like to see clothing torn, acutely aware of her own diminished wartime wardrobe. Blundering from trap to trap, the heroine succeeded only in further shredding the silk blouse that had been immaculate ten minutes ago, a carelessness that stabbed at Gloria's side. She leaned her head against Jean's arm, rolling her skull to find a soft dip in the hard muscle.

'Wake me up for the newsreel,' she murmured. 'I'd rather see old funny 'tache than this lot.'

★ ★ ★

Outside, two young GIs with an evening pass paused to look at the movie posters. They were among the first of the Americans to land, pockets bulging with chocolate, gum and confidence. They talked for a minute or two, one circling the other, then stepped up to the doors. Meanwhile, in the jungle clearing, the natives danced around a cooking pot.

If Jean had not dropped the bag of sweets, it might never have happened. She'd plunged her fingers a little too forcefully into the bag and managed to push it onto the floor. As bullseyes rolled under the seats, and Jean dived for them, Gloria was bounced from her resting place, her blonde hair swinging. A thin stream of light fell across her as the GIs opened the back exit doors, as if she were chosen. The first man through the door saw illuminated the face of an angel and was hopelessly lost. He put his hand to his heart and whispered in the dark, 'Save me.' Gloria didn't hear that echo of her own heart; whether the echo was tinny or rich. She looked towards the door and saw only the dark outline of a man. As the door closed, he materialised in the smoky half-light of the cinema. Gloria couldn't look away; she was making him with her eyes. He was still, waiting to be made. As each detail took shape, Gloria found herself closer to laughing.

His name was Jack, he could fill in on a film star's day off and he had just found the thing he wanted most in the world.

Later, Jean would wonder if the seats next to them had been empty all along or if the people in them had evaporated under the pressure of destiny. Jack edged past her, never taking his eyes from Gloria. If he thought there was something strange about her companion, he never betrayed it. Jean realised she could have been stood there naked with a live ferret for a hat and still not merited a glance. This was beyond her ruinous influence, and she sighed with relief, not realising that she was exhaling into a second soldier, whose head was level with her breasts. She breathed in sharply and he moved past her

188

with a smirk. Before he leaned back in his seat he looked down the row at her and winked. Jean felt it like a slap in the face.

They sat through the last ten minutes of the jungle film and the whole of the drama that followed in which a young woman spent eighty minutes trying to avoid the man she had fallen in love with in the first five. Jack spent most of the film watching Gloria, who rewarded his attentiveness with occasional shining glances. Jean, in turn, tried not to watch them, but she couldn't make her eyes behave.

Once, when she was about six, her father had come into the attic and woken her in the middle of the night. It was the first and only time he would do it, and she remembered being surprised that he knew where she slept. He put a finger to his lips and then with his one hand led her to the kitchen where the window overlooked the small patch of neglected grass at the back of the house. He put his arm around her and helped her onto the stool she used when she was washing up, then he gently pushed her head towards the window. At first she thought he wanted her to wash and so she put her head in the sink; he put his hand under her chin and lifted her head, again pushing her towards the glass. Jean leaned forward and pressed her forehead against it. The moon was full, and so low it seemed caught in the trees. A family of foxes were playing outside, the moonlight running through their fur in wet silver ribbons. They were more brilliant than anything she had ever seen: fast and sleek with beautiful, sharp heads. They scampered in the grass, nipping at each other, leaping over one another like a practised troupe of acrobats. Jean and her father watched them together until a neighbour's dog broke the silence with its barking, and the foxes disappeared under a tangled hedge. She remembered how sad her father had looked at their departure. He left her standing in the kitchen and went back to his makeshift bed, a ghost again. Jean stayed with her face pressed to the window until her nose went numb and her whole head ached. She had witnessed something marvellous and though she knew she would get a hiding if she was found, she couldn't move away. It was as if the possibility of it existed only within a certain radius, and there was no chance of it returning if she moved. That was how she felt next to Gloria, watching her and Jack. Something extraordinary was happening, and this might be her only chance to witness it. They were both so golden, even in the smoky dark of the cinema Jean could see that. For some reason she thought of a double yolk.

★ ★ ★

When the lights came up, the tall GI stood up and held out his hand to Gloria and, Jean assumed, introduced himself. His voice was not so much quiet as intended only for Gloria; it seemed not to stray from her. Jean could make out the unfamiliar rise and fall of the accent, the occasional letter drawn far beyond where she would usually leave it. Gloria nodded and then turned to Jean, she would have to translate from now on.

'Bingo,' she whispered. And then winked.

The friend, Denny, was five feet and four inches tall and had the small man's reverence for size. When he was a boy, he had fallen in love with a proud, naked woman who stretched the entire length of the wooden bar it was his job to sweep around. It had taken a single man six weeks to paint her and four men to hang her. Denny had wanted to climb over every inch of her. Jean was her first serious rival in size and had the added dimension of flesh. On first seeing her, he badly wanted to whistle and hoot.

Just as Jean was not Gloria's first experiment in benevolent friendship — a girl with a foreshortened leg came first, to be replaced, when she failed to return from a routine hospital visit, with a pockmarked simpleton whose favourite game was making shapes in dirt with her wee; she was too much of a project even for Gloria — Jean was not Denny's first attempt to recreate his painted woman. But while he had found sturdiness before, found breadth, found length, found examples and combinations thereof, he knew he had found something else in Jean. For both him and Gloria, she was a culmination.

As the cinema emptied, Jean watched the handsome GI steer Gloria to the exit, counted to ten, and then made to follow. She stepped over the rows of seats as easily as if they were a kerb. She didn't notice as she stepped away from the small American that he traced the length of her arm with two fingers. Sometimes her scars hid things from her.

He walked behind her, watching her slow progress to the aisle, where she took the stairs two at a time. She paused at the exit doors, rolling her neck and shoulders as if something was bothering her and she was trying to shrug it off. She was used to people walking anywhere but alongside her, but what she wasn't used to was the heat on her back from his gaze. She felt as if she were being X-rayed.

Outside the cinema, some women stayed to stare at their first Americans. One called, 'I see you're late again. Just the two of you coming this time?' That got a cheer from her friends. Gloria glared furiously, but it was Jack's indifference that smothered the laughter. No one there mattered to him but Gloria. The women felt their irrelevance, and it silenced them.

Jean and Denny stood apart from them, she sneaking glances at him, he openly ogling her. He had the kind of face she might have glimpsed in an old photograph, a street child peering out from under a battered bowler hat: a boy's face, but preternaturally experienced, full of rat cunning. His wiry body exuded energy; though he was standing still he appeared to flicker at the edges as if he were moving too fast for her to see. He made her want to hold her breath.

There was something familiar in the way he looked at her, as if she was no surprise to him. His eyes swept upwards from her feet, over her thighs and stomach to her breasts. His gaze was so penetrating she had to touch the fabric of her dress to make sure she was still wearing it. Finally he reached her face; a marvellous grin broke across his tough little face, and he leaned in close to her to whisper.

'I'll say it. There isn't an inch of you I wouldn't lick.'

Jean blinked and gazed down at him, amazed that such words could have been meant for her. Here it was, offering itself again: experience.

'Not one?' she asked.

★   ★   ★

When they got back to the camp, Jack asked Denny if he minded taking on the other girl. He explained about the blonde and her insistence on taking her friend along on any date. He laughed and said he was frightened of the friend and needed back-up. Jack and Denny had met at a brawl, the way some men might meet at a game of cards. It was their third day in England and a surfeit of orders had left Denny itching for an outlet. When he saw Jack rolling in the mud with three other men, inferior in size but dirtier in technique, he had decided to make things a little more democratic. Their friendship was sealed with a thorough beating, but was no more odd than any other made at that time; so much was being swept away that almost anything could be built upon.

'Did you see her?' Jack joked. 'I don't think I can take being beaten with the force of three men twice in a month. I need ya, buddy.'

Denny shrugged and said, 'Sure, but you hear

me screaming, call the MPs.' He then went back to picturing Jean naked surrounded by a gilt frame.

That night, Gloria climbed in with Jean so she could whisper more closely. She breathed Jack into her ear until it was damp and overheated.

'Hammell. Gloria Hammell. John Hammell the second. Wasn't he wonderful? I think I'm in love with him. What about the other one?'

'The other one looked at me as if I wasn't wearing any clothes.'

'What did you think of that?'

'I think I didn't want to be wearing any clothes' travelled across her brain; she shunted it into a neural siding before it could reach her mouth. She was not so sure now, in the familiar-feeling dark, the same old tickle of the blankets under her chin. What could he have been offering her anyway? Perhaps nothing, nothing more than a joke. She wished Frankie was around still. She would know.

'Very forward,' Jean lied. 'I thought he was really very forward. I suppose I was quite shocked, really. Still, we won't be seeing him again, will we?'

Gloria's tone was pleading. 'Don't say that, Jean, try to like him, please. Jack's taking me out next week, and he said the other one would come too.'

Jean's mouth fell open, her lips giving a wet smack of surprise.

18

Gloria spent a week quite stupefied with love; one of her symptoms was that she seemed able to only turn things on. She would walk away from a blaring radio, a warming iron or a blazing light. Jean appointed herself Gloria's warden and would follow her, turning off gas and water taps in her wake.

It was starting again, Jean realised. She was glad that she had rubble to sort. Each night she would lovingly prise the dirt from under her torn nails, rinse her cuts and draw her bruises out. Pride welled from her continued ability to sustain breaches and heal; her perfection was in her regeneration. She would allow herself extra minutes alone to trace the progress of her riven skin and wonder if she was ready. Gloria's wholesale abandonment to her future was unnerving; she was already passing out of Jean's orbit into the control of a stronger force. The week felt like a countdown to something more than one evening; Jean braced herself for the impact.

A walk was proposed. There was nothing new at the cinema, and Jack said he didn't want to dance; he didn't want to run the risk of losing Gloria to someone else for even a second. Gloria decided she and Jean would show the GIs the seafront and the view from the rise, and then be taken to a pub for English beer and Spanish sherry. It would give Jack at least three hours of uninterrupted viewing of Gloria, the effect of the fading light on her face and the movement of her hair when she walked. He would drink her in with the evening air. He agreed to it all. Walking helped; walking was good, he told himself.

After the pub, where Jean sat silently smiling as Gloria giggled at the stories Jack and Denny told, they walked back up the rise towards the Smiths' shop. The sea was oily black behind them, with spirals of barbed wire littering the beach like old bed springs. The light was almost gone; pockets of dark spread out from under trees and washed down the streets making them glitter cleanly. Jack and Gloria were ahead; over the distance of a few yards, it was if they had passed through a screen and were now untouchably remote, a projection. Denny and Jean were united in superfluity.

It had been a busy week, with raids most nights, and Jean had not had time to think of anything to say. She had been meaning to put something by for the occasion, but was just reminded by the deliberation that nothing of her life was of interest to anyone, even the fact she had walked free from a ruined home. Her miraculous survival had been tarnished some-what by the continuing war; better people than her were every day suffering the mundanity of violent death, and it would be like gloating to comment on it. Jean couldn't recall ever having said or thought anything original or amusing. She wondered if anyone had ever told her a joke. She maintained her silence, trudging alongside the little GI.

Denny didn't like to talk about himself and knew little of Jack. He thought his new friend was tough and reckless, and that was enough — though it was not the only way they were alike. Jack was from money so old it no longer had any value and lived in a small town that had been mostly built by people that worked for or were part of his family. Denny grew up near the docks of a big city and, when asked, said he couldn't trace his family back past lunchtime and suspected he was the offspring of a ship's rat that had lost its tail. But both had something they didn't want to go back to: a past self.

Jack was charismatic but weak; it was not in his character, but deeper, as if there was a hole in the wall of his heart that you could sense from looking at him. War was the place for him, he had decided. He had a way about him that made men either want to follow or fight him. Denny wanted to follow; he wanted to see where someone smarter could lead him; he was tired of being dumb, and having to struggle for everything because of it.

Though he was quiet, Denny was full of interest; his eyes were dancing around Jean. She aroused his curiosity, which was rare in anyone he encountered and almost unique in a woman. He wanted to know how she knew to be exactly what he wanted. He wondered if she was even aware of it.

'Can I ask you something?'

The pavement was narrow, so Jean walked in the road. They had tried it the other way around, but the gutter was deep, and her hip threatened his head. She looked only slightly down at him to answer.

'Course you can.'

'How tall are you? I mean exactly.'

'I don't know.'

'No?'

'No. Never been measured.'

'Really.'

He imagined unfolding a tape along her naked side, climbing a ladder to mark her on a wall. The image of the gilded frame returned to him.

'My mum said it was best not to know. *No question about you has an answer anyone'd want to hear*, that's what she said.'

'That's a damn shame. You should do it. Could be breaking some records there.'

A giggle escaped her, something wriggly and girlish that tickled its way out of her throat. Jean felt suddenly indecent, as if she had flashed him her slip. She stole his question, not having one of her own.

'So, um, how tall are you?'

'Tall enough. Least I was.'

At this, Jean gave him a smile. Rich and sweet, distilled from all the ungiven, fermenting smiles left in her, it could have stopped the heart, but instead slowed their steps. Jean was approaching her favourite time, the onset of enveloping dark. Unconsciously, her limbs straightened, her head lifted and her back arched. Denny wondered if she was presenting herself to the night, or to him. The trees that lined the path cast shadows that looked soft and inviting. Jack and Gloria were nowhere to be seen. Denny took Jean's arm and began to gently steer her into the blackness. He was in the process of trying to work out whether her arm was taut with resistance or fear, or was simply muscle-bound, when it happened.

If you are modest of size and feature, the ridiculous does not cling to you as it does to those who are irregular. You will not have the same attraction for litter, power lines and nesting gulls. Jean wore light fittings more often than she wore a hat. It was inevitable, really.

A loop of telegraph cable loosed by malign fate was hanging down like a noose from between the branches of the trees. As Denny guided her from the path, Jean walked into it like a rabbit into a snare. She immediately stumbled, pulling it tight about her neck; her head snapped back, her arms shot out like spring-loaded traps, and Denny sailed off into the welcoming embrace of a hawthorn bush.

Trying to wrench the cable from the trees, Jean began to back away with it still around her neck, her dazed legs taking her in circles. Never having had a go on the swings, she did not realise the folly of twisting a cable you are attached to, and in her panic she turned like a donkey driving a millstone and screwed her head firmly into its grasp. Denny crawled out of the scrub to find her bent nearly double looking ready to spit her tongue onto the pavement where it would cushion the landing of her eyeballs.

'Hold on, I'll get you out of there.'

He grabbed a stick and scrambled towards her; she was swaying backwards and forwards, wound so tight that the fingers she had wedged under the cable were purple at the tips. Denny leapt about with the stick in his hand trying to knock the cable from the tree. Anyone passing might have thought a gypsy had taken his dancing bear for a walk, and they had stopped to caper under the rising moon.

'Please,' Jean whispered. 'Please do something.'

Denny hesitated for a second then grabbed Jean's rump with both hands and gave her an almighty shove. Her look of surprise turned to one of terror as she spun full circle, her legs getting skinned on the paving stones as they collapsed beneath her. It took a few seconds for her to right herself and see that a single twist was undone.

'Again,' she croaked. 'Again.'

He drove her round against the grain until the cable began to loosen. Jean's feet were flopping like fins trying to keep up with the pace her behind had set, but her breath was returning. With one final shove, the cable came apart, and she ran out of its grip and straight into the side of a hedge. She lay face down; Denny sank to the ground next to her, exhausted and rumpled, and successfully fought the urge to give her backside a victory slap.

Jean's dress was pulled up and he could see where her fake seams ended. He felt bad about it but couldn't help the grin that pestered his face. It was a while before he could speak without the certainty of laughing; when he could, there was still high amusement in his voice. 'I have never,

ever seen anything like that in my whole life before.'

Jean rolled around to face him and smiled weakly. She had only the truth to tell. 'Happens to me all the time. Or things like it.'

She pushed down her dress and sat up. It was too complete a rout to care anymore, she hadn't a shred of dignity left. Denny took a crushed pack of cigarettes from his pocket and offered one to Jean.

She shook her head. 'Haven't the breath yet.'

He lit his cigarette, and they sat in silence while he smoked it, neither making an attempt to rise. Jean lightly touched the raw patches where the skin had been rubbed off. Denny watched her thick fingers exploring her neck, an expression of neither shock nor anger on her face, just acceptance.

She turned to him and smiled. 'Be all right in a minute. You get off if you want to.'

'Leave you here? You damn near lynched yourself back there. Are you sure you're going to be OK?'

Jean nodded. 'Oh yes. Worse things happen at sea, I'm told.'

It seemed unlikely to him, short of a torpedo, but Denny nodded anyway. He ground out his cigarette and looked up at the sky; stars were starting to show against the velvety blue. Her face was returning to a normal colour, though her eyes were still pure liquid. The heaving breaths she took caused her chest to rise spectacularly; he was mesmerised by the workings of her ribcage, the theatricality of it. He found he didn't want to go anywhere. The way she had felt under his hands, strong and pliant, had confirmed his interest. But still, what he said next surprised even him.

'When I was four, a dog ran off with me.'

Jean, who had been sitting patiently in expectation of his leaving, was confused. She couldn't understand why he wasn't going.

'Sorry?'

Then he realised; he wanted her to feel better. He wanted her to know that this was a good time. 'When I was about four years old, a dog ran off with me. I was a real scrawny little fella, no bulk at all, and I had all this grease and stuff all over me from the back of the diner where I was kicking around. I was looking through the garbage really. I think maybe he thought I was a bone and he picked me up between his jaws, my shirt. He was a real big dog, and he carried me off. My legs and arms were draggin' and my head was bouncin' all over the sidewalk and I was yellin' and everyone was laughin' and he had me; he wasn't gonna let go.'

Jean laughed. She had no idea things like this happened to other people. It was perhaps the most exciting story she had ever heard.

'Where did he take you?'

Denny's mouth pursed in a reluctant smirk. 'To his doghouse.'

'No!'

'He stuffed me right in there. I was kickin' and screaming, and he just kept pushing me in there with his big nose, snout, you know. He was a really big dog. The owner, big fat guy, arms like ham hocks, came and pulled me out. I was disgusting, all covered in hair and stuff. He hosed me off in the back yard and then kicked me back to where I came from.'

Denny looked down at his uniform, mud-smeared and scattered with thorns. He had no idea how he was going to explain this to anyone, or even if he wanted to.

'I never told anyone that. So now you know, worse things happen on shore too.'

He stood up and began to swipe at the fabric with the flat of his hand. Jean watched him ineffectually brush the muck deeper into the weave. She studied him, the mystery of his continuing presence. There was something new here, a chance. He was so beautiful in his nearness, his submission to her gaze, her being. Had he taken her arm before she had accidentally garrotted herself? She thought he had; she thought he had been about to lead her somewhere. She thought she wanted to know where. Not every action of hers need have a dreadful consequence. And Frankie would never forgive her if she didn't find out.

In a small act of mutiny, of revolution, Jean placed her hands on his back. Denny stopped his hopping and twisting and stood still, suddenly becalmed by the unexpected weight and warmth of her hands on him. Jean let them lie on his back for a few seconds, then she began to brush away the mud and leaves, picking at the damp rolls of earth that he had distributed over his jacket. As she smoothed the rough uniform, she felt muscle and bone through the fabric, could feel them move as he breathed; she marvelled at what a complete work this was, a body. She took a dry leaf from his collar, and it brushed his neck like a nervous kiss.

Denny's hands hung at his sides as he gave himself over to her touch. He had not done badly with women; it sometimes paid to be closer in size to a child than a man. He would get pulled onto laps, pressed into bosoms and petted. He would then surprise them by petting back and knowing how. It was a kind of devilishness masquerading as innocence that appealed. But Jean wasn't petting him; she was finding him, trying to know him. The heat of her hands passed through him like light, and he felt himself become clear.

She picked at the burrs that clung to him; Denny took a breath as he felt his shirt lift from his skin where her fingers tugged at the uniform, he could feel her breath on him, around him. Her hands were in his hair now. Jean drew some twigs out slowly; they scraped his scalp like long, painted fingernails and he breathed deeper still and closed his eyes. Something was evaporating from Jean's skin and taking to the air. He would be able to name it only when he saw the women running alongside the trucks and tanks, throwing flowers and screaming from the insane joy of being free. Liberation. To her it felt like flying, though the earth was wonderfully solid beneath her. She understood suddenly what it would have been to die in the rubble of the house. She understood that death was not individual. That the battlefields were littered not only with the present dead but also with those that would not now be born, be loved, be changed by the possibility of another. She would have been one of those, a ghost child who was not even a memory, not even a hope. She understood that she was only now coming out from under: that she would have died without knowing this.

She wanted to gouge her fingers deep into his flesh, turn him inside out and see what he was made of. She wanted to taste his skin. Her fingers seemed more deft than they had ever been as she slipped free the buttons of Denny's tunic and pushed her hands inside his shirt. His torso was firm but still malleable, clay that wasn't quite set. She did not know where to go next, but to speak, to ask, would break the spell. She believed he must be in some trance to allow this; if she spoke, he would wake, and she would be discovered. But she needed help.

'What can I do?' she whispered.

He took her hand and moved it to the base of his spine; it was impossibly warm.

'Anything,' he replied. The buzzing in his veins moved under her hands like iron filings on a magnet. It filled his ears and mouth. Jean felt the skin on her palms melt into his flesh; there was nothing between them now. She had found a gravitational pull greater than her own, and the forward motion was unstoppable. She turned his face towards hers, and covered his mouth with her large, soft lips. As she drew near to him, he was surprised to see his whole head contained in the dark of her eye.

19

The dial of his watch was luminous and it told them he was late. They had worked their way down the bank from the pavement and had to clamber back up. Jean's long legs were trembling like a foal's; stepping out onto the pavement they bucked twice then folded, and she hit the floor.

'Look,' she whispered in undisguised wonder. 'You leave me weak.'

He had smiled at that.

★   ★   ★

Back at the Smiths' flat, with Gloria asleep in bed, Jean scrutinised her face in the blue light of the cold bathroom. She studied every angle, wanting to see the evidence of experience. Her face didn't change, the mirror still threw her reflection back at her, but clear as the day to come she heard her mother's voice.

Think you know it all, now. Don't you?

'Bloody right,' she told the glass, pleased that someone knew.

This is what it means to be just cooling off, she realised, remembering Frankie; this was truly off the ration and to be savoured, for it wouldn't come again. Experience, finally. It didn't occur to Jean that things enjoyed were sometimes repeated. Her few pleasures had been singular and strange, existing only in extreme conditions, and so this could be no different. He wouldn't come to her again, she knew. After their walk, Denny dropped over the compound fence at midnight into the arms of an MP and lost out on the next pass. But Jean had already suffered the disappointment when it came. Although that left her unprepared for what did come.

The next week, Jack visited Gloria at the flat. Her parents were won over cakes and cups of tea, though they had decided in advance to dislike him for at least a month, just to be sure. But Gloria had irradiated them with her happiness and they were riddled with hope. Jean lurked in the doorway like the smell of yesterday's dinner, an envelope, passed from Jack to Gloria to her, growing damp in her hand.

Gloria and her parents were so pleased with the handsome GI in their midst that they failed to notice a faint hum in the air, emanating from both Jean and Jack, but on different frequencies. Anxiety threatened to light the oxygen in the air. When Gloria's mother suggested the four of them go for a walk, Jack and Jean nearly screamed their unified agreement. Alone in a Gloria-less bedroom, Jean tore the envelope open with her teeth. It contained an obscene drawing. He had remembered it all and rendered it in greasy pencil; Jean thought she might weep from the romance of it.

For her own lust, Jean was unprepared. Believing it to be another symptom of her freakishness, she was kind to it, as she was forgiving of her height, stoic about her hair and accepting of her fate. But she knew it had to be kept a secret; somewhere in her that was certain. Even Frankie had been afraid of judgement, and with Jean it held hands with ridicule. She wouldn't expose him to that. She placed the drawing, the *evidence* of it, of them, between the leaves of a book, then under the mattress, then behind a photograph. Finally she ate it. An act that was strangely pleasurable.

The ones that can go for ten years on a touch, a glance — they're the ones to watch out for. Since she had been shown what was possible, Jean had spent every spare moment back in that night.

Jean wondered what magic Denny had performed to dissolve her; at times she existed only on the tips of his fingers. She had never felt so small, so concentrated and yet so universal; she had bled into the night and floated on its cool currents. When the magic faded, she regained her form, became solid again. He had made her a changeling, realising what had always been suspected about her. She had no idea it was going to feel like that.

With the picture safe inside her, she lay down on the bed and closed her eyes to better see her dreams. She again saw the darkness, his back, the feel of rough fabric under her hands, the snake roll of muscle as he moved, her knee pressed into his side. She drifted off to sleep deep in the contentment of knowing what had been real. She would never let herself forget, she promised.

★　★　★

'What did the note say?'

'Hah?' Gloria had climbed over her and was getting into Jean's bed with her shoes on. She struck Jean with a heel. Jean pulled away from the dream that held her, and wiped her mouth. It was dark, and she had been asleep for hours.

'Oi, take your shoes off.'

'Oops.' Gloria giggled then shucked the brown lace-ups from her feet and threw them into the corner. She wiggled her toes against Jean's calves; her socks were damp.

'Did you walk home without your shoes on?'

'I think I've got blisters. We went to the seafront, got all the way down to the water. My shoes were soaked.'

Jean pulled the blankets around her. 'You getting in your own bed?'

'In a minute, pushy. What did the note say? Is he going to see you again?'

'I don't know,' she admitted.

Gloria wriggled, as she always did when she was pleased with herself.

'I do. Next Sunday. They have the whole day free and they're coming to see us. Jack and I are going to have tea at a hotel. We might even have dinner there.'

Jean turned to look at Gloria. She had on a fresh coat of lipstick and a smile so wide a person not in love would be in agony. Her hair was hanging down close to Jean's face; Jean took a thick strand of it and wound it round her finger where it made a band of gold. The day Jack and Gloria would spend together was hardly needed. The look that washed over Jack when he saw

Gloria at the picture house had made Jean's own heart pound. It was joy and disbelief and fear and gratitude. Gloria had sunk into the promise that look held, as if it were soft as feathers and strong as steel. Jean saw her friend walking away from her while her own feet grew roots that drove into the ground, breaking paving stones as if they were no more than wafers. Her stomach burned; this girl had raised her and now wanted to be free. Jean felt abandoned and inevitable; she had finally been orphaned. The ribbon of hair slipped off her finger.

'Tea sounds lovely. What should we do?'

'Whatever you want.' Gloria shrugged and then winked. Jean panicked; she couldn't know. Gloria planted a sticky red kiss on Jean's forehead and jumped into her own bed. Jean stared at the ceiling and tried to slow her heart down. She couldn't possibly know.

'No, really.' She tried to sound casual. 'What?'

'I dunno. Can't you go to the pictures?'

'You don't mind?'

'Course not. What's going to happen there? Not scared, are you? He's only a tiddler.'

'Me? No. It's not that. I just thought you might want me near you.'

'No fear. Jack wants me all to himself, he says. You'll be all right, won't you? Jack says that he — the other one, whassisname — will pay for everything; you don't have to worry there. And you can always come home early and wait in with Mum and Dad. They won't mind.'

Jean tried hard not to smile. 'No, I'll go. It's all right.'

'Good. Sorry he's not much, Jean, but there is a war on. Maybe next time, eh?' Gloria reached over to pat Jean's head, and then rolled over to sleep. Now wide awake, Jean stared at the ceiling and wondered what else there was to know.

★ ★ ★

When Jean was eight, a Christian woman of stout appearance with ideas about health and efficiency, as well as an ability to tolerate tweed in summer, had started a swimming club. It was for the poorer children and would take advantage of the limitless pool on their doorstep, the cold green sea. On Saturday mornings, she would lead stick-limbed hellions into the purifying waters and they would emerge well-muscled and disciplined, believers all. A notice had gone up in school.

Jean had seen people swimming, cutting through the water, sometimes just lying on top of it as if they weighed nothing. She asked her mother. At that time, Wisteria let Jean out of the house only on her business. She didn't want her to get sick playing with other children.

'You'll just bring something in that could kill us all. You're like a great vat for disease, you are. Brew it all up inside you and then spew it all over the rest of us. Won't get you, no nothing does, but I'm left delicate because of you, and where will you be when I go?'

The notice said something about health, and so Jean had thought it might pass: a way to get rid of all those germs. They were walking along the promenade at the time. Jean had the shopping bag slung across her; onions were beating a tattoo on her stomach.

Wisteria took her daughter by the hand and led her onto the pier, stopping on the beach to take one of the larger stones. Halfway to the end, Wisteria stopped, made Jean stand against the railings and bent down close to her. She held the stone up to Jean's face and then threw it into the water where it made a great splash and then sank without a trace. Wisteria turned and breathed in her daughter's face.

'And that's not even a tenth of what you are.'

Whenever Jean could get away to the beach, she stood in the shallows, steady as a breakwater. She would later feel a strange affinity with the first mine to wash up.

Jack and Gloria left the tea dance early. He already had an intolerance for noise, but it was easily covered by the greater truth; he wanted to be alone with her. They walked away from the sea and climbed through long grass towards full trees that promised shelter. The spring had taken a leap into summer from where it would fall back with a thump in a few days, but for this afternoon it was steady. They lay down on his army tunic, and she knew that he loved her then because he touched only her hands and face.

In the weeks they had been there, Denny reckoned he had covered about every mile of countryside surrounding the shitty little town, crawling through it, staging mock raids and digging holes in it. He had not wasted his time, however. They walked for more than an hour,

212

Jean's clothes clinging to her in the unseasonable heat. Denny made her walk ahead, though she didn't know the way. He said he would tell her when she was going wrong. Walking somewhere other than to work or a shop was something of a novelty, and Jean found her legs liking it, becoming loose and limber. She took off her shoes and treated the soles of her feet to the feel of wet grass and warm dirt.

The object of the mission was a pool, green and cool and ringed by obsequious trees that bowed low, dipping their branches into the water. Beauty had not been pointed out to Jean before — except as a reprimand — and she accepted it as a gift. She thought that was all there would be, and didn't know quite what to do when Denny pulled off his clothes and waded into the opaque water. He turned to see her standing on the bank, the hem of her dress twisting in her palms.

'What are you waiting for?'

She had not yet seen all of him without clothes. Her mind no longer had to fill in the blanks between the memories of her senses; there he was. He ducked under and quickly surfaced again, streams of water running from his sandy hair, dribbling over the slight shelf of his eyebrows, pooling in the hollow of his shoulder blades, gushing freely down his chest to the darker hair between his legs. She followed the course of that water so closely she thought she could taste each part of him it skated over. He was so incredibly beautiful she feared she might vomit. He noticed her sharp interest and crouched down in the water.

'You can't have me if you don't come in.'

Jean blushed and looked at her huge muddied feet.

'I'm not sure.'

'You didn't like the last time?'

Jean shook her head. 'No, it was . . . lovely.'

Denny laughed and swept his hand across the surface of the pool, drenching her from the waist down; her dress melted onto her curves.

'Lovely.' He liked the word. 'All right, then. Get in the water.'

Jean shook her head again, more worried this time.

'I'll sink. I know I will.'

'You don't know how to float?'

Jean shook her head. 'A stone sinks, and I'm more than a stone, more than a sack of coal. My mum told me; she showed me too.'

Denny stood up in the water.

'Do I look like your mother?'

The connection of the two nearly floored her.

'Oh no, you're . . . beautiful. She was . . . I can't even say.'

He liked being beautiful. He liked the way she took him in. Her gaze was uncomplicated and honest, the attention of a doctor combined with the unfocused lust of a teenage boy. 'OK. So who do you trust, me or her?'

She couldn't say neither. 'You.'

'You won't sink, I can promise you. Come in, I'll show you.' Jean took a squelchy step towards the water's edge.

Denny threw in the free gift. 'Then you can

have your wicked way with me.'

Jean summoned the self of that revolutionary night by the road, closed her eyes, pulled off her clothes and waded in.

★ ★ ★

To be weightless was something Jean had considered as possible as unaided flight. His hands were no more than lily pads beneath her; there seemed to be nothing holding her. She joined the select ranks of things that could float: cork, leaves, dust, her. It hardly seemed credible; he could balance her on one hand. This was dark magic, and good. Jean wondered how he knew what to do with her.

'Just relax, or you'll go under. And don't hold your breath. You want to go in a circle?'

Jean nodded, the water massaging her head with a cool hand. She fanned out from him like a sail, sending huge ripples out to the bank. Water dashed over her body; she giggled as it sluiced seemingly unreachable parts of her. From a cupped hand, he poured water over her torso, sending a stream of it running down between her breasts to pool in her navel. Jean felt the current change under her head; they were moving.

'Where are we going?'

He was walking her towards the bank. When the water was too shallow to support her, she put her feet into the silky mud. He pushed her back into the bank and walked up over her on his hands, his legs streaming behind him like pale fins. She clawed the soft wet earth as he drove deeper into her, the water rising and falling like the tide on his back.

She returned home from the swimming pond shaking; her blood bubbled and popped in her veins. She went to the bathroom to rinse her face and saw that Gloria had drawn a bath. The six inches of water caused an inexplicable erotic charge that coursed down her legs with such speed and ferocity that it nearly knocked her over. She ducked her head quickly under the cold tap and left the bathroom with the water dribbling down her neck. As Gloria bathed and related details of her day through the slightly open door, Jean shivered in the hallway. Gloria's parents were out visiting friends, the girls had the flat to themselves and had no need to censor their conversation, but Jean knew that this was not something that would bring them together. As she had seen Gloria striding away from her, she now saw herself striking out towards something else entirely. It was not ruin, exactly, but it was not the opposite of that. The sound of the water as Gloria rolled in the tub was unbearable. Jean had run up and down the stairs three times and downed two brandies by the time her friend emerged. Gloria looked at the sweating wreck crouched like a derelict outside the bathroom door.

'What's got into you?'

Jean gave a weak smile, though it was all she could do not to vomit the brandy onto her own feet. She was no longer unshakeable. Neglect, poverty and near starvation had not taken her legs from under her, but now the sight of water could.

Deep into the night, Jean lay awake, unwilling to surrender control of her mind's eye to the unpredictability of sleep. She wanted to see him, in the bright sunshine of that day, until her mind faded. Wisteria was most active at night; her voice had never been suited to daytime. She whispered in her daughter's ear, threatening to climb in and scoot through her dreams, trailing the usual sour destruction. Jean redoubled her efforts to make Denny appear and tried to ignore her mother.

In daylight. Really. Was there any reason to let God get an eyeful of that? Hasn't He suffered enough?

Jean blinked and tried to regain the image of Denny's shoulder she had been enjoying. She grasped the bedsheet tightly; Wisteria had always made her sleep with her hands above the covers, even on the coldest nights.

Well, you've done all there is to do now, haven't you? We won't see any more of him. Why buy the cow when you've had the milk for free?

Jean pulled the sheet up to her neck. She heard the distinctive death-watch beetle tapping of Wisteria's disapproval. *Tut, tut, tut. Ruined already. Who'd have you now?*

'Who'd have had me then?' Jean thought. 'You can't ruin a ruin.' A draught chilled her neck; Wisteria was displeased at her inability to shame her daughter. Jean wriggled in the sheet, trying to build up some warmth. She was not a natural addict. The one night and the one afternoon had been more than she had ever thought possible. She inherently understood rationing and was one

217

of the few people who could genuinely make do and mend. If this was all, then she would be sad but she would not be broken. She had drunk at the pool, aware inside herself — in her bones, her teeth, her eyes — that it could be a long walk through the desert.

★　★　★

But he did come back. Time and again. He had known plenty of girls, to various stages of erudition, elementary and advanced. But nothing like her. It was more than her size, though she pushed at the parameters of his fetish in a way that was almost unbearably good. She was not yet confident or skilled but still explored him with a hungry curiosity bordering on worship. It was the intensity of the attention paid that he repaid with intensity. He enjoyed her enjoyment: eyes struggling to stay closed, embarrassed by and unused to her own reactions. Sometimes she would gasp with surprise at herself. Then he would feel like he'd invented the whole deal, just for her. So he returned. He still had a few tricks he wanted to show her.

As the spring warmed into summer, she studied. The sun browned her arms and neck as she worked, matching the warmth she felt inside her. Denny had turned the skin she lived in into a source of pleasure and for the first time in her life she was glad she inhabited quite so much of it; it began to sing under his touch. Jean fell in love with her flesh. She came to appreciate her long legs independently of him, bristling as

Gloria drew on her stocking seams from ankle to thigh, reflecting how much sooner that particular pleasure is over for short-legged girls. Wisteria would still whisper at night, reminding Jean that she chose to celebrate the horrible death of her own mother by dragging her name through the mud. This realisation would occasionally creep into Jean's mind, soft-footed and wreathed in shame, and Jean would have to close the door on it. She was too glad.

She enjoyed her dinner-plate hands, as they could cover half of Denny's back. She would sit by him while he bathed in the sun and soak up his warm skin through her fingers. She wished she could absorb him into her body, carry him with her always. They would take mornings, afternoons, any time that was on offer. Her week was divided into pre- and post-him. Her world that had seemed so slim was now crowded with activity. There was each new find — what could be done with toes, or earlobes — and the time required to process and catalogue it.

The discovery of sex warps time. For the short weeks she had him, Jean lived years of her life. There was no timetable to adhere to but their own. The pieces of her had not yet fallen to the ground and formed a shape, a map. She felt the force of the blast still at her back. She had coincided with a period of the unusual and could only be grateful.

The hot summer gilded her; her scars were white against browned flesh. Swipes of nougat on caramel, Gloria's father said, before disappearing behind the counter in a cloud of confusion and embarrassment, leaving Jean to continue unloading the deliveries alone. He secretly saw Jean as the son he never had, a protective brother to Gloria, and could not help but admire how her body had pulled itself together. It gave him hope for the many more who would be broken.

Denny invented a game where he would map and name the marks on her, now more visible than ever. A raised circle on her shoulder left by a piece of hot metal was Half-Dollar Hill; on the inside of her thigh, two parallel lines with three short lines scored across them were Cupid's Ladder. He tired of it before even a quarter of her was claimed, but it was a glorious exercise in empire-building while it lasted.

One morning, as they lay outdoors, her hand on his chest, the sun burned his skin around her fingers. When she took her hand away, its imprint was pale and edged with red, as if the ghostly fingers could give out heat long after Jean's hot hands had gone home and turned cold. The next week, his last week, Denny lifted his shirt to show Jean. The marks were still there, softened a little, her spirit hand melting into his tanned flesh.

'There, you see? Still there. I'm branded now. I'll take it with me, wherever I go.'

She understood that he was saying goodbye. She had seen lives end as suddenly, and had wondered how it would feel. Inevitable, she decided. Jean traced the outline of her own hand with a lightness she had never before possessed in her thick fingers. Denny shivered and smiled, and she smiled back.

'Is this love?' she asked, before testing the warmth of his skin with her tongue. She wanted to know, and to warn him that any kindness shown to her would graft her to him for life. She resolved to be left by him, to let him do that. It wasn't much, considering what he had given her. But she yearned to know what it was that existed between them; the experience demanded a name.

'No,' Denny replied. 'It's not.'

Part Three

TRANSLATION

20

The ship was a floating academy of Americanisation. More than four hundred GI brides attempted to shed their nationalities into the Atlantic Ocean over the course of a long voyage plagued by heavy swells and the failure to understand what constitutes a decent cup of tea. The women took daily classes in the country: the workings of washing machines and Congress, and a version of history new and occasionally insulting to British ears.

At the dockside they had waved to hundreds of people they didn't know and shed genuine tears at never seeing any one of them again. Gloria had surveyed the faces far below her, all bitten lips and rapidly blinking eyes. 'Brave little England,' she thought, just as they had been saying all those years; poor, brave little England. Everyone so pleased to leave and so sad to be left behind. It felt a bit shabby after all that had been said and done. Half the town was missing or had moved on; there would be no one left for even the ghosts to haunt. But this was her destiny, and Gloria accepted it. For Jean, it was like winning a competition she had no memory of entering.

★　★　★

They were married in minutes, the four of them. Jean staggered out onto the town hall steps, the sun skewering her eyes, an unfamiliar tightness round her finger. Curtain rings and commitments were now to be worn. Denny stumbled out next to her, fumbling for a cigarette. They had the air of puzzled defendants who hadn't properly understood the verdict and did not know whether to wonder at getting away with it or rail at the severity of the sentence.

He had left her, as he was supposed to. It had been perfectly clean, with no tricks. But then Jack had got a licence, and he and Denny had got drunk together, and suddenly death seemed very possible; Jean had proved to be an effective barrier between him and the real. Realising that he would be sent to face entire armies without her magnificent body as a shield, Denny felt stupidly alone. So he asked her. Later, he cursed himself for this weakness, complicating life with the fear of death, but somehow he couldn't take it back. She had to be good luck, he reasoned; what else could she represent?

They would get to share a bed, be naked under sheets, and wake up together; it was worth a curtain ring. Jack and Gloria had been inevitable; he and Jean had been accidental. Inexplicable. When Jean said yes, she felt as if she were duping a blind man, a backward child. He doesn't understand, she thought — but still said yes. Gloria kissed her friend a dozen times, incredulous and happy. 'She thinks it means I won't be left behind,' Jean realised, but kept quiet. She could hardly expect Gloria to know about her and Denny, when she herself hadn't known him well enough to catch his last name prior to it becoming hers. Curnalia. It sounded like a country, one no one much would want to visit, or a condition that afflicted the feet. And now she was to put Mrs in front of it. Funny, this war, she thought. You never knew where things that had been dislodged were going to land.

They smoked in silence on the steps of the town hall, anxious to get to the point of things and have their night in foreign sheets. Gloria had come clattering down the steps behind them in smart, almost-new heels, Jack and her parents after that. Mrs Smith was brandishing her camera; this day would not escape her wall.

'Come on you lot, stand together.'

Denny slipped an arm round his wife's waist. 'Last day, big girl. No telling what after this.'

Jean nodded, smiling for the camera. She wasn't so used to smiles that they didn't look like the desperate grimace of a kidnap victim forced to put on a show of health and sanity.

'Funny way for it be over.' She ground the words through her teeth.

'I know,' her husband replied, no looser-jawed. 'But everything has to end, right?'

Jean showed her teeth in the widest smile her face could accommodate. He was convinced of his own death; she was equally sure of a long existence without him. It had been a perfect wedding. They were all grinning like death's heads, but Mrs Smith was not impressed.

'Look happier than that, you lot, it's for the *photograph*.'

Gloria leaned in and whispered in Jean's ear, 'I knew it. I knew things would come right. I felt so awful I was going to have to go without you.'

Because, of course, she would have gone. Jean's smile began to ache around the edges. They all pressed their heads together, and Mrs Smith pressed the shutter.

⋆　⋆　⋆

The morning after the wedding, the men were disappeared. The army took Jack and Denny and left photographs in their place, phantom husbands that hovered over Jean and Gloria's beds but did not warm them. When the wedding picture came back, they looked windswept and enthusiastic as if they had been on an enjoyable bicycle ride. Gloria decided it wasn't proper, and that she and Jean should wear wedding dresses and have a real photograph taken, stiff and formal and convincing. She wouldn't feel married until she looked married.

Gloria had the official portraits, in uniform, caps in hand, enlarged and framed, and she and Jean lugged them down to the front, where the brides posed for a paid photographer. He had suggested getting the pier in the background, saying they might want a memento of their hometown in days to come. Gloria had snorted at this, which caused Mrs Smith to look pained, and so she assented. It was not the backdrop she had in mind. She had wanted the painted silk screen in the photographer's shop, and instead got seaside sky, grey and slack as an overwashed sheet. Swathed in white — Jean's borrowed dress open at the back and in daring proximity to her knees — the two brides snapped in the chill breeze like ornately dressed flagpoles. They had chosen the largest size of portrait for Jack and Denny, to make sure that the men showed up properly in the second photograph. It now looked as if they were marrying into a race of supermen as they grappled with the outsize heads in their heavy frames. Gloria had to rest Jack on the promenade railing as she couldn't hold him up for long and kept hitting her foot with the lacquered frame; Jean was attempting to hide as much of herself as possible behind her husband, bending away from the photograph with such a pained expression that she resembled a bashful hunchback accepting an oversized award for bravery.

When the photographer poked his head out from under the camera's big black skirt and shouted 'Ready?', a shaft of sunlight broke through the grey, as if commanded. It fell over a loose length of Gloria's pale gold hair and sent it streaming into the sun as if she had been spun from it. When the picture came out, it would appear an act of Victorian trickery, a fairy photograph, with a decidedly earthbound Jean stood next to a gossamer sea sprite who looked as though she could dance in a human's hand.

★ ★ ★

The curtain ring turned Jean's finger green, and she removed it. She went back to work and gave no sign of having been married. It felt like a lie that would be easier to undo if it didn't travel

229

far. Gloria at least seemed to be changed. She radiated such an absence of need, it was irresistible. In the week following her wedding, a dozen people fell in love with her. A woman with twenty years of marriage and three children behind her found she dreamt of Gloria every night for a week after seeing her run for a bus and hop onto the back step like a goddess in flight. All twelve could have walked past with hearts aflame and scorch marks on their shirts for all Gloria could see. She was Jack's.

For the first year, she worried he would die. In the second year she worried he would forget her; at the end of the third year she worried she no longer remembered him. Jean had it easier. She felt the hunger of the sudden denial of Denny, but was still too stunned by the fact of him in the first place to count the weeks and months and years. She was accustomed to the sudden removal of comforts; Gloria was too used to being indulged. She thought she could influence death; Jean, having had more dealings with the entity, was passive, unconvinced from the start that she could prejudice any outcome. Her own continuation made no sense, so she didn't see what she could do about Denny's. She hoped instead that he found deep holes to hide in and marched alongside tall comrades who would shield him from fire. And she worked; occupation was everything.

Time lengthened again, the urgency of the beginning all but disappeared, the slow trudge from day to day all that remained. Death was present but almost diminished, strangely neutered in its inability to overwhelm the small worries and minuscule pleasures of existence. They disposed of week after week, absorbed by routine, as even the chaos had become. Gloria no longer protested at the waste of her life within the confines of the shop; she was happy to have comforting repetition around her, repelling the unexpected. She attended church, just to be sure, but found more solace at the cinema. Of all the war films Gloria saw, not a single one killed off the most beautiful of the men. The small, lucky one often survived too, Jean noted. While Gloria clung to routine, Jean relied on the regular occurrence of the unexpected to alleviate the dread of normality, to which she had no in. She knew how to respond to the demolition of an entire street better than she knew how to darn a sock.

They were what was required; the war had bent them to its fire. The lifesong in Jean passed into the background, where no relief of it was expected. The itch of frustration became no more than the chafe of monotony. They no longer expected a conclusion. But they hoped — Gloria for Jack, Jean for herself.

Then it ended. Like a drum that has rolled too far, the world righted itself with a nauseating lurch. It was no longer normal for trees to be festooned with underwear from bombed shops, nor for the guts of buildings and people to be on show. It ended, and Jean was told that she was no longer needed; a returning soldier would take her job. She felt the loss in her body, as when something warm — a baby, a love, a hope — is snatched away. She stood outside the ministry, leaking purpose like air from a defective tyre. No one thanked her. They seemed to despise her for having done well, as if it was a criticism of those who had been absent.

Jean briefly fantasised about doing away with the soldier usurper who had taken her occupation, but realised that wouldn't keep her in work. And once the rubble was cleared, the soldier would be as useless as she. 'I want it to take me with it,' she thought. 'Wherever the war goes, I want to go, too.' She gave a shudder at this, a little shocked by her own savagery, and wiped her mind clear of the staining thought. There were things Denny had shown her that made her grateful not to be dead; she resolved to attempt gratitude at now being alive. The time had come to surrender. Jean returned everything she was ordered to, but her overalls; these she put away, uncleaned and wrapped in waxed paper taken from the sweet shop. She could not have missed her skin more.

The victory was celebrated for a full day and a night, many of the women wearing bright crêpe-paper dresses over their own dull utility clothes. Gloria represented America in red, white and blue, a shower of stars tacked on to her skirt. Jean had lost out on being Great Britain and was instead Russia, all in red with a white hammer and sickle across her chest. They called her Uncle Josephine. A photograph was taken of the street party, the children giving double-handed waves, their fingers lost in a blur of movement, arms ending in excitable rotary blades. The women were all curiously still; bent over the table to refill a cup or balancing a child on their hip, they were caught in perfect detail, the lines of them fine but deep, their expressions clear and knowable. The uncertainty of life was giving way to the certainty of it. That was what stopped them dead, rendering them forever sharp against the shimmering background.

Everything slowed, feet fell less rapidly and jaws worked with less urgency. There would be time, after all, to get everything done, to get everything said, and what was to be said and done seemed less important because of that. Jean felt her insides fall in step with the after-world, her blood thickening, her heart quietening, her muscles cooling. They were entering stasis, and she didn't know how to struggle against it.

It felt as though the women had been put in a pool of water and left to bob. They floated off to their jobs, but the gates were locked, and they bumped against them before returning home. They trod water to and from the shops that had nothing in them and reined in the children that had grown free and wild, tethering them to the home. Jean saw her reflection in glazed, watery eyes and understood. The thing that sped them on was gone; they were becalmed. Men would return; uselessness would, too. She was too young to no longer be required, there was too much of life left. But the unexpected was over with. And if that were so, he wouldn't be coming back to her.

Jean returned to the shop where she ordered the glass jars with the same care she had shown the broken bricks she salvaged from the bombsites. Some of the bricks had still been warm, not from fire, but from living. They came from behind ovens or had pipes running through them, and cooled more slowly than a body. She would hold them to her face and try to imagine growing up in a house where there was warmth. Jean was more help than was needed but she worked all the hours she was allowed to, trying to seem indispensable.

'You don't want to be starting that,' Mrs Smith told her, when Jean began to alphabetise the cellar stock. 'You'll be off before you know it.'

Jean finished the cellar and began repainting the shelves, while Gloria waited for word from Jack. 'You'll leave them half done,' Mrs Smith worried. 'And we won't find anyone to do the rest.' Jean had smiled and shrugged and carried on. After the shelves, she started on the window frames, keeping the satisfaction close that she had managed to find tasks enough for a month or two. She wondered if the Smiths would let her paint the flat, too. 'They'll need you,' she told herself. 'With Gloria gone, they'll definitely need you.' Jean's heart twisted at the thought of losing her friend, but she knew she could only ever step into a vacancy. There would at least be that.

They were sheltered from the worst of it. The shop was Jean and Gloria's personal tank where they bobbed along together and waited to be fished out. They were back in their pre-war state of waiting to be wives; Jean prepared for a longer wait than Gloria. As the days after the end ticked by, Gloria cheered herself imagining how she would take flight in America, where beauty was prized and never suspected. Jack had told her she would rule there with ease. She spent the time between his letters wrapped in that thought, and it kept her sane while wild imaginings of Jack's destruction prowled close by. One evening she traced the scars on Jean's arm to see if she could 'get used to it'. Jean guessed she must have seen some new disfigurement walking the street. Gloria would often return hysterical from a shopping trip or library visit, imagining Jack with the affliction glimpsed on some other soldier's face or body. She was nervous at first, and Jean realised she had always laid a hand on some untouched part of her arm, as if the scars were communicable. Jean submitted to the attention, grateful for the benign contact. It seemed that in its ragged resourcefulness, her skin held some answer to their fears. Gloria found she might bear more than expected; Jean knew she had not yet found where her own limit lay.

'It's finally here,' Gloria sighed, as her finger swirled round a long-ago wound. 'I started to think it would never be. I started to think I'd be old before this was over. Aren't we lucky?'

Jean nodded. 'We are. All that time, and not one of us hurt.'

'I wonder what would have happened in another year, another week, even?'

At that, Jean felt ashamed for ever having longed for the end to be postponed, for her usefulness to be extended. The high price of it had been paid by others; her time was the remainder of theirs, unused and forever lost. She prayed with Gloria then, for the first time, for forgiveness.

As the losses were counted, Jean felt her obscene luck in not having been loved much. Her grief was limited. Frankie's name had been entered in the book of remembrance, and while it was not the only name Jean knew, it was the only one to whom she had become known. She wanted to kiss the page when they filed past. At the thanksgiving service, prayers floated up like burning twists of paper through the shattered roof. Jean thought she could see them rise, as those around her seemed certain their words would find their way to God. Jean was silent. She tried hard to feel chosen, sitting among the others that didn't die, but couldn't. Boys that used to throw stones at her were now dead, their lives rubbed out while they were protecting her. She wondered if they had realised that. She wondered if it would have mattered. Jean closed her eyes and whispered her thanks to the dead; she thanked them for taking her place, and tried to believe she made a worthwhile trade.

Gloria was unable to attend a single service until she knew Jack was alive; her gratitude was conditional. Eventually she received proof of him, a letter and a photograph in which his outline was sharp but he was still somehow out of focus, smudged by age and experience. His hair was sun-bleached almost white, and his eyes glowed; he looked like an exhausted angel. There was no word of Denny. They knew only that he had not been killed, and nothing of his intentions. As Gloria began the long process of emigration, Mrs Smith allowed Jean to begin painting the kitchen. The day Gloria went to obtain a passport, her father set about teaching Jean how to ride the delivery bicycle. Gloria alone believed that Denny's silence was down to a fault with the postal service.

If the government hadn't been paying the fare, Gloria might have been proved wrong. But Denny decided he liked the idea of having a woman delivered. Jean received a telegram, sent in a haze of lust only partially sated by a blonde with bad skin but the requisite form. 'NOT DONE WITH YOU YET STOP'. So she would be a wife.

21

From the back of the ship, Jean and Gloria watched England shrink and disappear from the horizon like a dull sun setting. They held each other tightly, aware that everything they knew and could name disappeared with it.

Jean felt unprepared for America. The orientation classes left her more bewildered than before, and bad weather drove everyone below decks after only a few of those. The corridors soon ran with vomit every time the ship rolled, and the film presentations sponsored by manufacturers of cars and refrigerators went unwatched. Nothing on the ship could tell Jean what she needed to know: what did he want with her?

She adjusted to the bucking of the ship faster than most; her long, sturdy legs absorbed the different rhythms of the sea before they could pull her centre off balance. She would walk around the deck, leaning into the fierce winds, practising resistance. She envisioned a waiting crowd at the other side, dead set on pushing her back into the sea lest she contaminate their shores with her strangeness. She would be ready for them. The American crew thought she was being terribly brave and British and gave her mock salutes and winks. She would return the salute if she could let go of the rail long enough, but rarely trusted her bulk to one hand and so instead would dip in an odd curtsey while clinging on. One ship's officer thought of a ballet-dancing gorilla he had seen in a comic short, and unthinkingly applauded.

They restarted the classes when the storm eased, but most of the brides had lost interest, preferring their own imaginings to those of the refrigerator company. For Jean it was simply too late. Automats and subways scared her less than the realisation she could no longer remember the colour of Denny's eyes. While Gloria slept (she had been particularly ill, and stayed in bed through even the calm days, trying to regain her former temperament and complexion), and the other brides danced or played cards, Jean tried to remember the face of her husband. She would lay the photograph of their wedding day flat against her stomach, close her eyes and then try to trace every detail of him in her mind, then check to see if she had forgotten anything. She revised him; learnt him as if he were a foreign language. It had been more than three years since she had seen him. She should at least know his face; she had little other information to go on.

They arrived before dawn at a city wreathed in mist, watched over by a giant superior even to Jean. Denny hadn't lied to her when he told her everything would be bigger here. Except her, Jean thought; perhaps she would finally shrink. The brides waved at the ghost city and in reply felt the cold roll off its skyscrapers towards their suddenly small boat. They were sailing into the iceberg they had all secretly dreaded for the whole voyage. Jean felt Gloria's hand slip into hers and rattle a little inside her great paw.

After they had been processed, the women were divided like packages into their postal districts. Some were claimed dockside, others forwarded in the care of relatives. Jean, Gloria and twenty-eight other brides were loaded onto a bus and taken to the station to catch the trains running further into the unknown; most of them hadn't learned how to pronounce their destinations yet and had them written down phonetically. Some of the girls going upstate were close to tears. The others pressed their faces to the window, twisting their necks to see how high the city went up. It disappeared over their heads, and they ran to the other side of the bus to catch it. The cars were as sleek and rounded as beetles; they moved between the lights in timed bursts, the streets an endless conveyor belt of people and machines. Jean saw a woman getting a permanent wave in a salon, on show in the window, metal suckers clamped to her head; she looked as if she was being mechanically milked. The brides broke their nails on the windows pointing too suddenly, too forcefully at everything. They slid back the glass so the smell of the city could surround them: petrol and cooking fat, cigarette smoke and sweat — it smelled so *rich*. So abundant. There was too much of everything; noise, people, traffic. It would never run out.

The city's stations were as grand as museums; movement was its art. Jean wanted to be part of the rhythm of this brilliant piece of engineering, even though to slip or falter would mean getting trapped in its gears and ground to dust. She liked the feeling of danger and urgency; it was oddly human. It made her pulse quicken, the way a siren used to, the way she missed, in the peace. The city's heart was hard, not cruel but indifferent, and it beat strongly; she felt it through the thin soles of her shoes.

When the chaperones shepherded the women into the station, Jean felt the city reluctantly give up its grip; the dense air of the street thinned and cooled. The thing she had enjoyed most with Denny was their faces close together, the air between them thick and warm, as it was in the city. She wanted to run into its embrace, disappear into the fog of breath and not face the cold, thin future. This joke had already gone too far.

A steady stream of fedora-topped grey flannel poured into the station: men come to claim the brides they had met when they were young and knew who they were, and what they were for. It was a meeting of ghosts, of people who no longer existed in the world but in fiercely guarded and cherished memories: a meeting of people who might breathe life back into each other. The women stood under the clock and waited to be claimed. They were always, it seemed, pitting themselves against time.

Denny and Jack rode the train in from Jack's hometown, a few hours' grace in which to consider what would and wouldn't be a mistake. Denny's first train east had taken him through a hundred small towns, a hundred destinations belonging to other people, destinations he could make his own. Some men jumped when the train slowed and headed into the dirt, the urge to desert taking them over only now the war was done. Denny understood that. He didn't want to be known. But he wanted her at least once more; that at least was worth the journey.

He and Jack sat in the observation car, smoking cigarettes with shaking hands. Denny didn't shake often, and when he did it was more from a desire for movement than from internal tremors, unlike Jack's constant oscillation. He busied his hands with a pack of cards while Jack steadied his the way he knew how. The scenery ran across Jack's glassy eyes like a strip of overexposed film, while whisky simmered in his pores.

'You thinking important thoughts there, Jack?'

Denny liked to interrupt him now. He used to leave him alone, used to think Jack had some privacy to be respected, but now he came close to mocking him. Jack didn't seem to notice or care. But then, Jack knew him; they knew each other after four long years, knew what liars they both were. Denny wondered how long it would take to exhaust his marriage and get on his way; he hoped it wasn't too long.

'You thinking big there?'

Jack nodded, smiling to himself. 'Thinking about my Glory. It's all about her from now on.'

Denny let a brief snort of air out of his nose and went back to his cards. It had taken him a while to work out that Jack wasn't trying very hard to survive. He threw himself into war as if it was clear water. Every act of bravery was just suicide gone wrong. He was given commendations as he was stripped of promotions; fond of charging machine-gun nests, he was not to be trusted with preserving the lives of men, only taking them.

When Jack saw Gloria, he thought she could anchor him to life and he would come to love living as he loved her. He didn't know why he couldn't care for it, only that he never had. At fourteen he had started to drink, at fifteen to fight, at seventeen to race cars, with the headlights blacked out. When he saw Gloria, he told himself it was her absence until then that had caused this dislocation, and that it would now be healed. But then he found how well the war suited him. In it, no one cared who he was; he was metal embossed with his name, khaki stained with his sweat, and a gun. Jack saw the fact of his death wasn't so stark within a slaughterhouse on this scale, and breathed easier. He had embraced the removal of choice, and now missed the opportunities for a beautifully blameless death the war afforded.

Denny had never thought enough about his existence to want to end it; he didn't consider it, just took one breath after another and responded to hunger, thirst and lust. He was a simple animal and knew it. Denny no longer saw Jack as smart, more as an idiot brother, born stripped of the skills for life and needful of his protection. He was tired of him. But still he said yes to Jack's offer of a home. He said yes because he was a liar, and Jack knew it.

Denny was halfway through a hand when the train pulled in; he left the cards on the table for someone else to finish. They moved quickly along the platform, holding up their tickets as if claiming a prize in a raffle. They had survived; they got to take home a wife and a shiny new future. It was a long platform. The past few years had been spent scurrying, scrambling, covering only a few yards, a hundred at the most. Something about walking such a distance — the length of a twenty-car train — made Denny talk faster; talking felt like some kind of cover.

'She wrote me a letter saying which outfit she'd be wearing so I'd know her.'

Jack nodded and carried on walking.

'Hat. Gloves. Purse. The whole thing. She's a hundred feet tall. What do I care what purse she's holding? She only has one purse. It's green.'

'She probably bought a new one,' Jack murmured, his eyes darting from left to right though he had stretched his mouth into an approximation of a relaxed smile. 'She's not going to take an old purse to a new home.'

'Did Gloria tell you what she was going to be wearing? You going to be able to recognise Gloria? Did you think of that?'

Jack had Gloria burnt on the inside of his eyes, dancing round his head, imprinted on his heart. He had managed to convince himself that he had thought of nothing but her. Her face had always been before him, but it had been as sheer as a veil and, as a restraint, about as much use. He knew there was nothing that could really hold him back, but he had tried. A spasm pulled at the constructed smile and his fingers tightened around the flask he carried at all times. He had emptied it on the train and tried not to tally the hours till he would be able to drink again. There would be too many.

'It hasn't been so long. She won't have changed. There's no one else like my Glory.'

'We sure do got a couple of individuals.' Denny laughed, almost bitterly. 'We sure do got that.'

They merged into the throng of sweating, suited men, some carrying wilted flowers or crushed chocolates or even nylons, as a nod to the past and because they didn't know what their wives liked beyond flowers and chocolates and nylons. Denny could see the women under the clock; their women, the ones they had tried to stay alive for, so they had told them in their letters. If he was honest, he wasn't sure what he was staying alive for; he just wanted to so much it was easier to give it a name. Give it her name, if that's what it took.

As they approached, the women began to bristle; the cluster of wives in their best non-utility suits became a multihued anemone swaying softly in the thick air of expectation. For a moment, each forgot who had come to collect her and just hoped to be picked by someone and not left behind. The first man to approach found thirty pairs of pleading eyes on him and had to walk away again to collect himself.

22

The landscape slunk by in a funk. In the February cold, the denuded trees looked like burned witches; Jean had heard they did that hereabouts, a long time ago. She wondered what they did to giants.

She was glad they were going to Jack's house by train, it would take longer to get there, to be at an end. The motion soothed Gloria into sleep. She had exhausted herself in a spaniel-like frenzy at the station, jumping up at Jack, planting wet kisses on his chin and cheeks, anywhere she could reach. Her teeth had grazed his throat and that's when he set her down and enveloped her in a calming hug that caused her to burst into tears. Jean and Denny had stood by like children, waiting for something they didn't understand to stop. The way Denny had looked at her, Jean knew. He had sent off for an erotic memory, and the fleshy, scarred present had turned up.

The train journey to the boat had been the first of Jean's life. The locomotive swayed like an old horse and smelt of coal and cigarettes. They had crossed from one piece of coast to another, through miles of grey: sock-coloured skies hanging over frozen slate-coloured fields. She had stared hard at the passing countryside trying to fix it in her mind, her last glimpse of home. She tried to conjure the landscape again here, on the other side, but what faced her was too much the same, and it contaminated the memory. She had lost it already. Instead she listened to the train murmuring as it carried her away from the sea. She would miss the sea and wasn't sure how she would live only on the land, with nowhere to hide. If she separated out every sound — the scrape of the rails, the soft exhalations of the leather seats, the voice of the porter calling out stations, Chesters and Shires far from where they should be — and concentrated on each one, following it as with a tangled line in a newspaper puzzle, she might not lose her mind, she thought. She listened to Jack's breathing as he pretended to sleep, his head touching Gloria's with a deliberate, concerned lightness. She listened to the soft smacking of Denny's lips as he ignored her, chewing at the inside of his mouth. She listened to her heartbeat, resolutely strong. She never felt how she felt.

The station still had a 'Welcome Back Our Boys' banner hanging from the rafters, a little tatty now. Jean thought someone should add, 'And who's that with you?' The snow had melted and frozen again in grey ridges, irregular but never wide enough to be able to place a foot flat on the floor. Jean crushed her way through, Jack carried Gloria, while Denny tiptoed like a high-wire artiste, balanced by a suitcase in each hand. Jean sat down heavily in the back of Jack's fragile-looking car and hoped there weren't too many hills to come.

Denny kept his eyes fixed on the window, not seeing beyond it. The ringing inside his head was threatening to split it open; he clenched his fists to stop himself from squeezing his skull until it cracked. He wanted to get out of the car, to stand by the side of the road until the cold froze his brain. The noise of the station could have set it off, or seeing her. Jean felt herself fading like a photograph as he kept his gaze from her.

They turned through pretty streets of identical wood-frame houses; Gloria was wide awake now and chattering excitedly about which one would be hers, and Jack had yet to tire of saying wait and see. Jean was silent, returning to an old standby; she mentally drew lines around herself and concentrated on keeping inside them. Denny was fighting the urge to scream.

Mrs John Hammell Sr stood at the door with her arms opened wide, a pose she'd decided on well in advance. She wanted her son's bride to feel welcome; the girl was going to need her, she thought, going to need someone to talk to. She had wanted her son back so much that for the first few weeks she had pretended not to notice the impostor in his place. Someone had taken her son's clothes and stuffed them with straw, and through some terrible kind of witchcraft this dummy could speak. But when she held him she felt only a clock ticking inside a bed of straw; she could not feel his heart. When she looked into his eyes she could not see his soul. She told herself she used to be able to. She had practised smiling for hours the previous day, opening her arms to the mirror and mouthing words of welcome.

Jean exited the car first, and Jack's mother gave a little at the elbows.

'Now, Sally girl,' she whispered to herself. 'Courage.'

She had put on her best winter suit, which was also giving at the elbows. Her thick silver hair, of which she was girlishly proud, had been set into a wave, and she was wearing her pearls before five for the first time in twenty years. She had her armour on, such as it was, and nothing would penetrate it. She spread out her arms and reapplied her smile; she could and would cope and be charming about it. Jean stood by the car, not wanting to lead the charge. She gave a shy wave; Jack's mother waved back with both hands. Then Gloria emerged from the front passenger side; a crown of gold hair swept back from her sweetheart face, which had been polished pink by the cold.

'Oh thank God,' the silver-haired woman breathed through her teeth.

★   ★   ★

An exotic impulse buy from a foreign bazaar, Jean didn't suit the room. Any room. She had been in this new world for just a few hours, and already it was clear to Denny that she did not fit. Neither of them did; that was what happened when you lived someone else's life. With no desire to be married, he had collected a wife; with no thought of a future, he had become part of hers, Jack's and others he had yet to meet. He felt institutionalised again, part of a great tide of men that were pulled one way or another and had no say.

The house was solid and comfortable in its sixth decade; the milky grey paint that washed down the walls outside and in was the colour of an old woman's eyes. The ceilings were high and the furniture low, creating vast spaces into which conversation evaporated. An upright piano clung to one wall, unplayed but still cared for. Objects past use were retained here.

Jack and Gloria took rooms across from his mother. It had been agreed that they would all live here until the men had enough money to provide proper accommodation for their wives. Denny knew he was being bribed to stay close. Jack's mother showed Jean and Denny to their rooms, the old servants' quarters, joining on to the back of the house. A bedroom, a bathroom and a kitchen, all for themselves. She left them alone together, and they stood in silence. Denny thought that if he didn't say anything for another hour, he might never speak to her again.

Though the ringing was fading to an angry hum, he had yet find a space in his head to form words. He put his wife's suitcase in the bedroom, and they loitered in the doorway, looking at the small, saggy bed. It had a deep, solitary dip; someone large had spent too many nights alone.

'Shall I make us a proper cup of tea?' Jean offered.

'Sure,' Denny's voice cracked but he was relieved to hear it come out at all. 'Why not tea.'

From the suitcase she took a small, decorated caddy, given to her as a leaving gift by Gloria's parents, and headed for the kitchen. A long wooden table, as thick as a butcher's block,

250

dominated the room; it belonged in an older, grander kitchen that might have provided heavy meals for solid, respectable families. Denny watched her fill the kettle and rinse cups; her dress was too tight and too thin for winter, and he could see the play of muscle across her back. The ringing in his head finally stopped, a sharp pain in one eardrum its exit music. He exhaled in relief and massaged his temples, closing his eyes to luxuriate in the sensation of no longer feeling his brain outlined in fire. When he opened them again, his wife was watching him.

'It was the same for me, for a bit — after the house. I used to play Gloria's records or go for a walk by the sea. The sea worked best.' Jean gave him a brief, uncertain smile then turned and continued to spoon tea into the pot. He sometimes forgot that she had also had a war. The unconscious shimmy his wife's behind was performing called to him.

'Remind me,' he said to her back.

★   ★   ★

Like everyone else who returned, Denny had a list. It was all they talked about: the girls they would have, the food they would eat, the long, hot baths they would take. They were pitifully alike, these tallies of life's pleasures — little sketches of indolence and indulgence in which puppet men stuffed themselves with prop food in a cardboard version of home. A few days after Denny got back, he had put a strike through every line. He had drunk cold beer with breakfast; found a woman for the afternoon; paid extra to have a deep, steaming bath and his hair washed by soft hands with long fingernails that scraped his scalp; been to a diner for hamburgers and banana cream pie. On his second slice of pie, he had started to laugh; he opened his mouth wide, threw his head back and roared, great hacking laughs that flung gobs of cream up into the air.

'What's so funny, pal?'

Denny looked at the cook: white apron, white shirt; white cap shaped like a soldier's but made of paper. Denny closed his mouth, crumbs of pie and laughter wheezing out the sides.

'Banana,' he said. 'It tastes like banana.'

The white-capped cook shook his head and walked away muttering, 'What the hell did you expect?' Denny couldn't explain; it was already ordinary.

★   ★   ★

Jean turned, a full spoon of tea in her hand. 'What did you say?'

'Remind me. Of you.'

Jean wiped her wet hands on her dress. She knew he didn't want a recitation of her characteristics or achievements.

'You want to go to bed?'

'Not to bed.' Denny patted the table. 'About your size, I'd say.'

'In the kitchen? It's still day.'

'You didn't mind it being day in the field ... under the pier ... '

252

'That was different . . . that was . . . outdoors. And there was a war on.' She pulled her dress tight around her.

Denny looked pleased. 'You English are so weird. You can only have fun if you think you might get killed for it. If you like, I can throw you out the window after.'

Jean laughed, her grip on her dress and her objections loosening. 'We're on the ground floor.'

He patted the wooden block again.

'Get on the table.'

The ground beneath her feet suddenly felt strangely familiar. Jean left her clothes and her nationality on the floor and clambered onto the block. In the blue cold of the kitchen, she stretched out like a cat in sunshine, feeling his gaze pass over her and warm her neglected skin. Denny walked slowly from one end to the other of her, chin in hand, like a curator in a museum, appraising every inch. He took two circuits of her. Tears pooled at the back of her eyes. Four years of hope and fear for one moment, a moment that was not quite there, but, she knew, already not far from over. In this one moment, he would decide. He took another tour of the table.

'Takes me five paces to get from one end of you to the other. I never measured it before.'

There was some wonder in his voice, she was sure of it. She could surprise him, dazzle him almost. The tears spilled from the corners of her eyes. In his mind, he saw again the gold frame, her flesh sinking into red satin cushions. He raised one of her knees and moved her arm to behind her head, she twisted under his hands, rising and falling, casting shadows, her body like countryside under fast-moving clouds.

Jean barely spoke before she was six years old, and remained uncertain of words. Language is a slippery article; like a love on the turn, it can go to bed one thing and wake up another. It was easier for Jean to communicate through her body. No ambiguities, no double meanings. She trusted it. She had endured too many words already. In the borrowed kitchen, they would lay down the language they could use with each other, clear, precise and known only to them. She let her body speak; its form was not dissembling.

Steadying himself with one hand on the edge of the table, Denny pulled his trousers off over his shoes with the other. When he was naked, he bent down over the table and lifted Jean's foot to his mouth. 'Better than banana cream pie,' he whispered, and slipped her big toe between his lips. Five paces away, Jean's eyes rolled back into her head and a smile spread across her face like melting butter. Everyone should be adored, in some small way, some time.

23

The morning after Jack went finally and irrevocably crazy, Jean would wonder if the course of her life would be changed by anything other than misfortune. She thought it must have to do with her having no place in life; that she lived by displacement, beginning with the shoving of her mother into the afterlife. Perhaps a smaller girl would have needed to make less of a production of it.

What Jean couldn't tell anyone was that she had been longing for something to happen, and had been misunderstood yet again.

It had not been as they expected, America. Where Jean and Gloria had landed seemed strangely like the place they had left behind. There was a mask of difference, in currency and words and accent, but behind it things seemed much the same. They had no occupation, they had no friends. Time was treacle, and progress was nil.

Their timing was off. The men had gone to war and returned whole, damaged or not at all; the town had swelled with expectation and shrunk with disappointment again and again. Many felt brittle from this wear and tear, a little pulled out; they just wanted to settle back into shape. By the time Jean and Gloria arrived, stories had been told and souvenirs distributed, and everyone was quite tired of everything foreign. The country had looked outwards for a while, not much liked what it saw and turned its back again. Jean and Gloria felt that, even when engaged in face-to-face conversations, they were tapping on shoulders. Since arriving, they had engaged in the industrious shuffle of the migrant; sitting down, even on a hot day, is a birthright.

In anticipation of the brides' arrival, Jack's mother had taken the money formerly spent on servants and put it into appliances, freeing herself from reliance on flighty girls and psychologically unstable spinsters. Gleaming with the rounded edges of the latest automobiles, two objects of near-architectural beauty were the first to arrive. A refrigerator resembling an upended sarcophagus dominated one corner of the main kitchen. It hummed fiercely all day and night, as if bees had made their home in its interior. Occasionally it shuddered as if in disgust. The equally monumental washing machine emitted high-pitched whistling screams not dissimilar to a V2, and Jean and Gloria preferred to wait out the wash in the safety of the garden. Two vacuum cleaners rounded out the domestic bonanza. Jean and Gloria both fiercely resented being undercut by these mechanical interlopers that highlighted the emptiness of their days. So, walks were taken. Cutlery was polished. In desperation, hobbies were gained. They learned to arrange flowers, bake pies and crochet booties, like women still in hope of marriage. This was not like the work they had performed in lieu of peace; this was a frantic scramble to conceal, and brought no satisfaction or relief.

As her fingers stumbled over small stitches, or snapped flower stems by the dozen, Jean thought she heard the contemptuous hawk of a phlegm-swaddled throat, or felt a whispered curse snap her ear with the fierceness of a rubber band. But she kept her head down and never looked round; she had enough to worry about without considering whether ghosts could swim. In any case, Jean knew her life now would please Wisteria, sliding as it was towards disappointment. She was no longer of use. She had Gloria, she had a husband, she had an ability to continue on with life whether it met with the approval of the majority or not. But somehow being valid had slipped away from her. She felt marooned in her new home, stuck high up on a sand bank, waiting for the tide. There was nothing for her to do.

She was not taken to, either. The enormous woman at the port had been a blind, a trick. Things were larger, as Denny had said — beds, cars and houses; buildings, lakes and roads. But people were still people, and she was again uncommon among them. If only she had charm, she thought.

If people can't find you attractive, they will expect you to entertain them as a return on their time. Jean was truly terrifying attempting to please when under pressure; even a smile could go off in unexpected directions, like a faulty firework. Fearful of repercussions, she became again silent and watchful; she loitered.

Gloria, meanwhile, exhibited. She made herself known, embarking on goodwill tours of every club, association and social circle that would have her. She let her beauty be noticed, hoping it would draw others to her and pull her out of the isolation she had landed in. But even Gloria had no luck. No one was unkind; she was not despised, or disliked, but pitied. Jack had made her untouchable.

At first she thought her presence alone could cure him, that he would find her preferable to oblivion. She wondered what he found there that was so much more desirable than his wife, who slept alone and was driven to steal the sensation of his skin. She would find him in the night, put her arms around him and press her face to his chest and know that he was submitting to her, that he allowed rather than wanted this contact.

Jack was trying hard to live. When wounded, he had been dosed liberally with morphine which went through his veins like love — he felt warmed and wanted by it. He joined this new passion to his deep and endless thirst, and brought them home. The morphine made the night soft and painless, alcohol brightened the day. Between the two existed perhaps an hour when he felt everything balance, when he thought he could see her, to explain to her, to ask her to save him from it all. But the thought of it made him take an extra drink, and the hour soon passed.

Gloria would watch him, sitting alone, lightly tracing his features with his fingers, or staring at a cigarette burning down. He was still so beautiful. It was a mistake, she thought; no one could look like that and be broken.

The end of the war seemed to be just the beginning of the terrible news about human beings. Gloria could never resist the pain of others and, as the accounts from Europe reached them, she would weep for the murdered, the starving and the dispossessed, her arm slung over the radio as if it could absorb and broadcast her comfort. Combined with her own grief, it wore her down faster. She badly needed the peace to begin.

The anniversary was to be a new start, Gloria hoped. Things would be different afterwards; they would celebrate, because then it would really be over. There had been too much waiting in the house; others had their resolutions, Gloria wanted hers. She had not gone through a war for this. She and Jean took every liquor bottle in the house and buried them all in the woods. Gloria emptied the medicine cabinet, Jack's wallet and the petrol tank of the car. He nearly knocked her down for it, but she stood her ground. He had woken that morning in a ditch, his clothes torn and his forehead bloodied, and had walked home through the centre of town.

'When did you start to hate me?' Gloria asked. But he wouldn't give her an answer.

On the day of the anniversary, flags and elderly veterans were taken out of storage and had the must shaken out of them. After a couple of hours in the sunshine, they barely smelled at all. Clockwork women whirred between picnic tables and kitchen doors, bearing an endless succession of baked goods. Gloria stood on Jean's back and hung paper doves from the branches of the trees that lined the village green; she needed to feel as though something had been won. It hadn't counted before, she told herself, as she and Jean had been in England. That's why it still felt so unsettled, so much like losing. They had not ended the war together, she and Jack. They would do that on this day, this anniversary. She stretched up high and left symbols of hope in the air.

Jack had gone twenty hours without the softeners that made the world less intrusive. It rushed through him now. Piano wires had replaced the fibres that criss-crossed his body and fastened the skin to muscle; they vibrated with the strain. Gloria had kissed him before she left in the morning and promised him everything would be all right. All he had to do was get to the end of today, she told him. All she was asking for was a few more hours. In his pockets, his fingers picked at each other, and blood wet the nails.

By late afternoon, the doves were wilting as the humidity sat on their wings, the ice in the buckets of beer had melted and was overflowing onto the grass. Jean had retreated under a tree to wait for the speeches and music to begin. Gloria was still working hard, doling out lemonade and charm, winning back as much as she could of what Jack had been throwing away. Watching her made Jean tired.

She rolled her beer bottle across her forehead. Every inch of her clothing was lying against her skin like wet, warm newspaper. She disliked the daytime. Her marriage was no more tangible than Gloria's, taking place only in the dark. Her own imagined night-creature self was elusive yet commanding. In the day she retracted, hoping to escape the notice of the town that, she felt certain, knew her to be a useless import. Denny ignored her, too, concerning himself with making enough money to escape from Jack and respectability. But maybe it was for the best, she thought. She didn't want him to use up what little desire he had for her; she would remain forever on the ration.

She looked for Denny but couldn't see him, only Jack was in view. He was with some of the other veterans. He was doing most of the talking, and looked pretty excited about whatever it was they were discussing. He glanced her way and for a second locked eyes with Jean. She saw in his such a desperate need to be contained that it made her catch her breath.

Jack had managed to find his mother's diet pills that she had refused to let Gloria throw away. He had wanted to be good, but there were no words without a drink, or a pill, or something. He took half the bottle and now felt terrifyingly able to carry on a conversation. Words were spilling from him uncensored, he struggled to draw level with them, to understand or restrain them. His heart was racing and he felt his skin draw tight about his face. He could not remember a time before this, before what he was now. He could not see it in the faces of the men surrounding him. 'Do you remember me?' he wondered.

This was why he didn't speak. Why he didn't risk splitting the skin of the blister and letting it all seep out. He had a feeling Denny knew, from the way he looked at him. From what he had seen him do. Poor dumb Denny who had tried to stop him getting killed. (For what, Jack wanted to ask him. For what am I to remain alive?)

He sought out solitude, leaving his bed in the night, returning before the house was awake to maintain the fiction of a marriage. One night, when Gloria had come looking for him, as she always did, they had sat together in an old armchair, she curled in his lap, her head pushed under his chin, her heart against his.

'You can tell me,' she whispered. 'You can tell me anything.'

And he had imagined opening his mouth and a great tide of blood and shit and trenchwater pouring out of it and sweeping her away, screaming and kicking against the filth. So he said nothing, though it drove spikes into his brain to keep it all in.

But he was talking now, to people he had known all his life and who might even know him. He was talking and talking and any second he might say something. He might say something true, and indelible. Jack wished one of the surrounding men would hit him. When he was younger, it had amused him to see how far he had to push before someone stopped him with their fists; now it tired him. Indulgence did him no favours; even favourite sons must run out of rope eventually.

'Why don't you take a breath there, pal, let

someone else have a say?'

Denny was next to him, as ever, to hold him back. Jack looked at the small man by his side — small, but solid in the confidence that he could stop his friend, if that was a word they could use about each other. Watchdog, keeper, ally, enemy. Denny knew his best chance was to get the first punch in. Jack wished he would.

'Do it,' he said. 'Do it now.'

The watchdogs always drifted away eventually, sick of the trouble that loyally attended Jack. Denny had taken longer to sicken than most.

'Jack, you're being an asshole. Cut it out.'

Denny very much wanted to hit him. Not out of any real anger, but for some peace. How many months had he spent listening to this hot gush of nothing at all? It was just air and spit; it never made any sense. That was the thing about not having so many words, Denny decided; they didn't queue up waiting to spew out and make you sound like an asshole in front of everybody.

'Fuck you, soldier.' Jack laughed at him.

That's when it ended for Denny. He was going to stop saving someone who didn't want to be saved; all the men that had begged him to, all the men he had failed, would not be compensated by it. It was as if Jack was his phantom leg that had been blown off, still itching, still giving him cramps in the night. Denny, at least, could remember the man he used to be, and decided to be him again, to cut himself free after all this time. He couldn't remember what he owed Jack anyway. Nothing he hadn't earned. Denny didn't say anything; he just began to walk. He saw Jean

263

standing in the shade, and wanted to be next to her. Being with her was like pressing his forehead against cold glass; he didn't think, he just appreciated the change in temperature. He would cool off with her, and then decide what to do next. Jack, relieved to see him finally go, made sure of it.

'About fucking time, *soldier*.'

Denny looked a hundred miles away in a couple of steps. 'Don't turn around,' Jack pleaded, inside himself. 'Let me do it. Stop keeping me alive.' Jack felt the weight of his life pull on his limbs. He looked down at his arm; it seemed elongated and loose, flying around in the air in front of him. He wondered if he was hallucinating. When he was so tired that he thought he might cry from it, little ghost dogs darted around the corners of his eyes, and he was always turning his head to catch them but they were too quick, panting and laughing that hoarse dog laugh. Denny was gone, and the air around him was thick with hostility. It was time. Jack's voice scraped his throat, and he realised he was more barking than talking. It made him grin; that was all he was doing, just barking at the moon.

Attracted by Jack's rhetoric, a dog had begun to yap at his heels. Grateful for the distraction, a couple of the men poured beer into their hands and flicked it at the animal. It chomped at the droplets but wouldn't stop its bark; it seemed desperate for Jack's attention. And the more it barked, the more Jack did. He was flailing, laughing and barking at the top of his voice, but pawing at the men's shirtfronts as if he were addressing them in a heated debate, as if he didn't even know he was barking like a dog. Some of the women giggled but they were soon stifled by a look from their husbands. Jack started to tear at the collar of the town mechanic, a man ten years and forty pounds his senior who had served in the Pacific. He was keeping Jack at a distance with one arm, while his free hand tightened around the neck of a beer bottle. This attempt at restraint served to rile Jack; he was fierce, his barking rabid, his spit all over the mechanic's face. The stray jumped at his heels, overexcited by the crazy man playing his game. The circle of men began to sway in a tipsy scrum; all had a fistful of someone's shirt, holding them up or holding them back, they were all connected. They lurched together, Jack at the centre, screaming at the dog who was jumping up at him, almost insane with excitement. Jack pulled at the hands that were fastening on to him; he barked and bit at fingers while aiming wild kicks at the dog. The scrum became a wild folk dance, with boots, shins and foreheads knocking together.

Jean watched; they all watched: helpless, fascinated, guilty. Jean looked for Gloria. She was standing motionless by the empty benches. A serving plate hung from her hand, a pile of sandwiches at her feet. Denny was striding towards Jean; she knew he meant for them to leave.

'No.' She wanted to stop him before he reached her, before she might give in and do as she was told. 'Gloria.'

Her expression was anxious and pleading, the kind he found easy to ignore. He shook his head and took another step, eyes on his shoes. This time her voice was like a hand on his chest.

'No.'

Her brow was lowered like a bull's. She wasn't moving, and no one was moving her. He felt a momentary twitch of pride at the thought of her tearing Jack to pieces on his command.

'I won't. I won't leave her to this.'

'I can make you move.'

'You can try,' Jean assured him. As she saw it, it wasn't disobedience, just a fact.

It was enough to persuade him. One last rescue, then to hell with everyone. 'You get Gloria. I'll do what I can.'

Denny turned back towards the heaving group. Three men held Jack now; only his legs were free, and these he directed, with curses, at the dog. He was slippery and twisting, a snake in oil. He was screaming, his rage focused, as it had not been before; he usually worked hard at passing out before he could flay anyone with grief and fury.

'Stop barking, soldier!' Jack screamed. 'I said stop fucking barking, soldier!'

As Denny got closer, he held up his hands as if he was pushing something towards Jack. It wasn't surrender, but it wasn't violence. Jack snorted at his approach.

'Is that all you got? Bring me something else, Denny, bring me more than that!'

Denny cursed under his breath and wished the

dog would bite Jack some place he'd know it. Denny decided he would give Jean enough time to reach Gloria and then back away, leaving Jack to his insanity. He patted the air again, half-hearted motions of peace. Jack pleaded with him, but Denny missed the agony in his voice.

'Bring me something more than that. Christ, Denny. What the hell?'

Jack saw apprehension in Denny's eyes, when he wanted to see his own end. 'Leave me to them,' he thought. Jack lost his will for a second and the dog got cocky, nipping at his leg.

'Goddammit! I am ordering you, soldier, do you hear me?'

Jack lashed out, and his foot made contact with the side of the dog's head, not a crushing blow, but enough to knock it on to its side. It scrabbled in the dirt, all illusions that this was a game gone, then lunged and sank its teeth into Jack's leg. Jack screamed and grabbed at its jaws. He lifted the dog up, still attached to his leg, and they both crashed to the floor. The human bonds on him loosened, Jack scuttled away on all fours, scattering the bystanders. A natural arena formed. The dog crouched low and snarled, Jack did the same. Denny was creeping forward, looking for a way to grab the dog or push Jack out of its way.

A baseball bat, left out for the friendly game some had hoped would materialise, lay on the grass. Jack's fingers closed around it. He would make everything quiet again. He lowered his voice, but the command was clear and strong.

'Stop barking, soldier.'

Denny heard it and stopped moving. He knew the voice. The dog didn't.

'Put it down, Jack. It's just a stupid dog. Put it down and get out of here.'

Jack ignored him; as much saliva dripped from his mouth as the dog's. His eyes were burning and wild. In his head he heard nothing but barking: incessant, overpowering. He didn't want to do anything except make it stop, he couldn't remember anything before it had started. It was just a thing he had to do. Like the things he had done for four years. From one place of safety to the next, looking for one man to kill and then another; not thinking about an end to the killing because after a while it seems there won't be one. He had been careless, reckless, brave, stupid, and none of it mattered. Now he just had to stop this noise, just this, and then he would think about the next thing. Jack raised his arm and brought it down. The blood slapped his skin like a hand. He raised his arm again and brought it down again, and raised it and brought it down again and again until his arm was tired.

Then there was nothing to be heard; he couldn't even hear his own breathing. No one spoke, no children cried, the air was still and his head was clear. Tears streamed down his face and washed blood onto his throat. He felt something wet slither from his palm and flinched, but it was just Denny taking the bat from his grasp.

'It's done, Jack. You're finished.'

'Thanks, buddy,' Jack whispered and then floated gently down to the grass, passing through it to the soft dark below.

Jack lay unconscious on the grass next to the pulped body of the dog, his side rising and falling with animal rapidity. Someone brought forward the doctor, and with the help of a few men, Jack was rolled onto a blanket and put in the ambulance that had been brought out for show. Brand new, it had replaced the one that had served the town for the duration, and had red ribbons tied around its headlamps.

Gloria lay a few feet away. She looked like a paper bird that had fallen, broken, to the ground. Jean had only been in time to catch her, not to shield her eyes from the first blow. Not to shield any part of her. Gloria awoke in her friend's arms and saw there was no point in pretending anymore.

A woman appeared at Jean's side and held Gloria's head as Jean carried her to Jack's car. They put Gloria in the back seat, where she curled up like a sick child.

'Damnedest war,' the woman muttered as they closed the door. 'Takes them useless and sends them back crazy.'

24

At the psychiatric hospital, Jack's mother watched as a gag was placed in her son's mouth and restraints on his wrists and ankles, and couldn't watch any more after that. She waited in the corridor, wincing at the squeak of rubber shoes on the linoleum as every nurse and orderly took a detour to get a look at the mother of the dog-killer. She stared every one of them down with all the pride she had left. She had always known she would sit here one day.

Jean was surprised to see the house still standing when they arrived home with Gloria. It didn't seem that anything familiar could have survived that afternoon. Denny went to lift Gloria from the back seat, and Jean felt a snarl form deep in her throat. Before it could escape, he withdrew his hands.

'You'd better.'

Jean nodded and carried Gloria through the house to her marital bed. Behind her, Jean heard the car start again. She didn't know if Denny was coming back, and at that moment she didn't know if it mattered. A pair of Jack's shoes was on the floor, and some freshly ironed shirts hung over a chair. It felt like returning after a funeral to the death room, its simple objects gaining significance yet losing purpose. She placed Gloria in the centre of the bed, but Gloria rolled to the edge and curled up, clutching the side. She didn't like to stretch out and take possession; she would always leave room for him.

★ ★ ★

Jean sat with Gloria, as Gloria had sat with Jean when she was broken. She mixed a sedative into hot milk and kept the covers tight around her friend. She wished she could take off her thick skin and wrap it around Gloria; it seemed ridiculous that she should need it more. Beautiful, blessed Gloria. She gulped down the milk, as eager for oblivion as her husband, then lay back on the pillow while Jean stroked her hair. Jean tried not to think of the madhouse with its slimy walls and clanking chains; she could never tell Gloria what Wisteria said went on there. Would they visit him, she wondered, and shivered at the thought. But Wisteria was wrong about one thing, at least: Jack, not her daughter, had been taken. Not because he was a nuisance, not because he was poor, or old, or ugly, but because he was mad. He would never be coming back.

Gloria's hand closed around two of Jean's fingers, the unconscious anchoring gesture of a baby. Her eyes were open but unfocused. She murmured something, and Jean had to lean close to hear. The perfect rosebud mouth was sticky with the milk that was turning her breath sour.

'Am I pretty?'

Love is a transference of power. The ability to see oneself fades, and one exists only in the eyes of another. Gloria had placed her faith in herself

271

inside Jack, where there was poison.

'Yes. Prettier than ever.'

Gloria licked at the corners of her mouth and lowered her heavy eyelids. 'I feel ugly. Everything is ugly.'

What could Jean tell her? Beauty was not immunity? Not even Gloria's? Something jealous of her perfection had saddled her with a lumpen friend and a cracked husband. Something in herself, even. Pity oozed from Jean's palm into Gloria's golden hair, where it clung like oil.

'Be all right in the morning,' Jean murmured, and placed the gentlest possible kiss on her friend's forehead, her neck muscles straining with the effort of making her head light. Gloria's eyes fluttered as she succumbed to the drug and the exhaustion of supporting a lie all that time. At least now she could sleep. Jean left her in the dark, and kept vigil in her own room, watching the day decline through the colours the passing hours splashed on the wall: pinks, oranges, deep velvet black.

The sky was bruise blue, and the air was cool when Denny came back. Jack's mother had not yet returned, and Jean hadn't moved.

He climbed into their bed and lay against her. The alcohol in his veins warmed his skin; Jean put her fingers in his hair and felt his sweat condense and chill on her fingers. At first Jean didn't realise he was talking; she felt only the reverberation of his breath on her stomach, his lips were so close to her skin. She had to listen through herself to catch every word.

'I knew. I knew all along.'

'Why didn't you say anything?' she whispered, and felt him swallow.

'Because I didn't care.'

She couldn't tell if the moisture spilling onto her was tears or a cold sweat. She kept her eyes turned away from him; speaking like this, it was as if he was without his skin.

'I wanted him gone. I feel like I've been walking round with a live grenade in my pocket.'

'Why, then? Why stay with him?'

'I don't have a home; never did. He offered me a place to stay. It meant I could have things; I could have you.'

Jean tried not to gasp. She folded her arms around him and waited to see what else he could tell her about them. Seconds ached by until he spoke and she could breathe again.

'What did you do?'

'When?'

'When the war was over, before here. What did you do?'

Jean thought for a moment. 'I waited.'

'For what?'

'To find out.'

'What were you going to do if I didn't come back?'

'I . . . I was going to think about it later.'

'Yeah. So was I. I guess you would have been OK.'

'I guess.'

It was the truth. She would have survived. As Jack had. Jack had found his body, his luck, too reliable, and so his mind had committed the act instead. He had found a way out. He reminded

273

Jean of her mother, she realised: disgusted with life but unable to break fully with it. How could she not have spotted it before? Jean saw that she didn't know anything, couldn't help anyone. She didn't even know who it was she held in her arms. Her husband. It was an odd word to her. Her husband, her arm, her leg. She didn't know when he had become a part of her. Or when it would feel like he had.

'What'll happen to Jack?'

Denny shrugged; his shoulder blades could barely move under the weight of her arms. He was so light he made hardly a dent in the mattress; he still had the body of a scrappy kid, muscular through fighting, lean through starving. That's what she knew, his body. How it met her own. How long can a body fascinate? Jean asked herself. How long before you see what's really there?

Faint stirrings of panic carbonated her blood. Since she was born for the second time, Jean had thought she was in near-constant movement: the flex of her muscle when she worked, the rush of her blood when Denny was inside her, the swell of the ocean she had crossed. But perhaps it was an illusion. She had borne nineteen years of immobility as quietly as if enchanted. Perhaps her life had changed hands, not direction. What war would come for her now?

Jean closed her eyes to calm herself. Things were slowing down, dawn had yet to appear, drugged into lateness along with the beauty that Jean herself had consigned to sleep. Jean was grateful for that; she was afraid to face Gloria.

She had failed to protect her, again. Whatever poison was in Jack, she should have crushed it out of him. She should have taken Gloria and run. But to where?

'I got a new job. A possibility.' Denny reached for the cigarettes on the nightstand, freeing himself from her arms. 'I didn't think it would take this long. Out west. We can leave in a few days. I need to do some things. It's almost ready, just gotta put the last payment down on a car.'

Out west. And he had bought a car. She wondered how long he had been planning this. And how recently she had been included in the plan.

'West? How far west?'

'Far, about as far as you can get without hitting ocean. I got a contact out there, from the army. He's got a lot going on, real estate, transportation. He can fix me up.'

Half the world was on the move, the dispossessed trailing their roots behind them, painful and raw as nerve endings, some trying to drive them down into unfamiliar soil, others unable to get purchase. Jean had felt the burn of grit as she skimmed the surface, her heels skidding in the thin eastern dirt. There would be no digging in. She hadn't quite stopped yet; that was something. The monster in her was awake again, a snack of bad luck and it was ready to go.

'A few days. We can't . . . I mean, I don't see how we can.'

Denny exhaled smoke, sighing as he did so. 'It's taken care of. You think I wanna stay here? Why'd he have to go crazy now? I could have gone crazy plenty of times in the war. But now? Tell me the good of that.' He shook his head. 'That poor damn dog. I gotta get outta here, can't sleep, can't think. Jesus, what's here anyway?'

The name leaked quietly out of her mouth. 'Gloria.'

She would leave her failings behind, load up with guilt, and escape punishment again.

For the first time, Jean sought her husband for comfort; not to make love to her, but to hold on to, to convince. His body was like a bundle of sticks; it rolled under her grip. She couldn't fasten on him, and he threw her off despite barely moving. There was no comfort to be had. He stubbed out his cigarette and lay back on the pillow, eyes closed.

'You need to think about who you're married to,' he told her.

She touched the damp spots on her stomach and brought her fingers to her lips to taste. Salt. She would do what she was told. Things had stopped flying into her life to change it. She was postwar; it was time to go.

25

Jack was quiet in his chair, slid deep into catatonia. Still they kept back in case, like a malicious jack-in-a-box, he exploded rudely into movement.

It was a private room, with smooth plastered walls that bore no trace of manacles, Jean noted. But still it felt inescapable; Jean had flinched when the door closed behind them.

'Tell me something,' Gloria asked, not taking her eyes from her husband; she was watching delicate bubbles of spit form at the corners of his mouth. 'You haven't told me any stories for ages.'

Jean shrugged and picked at her hem. 'I don't think I have any new ones.'

They knew all about each other's days; the nights were not spoken of. Jean entertained Gloria as best she could — stories of her mother's eccentricities, of the things she found on the bombsites. She found that much of what had happened to her amused others, even if it had been painful at the time. It was all about finding the right tone.

'Tell me a secret, then.'

So Jean told someone else's. 'There was this coal merchant called Graydon.'

'The one on London Road?'

'Yes. Got done in that raid that took out the Methodists' hall.'

A bad smell drifted over from Jack, and Gloria wrinkled her nose.

'I don't think he ever used to do that.'

It couldn't have been true, Jean knew, but Gloria put everything she didn't like down to his illness, perhaps in the hope it would all be cured. Gloria fanned herself with a pamphlet one of the nurses had left in the room, something about Jesus, Jean couldn't see what.

'He lived alone; everyone knew that. No woman would have him — up at four, bed by eight, no life for a wife, he always said.'

Gloria nodded. 'I remember. He used to come into ours for sweets and Mum would ask him every once in a while why he was all on his tod, with a good living and no one to share it with. He just used to say the same.'

'So, I'm on clear-up, and we start finding all these clothes — dresses, drawers, hats, gloves, the lot. There's even one wardrobe for the women's clothes and one for the men's.'

'So he had a wife after all, sly old thing!'

'Well, that's what we all thought. Cheeky sod, we thought, he's been hiding her away all these years. Or maybe he's killed her and hidden the body.'

'No!' Gloria couldn't help but swing her legs as she thought of it. 'Really?'

'Well, we wondered. But then we found all these photographs.'

'What, of the body?'

Jean shook her head. 'Nah. They were photos of him.'

'Just him?'

'Just him. In his hats and his drawers and his dresses and the rest. He even had a tiara on in one.'

'A tiara!' Gloria exploded with laughter. Despite the setting, Jean was pleased with herself. It might not have been appropriate, but it was good.

'We never found it, though, and we looked all over. He had one wardrobe for work, and one for home. Boots for the day, bows for the night.'

Gloria clapped her hands together and her shoulders shook. Jean had sworn to keep all the secrets she uncovered, but Gloria needed one now. They had quite forgotten Jack, as they were transported back to the blasted seaside, when they were young and allowed themselves expectations. He was no more moved by the laughter ringing around him than he was by the currents of air, imperceptibly changing as legs swung and arms waved.

'Can you imagine?' Gloria wiped the tears from her eyes. 'Thinks everything's all safe hidden under the bed, when the next morning there it is in the street for everyone to see. What they bury him in — boots or bows?'

They gave in to the laughter again, knowing full well they had nothing under the bed. All they had was out in the open now; Gloria wore her husband's madness like a wart on her face.

Jack's eyes were fluttering but not closing. Gloria couldn't think what on earth he wanted to be awake for. She sniffed as the laughter ran out, then nudged Jean's elbow, ready to trade: a secret for a secret.

'I swore at him yesterday.'

'What?'

'Jack. I swore at him. I waited until the nurses had gone and I closed the door and then I called him every name under the sun. And then I just used some words I knew that aren't really about anyone, just rude. And then I said his mum was a mouldy old bumface.'

Jean was shocked. Though Gloria was capable of tantrums, Jean had never known her to be spiteful. It seemed ridiculous too, twenty-five years old and cursing like a child with something to prove. But the thought of those foul words coming out of that pretty mouth made Jean want to giggle. She had forgotten Gloria could surprise her.

'What did you do that for?'

'Just testing, I suppose. I wanted to see if he could hear anything. I thought if I said all those things there's no way he could pretend not to. Unless he really couldn't.'

'And?'

'Not a sausage. I don't think he even blinked.'

'Well. Good job, probably. 'Specially about his mum.'

'But you see, I don't think he's ever heard anything I've said — not really. He told me he'd been looking for me, something pure and beautiful and sweet. So I didn't swear and didn't get angry. I was *mostly* how I am, but I'm not like that all the bloody time. I was a bit knackered, to be honest.'

Jean remembered some of Gloria's rages, even when they were little — or young at least: her white-hot fits of passion about the right way to be the dragon in one of their plays, the scuff on a new pair of sandals, the world's inability to understand her need for a certain thing to be just so, whether it was the weather on her birthday or the set of her hair. Recently, Gloria had borne everything with a pained serenity. She swallowed her anger, and it had made her thin and anxious.

'I wish I'd screamed. And sworn. I was so careful. For what? He doesn't know what I think of anything. How much I hate or like.' She paused and ran a shaky hand through her dull hair. 'I wish I'd said bugger at least once.'

'You can tell him later, when he's better,' Jean offered. 'When he comes back home. Welcome home — you could say — you bloody, bleedin' bugger.'

Gloria screeched with delight, then covered her mouth with one hand and slapped Jean's arm with the other. They rocked together, their joint betrayal of Jack's dignity feeling so wonderful. Gloria wiped her eyes and leaned against Jean, who moved to accommodate her, and she curled into Jean's side to be held there.

'I'll miss you, Jean. When are you leaving?'

Jean felt the stitch of grief again; it stuck her under the ribs and weighted her breaths with guilt, they squeezed painfully into her body. Gloria knew when they were going; Jean had told her twenty times. It hadn't changed. However much they had hoped for snags in the plans, for the car to expire, for the house to be blown down, for Denny to break his leg, everything had gone smoothly.

'Tomorrow. Denny's packing up the car today; we're leaving at first light.'

'Such a long way away.'

'Not so far.'

'As far as it is to England, almost.'

'Really?'

Jean was shocked. How could anything be as far as it was to England? As far away as their past? Neither of them had talked of returning, knowing it was an impossibility, but Gloria still thought she might see her parents again one day, though she didn't dwell on how it could happen. Jean hadn't realised she was being taken so far — well into the realm of the forgotten. They would be friends who would wish they could see each other again but have no idea how to accomplish it. She was a wife, that most portable of possessions.

'I don't know where we'll be living. But when I do, you could come for a visit.'

'We'll have to see,' Gloria sniffed. 'Jack might not be well for a while.'

'When Jack's better, then.'

'Oh yes. The sunshine'll be good for him.'

Anonymous laughter played at the edges of Jack's consciousness. His view was of flower beds, colours that bent in the breeze. Like strokes of paint, they washed from one side to the other, the colours blending and then separating. He felt that soft, felty feeling again as the prescribed narcotics swelled in him, and sank into it as if it were the first bed he had touched after years of dugouts, benches, cots and dirt floors. He was home.

'What do you think he's thinking?' Gloria asked, watching the light play on those lovely eyes as the lids fussed over them, undecided on where to stop.

Jean rubbed her shoulder.

'I think he's thinking of you.'

Gloria ignored her own question and Jean's response. 'It's not quite as far as England. At least there's no ocean in the way. You can drive it.' She sighed and closed her eyes. She was so very tired, and nothing made any sense. She was beautiful and doomed, and Jean was lumpen and free; the changeling had displaced her and was going off to live a life Gloria could have imagined for herself. That's what she got for believing in fairy tales. She opened her eyes and managed a smile for her friend. 'I hope you'll be happy, Jean. I hope it lasts.'

Jean wondered how it could. 'I'm just a body to him. Do you think it matters?'

'Oh, Jean,' Gloria sighed. 'Buggered if I know.'

She slumped down further into Jean's embrace, and Jean held her until she fell asleep. Jack's eyes finally closed then, as if he had been waiting for her to go. Her strength had given first. But only just.

When Gloria woke up, she was in Jack's bed, and he hadn't moved from the chair. They were alone together. Gloria had not heard Jean whisper that she loved her and was sorry the better things had happened to her instead. Gloria had not heard Jean leave the room and begin the long walk back to the house where Jack's mother waited for good news that she did

283

not expect to come. ('I just wanted him back,' she told Jean. 'I just wanted him back so much.') Gloria had yet to wake when Denny's car went past the hospital, heading west. It all happened without her knowing.

Jack had been shaved by a nurse while Gloria slept. The morning light was strong, and it gave his face a sheen of health nothing inside him could. Gloria went to the washstand and splashed her face with tepid water. She then very quietly opened the door and looked out into the corridor where the starched rump of a nurse was just disappearing into the farthest room. Gloria closed the door gently then ran in her stockinged feet around the bed to Jack and slapped him hard across the face three times. He smiled.

26

Entering the West was like stepping from a darkened room into a dazzling morning. That's how she would remember it anyway, as nothing gradual; it was as sudden as an amputation.

They barely stopped for breath or gas. The sun baked them as they rattled along empty roads that stretched to the horizon. The limitless blue above was higher, clearer and more deserted than any sky Jean had ever seen.

She had once watched a film in which movie stars played movie stars not themselves and made their profession out to be quite the joke. Gloria had hated it. Jean remembered it because it revealed that scenery going past a stagecoach window was nothing more than painted canvas on a roll. She looked for the seams as the fields and deserts streamed past her, perhaps powered by a man on a bicycle.

If the car could have kept going for ever, she would have been happy, she thought. Some considerate stroke of man or nature had provided roadside attractions: rocks that looked like rabbits, umbrella-topped refreshment stands, Indian caves. These allowed her and Denny to exchange words at least, and words can be powerful burrowers. An attempt to describe a forest of dead trees they passed through led Jean to say that their twisted carcasses made her think of her mother. When he asked her why, she told him — as lightly as she knew how.

'Can't blame her, really, can you?' She grinned after recounting the least of it. He laughed out loud, as she had hoped he would; she didn't want more pity, not that any would have come from him.

For the first four years of his life, Denny had lived with his prostitute mother and six other working women in a series of interlinked rooms resembling a railway carriage that had lost its wheels. He had a dim memory of being chased through door after door before being cornered in the last room, where he would be wrapped in a threadbare dressing gown and tickled by so many fingers his skin screamed with sensation. He lived under a shower of intense female affection, his innocence compensating for every customer that was corrupt.

When Denny was four years old, an epidemic of tuberculosis cut through the city like a harsh wind, wiping out five of his maternal harem, including his natural mother. He was sent to a mission, given a bed, a bucket and brush to scrub the floors, a new name and, unbeknownst to him, two years on his age. That was when his memories became vivid.

'I'm an orphan, too,' he said. 'But I was young. Probably a good thing, right? I got my liberty early.'

She smiled, and didn't say that she was sorry for his loss. She wasn't sorry for anything that had happened to him, because she could never know which bad thing had brought him to her. Malnutrition had left its mark on his body, and living had already lined his eyes. He was, she thought, very beautiful. He was the damaged boy her mother had said she'd end up with, if she was lucky. And she had been lucky. Wisteria failed to see the beauty in damage, in being shaped by incident and wearing the marks. During the war, the marks didn't matter, it was enough just to survive. An underrated skill in peace.

Jean wanted to be buried in that car. It was a sacred space where she and Denny could speak. They hadn't mastered the intimate nothingness of lovers, the fearless banality of conversation between two people who have made up their minds about one another. Theirs had been a marriage of desperate quiet. But she knew something of him now. And knowledge was a little like possession.

They slept each night at the side of the car, wrapped in army-surplus bedding. The camp-grounds were cheap, but Denny didn't like the proximity of other tents. He could guess the sounds he made in his sleep from the soldiers he had slept alongside. The dreams hadn't stopped, so he had no reason to think the jabbering had. When the fear came, Jean used her bulk to overwhelm it. She pressed the dreams out of him, enfolding him in her strong embrace while he bucked and whimpered. She took whatever was in him into herself and let it dissipate in her veins.

Small villages of tourist cabins sprouted here and there at the side of the road. There would be nothing in the darkness for miles, and then a

scattering of lights, looking lost, but content to
be so. Jean stared longingly at each one they
passed, hoping it would be her new home,
magical and remote. On their last night on the
road, Denny finally stopped at one: the Bellevue
Vacation Village.

She thought she could smell the sea, the crust
of salt on wood, leaf and skin. The identical
wood cabins radiated light and promise; bathing
suits and towels hung from lines on the porches
and ashes smouldered in the brick outdoor
ovens. Inside, games of cards were in progress
while sunburned children slept two to a bunk.

'Are you sure?' she asked.

'See those lights down there, away from
everyone? Honeymoon cabins. We'll take one of
those.' Jean thought she might squeal for the first
time in her life. 'It's not like we have to prove it,'
he added. And she swallowed the urge.

Once in the cabin, Denny filled the washbasin
and watched her bathe, naked except for a string
of beads. They had been idling this last day,
nostalgic already. The necklace was from an
attraction billed as being full of artefacts and
wonder — Archer's Amazing Indian Cave,
admission free — and wouldn't last the week.
She sponged her shoulders and neck, knowing as
she did so that he would follow each drop to her
foot. She closed her eyes and let herself drift off
into a fantasy. In it, she was still in the cabin, and
she was still herself, but there was no tomorrow
coming for them.

'Damn,' he exclaimed.

'What?' Jean didn't want to open her eyes,

suddenly fearful she might find herself outside and in public.

Denny's voice was full of mock frustration. 'I had a bet on the left drop reaching your knee first. You'd better fill the basin and start again.'

Jean opened her eyes and smiled. It was some kind of miracle he continued to enjoy the spectacle of her, so she played up to it, stretching to her full height, until the cabin shrank around her, and she was all it contained.

After four basins of water, they went to bed. He turned his back to her, and she wound herself around him, ready to absorb whatever came for him in the night. She could feel the words in her drying up again; the suspension of the usual was ending. This was perhaps her only chance.

'Can we keep going?' she whispered. It wasn't just asking for permission. It was asking what was possible; what, for her, in this new world, was allowed. His chest swelled under her grasp; he held the breath for a moment and then let it go. The long exhalation bore possibility away with it. She knew they would give in.

'I don't see how we can, without hitting ocean.' His voice lost its toughness in the dark; he forgot to put in the fight that daylight seemed to require. 'We gotta stop somewhere. I don't know where else we could go. I know some places, some people . . . you wouldn't like 'em.'

He could go on alone, make his own living, but he couldn't manage her too. She was heavy baggage, no matter how she tried to make herself small and light. Just the fact of her slowed him down. She had to make him choose her. Jean squeezed her husband tight before he could think too much about the places that only he could go.

'I'm going to work very hard,' she promised him. 'I'm going to work very hard and be very useful.'

She hoped that being of use would be enough, and that the feeling of homelessness that plagued her would recede when they reached their destination. She had an idea that it was unnatural to feel displaced inside a marriage. So much of Jean was unique, she often failed to identify what was commonplace. Denny's breathing soon became even and slow; he slept well wrapped in his long wife. Jean gently freed her arms and pressed her fingers to her face, trying to fix the scent of the cabin into her skin. She had to remember everything.

Happiness should come with a warning. A brightly coloured label at least. If Jean had known what would be her last uncomplicated glimpse of it, she would have thrown a net over it. But it's impossible. It's like trying to hold music.

27

The billboard for the Phuture Homes development trumpeted that it was 'on the brink of
tomorrow', though a quick look around would've
easily confirmed it was on the edge of bugger all.
A horseshoe of white, vaguely Spanish-style
bungalows, from a distance it looked like a
freshly laundered wagon train corralled against
invaders, waiting in vain for the cavalry to arrive.

Jean and Denny stood on the edge of the
development ('The Threshold of the Phuture'
according to a sign that was lying on the ground
nearby) and looked down over the valley.
Skeletons of half-finished houses littered the
rocky floor; a dispute with the county had seen
the road linking them to the outside world peter
out halfway. It was a brand-new ghost town.
Denny gave a barely perceptible nod.

'Perfect,' he said.

Jean didn't know where she was. There wasn't
a single identifying mark: no station, no river, no
school. They were nowhere. Even the small city
they had driven through en route seemed to
disappear before she could get a look at it. Palm
trees, white stone and aimless traffic materialised
in an instant and then vanished just as quickly to
be replaced by vacant lots and fruit trees. An
elusive place, it hid from outsiders. They had
passed by a line of great houses, which were
tended by their inhabitants as worshippers do

temples. Jean saw more people in the gardens than she did on the street. After the grand houses ended, a sprawl of modest imitations followed, broken up by more empty tracts. Isolated houses sprang up to break up the emptiness, then surrendered to it again. And then there was Phuture Homes. The low buildings were so white and new, to Jean they looked like baby teeth. She couldn't think of who would live here.

Denny had chosen this place, he told her, because of a boom nearby. She thought Phuture Homes must be its echo. Not that it was poor; she found it neat and bright and untainted. But it was anxious, hoping to be noticed. It also looked as though you could dig a hundred feet down and come up with nothing but dust. Jean couldn't see roots going down into this, couldn't see how it might possibly support her.

A few of the forgotten properties were owned by a man called Charles Pace, with whom Denny had bartered for cigarettes and booze on cold nights in wretched locations. He was the only one who had replied to Denny's requests for leads on work, and was waiting for them outside a single-storey box surrounded by fenced-in dirt. An overindulged man of thirty-five, he had the reddened cheeks and sketchy breathing of a fat child who's just reached the top of the stairs. To Jean, he looked as if he had been caught at something, embarrassed and breathless, but unapologetic. He waved at them, tanned arms extending from a loose, gaudily printed shirt.

While she waited by the car, Denny and Pace

shook hands and slapped each other's backs; she fretted for Denny's lungs, which Charlie seemed to be trying to dislodge. He had a curiously English heartiness that made her not trust him very much. The thought surprised Jean. When did I turn against my own? she wondered. Charlie whispered in Denny's ear, and then turned to call to her.

'Don't be shy, Mrs Curnalia, go take a look at the house. I know you'll be itching to see the kitchen! The refrigerator's running, and there's some beers in there. I'll bet your husband's a thirsty guy, would you mind?'

She obeyed. Throughout the house, the shades were up and the sun flooded the house, making it a box of light. The grit on her tennis shoes crunched on the bare boards, and she noticed that piles of sand had collected in the corners of each room; five rooms in total. Jean had never commanded so much as one. She was the first person here. She would not be sleeping in another's bed, washing in another's bath, eating from another's plates. She had never lived anywhere with a past shorter than her own.

Denny and Charlie were sat on the swing chair, an incongruous courting couple. She delivered the beer. Charlie half stood and tipped his hat; it was made of straw, she noticed, like a seaside souvenir.

'So what do you think, Mrs Curnalia?'

'I think it's . . . '

Never been lived in. Died in. Loved in. Destroyed. Rebuilt. It was like her life now, all brand new and no looking back.

' . . . lovely.'

'Why don't you take a look around again, our business talk'll bore you silly. Can't hardly stand it myself.'

She looked to Denny and he nodded, so Jean smiled and left them to their beer and their talk, sensing a lack of ease between the two men that was not solely to do with her. She walked through the house, down the narrow hallway towards the glowing square of glass set into the back door. It looked like a very cheap church window. She approached it without superstition and stepped outside. The low, white fence continued around the back of the house, although the ground each side of it was the same: just dirt and rocks. Jean could feel the stones through her thin shoes. She sniffed the air for traces of the promised fruit trees and flowers and caught something sharp and synthetic, like a burn on a rayon dress. It was so still and dry she could hear her hair crackle in the heat. Her body hadn't adjusted to being stationary yet; a wave of energy went through her, and she lurched forward onto the balls of her feet, as if on the verge of falling into something. After days of constant motion, they were here, if nothing else was. An ocean in front of her, and madness behind; she was again sandwiched between the two.

She opened the gate in the pointless fence and walked into the desert, curious to find out where the nothingness ended, but still tentative, careful. Giants fell over the edge of worlds in the stories she knew.

If her husband's arrangement with Charlie Pace seemed odd, Jean wouldn't go so far as to question it. Whims and strange circumstances were the only motors she knew. While she explored her barren surroundings, Pace told Denny what work there was for him.

'Are you fuckin' crazy?'

Pace lifted his hands in a gesture of incomprehension. 'What's the problem? You spend your days visiting lonely housewives — the husbands are in a bar or out at work, if they came back at all. It's even better than before. In the war, you had to have something — some coffee, nylons, a chicken leg. Here, it's just promises. Smoke and mirrors.'

'But Chrissakes, lipstick? Perfume? What are you trying to do to me? I came three thousand miles for this shit?'

'I'm letting you in on something big here. What you gonna do, go on the line? Punch panels and rivet shit in two-hundred-degree heat? You would not believe this town. You got some little gal with stars in her eyes and three hundred teeth in her head, and she's gonna buy every damn thing you got in the case because it could be the thing that changes her into a proposition. You say, 'Honey, it's not the teeth, it's that shiny nose.' And you sell her some powder. And then some lipstick. And then some skin whitener and then some tooth whitener and then some peroxide and then some diet tonic. She doesn't have a hope in hell, 'cos along with the teeth she's bowlegged and cross-eyed, but she'll fix everything else first if you make it the worst thing about her. I'm telling you, it's the greatest medicine show ever.'

'Why me?'

'Why not you? Look, fella, you asked me what there was out here, and I'm telling you. I can make some serious money on this shit if you'd just get out there and sell it. I had a guy making two bills a week *commission*. The house is empty, so I can give you a break on the rent. In six, nine months, the road is gonna come down here and the rents are gonna go sky high. You want work, I'm telling you there's work. I'm asking you to sell the stuff, not wear it. You could make money, and make me money. And I need guys like you living here.'

'Paying you rent.'

'Paying me rent. And making the place look good. Returning heroes, all that crap. I wanna milk the GI thing before it's too late.'

'I thought it already was.'

'It will be soon. I'm telling you, the road comes down here, with the refinery not five miles away and the plant . . . you don't get in now, you don't get in. I'm giving you a deal here, Curnalia. Don't be dumb.'

★　★　★

The further from the house Jean got, the cleaner the air became; the synthetic tang disappearing to be replaced by the smell of warm stone. She had never seen so much space waiting to be filled. Jean stared at the horizon and tried to see her future.

Out there, a ball of dust was gathering. It was the only thing moving in an otherwise static world, so she watched it as it grew in size and travelled along the ridge, propelled by a distant wind. She fancied she saw a little house inside it, being spun like a top. Perhaps a girl inside the house, being flung from the familiar to the unexpected. Jean swayed with it, hypnotised, as it danced from side to side and sometimes even leapt from the ground, feeling a strange kind of affection for something wild and distant. When it paused, turned and began to advance, Jean stopped still, blinking against the light. She had never seen a ball of dust change direction with determination before. It was more alarming than she could ever have suspected, thinking that something was under the benevolent command of nature and then seeing it had intentions of its own. It was the way she struck a lot of people.

Jean had the sense that it was something unpleasant, like fate or destiny. And it was coming for her. She watched it for longer than she knew she should, and decided what was inside the dust. It was consequence. That was what happened when you stopped moving: things found you. As the ball drew closer, she saw that it had a powerful core where the grit churned furiously, and an outer haze that glittered as it was scattered to the wind. It was a malevolent planet with a stormy surface come to knock her out of orbit, out of the life she had stolen.

'No,' Jean whispered as it gained on her, its course locked. 'No, I won't.'

She would fight it. Stand her ground and repel it. She had earned this life, whether she deserved it or not. Jean took a step towards the shimmering mass, then another, her whole body shaking. The drumming of her heart sounded like hooves to her. Then she saw, emerging from the dust, four thin legs, one dark human head, and some bright feathers. It wasn't fate, it was mounted hell. She screamed loud enough to split rock and at last put her legs into motion.

'What the hell was that?' Denny turned suddenly, knocking Pace's arm.

'If memory serves, a woman screaming.' Pace was more concerned with the beer Denny had caused him to spill on his shirt. 'Damn it, this is silk blend.'

'It's Jean. She sounds scared.'

'Things scare her?'

'Shut up.' Denny sprang from the seat and started running. He ran through the house and out the back door, emerging in time to see his wife outpace a runaway mustang, an Indian brave clinging to its back. 'Good God,' he whispered.

It was a magnificent sight, Jean wailing like an air-raid siren in the path of an exhausted and terrified horse. She was running with the power of a locomotive, the muscles in her legs shuddering with each stride, her arms pumping the air. Denny wanted to cheer her on. He wanted to put a bet on her.

All she could see was how far from her he was, how he would never reach her in time. She whipped a look over her shoulder, and she and the horse fixed their brown gaze upon each other for a moment, doomed animals in the wrong place at the wrong time. The Indian's wig had slipped, revealing a strip of red hair and a line of make-up. His war whoop sounded more like the shrieking of a schoolteacher in defence of her honour and his arms flapped like the stubby wings of a hysterical chicken. He was a poor specimen to be done to death by. But soon Jean could no longer see him, or anything in front of her. Her eyes were blurring with tears. She couldn't believe it was going to end here, running blind towards a settler's death. She closed her eyes and whispered prayers to the empty sky. It was over. If she had seen the rock she might have avoided it, and had her skull split like a conker by a horse's hoof.

The earth felt no more than a rug that had been pulled from under her. Jean went down screaming; dust exploded around her, hiding everything in a shower of brilliant grains. She could hear Denny yelling and knew he was running because of her, and didn't want anything to come into her mind after that. She rolled and rolled, the earth throwing her up into the air each time she hit, tossing her as if on a blanket. The drumming of the hooves stopped as the horse reared, letting out a shrill scream of its own, matched by the Indian, obviously a convert, who gave a final cry of 'Oh Christ in heaven!' Then everything was still.

Jean's first sight after regaining consciousness was of the Indian bending over her, tomahawk in hand. She screamed until he passed out. Jean could upset the balance of nature and erase the line between art and reality. Before unpacking. Denny's hand closed over her mouth.

'There,' he soothed. 'It was just an extra.'

Jean was confused. 'An extra what?'

Denny turned her head towards where the Indian was stretched out. Jean flinched, but Denny kept tight hold of her skull and forced her to look. The brave lay on his side; she could see his face. He was about eighteen, a redhead, with buck teeth, unpromising ears and teary streaks in his brown make-up. His black wig lay next to him in the dirt, like the scalp of an enemy.

'You see? It's just a movie Indian. He's not real.'

With her in it, the West was still wild, and even pretend Indians went on the rampage. The brave stirred, and Charlie pulled him upright and slapped his face till he came to. He was unhurt but in a mild state of shock, which appeared to worsen when he saw Jean. He made a great pantomime of shaking his head and peering at her anew, until he seemed finally convinced she wasn't a symptom of concussion. Denny sneered at him in disgust and helped Jean to stand. Her legs felt as if they had been piped out of a bag, but it seemed she was not badly hurt. She stood while her husband circled her, checking her for damage, muttering.

'Jesus Christ, Pace. What the hell goes on here?'

Pace was unfazed. 'What? Nothing. The company leases some of the land back there to the movie companies. Great Western country,

300

this, lots of . . . space. And rocks. It's really very exciting. They make movies there. Location shooting.'

At this, the brave suddenly remembered where he was supposed to be. Unsteady on his feet, he began to look around. Jean could now see how pretend he was. His buckskin breeches were khakis with fringe glued on, and his war vest was made of paper straws. She felt quite sorry for him.

'Did anyone see the horse? I have to return the horse.'

Denny was unimpressed. 'Is this going to happen all the time?'

'What are you talking about? The horse bolted, it was a freak accident.' Pace spoke as one who had no idea how often they occurred around Jean. 'A million to one. It's perfectly safe. Tell you what, you take the first week for free, on me. A goodwill gesture, for you and your lady wife.'

Denny didn't turn the offer down, and so it seemed it was settled. What else could they do? Pace wouldn't believe they had anywhere else to go. No one would. The fake Indian was nearing hysterics over the horse, fresh tears making gravy of his make-up.

'Please, you gotta help me find it. I told them I could ride. I . . . I figured it would be like a motorcycle.'

'Well, that just makes you one idiot minus a horse,' Pace snapped, as he climbed into his open-top car, eager to get away before the deal could unravel further. 'Be seeing you, Curnalia.

Come by the office Monday to get the case; we'll start you then. Oh, and Mrs Curnalia?' Jean was picking the gravel out of her knees and looked up in time to be the recipient of an unexpected wink. 'Welcome to Hollywood.'

He left the three of them standing in the dirt, unsure of where to go next. Jean and Denny looked at the brave, his elbows scraped, fair shoulders colouring in the sun. He was twisting his wig between his hands and seemed about to ask a favour. Denny wasn't in the mood to grant any.

'OK then, goodbye.' Denny gestured towards the yellow expanse in front of them. 'Don't hurry back.'

'From where? I don't know where the hell I am.' The fake Indian's self-pity was turning to peevishness. 'I'm gonna catch hell for that horse, too.' He slipped his wig back on, as if that might help him find his way, took a few steps and then turned back to Jean. 'But I really am very sorry about all this.'

'Don't worry,' Jean said. 'Happens to me all the time.'

He took a step toward her. 'Really?'

'Keep goin'.' Denny crushed his hope of forgiveness and a ride to the nearest payphone. 'The highway's that way.'

They watched him trudge away, the paper straws of his war vest rustling against his chest. Denny lit a cigarette, whistling as he exhaled.

'What in the hell was that?'

Jean took the cigarette from his fingers. 'A reminder,' she replied.

Don't get too comfortable, it was saying. You can always be found. Jean passed the cigarette back and watched the smoke disappear in the sun.

'Are we really in Hollywood?'

To Jean and Gloria, Hollywood had been mythical, an island off the coast of reason, where everything was perfection.

'We're just outside. It begins over there a way. Or ends, depending on your point of view. OK, let's get this crap inside before the rest of the tribe runs over it.'

Where Jean had grown up, people moving in were usually doing so on their way down from somewhere better. They arrived with their possessions in handcarts and unloaded them, sighing, into the damp old houses that peered down over the town like uninvited guests. Even after the furniture was in place, the new tenants would walk around as if they had wardrobes strapped to their backs, so weighed down were they with misery. But here was a place you settled, rather than sank into. It seemed the sort of place that someone very different to Jean would live. She wondered if that meant she was becoming different. She measured her shadow against Denny's, and could see no change.

They hung their few clothes in the wardrobe of the first bedroom. In the bathroom cabinet, Jean placed a comb, a lipstick and a compact. He deposited a razor and a comb. They shook the grit out of their shoes and left them on the back porch. Once the house had digested their belongings, it seemed empty again. Between them, they didn't make much of a dent. They would have to buy some things. They walked through the rooms, pulling down shades, dropping their clothes an item at a time, claiming the house the only way they knew how. They managed three rooms before falling asleep. When they woke on the kitchen floor, it was dark, and Denny had forgotten to dream.

He drew a bath for his wife and washed her hair in beer. He felt relaxed and generous, which ordinarily he didn't like to; it took him off his guard. But there was a locked door between him and the world, and he for once had the key. Denny sat on a straight-backed wooden chair smoking cigarettes while Jean curled up in the tub, cleaning her latest set of wounds. He liked her best in water, but couldn't say for sure why. Perhaps it was because of the swimming hole he had taken her to back in England, where he first noticed how the water magnified her naked form. They had come so much further than they meant to.

'Will you make it?'

She nodded. 'Nothing much. Be all gone in a week or two.' Jean looked at the shapes the water cast on the walls and ceiling. Denny had fixed a candle into the lid of a coffee can, the better to enjoy her by. He followed her gaze.

'Looks empty. Sounds empty. It's gonna take more than us to fill this place.'

Jean felt suddenly a chill, as though an ice cube had dropped into the water. They had never spoken of children, and Denny had always been so careful. Frankie had been the first to ask Jean if she knew where children came from, and Jean had told her what Wisteria had said.

Just after Jean's father had died, the woman downstairs had given birth. Jean had started to divine that life came and went from somewhere, that there was direction, movement, outside of the strange revolutions of her household. It intrigued her, the idea that there were other tracks to run on, alongside her own. Where, she asked, did I come from? Wisteria had put a roughened hand on her cheek, brought her face close and looked so hard into her daughter's eyes that Jean felt them cross. 'From darkest sin through gates of hellish pain,' she whispered, her hand cold and hard as the smile that barely reached the ends of her mouth. Then she slapped the side of her daughter's head and Jean heard the ocean roar deep inside her skull for two days after.

Frankie had laughed at Wisteria's words. 'No,' she had said. 'They're from bloody good fun or bloody bad luck.' Her two boys had died with their mother, and Jean was no longer entirely sure of their names. It amazed her that she had let so much slip away already, replacing it with Denny.

'What do you mean?' Jean stopped moving so the sound of the water wouldn't obscure his answer.

She didn't know anything about what he wanted. The journey here had allowed them to start to know each other. Could decisions be made on such little information? They still felt less than married. Would a child feel less than

305

legitimate — not in name, or in birth, but in longing? In want? He held up his cigarette; she nodded, and he placed it between her fingers.

'You know, get more stuff. Stuff like regular people have. We got two suitcases between us. We're like bums. What d'you think I mean?'

Jean shrugged. 'I don't know.'

She took a drag on the cigarette and then handed it back to Denny, who dipped it in the tub to extinguish it, flicking the wet stub into the waste basket. As she watched him, she wondered if it could happen, and if he would find her so full of possibilities once she became heavy and inflexible with child. While she craved a piece of him, she also feared dividing him. Whatever part of him bonded him to her, she felt sure it was finite and conditional. Jean was also uncertain of whether she wanted to reproduce herself. Did she really want another her in the world? And what would the world have to say about it? There was always a chance a child would take entirely after Denny, but there was always a chance it wouldn't. She saw a baby dandling its father on its knee. Jean thought of all the virgin space around her. They would need to buy lots of things.

'I was worried you wanted to move already,' she said, feigning relief. 'Can I have another cigarette, please?'

He placed one between her lips and lit it. She didn't want it, but had no idea how else to move past the small mines she detonated in conversation.

'So.' Flakes of tobacco stuck to her tongue and

306

she pulled them off. 'What do I do here?'

Marriage was supposed to make her a woman, but it had made her a child again, idle and awaiting instruction. Jean was going to be completely alone for the first time in her life. No Wisteria, no Gloria, no factory, no Amazons.

'Do?'

'Yes, do. Shall I get a job?'

'What can you do? You ever used a typewriter? A cash register? Did you finish school? I had to come all the way out here just to get a break, Jean, and there's gonna be a lot of other GIs did the same. No one's gonna pick you over them. You can stay here, you know, be my wife.'

Work was another world into which she couldn't follow him. She had dogged his steps only to find him accelerating effortlessly away from her. She smiled and offered him the cigarette, wary of pushing him but needing desperately to know.

'But what will I *do* . . . '

'I don't know. Christ, Jean, what did you do before?'

I was of use, she thought, but could say nothing.

28

To Jean, America seemed to take place under a big sky; England under a damp hedge. This she gleaned from the paperback thrillers of her respective nations. Having missed out on the shipboard orientation lessons and discerned nothing of worth from her time in the Hammell house, she was educating herself.

England, represented by tweedy murders that spoke of tea-infused marriages crumbling like stale cake, morals, class, cold and bad skin, was replaced by America — gunplay under the hot sun and a lack of planning leading often to death. Jean caught the belief she could tell a great deal about a foreign country by the way people were murdered in it. Things seemed more direct here; there was more light on things. She would become fluent and fit in. Her basic assumption was that she was too strange to cope with, and should make herself as normal as possible. She had no idea where she was.

After two days' rest, Denny went to work. If the women he called on found it a little strange to discover this diminutive ex-GI on their doorstep toting a wooden case full of rose face cream and lipsticks in gold-coloured tubes, they were soon won over. 'Better than selling brushes,' he would tell them. 'Get to make pretty girls prettier.' He said he saw it as an extension of serving his country; parroting the script, whisking out the heavily doctored 'before' and 'after' photographs. They wanted false hope, and he sold it by the bucketload. He had never prayed or begged for his own life, but, had he been given cause to, he wondered if he would have considered this a reason to be spared. He began to drink indigestion tonic to take away the feeling of wanting to be sick. The time apart from his bride made him feel generous towards her, at least. He would stop at drugstores on his route and bring her the Western novels and thrillers she liked to fill the void he had left.

Jean displayed the books proudly on the living-room shelves, the illustrations of women in flimsy undergarments being menaced by sharp-suited men in leather gloves adding colour to their surroundings. On one return trip, a clerk asked what Denny had thought of the book he purchased previously, a particularly racy tale of a drug-fiend heiress and a ring of white-slavers. The clerk raised an eyebrow when Denny shrugged and explained he just got them for his wife. He had never thought of her as a nice girl; she didn't think of herself as one.

At the end of their first week, Denny drove Jean to the ocean; here was something she could recognise. He bought her an indecently small two-piece bathing costume and enjoyed its heroic struggle to contain her as she abandoned herself to the sea. They stayed out until it was dark and then went home to bed; when she woke in the morning he was back at work. She knew that should have been enough, but she wanted to be of use more than once a week, or after dark.

She wanted to know this country, and be accepted by it. If she felt at home here, perhaps he would feel at home with her, and she could be sure of him.

Phuture Homes was an island set in a dry sea. There was no store at which to congregate, no church, no bar and no doctor's surgery. Everything lay elsewhere. Jean didn't know where to start. There were porches, but no one sat on them, or swung in the chairs provided. The carports were positioned so that the occupants of the houses could exit dwelling and enter automobile without breaking cover. She heard the slams of various doors and the gunning of engines but didn't see a soul. In the mornings, she would walk as slowly as possible to the nearest supermarket, where tiny wire trolleys mocked her size and appetite. Her daily excursion would take her up the dirt track to the main road and then across that into what she thought of as the town, but was little more than the hem of an outskirt: a beauty parlour, a grocery store, a carwash and a few offices carrying out or offering unknown services. On her way, she would occasionally see groups of men at the side of the road, waiting to be taken away to work at picking fruit, laying asphalt or canning fish. Jean wanted to go stand with them. Someone could collect her and put her to use; she could be at ease out on the highway or in a field, instead of cramped and bottled indoors.

Denny set no limits on her during the day; she was free to come and go, and to spend what was left from the housekeeping money as she pleased.

She could have walked the five miles to the nearest picture house without breaking a sweat, but didn't fancy sitting in the dark on her own, in an unknown place; it felt too much like waiting for trouble to join her. She didn't suppose it was permissible to carry a half-brick in a sock these days. The clothing stores were beyond her means and measurements, and the city was too far to contemplate. She was a housewife now, she decided, and her future lay within the white walls of the bungalow and the estimation of her peers. She knew very well what happened to women who strayed outside these parameters. They ended up between the covers of lurid novels.

But how to become? She and Gloria had been the daughters of the house at Mrs Hammell's, taking their instructions from her. She knew to eat, she knew to clean, she knew to make beds. She didn't know how to make it enough. With no person for company, Jean turned to the radio for advice, and tried to imitate its confident tones. She listened to long dialogues between women, at the end of which one would recommend a product to the other. In the hope of meeting such women, Jean prepared herself, applying the veneer of respectability.

'I find that using tinned peaches instead of fresh gives a much better flavour,' she told the mirror, while attempting to flatten her unruly hair into tame conformity (she had heard that wild hair made a man wild with distaste). But she had never tasted a peach. Denny kept promising to bring home fruit; she would have to remind him again.

'Do you prefer to use butter or margarine in your baking? Margarine is the housewife's choice of today,' she continued, drawing in her eyebrows with one of Denny's pencils. 'My husband won't stand for any other brand.'

She had no idea what her husband would or wouldn't stand for. She studied marriage as if it were a dissected frog, teasing out the innards of the thing, the radio her textbook. But she unlearned as well, scratching over impressions with received knowledge, mass-produced and badly cut. She thought she should paint her nails, dye her hair and wear something called marabou trim. She wanted to ask Gloria what she should do, but Jack's madness was more obstructive than the miles between them; it put a stopper in honesty, and drenched everything in tact. Asking Gloria how to please a husband would be like asking someone who had lost their legs for advice on buying shoes.

Jean could still believe that she would see Gloria again, once Jack got better. So much was strange, it made the absence of her hurt less, though Jean could feel it grow and take hold. She wrote long letters to her and then picked inoffensive lines out of them to make shorter letters, and these she sent. Gloria read each one at least three times and held them in her fist until the ink bled into her skin. She made carbon-paper copies of her replies; she had to keep up with the fiction that was being spun across them and could never remember where she had left off.

She would write during her visits to Jack. With

disuse, his muscles had become slack. He was taken to rooms with great tubs of water where he was swirled around like an old shirt. Therapists worked his legs and arms and dragged him along on sticks in the swimming pool. He was led out into the gardens for walks and dutifully shuffled along, burrs sticking to the slippers that covered his soft feet. He smiled without vigour, and frowned without anger or passion. His expressions seemed to be those of a man trying to work a kernel of corn loose from a back molar.

They told her he could come out of it if he wanted to. It was clear to Gloria that this was the last thing he wanted. That she was. She saw him buffeted by gentleness from one place to another, never seeming at rest anywhere. She didn't see the harsher treatments, the ones that spoke to his sense of disgust and injustice, the ones that aided him in his quest for dissolution. He kept all signs of response hidden, until they had no choice but to push him into the oblivion he craved. The doctors sighed over the deterioration of such a fine man, unaware they were colluding in his slow mental suicide.

To Jean she wrote, 'All same here; got a job at a haberdashers' — it was called 'Button Up', which never failed to make Gloria wince — 'and hope one day to have the bus fare to come and see you. Jack very much improved, taking much more notice of what's around him and swimming like a fish in the hospital pool.'

★ ★ ★

313

As the days and weeks went by, Jean found herself becoming more anxious; nothing was happening to her. She felt not so much neglected as quarantined. Denny had stopped asking her what she did that day, bored of the same answer. She tried to tell him instead what the people in her books had been up to, and read to him, not minding when he made fun of how the hard-edged American words became soft in her English mouth. But she craved incident, to convey something that she had been a part of. To exist. She was going to have to do what, in her experience, people preferred her not to: approach them.

From her thrillers she learned the importance of the stakeout. After a few days' careful reconnaissance, Jean was sure that three neighbouring houses were occupied. The fourth one fooled her, as it had a car parked outside it one day, but it was just Charles Pace, come to put up a sign. She stood at her own front door, feet swelling in newly scrubbed tennis shoes, armpits itching in her tight best dress, which had been a farewell gift from Gloria. It was made from pieces of red, white and blue fabric left over from various patriotic projects and had a white bodice and sleeves, a red cummerbund and a blue skirt with red and white ribbon trim running round the hem. The puff sleeves were supposed to be stiff and full but lay on her shoulders like collapsed lungs. She would just knock on a few doors, see who happened to be in. But she couldn't open the door, not until she knew what she was going to say. She rehearsed again and again.

'How do you do,' she whispered to the window shade. 'I am Jean. I am Mrs Curnalia. How do you do?'

And there she faltered; she couldn't imagine what would come next. She couldn't tell the story of the coalman and his tiara. She couldn't mention Wisteria, or Paul Bradshaw or Frankie. She would not talk about the war, her war, at all. Everything she knew was covered in dirt and debris. She would have to edit herself into respectability.

The next morning, she tried again. Her hand was slick on the doorknob and she couldn't twist it. Jean saw that as a sign, took off the dress and went back to her books.

On the third morning, she decided to bake. An offering was required, she decided; she herself, alone, was not enough. She would make something pretty, something that was as inviting as she couldn't be, that would see her given a cup of tea and talked to for a while. Someone out of three houses would take her in, surely? That would be something to show for her days here; she could prove to Denny that she was acceptable. 'But,' the radio commanded her to ask herself, 'is it convenient?' Jean had turned on the housewife's hour, sponsored that day by a manufacturer of canned hotdogs who would have the listening audience believe that dessert was as good a time for its product as any. Jean happened to have a can, and one of pineapple too, as the recipe required. She felt herself assimilating even as she whipped up the sponge base.

At three o'clock, Jean was just easing herself back into her best dress when she heard the crunch of gravel under tyres. Instead of disappearing into the carport, the car was parking outside the house next to hers. Jean would at last be meeting a neighbour. She fastened the last of her buttons and rushed into the kitchen where the radio-inspired creation was cooling on a rack. She forced it into a dish and covered it with a cloth, which instantly dampened with moist, hotdog breath. She was not going to miss her only chance. Wiping her sweating hand on her dress, Jean opened the front door and stepped out onto the porch.

Jean was dazzled. The woman seemed a very bright jewel against the monochrome surroundings. But had she been naked save for her purple suede shoes, Jean still would have been awed. She had no idea that footwear could exist in such a colour or fabric. She forced herself down the porch steps. She had been brave once, she reminded herself; this couldn't be any worse than a bomb.

The woman was attempting to exit the clumsily parked car as if she were going backwards down a ladder, blindfold. Her fabulously shod foot searched for the ground. On contact, she slid to her knees, still hanging on to the inside handle, and belched, loudly. Jean hesitated. Sweat ran down her back and her dress seemed to contract. She wanted suddenly to be naked and alone.

The woman was still hanging by one arm from the car, but she didn't let this interfere with her attempt to light a cigarette. Jean was now in the relative safety of the shade in front of the house and had not yet been seen; she wondered whether to break cover and run back inside. The cigarette flared into life and singed a good inch off the fine net hanging from the woman's purple hat. She left it dangling from her lips and transferred her attention to pulling herself to her feet. Jean took a chance and turned towards her house; on an ordinary surface she was less than discreet, on gravel, she sounded like a boat running aground. The woman whirled around, nearly falling back into the car. Her eyes were covered with dark glasses but Jean was left in no doubt of the direction of her gaze.

'Oh my God, where the hell did you come from?'

Jean looked down at the veiled pineapple and hotdog sponge. 'I'm . . . I'm your new neighbour. I made you this.'

She held out the dish, and the warm breeze carried the sickly scent of processed meat and tropical fruit to the woman's nostrils, where it caused her to gag.

'What are you trying to do, make me puke?'

Jean blushed so deeply the scars on her cheeks stood out like white-hot electric bars; she felt the sweat bloom on her upper lip and her knees jump. She put the dish down and extended her arms in a gesture of peace.

'I . . . I'm sorry.'

The woman pulled back the net with a gloved hand and peered over her dark glasses. She looked at Jean as a wicked stepmother looks at her unwanted new daughter — quite put out by her existence but pleased to have something to go to work on. Jean had been stared at before, but this was like being lightly tasted. Jean caught the scent of alcohol and vomit as the woman spoke.

'Well, look at you, honey,' the woman drawled. 'You look like you belong on a float.'

Jean was suddenly ashamed of her dress, herself and her ridiculous attempt to make the acquaintance of this new world. She would stay in the shadows where she belonged. As long as Denny could keep her, she would be safe; her mistake had been in thinking she needed or had a right to anyone else. Jean considered herself dismissed and looked to home. But then she heard a screen door bang shut and turned to see a little round woman in an extravagantly frilled white dress come bustling out of the house opposite. Fluttery and full, she balanced a great deal of flesh on tiny feet, seeming to spiral up out of the ground like a miniature tornado. The woman in purple straightened and slammed the car door shut; she appeared suddenly invigorated, as if she had been feigning before a fight.

'Fuck,' she said, grimacing. 'Typhoid Mary, Jesus and Joseph.'

On reaching the bottom of her porch steps, the frilled woman seemed to gather herself up like a bull about to charge. Tilted toward conquest, she set off in their direction, a cannon ball in ruffles. As she neared the scene she raised a hand, half in stern greeting, half in command; in her other hand, pamphlets quivered like captive birds. Jean felt herself being pulled towards her, drawn out like a demon.

'Miss Witter! Miss Witter, I have something to say to you.'

The woman's high, breathy tone was prim and absurdly young for its middle-aged owner. Jean couldn't place accents yet, but this one made her think of hoop skirts and hardships.

'How are you today, Miss Mildmay?'

'Trollop!'

'Oh, so kind of you to notice.'

'This is not a matter for humour, Miss Witter. You will take back that . . . that *filth* you left in my home.'

The woman in purple smiled; her voice had lost some of its slur and rang out clearly. 'I told you, you Jesus jockey. You put another of those damn pamphlets under my door, I'm going to put one under yours.'

'I am spreading the word of God, Miss Witter. These are advertisements for a . . . a . . . '

'A titty bar, Miss Mildmay. Don't you pretend you don't know what that is.'

'You heathen, godless . . . slut!'

No more than five feet tall, the frilled woman was impressive in her fury. As was Jean even in her placidity — a fact she forgot as she took a step towards her, hoping to calm the situation.

'There, now . . . '

At the sight of Jean, the midget dynamo stopped dead in her tracks. Her little feet didn't stop moving, but the energy they produced seemed insufficient to propel her forward, and so she ground the dirt under her, like a tank stuck in the desert. Years before, Ermeline had been much affected by a horror picture, viewed by accident thanks to a confusion over tickets, in which scientists played at being God and created a woman of terrible proportions. As Jean emerged from the shade of the porch, Eva's cigarette smoke trailing from her vertiginous hair, she appeared to Ermeline to be that abomination, made real.

The woman in purple, Miss Witter, was laughing. 'Oh dear, Ermeline seems to have slipped out of gear.'

Jean took another step into the light; she was close enough to see the thick rolls of fat at Miss Mildmay's wrists and ankles, making her look jointed. If dolls could age, they would end up looking like this. At Jean's advance, the woman's round eyes widened in her round head. Her nostrils, set in her button nose by God or nature with the care of someone poking putty with a pencil, flared alarmingly.

'Pleased to meet you,' Jean called, smiling as broadly as she could. She had spent a lifetime trying to put people like Ermeline at their ease and knew it had to be done quickly if it was to succeed at all. She took another step. 'I'm Jean.'

Ermeline's jaw slackened as the fury went out of her and dumb shock took over. She began to twitter and push the pamphlets into her capacious purse, backing away as she did so.

Jean wanted to reach out, to calm her with a touch, but one of her great paws on Ermeline's shoulder might have brought on a stroke, and the woman was too busy crossing herself for Jean to get a hold of her. 'It's all right,' she pleaded, ashamed that she should be more trouble than the drunk. Miss Ermeline Mildmay was now as purple as Miss Witter's dress, and was puffing her cheeks out as if she had a hot coal in her mouth. 'God preserve us,' she whispered. 'God preserve us and strike down those who would harm us.'

'It's all right,' Jean persevered. 'There's nothing to worry about.' And then she said the most comforting thing she could think of: 'I'm English.'

At this, Ermeline took flight, Miss Witter's heathenism forgotten, only Jean's dreadful appearance on her mind. She ran as though her ankles were tied, but still made good time.

'All right, then. Nice to have met you,' Jean called after the departing bustle of organdie. 'Take care.'

The woman in purple was still laughing, throwing her head back and showing her teeth in a theatrical display of amusement. She stopped so abruptly it was if her throat had been cut; it startled Jean into turning toward her.

'English, eh?' A fresh cigarette had appeared, and she took a long drag on it, leaking smoke from her nose and mouth. 'I wondered why I couldn't understand a word. Thought I was drunk.'

She laughed again, and then stifled a belch.

'Well, welcome to the neighbourhood, English.' Her smile was condescending, without a trace of warmth and with more than a little bile, either from the drink or her reaction to Jean.

'Actually, my name's — '

'Sorry, don't care.' The woman cut her off. Turning her back on Jean, she stumbled in the direction of her door, leaving the car beached where it was. Jean picked up the dish of fruited meat. She was alone.

By the time Denny arrived home, the cursed dessert had been consumed (she found it preferable to waste and that was all she could say of it) and Jean was sat at the kitchen table, re-reading one of her books. Denny set his case down in front of her and went straight to the oven, finding it empty.

'You eat already?'

She felt a soft bubble of hotdog and pineapple break on her palette, and exhaled it gently into her sleeve. 'Yes, sorry. I was going to do a steak for you; there was only one.'

'Don't bother, I'm not hungry.'

He didn't kiss her forehead, or embrace her. That was for bed.

'I'm gonna take a shower,' he said on his way out of the room. 'It was hot as hell today.'

Jean nodded and turned down the radio so she'd be able to hear the water on him. There was so much pleasure to be had in just existing in the same space together, she realised. Water on skin, sunlight, a day at the ocean, her own stove, a bed. It was concentrated at night; if she could only stretch it over her days it would be all right. She caught her frizzy-haired reflection in the window, the tallest coconut in the shy. 'Make do,' she reminded herself, so quietly it was barely a whisper. 'Make do and mend.'

The sample case was open in front of her.

Denny had to replace the labels on all of the colours that hadn't sold yet. Pink Ice would become Warm Sunset to see if it did any better; Blue Lagoon would be Pacific Sky and Chartreuse would be just plain Green. Jean opened up one of the compacts and looked at her eyes, clear, dark and round. Unchanging. She dug a finger in a pot of blue powder and rubbed it across her eyelids, trying to imagine Denny selling it to her, what he would tell her it could do, how it would make a man mad for her. She took a tube of red lipstick and ground it into her lips, leaving a thick smear of colour, and then drew lines across her cheeks, filling the tiny trenches of her scars with crimson.

She didn't hear him come into the room, in search of a new bar of soap. The water still ran in the bathroom, a soothing domestic rain that promised everything would be clean and fresh again soon.

Denny watched her from the doorway, working her way through the case. Her hair was scraped back from her face, and her pale skin glowed under a bare bulb, the shadows pooling in her throat and eye sockets. The fabric of her sleeves pinched her arms a little, the waistband was too tight and her stomach sat above it in a soft roll that he wanted to bite. She made everything around her look small and petty.

'What are you doing?'

Jean jumped and then giggled, as if some secret had been discovered. With the stick of red grease poised in her hand, she turned to face Denny and then looked sheepishly at the mess she had made, powders and creams spattering the table.

'I'm sorry, I . . . '

She couldn't really explain, couldn't tell him she was painting herself in because she felt herself fading.

' . . . I was just playing.'

It was play. Every day she put on the apron of a wife and cooked for the body of a husband without ever feeling that she was a wife, or knowing what it was supposed to feel like. Like firm ground, she supposed. Not like holding your breath.

'Playing, huh?'

She was so nervous she could feel her blood fizz. The possibility of his anger still scared her, not because he could harm her, but because he could deny her everything she had come to crave.

'Yes. Sorry.'

He walked up to her, gently took the lipstick from her hand and held it in front of her face. Jean gave a pained smile, and tried to look contrite. She thought he would lecture her on how much it cost. Instead, he pressed the lipstick against the tip of her chin and slowly drew a line, down her neck, to the pool of her throat. When he reached her bodice, he opened the buttons and dragged the red tube down between her breasts. When it broke, he mashed the stick of pigment into her skin.

'I'm going to play too,' he whispered.

She was still fascinating to him. The workings of her absorbed his energy and imagination and left him exhausted. He was true without being faithful. The other women — and he met only women, day after day, lonely, bereaved and jilted women — were not her replacement; they were to confirm her uniqueness. Every woman unlike his wife pleased him, as none could quite match her dimensions or her gift for realising his needs, for creating a need in him. He saw that, as he painted her in the velvet reds he had dreamed of.

Jean let her shoulders fall as he pulled the bodice down to her waist, the tension evaporating.

'Did anything bad happen to you today?'

Jean shrugged, pleased that he noticed her moods, worried that he could detect anything approaching displeasure. She would not be ungrateful.

'No. Not really. I tried to meet the neighbours.'

He held the dress while she stepped out of it, folded then draped it over the back of a chair. His actions were as soothing to her as sleep. This was all she needed, she thought. As long as there was this, she was employed.

'And what happened?'

'Oh . . . ' How much to tell, she wondered. Is there really nothing to fear anymore? 'The usual, for me. There was some upset. I didn't start it. One was drunk and horrible. One was scared; a little one, though.'

Denny undid his belt. 'I don't think I understand.'

Jean sighed. 'No. I don't. I don't think I understand people at all.'

'Fuck people.'

She laughed at this, and held him as he stepped out of his trousers.

'So you came home to play.'

'Yes,' she nodded. 'I didn't know what else to do.'

'I know.' For a moment he sounded far away. 'I didn't either. But we do.'

Denny pressed his face against her body, smiling as he smeared the lipstick over them both. She felt the cold enamel of his teeth graze her ribs. Calm filled her, like sunlight flooding a room. It was certainty, there and then. Jean peeled the shirt from his back, streaking his skin with the lipstick on her fingers. His body had barely changed in the time she had known him — she had the marks he collected in the war memorised within a week of his return — but still he could surprise her. She could feel the texture of his skin change a dozen times between elbow and neck; had she forgotten, or had it ceased to amaze her?

'Remind me,' she whispered.

There were more ways to travel here. Propelled by circumstance, she had forgotten the most transporting thing of all, that she might not always do harm. That she could excite, soothe, compensate. Love. She had feared the cessation of movement, but there was movement around her still. He was returning to her, again and again. He was how she would travel: delving deeper into him, learning all the things she could only guess at now, naming and claiming all the undiscovered parts of him. She knew all the

326

wants she fulfilled, but could only guess at what was left. She had to ask.

'Am I enough?'

He lifted his face to hers. Her skin bore the rouged marks of his lips, and she wished it could always, that she could have the memory of him tattooed on her flesh.

'You'll do,' he grinned.

Part Four

EDUCATION

29

There was no underwear on the floor. That was how she knew.

★   ★   ★

The discovered parts of him included these: his hair grew in whorls from the crown of his head and in the morning looked like freshly stirred white coffee. He wasn't ticklish anywhere. He liked to sleep in his underwear, then leave it on the bedroom floor and walk naked to the bathroom. She wanted to tell the druggist when he handed over her aspirin. She wanted to tell the cashier at the market. She wanted to take a test in him to prove it.

Jean had memorised his habits so intensely that when she got out of bed in the morning, the first thing her body did before her mind was even awake was to stoop for that underwear. And when it wasn't there, she knew he had gone. She still made herself conjure other possibilities — that he had slipped in the shower and knocked himself out, that the car had broken down and he was fixing it. She let the first lift her feet from the sticky floor and guide her to the empty bathroom; the next commanded her arm to raise a window shade, revealing the absence of the car. He was gone, of course.

The sheet she was wrapped in looked like a

lunatic's flag. Makeup stained the pillows, and talc caked the bedroom floor. They had plundered the contents of the cosmetics case, pelting each other with cold-cream bombs, wielding boxes of talcum powder like flame throwers. They had chased each other round the house, skidding like ducks on ice, not caring who heard. They were home. He had said, 'You'll do,' and it was enough.

She could feel her lungs compress and thought her skull might shatter. For the second time in her life, the house had fallen down. She was reminded of the scouring, the hot rasp of being licked by grit and splinters. It was happening again, inside her. Everything she was, was in the past.

Her veins stiffened as loss coursed through them. Her skin felt as though it might split. She knelt down and placed her palms on the floor, her head resting between them. Emotion swept her body, raw and uncontrollable and vast. Jean felt the cold floor against her forehead, and wished she was buried beneath it. Her mistake had been to love.

'I take it back,' Jean whispered to the bare boards. 'I didn't mean it, I take it back.'

A desperate howl brewed in her; she choked it by stuffing a towel into her mouth. It would have pleased Wisteria, her daughter ending up an abandoned, disfigured monster, with a heart that twisted and shivered in epileptic grief. Jean had fallen into the trap, and it was as deep and smooth-sided as sleep. She had hoped for too much.

This is how it would have been in the war, she thought. A sudden absence, after years of fearing it. To have waited until the moment she knew she loved seemed especially cruel, but not altogether surprising. Cruelty she expected. The kindness, the pleasure, had done her in.

'I could have gone without,' she told herself. 'I could have gone without ever knowing.'

Jean lay on the floor until the desire to scream ebbed, and she could pull the folds of cotton from her mouth. Her jaws ached, but she couldn't have risked releasing what was in her; she felt it could have turned her inside out. The bedsheet lay open and she could see clearly on her body the marks that he had left. With no strength to get up, she rolled onto her back and stared at the ceiling, the skirting, the undersides of chairs. She felt underneath the world, rather than of it. There suddenly seemed to be no distance at all between where things had ended and where she had started from. Only some time, and not nearly enough of that. She was without hope of change again. He had taken that with him.

She had thought herself adaptable. She had picked her way through life, being what was required when she could not be what was wanted. But she saw now that the world had become strange, briefly, to suit her. She had not adapted, it had been corrupted. She was lying on the floor of normal life, not knowing how to get up.

'What will I do?' Jean asked herself. 'What will I do, now the last person has gone?'

The first hour passed, and nothing stopped: not her breathing, not her pain. She watched the hand of the clock take the minutes away and didn't think of rescue. No one would know where to dig this time. The second hour saw the sun warm the room and her flesh, and Jean wondered who she should tell not to bother. The third hour she might have spent wondering why, but that was the first thing she had known.

The next thing, what now, was so vast as to paralyse her brain. It was like trying to imagine the edge of space. So she counted the fine cracks in the paintwork, the insects on the ceiling and the birds that flew past the window. Under the house was something Denny had called a crawl space, and she couldn't imagine a more comforting name for a thing. There was very little between her and it, the thickness of a few boards, and she could hear the bugs, beetles and snakes that enjoyed the cool dark of it, a rabbit scuttling through on its way to the desert. She wondered if they would accept her among them, a human transformed by the magic of bad luck. It wouldn't be like a curse at all, to escape notice, to become something small that wound its way through the earth — it would be like being given wings.

At least she had waited this long, Jean told herself. At least she had waited this long to forget everything she had always known. The last warning had been so recent, and she had ignored it. Fate's Indian had run her down, and she had turned her back on him and gotten cosy anyway. Perhaps if she hadn't, a smaller reprimand would have been delivered. 'No,' Jean told herself. 'This has been a long time coming.' She was never meant to have been born once let alone twice, and she had left others dead in her wake. How could she think there wouldn't be a price, or believe that she had already paid it? What was she to do with all that was left? She was too strong, too able to continue. It might be years, hundreds and hundreds of days. At this, Jean felt the tears come again and the grief swell, and forced herself to count the cracks again.

Hunger pulled her up eventually; her body never could defer to events. She tried to prolong the feeling as long as possible, grateful to have its gnawing insistence to focus on, but when her stomach began to burn she got up off the floor. There would be much more pain to bear; she knew she shouldn't take on too much at once.

The lunch she had made him was still in the refrigerator. He hadn't taken one thing of hers to remind him, only that which he didn't want and probably didn't know he had. Her heart. He would have thrown it from the car if he could, she thought. But it was in her, it beat still, although that didn't seem possible. She ate his lunch and then regretted it. He couldn't come back for it now. She put the core of the apple she had chosen for him in the refrigerator. An hour later she took it out and threw it away.

She couldn't believe that he had removed himself so completely before she was even awake. It was as if he had never been there, as if she had invented him. His clothes were gone, his toothbrush, the car. She thought perhaps she had been deluding herself all these months, thinking that she had a husband when he had been nothing more than a figment of her imagination. Perhaps there had never been a war either and she had just gone mad in her mother's house, and was there still, crouched in a damp attic eating the paper from the walls and birds that got caught in the rafters.

The dishes from their last meal together were dry and stacked away, the cup he drank coffee from was still in its place. She took the towels from the rail in the bathroom and pressed them to her face, hoping to feel the damp of his body in them. Everything was clean and dry; nothing lingered out here. She searched every room but found him only in a photograph, frozen in the past. She was there with him. It was her only proof they had ever met.

The sounds that used to send her rushing to the window made her duck down under the sill — Eva's car pulling in, Ermeline's door closing; she didn't want to be seen now. The sun departed from the back rooms, and she shivered, but didn't go outside to warm herself. She didn't want to break the spell. If she stepped outside, she would be seen. She had to stay invisible; it was her only hope of making it not so.

Jean went back to the bedroom and curled up on the floor among the powder and scent they had spilled so carelessly. She picked at the grain of the floor to keep her fingers away from her scars. They were fierce with longing, and she would pick down to the bone if she started. She scratched at the wood until her nails flaked, focusing her mind on the meaningless task, letting it bear the responsibility for keeping her sane. The day washed over her without leaving a stain. When the darkness came, she didn't turn on the lights. Best save on the electric now, she told herself.

The lifespan of a hope often depends on the hour of its birth. When she woke just after dawn, the weak shadows painted a room different from the one she had fallen asleep in, and for less than a second Jean could believe that the previous day had never happened. But the cold from his side of the bed was already rushing from the palm of her hand to her brain, the increasing light was sharpening the room to one more real than desired, and her body bore no imprint of his. She pulled the dirty sheet over her head and waited for sleep to return.

When it didn't come, when the bed became too empty of him to bear, she went to the kitchen. There she could pretend to be waiting for him to get in from work, letting a succession of neglected cups of tea cool in front of her. The refrigerator hummed; it sounded happy to her. She wondered if she could push it over. She pulled open the heavy door and totted up the contents. A couple of pounds of hamburger, a gallon of milk, six eggs, some bacon, butter, a bottle of beer, two heads of lettuce, five tomatoes and some yellow cheese. She took the beer and sat down to watch the contents of the icebox lose their chill as the warm afternoon crawled in.

'Waste,' she muttered. 'Waste.'

With the sheet wrapped around her, she took another tour of the house. Passing the bathroom mirror, Jean flinched at what she saw: the last inmate to hear the fire alarm, woken too late to escape with the others. She was supposed to go with him.

She had been given her life at the very beginning of the war and had not known what to do with it, so she gave it away to the first person to ask for it. All waste.

In the rubble, Jean had not thought what she should do. She had waited, making tiny movements that neither freed her nor brought the house crashing down. In her marriage, she had made tiny movements that neither freed her nor brought the house crashing down, until the night she had somehow reached up and pulled down the rafters. And no one was coming for her this time. She had allowed herself to be blown about like litter, and now she was stuck.

For the second night in her life she slept entirely alone, the only person under one roof. The only living person.

The next morning, two policemen came to the house. The car had been found abandoned; the tyres were missing and twenty boxes of rose face cream had been left to melt on the back seat. No, Jean told them, there was no note. She had no reason to believe her husband had taken his own life. She knew of no mistress, no friend he could be staying with. The policemen's shoes stuck to the floor. The sweet smell of the house was sickening. No, they hadn't had a fight.

338

They'd been playing. They asked her what she meant. 'Like foxes in the moonlight,' she said, and they had looked at each other. Since he left, Jean hadn't bathed or pulled a comb through her hair, and as she sat in the kitchen listening to their questions she felt her body tell them all they needed to know. She knew they were listening, taking in the grease smears, the one sock, the shine on her nose and the sour breath; her bovine face betraying her stupidity in not preparing for this day — how could she not have known it would come? How could she have fooled herself for so long? He had run away from his big ugly wife, that was all. They asked about suicide only because they had to. They knew what had happened as soon as she opened the door screaming her husband's name. Jean felt like a prophecy fulfilled.

The policemen stayed for less than an hour; they made few notes. She was told to contact them if he returned. The last thing they asked was for a photograph. One of the policeman gestured at her wedding picture on the wall.

'You got a copy?'

'No,' she replied. 'That's the only one.'

'That's it?'

But she had forgotten. At the end of their first week in California, he brought home a camera and took pictures of her wearing the two-piece bathing suit in the back yard. She had hung sheets on the laundry lines to shield herself from the neighbours. Then he had handed the camera to her. She remembered that her hands were shaking as she held it, and she had to wait for the tremors to pass. He was giving her something she hadn't dared to ask for: proof of him. The wedding pictures were counterfeit; in one, he was a stolen image, in the other, a bystander. But this would be her photograph, hers alone. Because in it, he was willing. She had hidden the wallet at the back of a drawer so her immodesty would not be accidentally displayed should anyone come to the house. She raced to the bedroom and pulled the drawer from the chest, tipping its contents onto the bed. The wallet was there but had been emptied. She felt it as keenly as a kick, the force of it bent her double. He didn't want her to have anything of him, not even a memory.

'That's it,' she confirmed.

The policemen took her words instead, and left her to mourn her lost husband. Happiness had not been so total. If she cut herself, she thought she might bleed misery.

She slept as much as she could and ate as little as possible. She didn't have the energy to clean the floors, though she ran herself under the shower after the police left, cruelly aware of her own stink. When the milk was gone, she had her tea black in the same mug; she couldn't catch her own germs. She drifted between their bed and the kitchen, waiting for her head to clear. It was too full of pain to let anything else in, so she slept and starved and waited. She couldn't think what else to do. If anyone wondered at her situation, they didn't betray themselves with an enquiry. Jean went undisturbed for six days, after which her food ran out.

She knew it was coming. It had seemed

unimportant, relating only to when she would next have to go to the store for supplies. If she went to the store, and he came back, and she wasn't there, he would think she didn't care. He would turn around and leave again, and she would lose him for ever. If she left a note, it might come away in the wind and float to some other door where no one knew him. She had considered these possibilities, but not that there would be no money. Her housekeeping was left, every week, in a jar under the sink, from where she would take what she needed. How could she have thought it would refill itself without him? How could she have thought he would have made sure she survived?

Jean began to tremble; her whole body rippled with the most concentrated fear she had ever felt. Stronger than childhood, stronger even than being buried in the house, it was the piercing fear of the total unknown. Tears pooled in her eyes and burned her cheeks. The split second when a person wakes in the dark, convinced the world has ended and left them behind, was now the rest of her life. Jean's voice was high and thin as she addressed the night.

'Mum?'

She felt nothing but a cold satisfaction, somewhere in her past, somewhere in her mind. Wherever she was, Wisteria was rejoicing.

★   ★   ★

On the seventh day, Jean ate the last of the tea. She drank pints of water to make her stomach

341

feel full, but it just growled at her in disgust. She tried to sleep, but hunger held her back. In this half-state between hunger and sleep, she dreamt him back into the house, thinking she could see him in the shadows. But she couldn't make herself hear his voice or feel him on her skin; she was not far gone enough for that. It couldn't be much longer though, she was sure. She had made him her reason, and her reason had departed.

But she had her body. Her map of time and incident. Jean sat in front of the mirror and plotted her course using the firework bursts of abraded skin; the deeper cuts with their scalloped edges; the gathered pink crêpe of the burns. In that landscape, she set out to find him. Some marks were as familiar as sight; she had carried them since before she had a memory to recall them. They told her this was inevitable: she was not made to be preserved, but to be torn down from time to time. They told her not to ask why. The more recent inscriptions — the delicate lattices on her arms and thighs, the deeper trench in her calf — spoke of pain giving way to pleasure, of how much sensation was contained in her. He had discovered her when she was discovering for herself what could be achieved, and he had left her when she thought there was nothing more to know. In recognising love, she had closed herself to possibility.

She could not imagine a way out, because she could not imagine herself anywhere else. So she would go back to where he found her. Like Victorian castaways who wore stiff collars over bare, sunburned chests and sang the national anthem before going to bed under banana-leaf roofs, she would go home, as best she could. If she could recreate herself as she was then, perhaps he would return to her. To when he wanted her. Jean unplugged the radio and the refrigerator. She observed the blackout and slept under the table, crawling back to bed at dawn. She whistled in the dark and prayed for a bomb.

On the evening of the eighth day, Jean found four bottles of beer under the sink. She had been looking for her gas mask, hunger having worked quickly on her. In the absence of food, her body had started to feed on itself, and Jean was hallucinating on and off. She had already tried to eat her cold cream, thinking it was a forgotten jar of rice pudding. When she realised what she was doing, she continued for a couple of spoonfuls, to see if she could bear it. She could not. Dropping the bottles of beer into a sink of cold water, Jean wondered what would happen next. She wondered if she would die.

She had seen it before, women dying from pride, refusing to ask for handouts. Those with children were quicker to ask. Why should she be kept alive, with no one's life depending on hers? Could she ask for herself, just for herself? She could walk the short distance to one of the other houses, crawl it if she had to, and ask them for food. But if where would it end? What could she pay them with? It would be like the societies again, carting herself around for charity. She had been young and strong; he had made her old and weak. Dependent. She wouldn't go through that again; she didn't want to be exposed for the waste of skin that she was. Denny would appear with some food, or send her some money. He couldn't let her die; he was the only one who knew where she was. He was the only one who could come to her funeral. She wondered if he would. That had been Wisteria's concern, that there would be someone to bury her; after that, Jean could go hang. She had buried her mother, and now there was no one to uncover her. She was beyond all people and all things now.

★   ★   ★

After the third beer, Jean's hunger eased; her stomach still gurgled but the pain was less. Her head rose on a current of air; she found she was unconsciously nodding along to some unheard rhythm. The beer warmed her cheeks and chest. She decided to take her slip off — she had stopped bothering with outer clothes days before. Sitting in the kitchen in her underwear, she felt much better. She could still see caked powder and cold cream at her feet. She poured a little of the beer onto the floor and whisked it into a paste with her foot. Staring at the boards made her head spin, the wood began to undulate in large waves. She felt as if she could dip a toe in; the floor had become liquid, a deep, dark sea that she could dive into. That's when Jean realised: she could disappear.

Though she hadn't eaten for three days, and her mind was scraped by grief, things were suddenly clear to her. Her family was dead, her

344

husband was gone and the only other person she knew and loved was thousands of miles away, chained to a lunatic. There was no one left to care. It would be so easy to just fall between the cracks and never be seen again. To be no one's responsibility, no one's shame. She was free. She at last understood the freedom in not being wanted. There was no reason to extend this. No reason to pretend she had expectations of anything better. If no one else wanted her life, it was hers entirely.

Jean finished the last beer. Her legs were lead, but the rest of her was whipped froth, ready to blow away in the wind. The night sky was an inviting velvet blue, with just a few stars resting against it, diamonds on a pillow. Jean looked down at her roomy, greying underwear; she couldn't see that it mattered for a walk in the dark.

There had been too many false starts. Jean opened the back door. Though the night was mild, there was a strange tingling in her body, and her hands and lips were numb. She stumbled down the steps, slipping onto the desert floor. She felt the cool dirt under her bare feet and flexed her toes. A breeze lifted her chin, urging her on.

'Yes, yes,' she muttered. 'I'm coming.'

After three strides, she felt herself evaporate into the dark.

30

Eva Witter's first thought was to poke her with a stick, as with a stranded jellyfish. Beached, it became clear how far out of her element Jean was.

The sun had been on her for a little over two hours when her neighbour first noticed her. Eva had staggered to her kitchen to medicate the excesses of the night before, and was pouring gin into a jug when she spied Jean. Though her stomach churned and her hair bristled like an ill-fitting wig of steel pins, Eva was curious enough to wander onto the back porch for a closer look. She was used to public displays of instability and usually assumed a strongly non-interventionist stance: she had once hauled an actress off a window ledge and been kicked near the teeth for her trouble. She did hesitate when she realised Jean would be able to manage much more, but when a bird stopped for a rest on Jean's knee, and she failed to stir, Eva decided to investigate further. Not that she was happy about it; Jean felt like bad luck.

Jean was just crawling up the bank of consciousness when she became aware of a shadow over her. The light was like molten lead on her eyes, but she forced herself to open them and look into the face of her fate. Poised over the prone form, Eva — wearing a kimono over her evening gown, dark glasses and a wide sunhat

— held an ice-cold pitcher of gin and a picnic umbrella. Jean tried to make sense of what she saw, couldn't, and tumbled back down the bank. Eva raised the spike of the umbrella high above her head, closed one eye and, in a single movement, drove the spike deep into the ground beside Jean's head and opened the canopy. It made a sound like a great seabird settling its wings. Eva then threw the cold gin in Jean's face.

The icy liquid stung her out of oblivion; Jean rolled onto her side and coughed until she vomited a thin stream of liquid, all she had left in her. Wiping her mouth with the back of a dusty hand, she looked up towards Eva, whose balled-up fists were plugged into her hips.

'What happened?' Jean's voice was small and frail; she had never heard herself so weak.

Eva was perplexed. 'How the hell should I know?'

Jean nodded. It had not been a fair question. At that moment, all she knew was that it was sometimes impossible to argue with life: it seemed very emphatic around her. Jean shaded her eyes and looked around her; it was familiar again. Eva tapped her foot on the desert floor, sending up little puffs of dust, like smoke signals. They told Jean to pull herself together. She managed to push herself into a sitting position, and waited there for word from her legs. She couldn't quite recall what had brought her to this — any of it. All she knew was that the purple woman had saved her: not only was she alive, but she was someone's again.

'OK, English. Get up, get dressed and come to

breakfast. I hope you like hamburgers.'

It took Jean forty minutes to wash and dress. She had to sit down to put clean underwear on, not daring to risk standing on one leg, as she had nearly fallen out of the shower twice. Her feet were sunburned, so she wiped the paper the butter had been wrapped in around the reddened, swelling flesh, then cut the sides and toes out of her tennis shoes so they wouldn't chafe. She suddenly knew how to take care of herself again, if only a little, too late. Once reconstituted, she went to Eva's.

Jean was somewhat hazy on the last few days, but she remembered the scandalous Miss Witter and trod as lightly as she could between her porch and Eva's, hoping not to invite the interest of the hysterical Ermeline. Jean could not imagine she looked less dreadful on this day than that.

An hour after she had been brought back to life, Jean was sitting at Eva's grand dining table, her feet soaking in a bowl of cool, oily water. She was too tired and hungry to feel the embarrassment she knew she should, and sat in grateful silence, observing her surroundings while Eva made drinks for them both.

'Come in,' she had said. 'If it's too early for you to drink, come back later.'

'It's all right,' Jean had assured her. 'I don't know what time it is.'

That seemed to work. The Eva that let Jean into the house was partially restored to an elegant if not entirely sober self; she had replaced the evening gown with day pyjamas and applied fresh makeup to her newly washed face. Her wet

348

hair was dark and curled at the edges, and as she turned away from her, Jean noticed the glitter of diamonds in her ears.

While the interior of Jean's house was as smooth and white as bone, Eva's was stained as a front tooth. A wash of nicotine and neglect coloured the walls; Jean thought she caught a whiff of her childhood rising off dirty plates and old ashtrays. The furniture was simple and expensive: leather couches, the dark-wood dining table, curved glass cabinets holding yet more glass that had been blown into sensuous shapes. But even to Jean it looked somehow out of date and prewar, a movie from when there was no colour. She noticed that some of the glass pieces were chipped, that there was a tear on the arm of the couch. A gold compact lay on the floor, its contents now nothing more than a heap of beige dust. Everything was expensive, but nothing was prized. She had never seen a house like it; neglect was easy enough to understand, but this was closer to abandonment. A typewriter was positioned in one corner of the table, where it had collected a fair amount of dust. When Eva came back with a tray holding a pitcher and glasses, she saw Jean's interest and moved the machine to the sideboard and replaced its cover.

'The artist at work,' she smirked. 'Who knows what genius you've interrupted.'

'I'm so sorry.' There was so much to be responsible for, now she had ruined Eva's day just by living. 'I didn't mean to inconvenience you. Are you writing something?'

'Only the Great American Novel.' Eva's top lip

was breaking rank with the rest of the smirk and twitching slightly. 'It's a collaborative piece; around ten thousand poor slobs are working on it at any one time.'

She paused for a reaction but Jean was as blank as new-fallen snow. Eva sighed, she had been waiting to use that; she hoped it was vague and clever enough to fool someone into believing her. Faced with Jean's incomprehension, Eva shrugged and momentarily dropped the worldly pose she had perfected across years of swallowing down disappointment and pretending not to mind the taste.

'Doesn't matter, it was a joke. On me, I guess. Ask me, what am I working on.'

Jean obliged; her voice was getting stronger though her lips were swollen and she had a raging thirst. 'What are you working on?'

'My third martini. Join me?'

Jean smiled at this and, despite herself, Eva was pleased. She had perhaps seen too many women lying outside in their underwear. She had perhaps too often been one. She took a long gulp of the drink and felt it calm her warring insides. Soon, the pain would be all gone. Jean took an equally large gulp and had to suppress the urge to cough as the cold, bitter liquid raked her throat. On reaching her stomach, it exploded into flames.

'That's good,' she croaked.

'Thanks. It's a rare talent, I'm told. How are you feeling?'

'All right. A bit silly. Thank you. For finding me.'

'Don't mention it. Just don't try it again. It's frowned upon, legally speaking. Socially, too.'

Jean wasn't even sure what she had tried. There had just been nothing, nothing to hold her back and nothing to go towards. If that was death, she was there already. But she didn't remember deciding.

'No,' she said. 'I won't.'

'Good. So what's the story? Husband? Let me guess, the secretary?'

Jean shook her head. 'He doesn't have one.'

'Maybe not in his office.' Eva managed to sound as if she knew everything Jean didn't. 'So, he's gone for good.'

Jean took another gulp of her drink. Someone at last was talking to her, she only wished it was something she wanted to hear. She could no longer keep it from being official, Eva had confirmed it.

'Did you have any idea?'

Jean blushed, which was answer enough.

'Here.' Eva raised her glass. 'To rats. It's only when they desert you know the ship is sinking.'

Tears formed in Jean's eyes. Eva groaned inwardly. She found dialogue easy, but conversation hard. Why couldn't it be like a movie: all talk, talk, talk and no harm done. Perhaps this had not been such a good idea. There was an unexpected strength of feeling in Jean; it threatened to wake her own. 'Cheer up, at least yours didn't . . . ' Eva wanted to say, but stopped herself. She wasn't going to be that woman.

'Hey there, good riddance. You won't be the first gal to be left in the lurch. You're not . . . ?'

Jean shook her head, assuming Eva was asking if a child was involved. No, he hadn't fled in fear of her duplication. Not specifically.

'Well, that's something, isn't it?'

'Yes.' Jean lowered her eyes to drink, fighting the urge to cry.

Looking out of the kitchen window at Jean, Eva had contemplated calling an ambulance and leaving it at that. Of all the problems she had, this Englishwoman was not one of them. But she had changed her mind. There had been something almost appealing about the way Jean lay out in the desert; it had seemed honest at least. It made Eva give her a chance. But now she wondered if it wasn't too soon to let Jean go; it had to be done before their misery got together and bred.

Puffed up from the sunburn, Jean seemed harmless, a shiny buffoon. Eva wondered what she did. She had seen some novelties in her time, but she couldn't work this one out at all; there didn't seem to be anything theatrical about her, past the size, and Eva couldn't see how she would make use of that, unless she just pulled weights, carts full of donkeys, that kind of thing. Perhaps she was just here for the factory work, like half the country.

Jean's drink seemed to be going to her head or, more specifically, her eyes. With each gulp, they got closer to spilling over. She sniffed loudly, bringing Eva out of her reverie.

'Well, do you want to call anyone, Mrs . . . '

'Curnalia. Sorry. I didn't introduce myself. I'm Jean.'

'There's a telephone behind you.'

Jean turned. In the hallway, there was a small table with two telephones on it. A white one, its cord ripped and frayed, sat next to a functioning black one. Jean wondered at the extravagance of a broken telephone. She thought of how many days it had been since she heard Gloria's voice, and her heart stilled. She tried to summon that familiar candyfloss tone, soft and sticky, to her ears. Mrs Hammell Sr was against telephones; she said they brought bad news into a home.

'No. Thank you.'

'OK. Eat something then, English. You'll feel better.'

Jean smiled, gratefully. Eva emptied her refrigerator of food: four cold hamburgers, purchased hot late at night and forgotten after too many drinks. The hamburgers tasted of fat and paper and reminded Jean of the rare treat of white bread and dripping. She attacked the food without mercy and made such noises of appreciation that Eva was almost embarrassed; she lit a cigarette and watched Jean wolf the burgers down, then lick at her hands. The few days of starvation had reduced her back to a feral thing. Gloria had taught her how to eat properly; she had sometimes made herself sick gorging on the food denied her at home, and had to be told to slow down. Gloria was not there to tell her now. Jean noticed Eva's attention and hesitated, feeling self-consciousness creep back. She was in the world once more. Eva proffered a napkin.

'Stop before you chew down to the elbow, won't you?'

Jean took the napkin and wiped her hands. The white cloth was heavy, of good quality. Eva refilled Jean's glass and her own. Jean wondered if she remembered their first meeting, how Eva had laughed at her. With good reason, she thought, looking at herself now.

'About the other day,' Eva began, lightly.

Jean feigned ignorance. 'The other day?'

'Oh, I remember, some anyways. I was stinking. I didn't mean anything by it. Anyway, I didn't know you were . . . in trouble.'

'Neither did I,' said Jean, and Eva laughed, a little bitterly.

'We never do, do we. Didn't anybody tell you that this is where husbands come to leave their wives? There are hundreds, thousands of us here. We're the old wrecks they arrive in, and then they trade us in for something shiny and new.'

Eva laughed again, so Jean tried to as well. She thought of Denny, bringing her this far just to leave her alone, taking her away from Gloria. She had been done out of two homes at a stroke. Why couldn't he have just left her where she didn't expect anything. She sipped the bitter liquid from her glass and grimaced, then sipped again. Emboldened, Jean wondered if she and Eva might have something in common, something that would work better than pineapple and hotdogs combined.

'Did you have a husband, then?'

Eva took a deep breath. 'Oh, I had *the* husband. The original bastard. Loved him horribly, of course, but I was just a stepping

354

stone to him. Never in my life . . . '

Then she caught herself. Never let a beaten stray into your house; don't feed it; don't listen to it. Or it might never go away. She stubbed out her cigarette to break the momentum, and lit another.

'You pay rent on that place?'

The chance to find out more was gone, snatched away so quickly Jean strained to catch up. 'Yes. We . . . I . . . Charles Pace owns it. I suppose he'll be expecting his money soon. I don't even know where to find him.'

Eva refilled their glasses, hers to the brim. 'He'll find you if you owe him money, you can be sure of that. Have you got a job? What is it that you do?'

'Nothing,' Jean admitted. 'I don't do anything anymore.'

'And I take it there's no one to pay for you.'

It seemed to Jean that most people she knew had paid in some way for knowing her. But there was no one to support her, that was true. She shook her head again, thinking she could feel the oiliness of the burgers in her stomach; there seemed to be some of that oil on her eyes, too, everything was getting filmy. 'I should find him, explain. See what's what. He might . . . have an idea.'

'You're not thinking of staying, are you? How will you live?'

'How do you live?' Jean asked. It wasn't a challenge, she needed instruction.

'Independently,' Eva said, grandly. It was useful, sometimes, to have someone new to lie to; the lie itself could feel new, she could believe it for a second.

Eva saw that the pitcher was empty; perhaps she would make another, or sleep until it was time to go to a bar. Because that's what it was to be independent. The ache in her skull, not fully put down by the medicinal martinis, was gaining in strength, and she suddenly didn't want to be talking about this anymore; it felt too much like a rehearsal for what might come if she herself ever fell from favour. But she decided to give Jean a small morsel of truth to be going along with, for all the good it would do.

'You know what you should do?'

Jean was fighting the distraction of her face seemingly separating into factions. She became suddenly aware of just her sagging lower lip, then only her right eye as it was strummed by a twitching eyelid. She tried to ignore these strange sensations and focus on Eva's mouth; this was important, she couldn't afford to miss it.

'Get out.' The crisp harshness Jean had first encountered had crept back into Eva's voice, it made her flinch. 'Get out of here and go home. One day, you'll thank me for saying it: this is not the place for you.'

'But . . . I can't,' Jean replied. This, too, was the truth. How could she go back to what wasn't there?

Eva shook her head, then shrugged. 'Well, I tried; no one can say I didn't. So you'll get a room, and a job. Dressmaking.' Eva shot a glance at Jean's hands. 'Or something in a laundry, perhaps, and you'll never go home again. I'll even take you if you like, shouldn't be too hard to find somewhere cheap.'

'Thank you,' Jean said, with effort; then she thought of Denny. 'But . . . if I move, how will my husband know where to find me?'

Eva hesitated, but cruelty is best delivered all at once, drawing it out just lets it infect deeper, as she well knew. She fixed Jean with the sad smile reserved for the simple and the alone.

'But he's known all along, hasn't he?'

31

When Jean let Eva drive her away from her home, she felt her insides pull, as if her stomach was full of hooks.

It took so little time to pack her case, Jean couldn't bear to close it until the last possible minute. It contained a situation that had too quickly become real and she had to let it breathe a while longer. So she shut the bedroom door on it and went to the kitchen to write to Gloria. The attempt consumed a whole pad of the delicate onion-skin paper that was made light in order to fly great distances, but to Jean seemed too flimsy for actual events; it would have to shed her words halfway to carry on, with only a blank page landing at Gloria's feet. Sheet after sheet ended up crumpled in Jean's fist. Jean discarded even what she didn't tear with a misjudged swipe of her pen. She didn't want to write of leaving, but of arriving, of finding occupation, not losing ground. Gloria had burdens enough; Jean would wait. She burned the letters in the sink and rinsed the ashes away.

★ ★ ★

They drove, Eva powered by a furious hangover, Jean by a dull, regretful ache, to one of the dozens of single-sex establishments run by ex-actresses and showgirls for actresses and

358

showgirls to be — as blatant a prophecy as was ever ignored. There was a parlour at the rooming house in which doilies and antimacassars clung to surfaces as anemones cling to reefs. Webs of white thread smothered the arms and backs of chairs. The bookcases held mostly glass and china animals, along with a small selection of well-used paperbacks that were picked up each night by a different woman and put back half read; the next night a different one would be picked up in its place. It was all restlessness. In a room somewhere above them, someone was playing a piano with the fervour of a dying concert pianist in a women's picture, pounding out the music with such force that it rained down from the ceiling like a shower of bricks.

A blanket of unhappiness lay over the place, unrelieved by camaraderie or sympathy. Jean and Eva wandered through the public rooms; Jean noticed that those who smiled or nodded in greeting did so at her; there was no question of it being Eva who was moving in. Jean had picked a fine time and place to finally belong.

Wisteria glided into the wings of Jean's brain. She was silent, but her amusement made the back of Jean's neck prickle, the joy that she had at least managed to avoid this: the non-denominational convent of a women's boarding house, with all the fervour, repression, hopelessness and spite contained within such a proposition. Wisteria had kept her misery for herself and had not been forced to share it with anyone but her daughter, which is what she had made her for.

Wisteria's reservoirs of anger were her one

true possession. By the time she contrived to marry, she had worked for over twenty years and was getting poorer by the year. She wouldn't have been able to afford them for much longer. The unenjoyable horror of single rooms as damp as a lung, and dark dormitories where gratitude was mandatory, loomed. External forces had been about to overtake her. She didn't want to be surrounded by others like her, cheapening her life's defining characteristic. Nor did she want misery that was total and uncontrollable. What she had was to be hers alone. Wisteria wasn't able to sustain the balance for ever, being, by the end of her life, quite mad, but she attained a privacy of the mind rare among her peers.

Jean felt Wisteria more keenly than on any day since her deliverance; her mother was at her back, urging her on, into the smoke- and face-powder perfumed air of the boarding house where women lived two to a room, each in fear of being the one left behind. Jean thought she had escaped the destiny her mother had carved out for her; now she saw that she had merely backed into it while creeping around in the dark.

In Jean's desert house, the walls were white and smooth and innocent. They absorbed nothing of her; she woke up each morning in awe of their neutrality. There, her loneliness could be paralysing. She could spend long periods staring at dust on the floorboards, compelled neither to clear it away nor form an opinion on it. There she could cry in the afternoons, in the open, bare kitchen. If she moved to this house of women, where there were

360

others like her — who could perhaps understand her — she would have to give up her grief. She would instead spend her life in bitter little fights or brave pretence, trying to look as if she hadn't been kicked in the guts when she could barely walk from the pain.

Eva sauntered through the hotel as if her hide were leather; if she felt even a tremor of fear or premonition she didn't show it. The owner was showing off the sun porch, an enclosed box of unbearable stuffiness furnished with wicker chairs halfway to baskets and hothouse flowers that seemed to be pleading for mercy. A couple of the older tenants were snoozing there, mouths slack and uncaring.

'Isn't it just a dream?' The skin under the landlady's chin and arms swung together in merry agreement as she turned a full beam, store-bought smile on to Eva.

'The nightmare I wake screaming from,' Eva murmured, forgetting the brittle smile that would make it less of an admission.

The landlady's smile puckered, sourly, but she rallied when the thought of hooking an extra boarder crossed her mind. 'I can give you a great deal. Your friend's odd but you'd look good about the place, bring in the career girls. You'll pay just seventy-five per cent of what your friend does.'

★ ★ ★

Eva turned on a well-polished heel and fixed the woman with a glacial stare. 'If I return,' she

361

whispered, 'it will be to burn this place down and perhaps piss on the ashes. Now if you'll excuse me, I have somewhere to be.'

The woman's jaw worked noiselessly as Eva strode away from her, yelling Jean's name. Jean jumped at the sound of Eva's voice and crushed the plaster animal she had in her hand. It had been a Chinese dog with a green smile that reminded her of Wisteria. No one had seen her pick it up, and no one saw her place the crumbs of it in a plant pot and wipe the fragments from her palm.

'Mrs Curnalia!' Jean hurried into the hallway just in time to see Eva reach the door. 'Good luck,' she called, without turning round. There was a flash of brilliant white light as the door opened; the snap of it closing was like a bulb exploding. Eva was gone, and all was gloom again. Jean suddenly saw what this was: a magic box women stepped into that made them disappear from the outside world.

The house in the desert was clean and empty, Eva had the keys for when Pace came collecting. Jean had been transferred in a minute. At that moment, she didn't feel to be much more than a lamp. Her suitcase had been left next to the stairs; Jean carried it to her second-floor room, which was overpoweringly familiar to her, right down to the faded roses on the walls and a woman surrounded by a bitter and long-cultivated air of resentment. Her room-mate was sat up in bed smoking a cigarette, a once-pink bedjacket round her shoulders and a fan magazine spread out on her lap. The door was open, so Jean knocked on the frame; the woman raised her head.

'Who the hell are you?'

Jean didn't, couldn't answer. It was the small dark room where no one would ever come for her and her screams would go unheard, and she was walking into it of her own accord. There was no doctor, no committal: just a smooth quiet ride to the edge of town and the affordable entrance fee of having been abandoned. That was enough to secure Jean's place, alongside a woman who near as dammit was Wisteria. She thought of being back in her mother's kitchen, asking her reflection what purpose she had. 'What are you for?' she had wondered. 'What are you for, Eugenia Clocker?' she asked herself again now, the answer having more urgency now than ever. Jean could hear Wisteria's familiar coarse tones worming their way to her ears, cruel and mocking. 'Yes, you lumpy bitch. Just what are you for? What are you for, eh? What are you for?'

It roared out of Jean before she could stop it — 'A sight more than this, you old cow!' — startling the cigarette from the movie-fan's mouth. That room was the rest of her life. On the threshold of it, she made her choice.

★   ★   ★

It was dark when Jean reached the Phuture Homes Development. Her feet bled, and her throat burned, but she found her way. She would have her house and her grief and her solitude

363

because they were all she had left and she was built to endure. Eva was sitting on her back porch, holding a full glass and smoking a cigarette, when Jean returned. Eva was more rattled than she would have admitted by what she had seen that day; she knew where she could end up without patronage and feared the drab little places where a person's mistakes hung around them like stale smoke. She stared out at the desert, soothing her fears with stronger spirits than she.

Jean was audible long before she was visible; she sounded like a bear with blisters; the quick, jumpy steps of ravaged feet not disguising the obvious bulk they transported. Eva's windows cast slants of light across the dirt; she gasped when Jean stepped into one of them. Jean had torn the collar and sleeves from her red, white and blue dress, and let the bodice hang open; her scars were as livid as veins. Eva stared at them, convinced that Jean had turned herself inside out. Eva put her hand in her pocket and felt the chill of the keys to Jean's house. Without speaking, she took them and tossed them to the floor at Jean's feet. She didn't consider putting them in her hand; Eva couldn't be sure she would get the hand back. Jean crouched slowly and carefully to pick them up, her aching joints and tightening skin fighting her at every degree. Eva dug in her pocket again and drew out a couple of screwed-up small bills and some coins, which she threw after the keys.

'For breakfast,' she said. Jean collected the money without a word.

There was more joy in that turn of the key than Jean would ever be able to describe. More even than in the first. The house was very quiet and very clean, as Jean had left it. She got into bed and pulled the sheets over her dress, covering the flesh that showed through. She was still strong enough, she thought. She would go stand on the highway with the other aliens and drifters and wait for work to come. She didn't need anyone to find her a place. The underneath was where she belonged, where she should have begun. Her kind had always sought the shelter of bridges, glades and ruins. There was no need to dig; as long as everyone else kept their heads high, she could easily sink below. 'You belonged back there,' a harsh whisper told her. 'They're as close to your kind as you'll ever come across.' She ignored it, paddling slowly into the deep of an exhausted, dreamless sleep.

The only trick was persuading time to stand still on a moment, to reach the point where she was free and have nothing more after that. Extraordinary things had stopped happening to her, the bizarre no longer visited. Just the usual and the expected: absence and disappointment. As she disappeared under the surface, Jean wondered how to attract lightning into her life.

32

Jean took stock of her new situation. She owned one torn dress, three not torn, one pair of overalls, one pair of men's blue jeans, three men's shirts. Underwear. One cardigan. One man's jacket. She had the eviscerated tennis shoes, her brogues (all but finished off by the previous winter), two pillowcases, two sheets and one blanket. She gave back the radio and the refrigerator before she could default on the payments. She still had the make-up case.

It occurred to her only when she was looking under the kitchen sink for scouring powder. She had put the case there after he disappeared, the memories of a perfect night contained in its damaged jars and compacts, and found it again on the day she had been turned down for employment by every shop in the vicinity, as well as two ice-cream parlours, a bank and a slaughterhouse. He had not only left her; he had left her his livelihood. This was something for her to do. It presented itself like a last chance, she had to take it.

Jean carefully scooped the powders back into their compacts and pressed them down with a damp flannel before leaving them in the sun to dry into a cake. The lipsticks were harder to salvage; she moulded the ends with a butter knife, but they still looked stubby and irregular. She would have to drop the price considerably.

But if she could shift them, she would show Charlie Pace what a good saleswoman she could be. He would give her more stock to sell, and soon she would have paid the rent and got back the radio and might perhaps treat herself to some new tennis shoes. Using whatever small spills were left, Jean painted her own face in bright colours with broad strokes and set out to beautify the lives of women.

Had they burning torches they would have used them. Like villagers in pursuit of a monster, they chased her out. Not on foot — no one had their outdoor shoes on — but she had a mob on her heels nonetheless.

The place she chose to start was how Jean thought Phuture Developments might have been, or aimed to be when it grew up. It was the same bland, bone colour, but the houses had second storeys and neat well-tended front lawns with ornamental windmills that barely stirred in the humid air. Contentment issued from every house, from the people that moved inside them; even the lawns exhaled it. In these houses, women wore make-up indoors. It had taken Jean three hours to find such a place, and she was hopeful of success.

Air-conditioning units greeted her with a fanfare in monotone; they bulged out of every front window, humming like vast hives. Women paused in their chores to watch Jean move along the street, holding their breath as she cast about for her first victim, hands hovering over the telephone, ready to call the police, local asylum or zoo. Jean took a deep breath and knocked on her first door. She waited a minute or two for a response, and then knocked again. She thought she saw a shadow pass the window, but no one came. Still, there were plenty more to try. A curt 'Not today' was the response from the next three houses, the doors slamming in her face before she could say more than her name. It didn't seem to matter what she was selling; it wasn't wanted. Jean knocked on door after door, only to hear a vacuum cleaner start up or an interior door slam. The standard had been set; no one would admit her. One woman opened her door only to empty her dustpan over Jean's feet.

'This is a respectable neighbourhood,' she tutted, before closing the door again.

Jean was bewildered and then incensed by the hostility. She was trying her best; didn't they know that? All she wanted was to be part of it, to be like them. The next door took a hammering. She was not now knocking to be let in; she was letting them know what was on the outside.

'Bloody cows,' she muttered, tears stinging her nose. 'Bloody stuck-up cows.'

Across the street, a door opened and she heard someone call to her.

'Hey, over here. Over here.'

Jean turned, unable to believe it. Someone was giving her a chance.

'Coming!'

She sprinted across the road towards the door being held open by a middle-aged woman dressed in a very old housecoat; she had a cigarette burning in one hand; the other held a dirty cloth.

'It's too early, but come on in.'

Jean smiled and stepped over the threshold. She felt as though she had stepped into a billboard; the interior gleamed with modernity and wealth. The couches looked un-sat on, the kitchen not cooked in; the carpets spread from wall to wall and were unmarked by human traffic. It was a museum of the new. The housekeeper closed the door behind Jean, then looked her up and down seeming neither charmed nor offended, just slightly quizzical.

'If you're what they sent, the misuss ain't gonna like it. They was expecting the one from the advertisement, the one that's been on the TV show.'

'Excuse me?'

Jean couldn't work out what the woman was saying. How could she not be what was expected, when she wasn't expected at all? Jean held up the case.

'I have lipsticks, and powder too. Eye shades. Lots of colours.'

'Well no doubt, you've got half of them on you already, but you're still not the one from the advertisement. See, I'll show you.'

The woman shuffled off down the corridor and returned with a newspaper cutting. She handed it to Jean.

'The Jumbo Fun Agency,' Jean read. 'For variety and television appearances, lodge and country club events and children's birthdays, no job too small. Magicians, tumblers and . . . ' She paused, and the tears that had been threatening spilled down her cheeks, carrying the thick

369

mascara from her wadded lashes over the hastily applied rouge down to uneven scarlet lips. Jean raised her head. 'I am not,' she wailed, 'a bleedin' clown.'

★ ★ ★

Agnes — the housekeeper Jean had disturbed in her preparations for her employer's children's party — took two lipsticks and a barely distressed eyeshadow off her. She fished the money out of a tin in a kitchen cupboard.

'She won't know it's gone,' she assured Jean, and then held her thumb and forefinger at her mouth and leaned her head back to show that the lady of the house was a tippler. The sale of the make-up stopped Jean's tears. Agnes had paid her to shut up.

'Thank you,' Jean said. 'And do come again.'

'I won't say the same to you,' Agnes frowned, and hustled Jean out of the door.

★ ★ ★

She used some of the money to find Charlie Pace. His office took up an airless corner of a crumbling block; she guessed that he was not making as much as he would like people to believe. Climbing the stairs to Pace's floor, she almost lost her nerve. What was this but charity again, the exposure of herself as worthless and in need of pity? But pride had got her nowhere except laid out in the desert with the sun burning her feet and her underwear on show to

370

the world — and so she carried on. Jean had found that she was not entirely disposable, not by her own accidental hand anyway, and so had to find ways to continue. It wasn't charity, it was compensation.

It had to be someone's fault, that is what Jean had learned from Wisteria: no one will pay for something they didn't cause or contribute to. But Pace was unconvinced by Jean's claim that she was due another free week on the rent as she still had nightmares from the Indian attack (the best she could come up with at short notice). She had considered affecting a limp, but didn't wish to appear physically incapable of work. He listened to her story then shrugged his shoulders and spread his hands.

'What can I do, Mrs Curnalia? I'm a businessman. If you had come to me at the time . . . '

Jean felt momentarily lost, but Agnes had shown her the way. She took a deep breath and cried. She howled and barked, using her residual grief to power a booming display of distress. Pace could see the frosted glass of his office door crowd with heads. Jean carried on for minutes that seemed like days, and he squirmed in front of this font of misery as he never had in the face of gunfire.

'I just want a job,' Jean sobbed, when able again to speak. 'I'll be a good worker, I promise. Please, Mr Pace. If you give me a job I'll go away. Otherwise, I've nowhere else to go. I'll just have to sit outside your office every day, from eight thirty to five thirty. Every single day.'

Jean sniffed and an escaping string of mucus zinged back into her nostril. She wiped her nose with the back of her hand and then wiped her hand on her dress. Pace looked at her, sizing up his chances of getting her out of the chair and then the door unassisted. His chances were small and malnourished. Jean let her lower lip hang down to where it fell naturally into a tremble, that built rapidly to a near-spasm. Pace crumbled.

'OK, OK. You can keep the house, same rate as before, and, as it happens, I need someone to clean — I'm having trouble finding someone to go out all that way. You got the job, just don't bother me again. And you still gotta make the rent. You don't, you're out.'

★ ★ ★

Jean rode the bus as far as the lowest fare would take her, and then walked the rest of the way. She wept along with her blisters, but by the time she reached Phuture Homes, she was dry. She had no more tears, and was grateful for that. Thanks to the lessons of her childhood, Jean knew that weakness was a thing to be rationed, and rarely shown. There is a nuisance, and there is an affliction; one gets paid to go away, one gets forcibly removed.

372

33

She was glad she had kept her overalls, their
creases ingrained with brick dust. Small pieces of
England clung to her still. She covered her hair
with a handkerchief and cinched her waist with a
thick leather belt and felt a little more herself.
He had found her when she had been a worker
and being one again made her feel visible, a pin
point on a map. You can't come for what isn't
there.

Jean's duties took in Pace's office, his home,
the apartment of his mistress and the occupied
and unoccupied Phuture Homes in his possession. Occasionally a young married couple would
leave the highway, drive the gritty length of the
track to the little horseshoe and view one of
the empty houses. They would peer through the
polished windows to where the desert met the
horizon and their steps would echo on the newly
swept boards and they would fail to imagine
themselves living in such a spot. It was as if quiet
had moved in first. It lay strewn across every
floor; dislodged, it tumbled down from the tops
of wardrobes; it piled in drifts against the doors.
It unsettled those young married couples who
came looking for a place to raise screaming
families. This was a place for people who didn't
like to be reminded too strongly of life.

Jean began at Eva's. She had anticipated some
awkwardness due to her drop in status, but Eva

373

seemed pre-adjusted, geared already towards treating her like a domestic. She was grand and cold, as if greeting Jean on the steps of a marble mansion.

'Well,' she said, on opening the door. 'That makes sense. How much are you charging?'

'It's in with the rent,' Jean explained. 'Same as before.'

Eva looked puzzled, then shrugged. 'I don't handle that end of things.' She stepped aside. 'Come on in.'

Eva led Jean down the photograph-lined hallway to the kitchen. Jean was able to take in more of her surroundings this time, and saw that many of the glossy, framed prints were of the same woman. Walking past the same face sporting varying expressions gave the corridor the feel of being animated.

'Is that . . . ?' The name failed to materialise, but Jean was sure she knew her: a beautiful constant of Jean and Gloria's movie-going adolescence.

Eva paused. 'Yes,' she confirmed. 'It is. Varga James, *movie star.*'

'Me and Gloria used to love her,' Jean gushed.

Eva raised an eyebrow. 'She'll be so thrilled.' There was something in her voice akin to bones snapping. 'It's always good to know how people *used* to feel.'

Jean fell silent and tried to shrink a little. She followed Eva to the kitchen, bathroom and bedroom, nodding as Eva explained her requirements.

While Jean cleaned, Eva relaxed in a hot bath, from which occasional requests for a martini were issued. Jean put the drinks on a small wooden tray and slid them into the steam-filled room, turning her back when Eva exited in a cloud of soft cotton and perfume. While Jean collected the damp towels and emptied the sodden ashtrays, Eva sat at her dining table applying red polish to her nails, a silk kimono wrapped tightly around her cooling skin. Jean watched as she tried to control her hands long enough to get a straight stripe of colour.

She considered coughing, or asking permission to speak, wondering what her new position merited. Jean decided to simply begin talking and see how far she got. 'I hope it's not strange,' she said. 'Me like this.'

Eva paused, the brush hovering above her half-painted fingers. 'The bum who took my drink order last night was named box-office king three years in a row back when you and I were young and it didn't matter if you had a voice like a dying accordion. Never be surprised by who ends up at the bottom.'

'So, do you know lots of stars, then?' The way Eva spoke, Jean assumed she had to; and photographs were not given to just anybody.

'Sure, everyone does, here.' Eva replaced the brush in the bottle of polish and reclined in her chair; then she tapped her box of cigarettes. 'Be a dear, my nails are wet.'

Jean obliged, placing a cigarette between Eva's lips and lighting it for her. Eva took a drag, then removed the cigarette with two red-tipped fingers. She almost felt guilty at the amount of pleasure she got from being waited on, from imagining that Jean might think it usual. Jean, meanwhile, felt as if she had wandered into some amateur theatricals with no memory of her lines; she began to grow warm at the thought of ruining the scene.

'Varga James,' Eva gestured towards the hallway. 'I do all her dialogue. It's a secret, though; you won't find my name anywhere.'

'How exciting.' Jean was certain it was an appropriate response.

'Well, I guess it would be to you.' Eva laughed, and then frowned. 'But seriously, you're doing very well. You shouldn't feel ashamed.'

Jean felt on firmer ground; her only shame was in idleness. 'I don't mind the work,' she replied. 'I just want to be useful.'

'Really? I'll remember that.' Eva's sardonic smile pushed into one side of her face only.

★   ★   ★

Jean left Eva's with the feeling that she should tread carefully; there was now more than one person in her life to please, and they all had to be satisfied with her.

Mindful of their first meeting, Jean decided not to sound a warning when approaching Ermeline's house, but instead use stealth. She crept as softly as she could up the front steps, barely troubling the door with three featherlight taps. Jean felt that Ermeline would accept her when she realised what a good and quiet soul inhabited this giant's frame. When her knocks brought no response, however, she decided to go to the window.

The coloured celluloid shade Ermeline kept pulled down over her front windows rendered the outside distinctly otherworldly. Ermeline had been agitating herself with a particularly terrifying true crime novel — she took a strange comfort in tales of sex fiends preying on buxom young sluts in modern apartment buildings — and looked up from a particularly nasty strangling to see a vast, aqueous silhouette, at her window. In an instant, Ermeline commended her soul to God and her body to the floor.

Jean watched as the little woman dived below the window and then began a horizontal shuffle across the floor, her frilled arms like the forelegs of some extravagant newt in full display; dragging her towards the safety of the hallway. Jean was caught. To hammer on the window would only drive Ermeline further into a state. To retreat could mean the loss of her job. She decided she could only do what she had been instructed to: work. It was her shield.

Having already filled her bucket, Jean dipped a rag in the warm soapy water and threw it against the window, where it made a satisfying splat — not unlike the sound of a newt under a wheel. She reached to the full height of the window and dragged the rag downwards, dust and grime helpless in its path. She felt the satisfaction of the task and Ermeline's inability to stop her accomplishing at least this much. She rinsed the rag and repeated the motion; the sunlight danced on the glass, she was preparing a ballroom for it.

When Jean was on her final window, the back

door creaked open and Ermeline's bobbed head poked out into the afternoon sun.

'After that, you . . . you'd better start inside. I called Mr Pace, he said it would be all right.'

'Yes, Miss Mildmay,' Jean replied, smiling.

★ ★ ★

Jean's bungalow bore little imprint of her personality. She hadn't had the time to fix any of her life on to it and it seemed pointless now that Denny was gone. What did she care if a wall was bare or had a picture of a flower on it? Ermeline, however, had made her home her own. Everything in it was as squat and frilled as she. Anything that could not be covered with doilies had been knitted a cover. Jean had to guess at what lay under the woolly shrouds that covered each item. The larger ones, such as chairs and a piano, were easy, but there were many smaller objects that did not correspond to any shape in Jean's experience. It was commonplace to see a teapot covered in a cosy knitted from the offcuts of old jumpers but less so to see a birdcage similarly attired. A Bible as big as an encyclopaedia lay open on a wooden stand; it wore a white crocheted jacket and the stand was draped in white cloth fastened with green ribbons. Jean wondered what so offended Ermeline about furniture. And why, then, did she have so much of it? Each room strained to contain its quota of things occasional or ornamental and Jean moved in between them with tedious care. She vacuumed as if she were minesweeping.

The walls held at least a dozen yellowing photographs of Ermeline's past; from one Jean gathered that she was the daughter of a vicar and had lived somewhere with a porch strong enough to hold the twelve members of her solidly built family for as long as it took to take a photograph back then. They were a different kind of big to Jean, growing out rather than up; they looked puffed up and unhealthy, like the infected skin around a splinter. Ermeline appeared in other photographs without her family; usually standing in front of a church. She had belonged to many in her time, and was one for forming unsuitable attachments to men of the cloth. Some of the more bizarre artefacts in her collection, such as the prosthetic limbs, had been acquired as a result of these infatuations: she would become fascinated by a cause — and its instigator — for a while and would devote herself wholly to it. Ermeline took Jean on a tour of her concerns, pointing out the contents and possible recipients of each box.

'And these are the limbs I collect for veterans.'

'From who?' Jean asked.

Along with the artificial limbs were frighteningly disfigured secondhand dolls for orphans, and Bibles in foreign languages for delivery to heathen and Catholic nations. Jean made a mental list of oddities that she would send to Gloria. Though she wondered if, these days, Gloria would find it in good taste to laugh at someone who was mentally disarranged. She used to roar at Wisteria, Jean remembered with a smile.

'As for these,' Ermeline was pointing to a box of ladies' shoes, all at least twenty years out of fashion and, sadly, all too small for Jean, 'put them in the carport, they're no longer required.' The Reformed Women of Vice of America had fallen, once again — this time from Ermeline's favour. The minister who had enlisted her help in collecting used clothing for these used women had declared his intention to make one of the women more honest than the others. Ermeline's attachments would often end before the mission could be completed — a whispering campaign through the congregation, the pained appeal of the cleric himself, or his wife or spinster sister — and the fruits of her labours would go undistributed, to the detriment of legless veterans and heathens everywhere.

She read passages from the Bible — a smaller edition than the one in the woolly jacket — throughout Jean's visit, rocking slightly, her lips pressed together but still moving, as if she were trying to keep something small and alive from escaping her mouth.

★ ★ ★

Jean's routine was soon well established. There was one other occupied house, but this was taken by a nightworker at the plant who she never saw and whose presence was detectable only by the odour of engine oil, which, at a low level at all times, peaked when he was home and asleep. He kept his bedroom door shut and left no instructions. Jean cleaned what she saw and could only guess at the rest. Sometimes, when she felt daring, she would listen to his radio while she swept sand into the yard. It reminded her there was a wider world, and people in it that had some connection to her.

To supplement her income, she joined the fruit pickers and waited at the side of the highway to be chosen. On the days she was passed over, she stayed at home, and practised being still. She purchased a new onion-skin pad and set down fresh lies for Gloria. One married woman writing to another. Cleaning awarded Jean rights and liberties she would never otherwise have enjoyed. Moving freely about her neighbours' homes gave her the illusion of intimacy; in the absence of a life of her own, theirs would do. She told Gloria about Eva and the famous actress, promising to get an autograph should Varga James ever come to visit; she listed the colours of Eva's shoes and the contents of Ermeline's collection boxes. She described everything around her, only her letters came from the centre of a blind spot — everything but him. 'Best to Jack,' she remembered to end. 'Best to Denny,' Gloria knew enough to reply. Jean's bank was a jar under the sink, with a second, smaller jar next to it. The first was for rent and food. She would add to the smaller jar when she could; it was for finding him somehow. Because even with occupation, she lacked purpose. The 'what' she was for had lately become muddled with the 'who'.

It was only on making her second payment to

Pace that Jean realised she was surviving. One week was a valiant last stand, two was a declaration of intent. She demolished one day after the other, met it like an enemy at dawn and accepted its surrender each night. She understood being alone; it was not a new discovery, the knowledge was buried deep within her: work must never be finished. She scrubbed her own floors every evening and wished she had more clothes to wash. At least the desert had to be kept at bay, and she pursued every grain that infiltrated her home and cursed those that hid between floorboards, trembling at her approach. But a body such as hers was hard to decommission. There was still something pent up in her that she couldn't exhaust. So she ran. The impulse hit one night when she was pegging out clothes in the yard, and it spirited her away. She ran until her house was just a bead of light. And then she began to scream. Like a vent of steam in cracked earth, heated anger poured from her. She cursed him, herself and everyone in existence. She swore until she ran out of words and then sang at the top of her voice. She demonstrated life where no one had a hope of seeing it. She returned coated in dust, and fell into bed where she slept for hours.

Running, she felt her legs lengthen and the air rush over her body and the energy that had gone unspent come spewing forth. Energy he used to take from her, in their bed, even when he was asleep. Her strength was impressive but not endless. A night of drawing the horror from him, taking in his fear and filtering it through her before expelling it, harmless, with her breath, left Jean hollowed out. There was nothing here now that could consume her so. At school Jean had half heard a phrase she had never before understood about fixing courage to a sticking place. Now she thought of it each time she returned, breathless and burning. This was her sticking place and she needed every ounce of her courage to come back to it.

After five weeks, she asked Pace to let her pay by the month. He gave her the same speech he had given Denny about the road that would come and the prices that would rocket, and then agreed to fix the rent for a few months more. She now had to last more than a week at a time. She wouldn't sicken, wouldn't shrivel, wouldn't waste to an appropriate size. She would endure.

But on those evenings when the heat put a heel on the last rays of the sun so they struggled to roll up to the sky, and the moon was as thin as tracing paper, all but ignored by the overstaying day, Jean felt the world slow, and her sentence increase, and she wondered what it would be like to come apart. Whether it could really feel worse. On those evenings she rubbed emollients into her scars and flexed her obedient muscles and prayed to stay strong. She would never be enough otherwise.

34

When the Smiths' shop burned down there were fifty bags of black-market sugar in the basement. The smell of caramel hung over the site for days.

It was a beautiful fire; the shop was full of newly delivered rations as well as illicit supplies. Hard-boiled sweets cracked open and disgorged lit rivers of liqueur, jars exploding in the heat showered the flames with rainbow crystals that formed multicoloured flows of sweet lava, snaking down cabinets and across the linoleum. Chocolate poured from the shelves onto the burning counter, resin and confectionery bubbling together in a stinking brew. The shop melted like a witch's house. Days after the fire had cooled, and the ruins hardened into candy-lacquered shapes, the bravest of the local children would break pieces off and test the flavours with the very tips of their tongues.

The heat had pulsed ahead of the fire, coursing through the walls like blood, spreading quickly to the upstairs where Gloria's father and mother lay suffocating on sweetened smoke. Their treasured letters from her went first, they had been left in a bundle at the back of a bureau, pressing against the wall that ignited them. If lies were asbestos they would have survived the inferno; Gloria's lovingly deceitful words became mist as the ink evaporated from the paper. Her parents had not been told of Jack's illness; they would die believing her the happy wife of a handsome, healthy soldier. On the flock-papered walls, the photographs of Gloria, their painstaking biography of her charmed life, began to warp and shrivel. They had bought an expensive frame for their favourite, Gloria sitting in bright American sunshine, her hair as white as the sky, with a child of about six months in her lap. Their eyes were the same, pale in the centre with a dark outer ring, and his light hair disappeared into hers where their heads touched. There was so much of their little girl in him, they saw. And so much love in her.

Gloria had decided it was about time her parents had a grandchild and this one was as like her as any natural child could be, so she'd sent the lie to her parents for safe keeping. His mother was in her sewing circle, and was the only one to invite Gloria to her home. Gloria had memorised his every detail and embroidered upon them to make herself a son, who she called William, after her father. William came briefly alive in her letters, and Gloria did too. But fire can overwhelm even what isn't true and a single flame eventually burst through the centre of the photograph, as if Gloria's heart were ablaze.

When she received the telegram, Gloria thought she could smell powdered sugar on it, as she used to on her mother's cheek. There was nothing left to go back to now.

Jean's mailbox stood to the side of the house, like a lonely sentry. On the last Friday of her third month alone there were two items inside. One was a photograph of her. The sun had

385

stolen her face — a ball of white light sat where it should have been — but the body was unmistakably hers. It was from the reel Denny had taken of her posing in the two-piece bathing suit. The photograph had been sent in an envelope that was postmarked with a smudge, there was no letter and nothing was written on the back of the print, although there was space for perhaps fifty words. There was not even a pencil mark to suggest he had tried and failed. All it said to her was, here, have this back. I don't want it anymore. Jean knew from the war that some took disappearance worse than death. Or at least took it longer.

The other was the telegram informing her that the Smiths were dead. The shop was gone, the wall of photographs burned up. It was as if England had finally sailed over the horizon into the past. If it wasn't for Denny, Jean would have burned too. Or survived more people better than herself. Jean emptied the jar of the money put aside for finding her husband. He was not lost. He knew exactly where he was. But she was now adrift.

She squeezed herself into a drugstore phone booth and arranged the money on the shelf in front of her. She supposed she could have given the money to Eva and begged the use of her telephone, but the words she wanted to speak could not be heard by anyone else — they would be the first of love she had spoken for a while and were too fragile for the common air. The clicks and whirrs of the unfathomable technology it took to join her to Gloria seemed to mimic

386

Jean's fluttering insides. An unfamiliar voice asked if it could help, and Jean stammered out Gloria's name. A silence you could drop a coin into followed, but then Gloria whispered to her, and she felt her home rise from the waves.

'You go first, Jean.'

'I can't. You.'

'No. Not yet.'

'I don't know what to say,' Jean admitted. 'Everything's terrible.'

At this, Gloria broke down. Jean listened to the strangely dislocated sounds of grief; they were ugly and bare, gurgles and glottal stops spewing down the wire, stripped of humanity by the machine that carried them. It was a minute or more before Gloria could speak again.

'Oh, Jean, it's not been worth it, none of it has.'

Jean knew it was the last thing she should tell Gloria, but also that it had to be said. There would be no more pretending.

'I know. Denny's gone too.'

Gloria exhaled in a rush. 'Oh God, the joke's really been on us, hasn't it? Well at least I can tell the truth now. Finally.'

Jean understood and nodded sadly, then remembered she was on the telephone.

'Yes.'

'Just as well. I can't even invent good news anymore. I told Mum and Dad so many lies, I can hardly remember them all. I get so used to it. I go to the butcher's and I say, 'Yes, he's doing fine, thanks. Won't be long now.' I wait in line at the bank, and say, 'For the time being,' when they ask me if they're to deal with Sally or me instead of Jack. And I don't really mind. They think they're sparing my feelings but they're just wasting my time. So many lies, Jean; I should be ashamed. I go places, I get on the train to where no one'll know me and I tell people different names and different stories. I tell them I've got babies and a husband and that we go on picnics. I don't want to do it anymore. I just want my mum and dad. I won't even be there to bury them.'

Gloria started to cry again. Jean couldn't think how it must be for her; all that love slowly slipping away. First Jack's, then her parents'. It had taken so much of it to make her as she was, Jean wondered if she could be sustained without it.

'I wish I could be there; I wish there was something I could do. Shall I send a telegram?'

'I suppose.' Gloria sniffed. 'Auntie Midge is coming down to arrange things. Send the cable to the funeral parlour. It's Barkers off the High Street.' Gloria sniffed again, and then coughed, trying to regain control. 'We can never go back now, never.'

'No. Did you think you might?'

'I did, but then I started lying, and I couldn't see a way around it; it would have all come out. I've made such much a mess of it all.'

'Oh, Gloria, I'm so sorry.'

'I know. I wish you were here. No one else knows them. I can't say, 'Do you remember when . . . ' to anyone, 'cos they don't remember. They haven't got a clue. I'm worried I won't be able to remember it all on my own. Then they'll just be gone.'

'I remember. I'll write it down. In every letter, I'll put something down. Like the vanilla essence.'

'Vanilla essence?'

'Your mum wore it once because there was no more perfume and it had gone all funny, do you remember?'

'Oh my God, yes. She smelled like sick.'

Gloria laughed, a little snort of air from her nose. It amazed Jean that the phone could convey a breath over such a distance. She inhaled the sound, filling her lungs with Gloria.

'Will you really do it? Every letter?'

'Of course.'

'You're never going anywhere, are you? Take a bomb to shift you.' Gloria spluttered then sniffed again, while Jean smiled. Yes, it would take that much. Because there were better reasons than hers to stick in this place. Better reasons not to come apart. 'So, tell me all about it, then, while I've got you here. When did he go?'

'Weeks and weeks ago.'

'Bastards, int they?' She swore much more casually, now. 'We should have stayed English you and me. Did he tell you or just bugger off?'

'One day he was there, and then . . . I didn't even wake up.'

'Typical. How you doing for money?'

'All right. I'm cleaning, and fruit picking.'

'Oh, right. We'll see you on your holidays, then. Coming on the clipper, are you?'

'I'm fine, really. But I'd come see you if I could.'

'I know. Well, millionaires for us next time, then. But you're sure you're all right?'

'Yeah. You know. Surviving.'

She could hear Gloria draw on a cigarette, her next question came wreathed in smoke.

'Wasn't there any warning at all?'

'I suppose there was. But I got used to it in the end. It's like being in a raid. The first few times you stay up all night worrying about getting hit and then after that it's just boring and you get a bit tired and you sort of stop thinking about it and play cards till you fall asleep. And then you wake up, or you don't.'

'And one day you didn't.'

'No. I was just getting used to him.'

'That's rotten. Do you miss him?'

Jean was supposed to be no better than a cripple, meant to keep longing shut tight inside a ruined body. But however ruined her body was, it still craved him. The violence of it surprised even her.

'I do,' she whispered. 'I really do.'

'I hate Jack.' Gloria declared, quickly before she could change her mind. This might be her last chance in this life to say it.

'Really?'

'I do. I hate him. I can't stand seeing him sit in that chair and look at bleedin' begonias all day like the rest of us can just get on with it without him. My mum and dad are dead and he . . . It's not bloody fair.'

Jean was uncertain how to react. Gloria had always been so sentimental about weakness, back when it was her choice to surround herself with

390

it. 'I see,' she replied, weakly.

'Don't 'I see', Jean, please. Tell me I'm awful, or tell me I'm mad, but don't say, 'I see.' I get enough of that from the sodding doctors. They're always asking you how you feel and then when you tell them, 'Oh, well, doctor, since you ask I think I'm going off my head waiting for my husband to break it off with that pot plant,' they say: 'I see.' See what? They never bloody say. Don't say it, Jean. Don't.'

'No, I won't. I just . . . I don't know what to say. Is he that bad still?'

'Worse. He looks horrible, Jean. He looks like he just *melted*. His face runs down over his collar and his neck's somewhere inside his shirt and his hair's all long and stuck to him. It's horrible. He's nothing like the man I . . . He's changed. It happened really quickly, as well. I went for two weeks without a visit and when I came back he was like that. I thought they'd just left him in the window too long. I asked them to move him, I thought it would help.'

'Did it?'

'Of course not. He didn't really melt, Jean. He's not a toffee.'

'No, sorry.' Jean headbutted the wall to punish her brain.

Button Up's office was just a corner of the storeroom, partitioned by the curtain. The telephone was fixed to the wall and a chair had been placed next to it. A pharmacist's chest, dark wood with dozens of slim drawers, stood against the wall. Each compartment held a different shade of ribbon, with four inches or so hanging out of the drawer for easy identification. It looked like a tiny tenement that was having a parade. Gloria sat under the multicoloured streamers trying to work out how things had brought her to this. Sometimes she thought she should just move into the bathchair next to her husband and live out her days nodding and drooling. But it seemed her kind of madness wasn't the right kind for that, it was just despair. She ground her cigarette out underfoot, adding to the little heap of butts already there. This was where she would get her daily update from the hospital and feel the desire to run course through her; she would sit and smoke until it had passed.

'Jean?'

'Yes.'

'Do you think we're being punished?'

'Whatever for?'

'Paul Bradshaw.'

Jean's palms bloomed with moisture; she remembered the feel of his blood on her hands as she crawled through the grass.

'What made you think of that?'

'I think of him all the time. Don't you?'

Paul's front teeth, nestled in Gloria's handkerchief, rattled in Jean's memory.

'No. I mean I haven't, not for a long time.'

She tried to remember all of it, but only pieces of that night flashed across her mind, like heat lightning. In the second she thought she had killed him, the world ended. Everything that would have been ceased and was suspended in space for a moment. Long enough for her to

392

catch a glimpse. But he lived. The world began again. Changed.

'So, do you think we're being punished?'

The operator cut in to tell them the time they had left. Jean jumped, knocking her head against the light in the booth. She could hear Gloria gasp at the other end of the line.

'I hit my head.'

'I bit my tongue. Do you think they listen?'

'No. They don't know who we are anyway.'

'No. I s'pose not.' But Gloria's voice was lower, and Jean had to strain to hear. 'So, do you?'

The night she had run Paul Bradshaw into a tree was the night Jean learned there was a lack of consequence in the world. Gloria had been raised in a moral universe, where good was rewarded and evil punished. Jean, meanwhile, had been raised by a psychopath.

Gloria persisted. 'Do you?'

Jean didn't know. According to Wisteria, her birth had been an act of random, excess brutality. Jean was little better than a burglar that split old ladies' skulls *after* taking their silver — her existence had been crime enough, her size was uncalled for. If something is deserved, Jean wondered, does that make it inevitable? Should she be punished for running Paul Bradshaw into a tree when she had endured much more? It seemed to her that God, or something like it, played favourites. But what of Gloria? That wouldn't work for her. She was a favourite, or had been. No wonder it made so little sense to her.

Jean knew that Gloria must have whatever she needed from her friend. 'Yes, I do.'

'I knew it. For Harry too. For all of them. Maybe it's done now.'

It was a relief. Her voice was calm, quietly triumphant, though softened to a whisper for the seconds that remained for them.

'Do you remember how I was? How I couldn't wait to fall in love and get married?'

'I remember.'

'I used to think life wasn't worth living otherwise. Your mother always said I was more bosom than brain.'

Jean tutted, and thought she heard a dry, sour chuckle echo back to her along the line.

'I could live without this, though,' Gloria continued. 'I could well live without this. If I'd known . . . well, things would have been different, wouldn't they?'

Jean couldn't say. She looked at her arm, the scars laced round her forearm that told her that pain was better than death. Sometimes she believed them, sometimes she didn't. They had very little time now.

'I was happy.' Gloria sounded no more than twelve years old. 'I never lied. But in the end, I was happier with the idea of him. Proper fairy tale, eh? Didn't see it coming. But then I never could finish a book. Sally says we can't dwell on things, just have to get on with it. She sounds like my mum when she says it.'

At the end, all Gloria had cared about was protecting her parents from the truth and, now they were dead, she was left with the lies. They were poor compensation for the loss of her past. Jean had nothing to say, she just wanted to listen to Gloria for ever. She didn't want to be alone again without even a voice in her ear.

Gloria broke the silence. 'Am I good?' she asked. 'Even now?'

'Yes.'

'Am I pretty?'

'Prettier than ever.'

'Will we ever be together again? Like it was?'

'I don't — '

The operator cut them off before Jean could finish. The receiver that had just been lively with Gloria was inanimate again, a blackened bone. Jean replaced it in the cradle. Gloria was nowhere she could touch, nowhere she could see, but she was alive. Sometimes it has to be enough just to know a person is in the world and living.

The brief winter had arrived, damp and pawing. Unlike in England, the air didn't punish a person for going outside, but neither did they feel the relief of leaving its grasp. When Jean left the drugstore, it enfolded her in a charged embrace, lifting the hair from her arms. She could smell the coming rain. The storm broke as she let the road for the desert, water hitting her back like the insistent prodding of a hundred fingers: 'Do something.'

35

The rain was just the start of things. Winds whispered; sand crept, muttering, across the desert floor; Jean's scars bristled with irritation: 'Do something.' When she ran, she only gathered energy and saw it spray from her fingers onto the metal of the screen door. 'Do something.' I'm doing my bloody best, she thought, as pressures both atmospheric and psychic bore down on her. From Denny, more photographs arrived; her face eclipsed by the sun in each of them. Jean read the postmarks but her imagination couldn't create real places she had never seen, and so he remained in a colourless, dimensionless limbo, the swirl of not-quite black she saw when she closed her eyes.

With the rains, the fruit pickers moved indoors to the canneries, and Jean tried to follow. Lining up the cans to be sealed scared her, the machine moved as quick as a fist, and she froze, causing cans to pile up and fall from the belt, their contents floating free on a syrup slick. She went back to the highway but the skies stayed dark and no one came looking to hire. Luckily, some things are always in season.

Eva lived in a cyclone of drunkenness and regret that was independent of the weather. A week after Jean had been let go by the cannery, she discovered Eva unconscious on the thick rug she had swiped from the set of a high-society comedy. Eva supplemented her allowance with these thefts, decorating her home and expanding her wardrobe via the prop cupboards and costume rails of Varga's productions. She didn't think anyone noticed, and Varga stayed silent and wrote the cheques. Jean had passed days of inactivity waiting to go about her rounds; she had almost hoped for something like this. She carried Eva to the bathroom, where she stripped her — Eva was wearing one purple and one black shoe, a blue skirt, no underwear, a stained white blouse, a rose-pink jacket and a red hat; in the circumstances she could only be grateful that she had fallen over sideways on her way out and lost consciousness — and lay her on the floor while the tub filled. Her body was scattered with bruises, both fresh and faded, and gave off the scent of alcohol. Jean checked her head for blood, then felt her arms and legs for breaks. The god of drunks had looked out for Eva, turning bone to rubber as she fell. Her eyes fluttered open as Jean lowered her into the tub, Jean hesitated, fearful she had gone too far, but Eva blinked her assent, sighing as the water closed around her. Jean held her head and scooped water over her hair, face and throat.

'I have no idea who you are,' Eva slurred, then giggled.

'I'm Jean.'

'Then I have no idea who I am.'

'You're Eva.' Jean's tone was patient, but scolding, as when dealing with a child telling spiteless lies.

'Wrong!' Eva slapped her hand against the

water, scoring the point, then lay back in the tub, eyes closed, a triumphant smile on her face.

After a few moments, she smile faded; she was asleep. As Jean scrubbed at the nicotine stains on Eva's fingers, she thought how this was not so different from giving her grandmother a bath; just a body resigned to decay. Jean rinsed Eva's hair, then spread thick towels on the floor and placed Eva on them, wrapping her tightly before carrying her to bed.

Eva had been active since Jean's last visit, eradicating all traces of cleanliness and order. As she slept, Jean gathered the clothes from the floor and set the chairs back on their legs; photographs, torn from an album, were scattered about like stepping stones. In one, Varga and Eva stood at the edge of the ocean with their arms wrapped around each other, squinting at the sun that danced on the water behind them, their half-smiles making a perfectly symmetrical whole. Jean stared at it for a few moments before tucking it back into the album. There were some things you had to wait to be told. She put the album on Eva's dressing table and went in search of more to do. She emptied ashtrays and beat rugs and polished furniture; she found a cupboard full of stained sheets and scrubbed them all clean. (Eva could see into her yard from her bedroom and when she woke she thought she was at sea, with a view of white flags fluttering on lines.)

When the last sheet had been pegged out, Jean returned to her own home in search of a recipe; she would not repeat the disaster of the pineapple and the hotdogs, and carefully reviewed those culled from the radio. Eva was dressed and sitting on her back porch smoking a cigarette by the time Jean got back. Her wet hair had been pushed under a silk scarf, her eyes were hidden behind dark glasses; she was dressed simply in wide trousers and a loose, thick sweater. Jean knew now how thin and slack she was under the false shoulders and expensive foundations; a little of that showed through. Eva looked tired and a little bewildered; how someone must, Jean supposed, when they miss parts of their own life. Parts that might explain the rest.

'Hello.' Jean had hoped to have the food ready, making it an irrefusable feast. 'You're awake.' (Please don't send me away, she thought.) 'I thought I'd do you some breakfast. I usually let you sleep, but . . . I thought you might like some today.'

Eva tapped her cigarette and a flurry of ash fell. 'I forgot it was your day. I . . . I had an errand, but I wasn't well. I shouldn't have tried to go. This damn flu . . . '

She pushed up her glasses to rub her eyes, and Jean saw the green-blue flesh under them, as plump and sick-looking as an oyster on the turn. Eva pushed the glasses down again, gave a tight little smile, then took three pre-selected bills from her pocket and held them out.

'I'd appreciate it you not mentioning this to Pace. Morals clauses and so on. It's a dump, but it's home, and I hate moving. In fact, just keep it to yourself all round. Loose lips, remember?'

Eva's voice could change the temperature in a room and deliver the sweetest words with a sting, but today it housed an unfamiliar tremor. She could not quite manage to play the part; even Jean could see that, as she declined Eva's offer.

'No need. I won't tell. And no one saw.' Eva's shoulders relaxed a fraction. Jean smiled, and gestured hopefully towards the kitchen. 'What you need is a good breakfast.'

Eva's chin twitched. 'So you're going to look after me, is that it?'

Jean knew it suddenly. If there seemed little more than dogged inevitability to her own survival, Eva's presented a challenge. There was more to do here.

'There's no one else.'

'No one else?'

'No one else that needs me.'

Eva raised her chin, straining for an attitude of haughty defiance — difficult in one recently rescued from the floor and given a bath. 'I don't need you.'

Jean smiled, undeterred. 'But you could use me, though.'

She made for the kitchen before Eva could order her out. Eva let her go, lowering her glasses once more to give the departing Jean a hard, appraising stare. She had spent half her life in a place where self-interest paraded naked down the street; her marriage had been part of a stratagem, her confidence a business opportunity. This was novelty. She flicked her cigarette onto the desert floor then followed Jean inside.

'What do you want, English?' Eva folded her

400

arms and leaned against the doorframe, watching Jean's arm shake as she beat six eggs into submission. Eva could feel the trembling of her own fingers and pushed them deeper into her skin to still them; she was in control here.

'I told you,' Jean replied. 'I just want to be useful.'

'And that's all?'

Jean didn't turn; she didn't want the eggs to lose their volume. This would be a good breakfast, perhaps the first of many.

'That's all.'

And from Eva, it was all she wanted. What she wanted of herself, that was a different matter, lately.

Eva removed and folded her glasses; she was really going to do this. The last time she had invited someone into her and Varga's lives, the results had been disastrous, and expensive. But Eva sensed something different in Jean, the combination of an honest, willing disposition with a curious moral blankness. And it was only an errand, just something she didn't want to do herself; Jean didn't need to know more than that. 'About that errand . . . I don't suppose you could do it for me, could you? I'd pay you.'

Jean nodded, enthusiastically. 'Of course.' Of course she would: what else was she for?

'But I need to know I can trust you, really trust you.'

Jean set the eggs down. 'Oh, you can, cross my heart.'

'It's a medical matter, on behalf of a friend. It's kind of tricky, she can't go to the doctor for

401

herself. All she needs is a few harmless pills, anyone can get them, anyone who's trustworthy. I just wish I could tell . . . I just wish I knew more about you.'

Jean took a deep breath; if that's what it took, then that's what it took. Eva would have her assistance. 'Once, before the war, I ran a boy into a tree. He was going to hurt my friend. No one knows.'

Blushing, she turned her attention back to the eggs, wondering if Eva would now have her deported for being a violent danger to society, or just thrown straight into prison. Eva placed a cigarette between her lips to stop them twisting into a smile. It wasn't quite the insurance policy she was looking for — the confession sounded almost sweet to her — but she knew it was real enough to Jean, and that she had just been handed power over her.

'Well, OK, then.' She flipped open the lid of her cigarette lighter. 'Now we're in it together.'

★   ★   ★

Jean sat in the waiting room of a doctor known for his liberal prescribing of chemical joy; a week's rent, awarded in advance, sat in the jar under her sink. She had never made such easy money in her life, and wondered at, and was grateful for, the poor woman laid so low as to require her services. She was ignorant of the fact that it was Varga James.

Varga's acting style had evolved in tandem with her medication: opiates had carried her, heavy-lidded and seductive, from her first films to the peak of stardom. She seemed permanently ready to fall into or out of bed and spent most of her time in a kimono and glass-heeled slippers. By the time she was in her thirties — the amphetamine phase — she had tightened. Her hands clenched and unclenched constantly, her eyebrows were permanently arched and her mouth lost its sensuous curve. In her forties, she looked permanently on the verge of a scream. The studio doctor had nurtured each era, then introduced the next. But Varga was no longer his favourite child, and her needs were growing past his inclination or instruction to cater to them. Varga was being slowly cut off and found her fellow actresses to be jealous hoarders when it came to pills, they feared the cessation of their production more than that of peroxide. Eva was told to make up the shortfall however she was able. She had been many things since coming west to join Varga, but procurer was a role too far; at least, this way. So into the breach stepped Jean.

Jean ran through her prepared speech as next to her a child roamed over its mother, hot and discontented in knitted jacket and booties. Its splayed hand, resembling a soft pink starfish, waved in the air, looking for leverage. Jean swallowed guiltily and moved her elbow into its path, just enough to bring them into contact. Once the child's hand had found her arm, it began to drag itself toward her, eager to explore new territory. She felt the fumbling little fingers gather her flesh, squeezing and kneading as it climbed. Its head dropped into the crook of her elbow and Jean became aware of the wet hardness of toothless gums as it began to suck on her arm. She admired its audacity, taking on someone so many times its size, but the surge of feeling she expected did not occur. There was only relief when the child's mother pulled it away.

'I'm sorry, she's real hungry.'

The mother was young and very pretty, with the same dark hair and red cheeks as her child. Jean shrugged.

'It's all right. No harm done.' She subtly turned her arm in against her side and wiped the baby's spittle on her skirt.

'How many do you have?'

'Oh . . . ' Jean tried to remember the story Eva had provided her. She would be given a new background for each medic she saw — needlessly so as it would turn out: they were only too happy to dope or pep up the restless female population. She chewed on her lip and squinted then looked at the ceiling. The young mother followed Jean's eyes with cautious concern. Eventually she had it. 'One.'

The mother nodded and patted her hand.

'Seems like more, doesn't it? I understand. I don't know what I'd do without Dr Gillforth. I could sleep through a five-alarm fire these days.'

Her voice was filled with weary gratitude. She absently rubbed the child on its back as it stood up on her lap to get a better hold on her earrings. Jean wondered if she might keep a few of these tablets for herself. Sleeping a little longer each night couldn't hurt; there was quite a lot of day left at the end of the interest she took in it. Her nightly runs could be replaced by a pill.

A stout nurse in crisp white appeared at the doorway to the waiting room and called Jean's name. 'Mrs Curnalia. Come through, please.'

Jean smiled at the mother with her red-faced baby, which was now working hard on swallowing a green paste earring, and followed the nurse. The mother frowned as she tried to recall where she had heard the name before, everything was such a fug. From some reason she thought of lipstick; then she remembered. 'You see that lady,' she whispered in her baby's ear, 'she has the same name as mommy's special friend, the make-up man. Do you remember him? We miss him, don't we?' It had been many months since she had seen him, and she would be remembered by him for little more than the ways in which she differed from his wife, who held his imagination while his body ranged over time and distance. The baby cried as its mother took the earring from its mouth.

Jean recited her story as Eva had given it to her. It was an American tragedy; seduced, abandoned, working all hours in a sweatshop with the baby asleep beside her. She needed to be awake for her work, but at night she couldn't sleep, despite the exhaustion, because of the noise from all the other divorced mothers in the home, calling for their babies and lost husbands. Eva had wanted to make her scars the result of a tenement fire but Jean refused; for some reason she didn't want to lie about them, feeling she should have one true thing about her. Thoroughly unmoved by Eva's confection, Jean delivered the lines as best she could and waited to be laughed out of the surgery. The elderly doctor looked at her over the top of his half-moon glasses.

'Female trouble, eh? Well, let's take a look at you.'

He hustled her onto a table and into stirrups and examined her with the delicacy of a park-keeper clearing leaves from a gutter. When he was done, Jean eased herself off the table, its rubber cover sticking to her sweat-drenched legs.

'You're a healthy enough young thing,' he told her when they were sitting opposite each other again. 'You'll have another.' Jean glanced at the notepaper in her bag. Had she said her child had died? She couldn't remember now that she was feeling sick and dizzy.

'You need to rest. I'll give you something for that. And something for the concentration, keep you going at work. And something for those other times, you know. Time of the month and all.'

He handed her a piece of paper.

'Take this to the nurse, let her know if you want to take your repeat now. You have cash, don't you?'

★　★　★

Eva had directed Jean to a side entrance at the studio, and was waiting for her. The same dull grey as the wall it was set into, the door would have escaped the notice of anyone who didn't know it was there. In fact, the only unusual thing about it was Eva, dressed as a seventeenth-century French courtier, propping it open with an immaculately shod foot. Her small breasts had been pushed up into little domes, crowning the top of the richly patterned bodice; her skirt looked as though a sideboard was hidden under it and a packet of cigarettes nestled in her towering wig. As instructed, Jean had placed the bottles of pills in a lunch pail, and she presented this to Eva with a small sense of pride. She had done well.

'I like your dress.' Eva was calculating the haul, leaving Jean to make conversation. 'Are you in a film, then?'

Satisfied, Eva put the pail on the floor and took the cigarettes from her hair, offering one to Jean.

'Varga likes me to be on set when she's shooting, in case the script isn't going well.' Eva did not mention the medicine chest she brought to the set, on which Varga's initials were inlaid in gold. 'I got roped in to being an extra. You only see the back of my head, but the dress is fun.' She patted the newly formed mounds nestling atop the dress. 'It's nice to have something to lose your jewellery down, besides the couch.'

Jean agreed and took a deep drag on her cigarette. She let the smoke chase out the smell of the doctor's office that was lingering in her nostrils. She ached a little still, but felt she had indeed done well.

'You got three months', right?'

Jean nodded.

'OK, then, we'll send you back in a few weeks. Maybe somewhere different. And ask for these ones again, no diet pills, we want the good stuff.' Eva paused. 'Can you take it?'

Jean nodded again and Eva took the pail and discarded her cigarette.

'Thanks, Jean, I owe you one.'

Jean blushed with pleasure.

'Do you know how to get home from here?'

'I think so.'

'Here.' Eva pressed two bills into Jean's hand. 'For a taxi. Now get out of here. You're . . . memorable.'

'Oh. Sorry.'

Eva gathered her skirts. 'Help me with the door, will you? Manoeuvring this thing is like docking with a blimp.'

Jean pulled back the door. It was like raising the curtain on a world in flux; it dazzled Jean as it disorientated her — she had never seen so much life. Roman centurions in tunics strolled with dancing girls in nude net suits; white horses protested at their green-sequinned bridles as they were led by a red-wigged clown; a man with skin the colour of bitter chocolate performed a solitary dance, the silk lapels of his elegant tuxedo flashing in the sun, his feet a blur — so fast they were more sound than movement. Jean saw a dozen countries and a hundred ages in one glance, and felt the chaos pull at her. This was the overspill from fiction, where things were neither real nor unreal. A place to be lost in, if it would take you. She felt her weight shift to the balls of her feet, but before she could fall into its spell, the handle was pulled from her grasp; Eva, sailing through the door in a sideways motion, was closing it behind her. Jean stayed, waiting, hoping the grey door in the grey wall would open again and give up more of its fabulous secret, but it stayed resolutely shut.

★   ★   ★

She decided to save the taxi fare and walk to where the trolley cars ran, fancying a ride on the roofless top deck, where she might catch a sniff of the sea — if she went in the right direction. On foot, there was more to the town than Jean would have guessed: before it had seemed to consist only of mansions masquerading as temples; now she saw picture houses robbed from Egyptian tombs and department stores conjured from the shells of cruise liners; a Spanish ranchhouse offered cars rather than cattle for sale. Nothing played itself. Jean stopped outside a store, dressed down to resemble a mere automobile factory, that had a live demonstration in every window. A pre-fabricated banner announced the 'Woman of Tomorrow'; Jean moved closer to get a look at the creature.

There were several to choose from. In the first window, a lone housewife wearing a petrified grin performed a ballet of chores: she vacuumed around the edges of her voluminous gown; executed neat pirouettes in time to catch pieces of toast emerging at speed from a polished machine; dodged an ironing board that dropped from, and then raised itself back to, the ceiling; and basted a turkey that, every so often, trundled out of a remote-controlled oven with the solemnity of a funeral cortège — all choreographed to a feminised martial beat that poured from a tannoy attached to the overhanging canopy.

In the next window, a woman in greying underwear was being hosed with foam; the wide horizontal collar around her neck protected her hair and make-up, and also gave her the look of a performing poodle that had mastered walking on its hind legs. Fully covered, she took a turn around the display area, her arms raised, foam oozing into her high, white shoes, while another tannoy announced: 'The woman of yesterday had to scrub!' The woman paused, centre stage, and a jet of clear water was turned on her, washing the foam into channels cut into the floor and revealing snow-white underwear against reddening skin. 'The woman of tomorrow does not scrub!' crowed the tannoy, as the woman skipped off hurriedly to polite applause from the assembled audience.

The last window had drawn the greatest crowd; Jean had to shoulder her way through to the front, where marvels were found. There were perhaps a dozen women, some reading, others smoking and drinking cocktails, one determinedly knitting, all stripped to their slips and all carrying what looked like crystal-radio sets. Wires sprouted from the sets and ended in little

410

suckers, which were attached to the women's bodies and faces. A low-level hum emanated from the window; Jean touched the glass and felt the current tickle her fingers. A gold sign announced 'The Buzzy Bee Super Reducer' and a barker with a microphone moved among the electrified women extolling the virtues of the machines that hung by thick leather straps from their shoulders. 'It fits easily in your home and on your person,' he boasted, 'and is available *on credit*. It's electric, ladies, a real live current that melts unsightly fat. But be careful . . . ' He held up a finger and the crowd held its breath. From the back of the window display, a tiny woman, perhaps half Jean's height, rushed forward, flapping her hands and rolling her eyes. 'You don't wanna overdo it!' The barker stamped his foot and slapped his leg and the crowd shrieked as the little woman ran round and round, her blonde curls shaking as she mimed panicked regret at her overindulgence in electricity. The barker spotted Jean, and it was too much for him to resist: 'She was your size once, lady — no fooling!' The crowd screamed with laughter. Jean felt a cold sweat sweep over her body like an electric current.

411

36

The barker made her take a catalogue to show there were no hard feelings. A booklet of around thirty thick pages, issued by the Surgical Brace and Truss Company, incorporating Electrica Inventions, it began with a glossy, full-colour section, depicting women erupting with joy while gardening, sunbathing or socialising over cake and coffee — all the while being reduced. The climax was a supermarket scene in which a musical comedy appeared to have broken out in the aisles: electrode-spattered, full-skirted house-wives kicked their legs high while similarly wired checkout girls hurled fruit into the air in celebration.

The colour plates gave way to black type on roughly cut yellow paper, the equivalent of a back room where the more nightmarish contraptions were kept, and the company fell back from the present to the previous century. It started innocently enough, with drawings of men doing callisthenics, their movements drawn out from their bodies in dot-dash lines, like distress signals. The catalogue then progressed to illustrations of back-lengtheners and leg-straighteners.

'What do these do?' Jean asked the barker, who came outside with the catalogue. He was reluctant to leave the window, but he didn't want the crowd to turn against him for singling the big girl out. He had noticed a few dark stares and

412

some pursing of lips.

'Beats me.' He shrugged, looking back at the girls getting ready to go through the demonstration again — adjusting seams and shoulder straps where the weight of the battery was taking its toll. 'Change you. However you want. Taller, smaller, wider, thinner. Or just average.'

'Average,' Jean repeated softly, not quite daring to touch the picture of a leg brace.

'Where you from, honey? Out of town? You're in the right place. Here you can change your name, your face, everything. Just takes money.' He looked her up and down. 'Lots and lots of money.'

'She wasn't really my size, was she?'

'That's just a stunt, lady, a gimmick. Don't worry, the Buzzy Bee ain't gonna turn you into no midget.'

'Oh. Do these work?'

He glanced at the page Jean was studying. 'I'm no doctor — that's the medical stuff. They put that in the back hoping to shift it. Bad advertising, if you ask me; gives people the willies.' He then remembered his paymasters and flashed her a smile. 'But they couldn't sell it if it didn't work, right? Take the Super Reducer, or the Voltage Vanisher — top-of-the-range beauty items, satisfaction guaranteed. Ask inside for credit terms — excuse me.'

He scooted back inside, ready to entice another batch of women to the window. Jean looked down at the picture of a man happily playing golf with half his leg encased in what looked like a steel cylinder. 'On the mend!' the caption promised. The feeling of satisfaction brought on by successfully delivering the pills began to wane.

In Jean's childhood, rickets and polio manipulated the limbs of children as if they were balloon animals. It wasn't uncommon to see doorknob knees on pipe-cleaner legs and hips with the slant of a poorly put-up shelf. Just walking could be a bitter comedy of compensation, with built-up shoes and makeshift crutches pitted against nature at its damnedest. The young Jean had thought she might find a home among those who had been similarly betrayed by nature, but it was not to be. They scuttled away even faster than the others, anxious to protect their crooked bones from her iron grasp. Until now, she had never considered herself one of them — one who was correctable, able to be shaped by wires and struts.

She turned the page to what looked like a generator, spilling a fearsome tangle of cables and clamps like entrails. In the diagram, a man stood next to what appeared to be his own shadow, arrows shooting from the smaller to the larger form. 'The Atlasator', Jean read, 'improves form and presence through pressure-stretching, electro-massage and bone-moulding capabilities.' And then, 'Current can be reversed for female patients.' She almost tore the paper in her haste, but on the following page was a diagram of a woman, the arrows flowing in the opposite direction from her shadow self. She held the catalogue close to her chest. Would she, Jean wondered, be susceptible? She thought about that second smaller jar under the sink and walked as far as she could before getting the bus, pleased she hadn't gone to the expense of a trolley-car ride.

When she got home, Jean put the catalogue under her pillow and went to bed, too tired even to run. Her dreams were electrified; they brimmed with thoughts of metamorphosis that wouldn't crystallise, suspending her between states animal and mechanical, or solid and liquid, before evaporating altogether. The only thing that was clear in Jean's mind was the absence of a reason. 'What are you *for?*' She thought she might have shouted it on waking, it felt so fresh on her tongue and bright in her mind — her ears rang to it. Jean was superstitious enough both to move the catalogue, and, later, to see that day as fated. It was her day for Ermeline.

★ ★ ★

Ermeline was not her easiest call. She would follow Jean round the house, burning with righteous self-belief while emitting pity like methane gas. She had advanced from silently reading the Bible to quoting it out loud, and had tuned her radio to a station that broadcast beam-shaking services around the clock, often halting Jean in her work to make her listen to a passage or point of particular relevance, usually to do with the physical manifestation of sin, as if Jean's size was indicative only of the magnitude of her trespasses, the severity of which ran

415

roughshod over Ermeline's imagination. On the fated day, however, Ermeline was in a state of high excitement; her face was shiny with perspiration and her dark, deep-set eyes glittered like coal in a cave. She didn't want to see Jean at all.

'Oh dear.' Ermeline quivered at the doorway, hopping from foot to foot. 'Now is not a good time, not at all. I have a very important guest, a very *spiritual* guest.'

On another day, Jean would have simply sloped off. She could have come back after she had been to the office, apartment and then love nest of Charles Pace. She could have admitted that she had few other plans for the rest of the week and one day was much the same as another to her. But there on the step, irritated by Ermeline's springing and her own tormented dreams, Jean decided that she would not, for once, be accommodating. She wanted to do her job, that was all. It just happened to fall on a day she was looking for answers and wouldn't take no for one. She could have gone on looking, eternally and cheaply, but for the Reverend Jonas Hatchard.

He was the son of a minister, come west in pursuit of sin. He couldn't get enough of it. Jonas's graveyard demeanour masked a character that was a bubbling soup of perversions. It had taken a great deal of time and money to run them down — his dustbowl face that seemed always old and always to belong on top of mortician's garb made things very expensive for him that were often free for others — and he had ended up, exhausted and bankrupt, in the desert. He had driven himself there after a final bacchanal, intending to add self-murder to his list of sins. A career as an agent-cum-pimp behind him, nothing but a sunrise before him, Jonas Hatchard found himself without ambition. To save him, some new depravity would surely have to be invented; he felt he had sampled it all. With peyote-tinctured coffee, he sadly toasted a new beginning, whatever it might turn out to be.

That was the moment a young vagrant chose to split his skull with a rock. It could have been worse for Jonas, but the man who stowed away in his car intending to rob him at the earliest opportunity — and who was extremely agitated at finding himself in the desert with no idea of the route back to town — did not find the gun Jonas had put in the glove compartment, its hour close at hand.

People are slow to give their bodies credit. Their occasional ugliness and propensity to leak or otherwise disappoint seeming reason enough to doubt their ingenuity. It's not uncommon for those who have cheated death to feel spared for some lofty purpose; to feel that their character had something to do with it. As if you could kick a nun and a murderer and guarantee the nun would heal faster. Jean had struggled to find a reason for her deliverance. Her body had marked her out for survival, but while the animal in her wallowed in it — running, eating, breathing — the nagging, unsatisfied human was uneasy still, and thought of blame and purpose. Jonas Hatchard had the advantage on Jean, he believed

417

himself Chosen from the moment he opened a swollen eye and found that he was still alive, though relieved of his wallet, car and shoes. Jonas had spent his life running from God, unable to reconcile his liking for carnal and narcotic pleasures with the notion of the Almighty instilled in him by his father, a fearsome minister of the old school who believed God should be beaten into the malleable flesh of the young — as young as possible, so He could really take. Waking up alive, Jonas felt less pardoned than *endorsed*. He felt that everything was available to him once more, he had only to take it — it was *waiting* for him. It was a wonderful feeling. So good, in fact, he wished he were able to sell it.

One of the side-effects of Jonas's injury would be an inability to become excited by his old quirks and deviations, but even before his past life and its attractions began recede from his memory, its very particular nature signposted the way to his future.

Much of the society Jonas had formerly frequented had been necessarily secret; passwords and unmarked keys had been part of the routine. He knew of the vast underground network that existed to unite people with their particular pleasure. The more rarefied the pleasure the more dedicated the effort to wed seeker to provider. There existed no such framework above ground, in the open, for the commonplace. Jonas realised that if he could be seen to be the gatekeeper of these more banal desires, there would be no limit to the number of people who would join him. He aimed to fling open the doors to heaven on earth, and their heaven was now his: no longer dogged by his rather specialised lusts, he wanted only what everyone wanted. Money.

Jonas did not take to his father's faith of delayed gratification. But from it, he learned the communication of certainty. Clement Hatchard held his congregation fast, dangling on the unshakeable conviction that heaven or hell would be attained. Dollar after dollar went into the collection plate to maintain this man of God, who read from a book that was widely available for minimal cost; every public library had one, but still the literate came to hear him read. Clement Hatchard fed off God for seventy-nine years and died fat and in bed.

When his legitimate clients abandoned him after he failed to achieve their dreams, Jonas noted that they seldom abandoned the dream itself; they would just seek another facilitator, a better deal. They would leave with their belief in themselves undiminished, thinking that it really was a bad time for brunettes, or they were the wrong height for comedy. So few gave up, he should really have been a rich man. God, meanwhile, had been offering the same deal for over a thousand years. Humanity needed better representation. Jonas had run scams before, starting out. Send just this much money and receive a diploma, a hairpiece, a device to make you taller/thinner/younger. This necessitated the constant change of mailboxes and drop points, the cashing of cheques. And once scammed, twice shy. There had to be a return, eventually. A business must have goods to sell, a religion can have bare shelves and nothing on order: it's all on the never never. Its perfection brought tears to Jonas's eyes, and for the first time in his life unbidden, he prayed. He thanked God for showing him the way. It's how he was discovered — on his knees, hands clasped together, watery eyes turned to heaven — by the police who had found his car and were looking for his body.

★   ★   ★

Ermeline attended several churches to be on the safe side and was a regular presence at extramural gatherings. Jonas cruised these assemblies in search of backing. He was beginning to think that he had misjudged the appeal of his mission — the Church leaders were hostile to anyone attempting to filch their faithful, and their weekly contributions to the plate, while the congregations themselves seemed unsettled by his aggressively modern approach and language — when he met Ermeline Mildmay. In her, the Reverend Jonas Hatchard found the perfect woman to sit at his right hand: lonely, gullible, a touch conceited and not desperately clever. He took her to a very respectable tea house he knew of and, over the course of the hour they spent together, looked deep into her eyes and — seeing nothing more than his reflection there — used the language of seduction to draw her to his cause. He spoke of his need for her, his yearning to see God's will done, the passion he could divine in her, the temples they would build together. Ermeline fell for him as portly ladies fell for mad stranglers in crime novels. There was barely a knotted silk stocking between one of them and Hatchard anyway.

Jean had chosen a bad day to be assertive: Jonas let opportunity go by as often as a spider, and, with his first patron secured, he was keen to begin recruiting the lower ranks.

'You won't know I'm here,' Jean had assured Ermeline as she pushed past, using her bucket as a buffer.

Ermeline's subsequent flapping — she was as possessive as a teenager who has found herself accidentally alone with the school heartthrob — brought him scuttling to the hallway, where he blocked Jean's route to the kitchen. He stopped her with a smile, a broad yet shallow thing that could easily have had a live bird trapped behind it, so ravenous and insincere it appeared. Jean thought he had the greenest teeth she had seen outside of England, great long tombstones that were cracked and weathered. Ermeline's flaps turned to squeaks of protest, but he silenced them with a nod.

'And you are?' he asked, his voice a practised purr, neither kind nor unkind, but forceful.

Jean held up the bucket as if it explained it all for her. 'Jean. I've come to do for Miss Mildmay.'

The Reverend's strange smile seemed to dip slightly.

'I'm sorry, what did you say?'

'She's from England, Reverend,' Ermeline supplied helpfully. 'GI bride.' And because some

421

part of her, some jealous adolescent part wanted to discredit Jean, she continued: 'But he ran off . . . '

Ermeline stopped, aware she had gone too far, even though it was more stupid than cruel. Jean blushed but said nothing; the Reverend was pleased, he didn't need any more than that.

'I see. And here you are making your own way, out here in the desert. How impressive you are, practically a parable. But this is not all there is; there should be more, shouldn't there, Jean?'

Jean felt her eyes widen and the muscles in her face go slack with surprise, hurt, and something else — relief. Finally, someone noticed.

Early in his career as an agent, Jonas used to wait for people to tell him what they wanted, but soon discovered it all came down to the same thing. He could tell just by looking now, which was no great skill, since most people wore their wants on their sleeve. Specifics weren't necessary, 'more' usually covered it. There could always be more.

Watching Jean's eyes nearly spill from their sockets, he knew he was on to a good thing. 'Don't be afraid, Jean. And forgive my directness. I mean no harm, I only want to help. Won't you join us?'

Ignoring the urgent shaking of Ermeline's head behind Jean's back, he ushered her into the front room. The table was set for tea, with a layered chocolate-fudge confection crushing a cakestand and fine china cups waiting to be filled. In his faded black suit, the Reverend Hatchard resembled a stick of liquorice dropped in the dust. He was almost as tall as Jean, but weighed perhaps a third less and had concentrated most of that around a bulbous middle, leaving his limbs starved.

Ermeline grudgingly cut Jean a slice of the cake, then carried it back to the kitchen where it would be safe from further uninvited depredations. Jean watched it go with the tenderness and regret a mother might feel watching her child being carried towards adoption. She had tried not to get used to having extra, having learned her lesson with Denny. After years of rationing, she had binged on him; got fat on sentiment. She was hard on herself now, no sweet things, no pleasures. Only what was required to stay alive.

'I was just elaborating on my mission to Miss Mildmay, Jean — you don't mind if I call you Jean, do you? Miss Mildmay agrees with me that there is much to be done in this part of the world. People prosper here, Jean, but they use their riches to build swimming pools, not baptismal troughs — because it was sin that got them where they are today and sin they repay. Do you feel alone, Jean?'

The sudden change of subject seemed no more than a slight kink in the current, so smooth was the flow of his words. She wondered how many more times he would say her name. With each use it felt like a blow falling, but a soft one, just a compression of air.

'Unable to accomplish all that you are capable of? Well, Jean . . . ' His eyes were huge and very round, an odd shade of deep blackish brown, almost purple, and seemed to jump occasionally in their sockets. He was compelling, but in the way of a ghost story or a newsreel about an air disaster. You didn't want to take your eyes off him, no matter how little you were enjoying the experience of looking. 'There is more than heaven awaiting the righteous.'

At his signal, Ermeline fluttered up out of her seat and scurried into the next room — where the false legs and Bibles had been cleared to one side to make room for a mimeograph machine and a dozen boxes of yellow paper — and returned with a leaflet. 'Success Through Spirituality' was printed at its head, followed by 'Guaranteed'. That word again. Like the medically certified claims of the Surgical Brace and Truss Company, it was a promise. Jean felt as though both had been made to her personally. The rest of the leaflet was given over to a glowing report on the Reverend Hatchard's background. He was apparently the private spiritual counsel to some extremely important people, and had only recently been persuaded to impart the secrets of their success to the general public. Personal consultations could be had for a fee that was refundable against the cost of the Success Through Spirituality programme, which came divided into 'Steps to Success' and led to a spiritual graduation and immediate conquering of the subject's chosen world. A correspondence course was also available.

'Won't you join us?' he repeated, the new meaning of the words not lost on Jean; he soaked them in significance. 'You need be alone no longer. We are here to support you, to get you what you deserve.'

She had tried her best, but part of her knew: her best wasn't making anything better. She had survived, but somehow become part of the wreckage, hopping up on doctors' tables to pay the rent. She was unable to help Gloria; she was unable to do anything but wait for some resolution that might never come. All that was good — more than expected, she had to concede: two friends, of which one still alive; a lover — had happened some time ago. There was a lack of alchemy in her postwar existence. As Jean looked at the leaflet in her hand; a new feeling spread in her — she felt she might yet become lucky, an unheard of trait in her lineage. She, specifically, was being asked to be a part of something.

The invitation — and in particular the word 'Guaranteed' — sparked something in her. Even seeing it in smudgy ink on a yellow sheet was enough, it confirmed its existence. The world that floated into her atmosphere via the radio, where automobiles were given away like overripe fruit at the end of market day, or the department store catalogue (why be you when you can be better?) — that world of excess felt closer. Guaranteed. The Reverend watched her read, saw the light come on in her eyes. Success Through Spirituality was on its way to its first convert.

'There's no reason why you can't have it all, Jean.' And then he went for the kill. 'There never has been.'

All her life she had been looking for a crack in the world large enough to hide in. Life with

Denny had been a chasm she could happily fall into, but there had been a shift in the plates of the earth and it had closed, leaving her clawing at the surface. Jean had yet to find anything else that could so effectively obliterate her. Until Hatchard. He was promising her the end of her self. What she had been, Denny no longer wanted. She would present him with a new her, and capture him again. Capture the old life, where lightning struck.

'Now, Jean. I'm going to ask you perhaps the single most important question of your life. What do you think you deserve?'

Jean had no answer to this. She didn't deserve anything; she had never deserved anything, good or bad. She had never done anything good or bad enough to merit it. The Reverend Hatchard blinked and asked her again, his voice slow and deep, as if he were trying to extract a vital secret that could turn the tide of battle.

'Now, Jean. Don't think, just answer. What do you deserve?'

Jean blinked, and a fat tear hopped up unexpectedly onto the rim of her eye. Something stirred inside her, a distant voice like a ventriloquist's dummy trying to escape from its suitcase. Somewhere Wisteria was laughing. Laughing at the daughter that had become her, alone and unwanted, fighting only for her piece of solitude in which to run mad.

What did someone who had been freed by death, only to disappoint life, deserve? The confines of Jean's life had once been reduced to an upturned bathtub, and she had accepted them as her boundary. She had navigated her way through a changing landscape and revelled in the new joys it threw up even as it swallowed what was loved. She had loosed herself from familiarity long ago, but was clinging to any semblance of it now, no longer attuned to chaos. She had conditioned herself to endure, and now could do only that. But it was novelty that propelled her. The tear gathered momentum and rolled from her eye, down her cheek, flattening into its scored ridges.

'Nothing,' was her eventual reply. It pleased the Reverend Jonas Hatchard, though his face didn't betray it (he was practised at concealing pleasure). He lowered his voice still further and let it snake around Jean's shoulders like graveyard mist. She shivered at his closeness while Ermeline watched in wonder at how effortlessly he snared her. Truly, He was working though this man.

'There now, don't upset yourself. Why do you believe that when there is so much to tell you it isn't true? There is so much that faith can give you, if you have faith in yourself. What is it you want, Jean?'

'Me? I don't want anything.' She felt accused, as if he suddenly resented this demand on his time.

Ermeline was spellbound by the Reverend's technique. Had it not been blasphemous to do so, she would have compared it to hypnosis. Jean's sudden refusal unnerved her. 'There must be something!' she cried. 'Just look at you!'

Jonas's eye twitched with annoyance; he rolled

his shoulders, and Ermeline's outburst trickled down his back. In a second, he was again unruffled. 'We all have wants, Jean. I want to help the lost and make them see that they can succeed. Now, what do you want?'

'I want . . . '

She expected Denny, or Gloria, but no particular image came to her, just the feeling of what it had been like, to be bound by the equality of uncertainty.

'I want for it to be like it was before.'

'Before? Before when, Jean?'

'Before everything was set, decided.'

'I see.' The Reverend closed his eyes and nodded, as if he were viewing Jean's private thoughts. When he opened his eyes again, there was no doubt in them. 'You want possibility, Jean.' And then he spread his hands wide. 'That is all I have to give.'

'The possibility of what?' Her voice was no more than a hoarse whisper. Like the swiftest, smoothest pickpocket, he had already robbed her of scepticism.

'Change,' he answered.

She thought of the catalogue, and her voice was wistful. 'I saw a machine that could change you.'

He could see the longing in her. He had suspected it. A great big thing like her, abandoned all the way out here. The husband was a specialist, he thought. No one else was coming for her, but that wouldn't stop her trying. 'That's what my Church is,' he said, softly. 'A machine to change you. Don't you want to do something?'

Jean felt as if she was a target with a dozen arrows sticking from her — 'Do something.' 'Yes,' she whispered. 'But what?'

'Now, Jean' — he made as if to pat her hand, but patted the tablecloth instead — 'did you really think you would have to find those answers for yourself? They are here, waiting for you. You just find the right questions, that's all. That's what I, or rather the Church, is for.'

She would never be able to say why, exactly — perhaps a lack of food, a surfeit of loneliness, or a weakness of mind — but Jean looked into his eyes, eyes the colour and sheen of an aubergine's skin, and found she was ready to believe.

'Now, tell me again: what is it you deserve?'

Her lips parted, but no sound emerged. It was too much to ask, so he replied for her.

'Everything, Jean.' His tone was gentle and stroking, less foreign than the fake swamis he used to run into at parties, but as insistent; as persuasive, he hoped. He had worked hard on it. 'God has many gifts for you, but he doesn't deliver.'

She had never fought herself, that was the problem; she had been too ready to give in to her size and its destiny. You, he was saying, are not inevitable. Not anymore. She *would* be a changing thing. She *would* be malleable. She hadn't been able to grow so large she could hover above it all, become the creature of her dreams. So she had no choice but to relinquish her uniqueness, which remained a barrier to her

429

acceptance and happiness.

Jonas smiled. It was as if her skull had become transparent and the clockwork revolutions of her thought process were clearly visible to him. He had her. It was incredible how a lifetime of experience could be overruled by a simple question. The impossibility of change was her constant; it had taken dynamite to move her life a fraction of an inch, to leave her alone and unloved in the desert rather than by the sea. And yet she hadn't learned. The ability of a person to ignore probability in favour of the slimmest of possibilities was what Jonas was banking on to build his Church.

'And if I believe, I'll change? Is that it?'

'Yes,' he said softly. 'Yes, that's it.'

★ ★ ★

And so like the friendless and hopeless before her, Jean found God. She left carrying a box of leaflets and a large leather satchel that Ermeline claimed had belonged to a missionary, later cannibalised.

37

With all that Jonas promised her, Jean wondered that any other religion had done as well as it had. To begin with, a lot of confession was involved. Not of sins, but of desires. Where Jean came from, speaking of oneself intimately was as bad as touching oneself intimately, and, when done in public, just as likely to get one put away for the common good. In the Reverend's Church, she would discover, it was quite the reverse. The bald admission of want, and, by association, lack, was encouraged. Only then was admission to the Church granted. Jean surprised herself by admitting everything: that she had not made a success of the life that had been spared, that this had to be a greater defeat than succumbing to her injuries would have been. That she felt an urging at her back that would not let her rest, though she had proved incapable of fashioning any other life for herself but this. Through it all, Jonas nodded and smiled. 'Of course,' he said, finally. She was nothing, that was why nothing good would happen to her and nothing good came from knowing her. Her Success would be in becoming another, someone worthy of the kindness and attention she craved but dared not ask for. After her confession, she spent two hours in the desert looking for a stone that matched an exact description given by the Reverend, only to have it thrown back in front of her.

'That was a demonstration of faith,' he told her. 'You are convincing me I can trust you with answers.'

This did not suggest to Jean that he was making it up as he went along. She handed over the money she earned from Eva. It barely had time to warm in her hand before it disappeared into Jonas's pocket. For that, she received a brochure, printed in colour on thick shiny paper with Ermeline's money, containing the first Step.

'You are a foundation stone,' Jonas told her. 'Now it begins.'

As the first convert, Jean was dispatched to lure others into the fold. Bus stations, libraries and lunch counters were good repositories for lost causes, places where they could linger without a specific occupation. They were the fodder Jonas required. There was only ever one lottery winner, but millions still bought tickets. It was a share in the dream, not the reality, that he was selling. There were times he wondered if he even needed God, but he didn't know how long it would take to establish the business and ordinary investors didn't like to wait for results, while religious types were prepared to wait for an eternity. The useful fact of it was that there were always reasons why religion didn't work out the way it was supposed to. It was almost part of its appeal.

Jonas spent a day coaching Jean before letting her loose on the general public. She would approach crying women and angry men and simply offer them a leaflet, then ask if she could stay to talk for a while. Jonas knew he ran a risk here, that they could bolt for the hills or be too scared to move. He reckoned fifty per cent either way would be all right.

'Your life begins now,' Jean said to each of them, in conclusion.

Jonas's fears that Jean's appearance might be too eccentric to lure people in, that no one would want to ally themselves outwardly with the peculiar or dispossessed, were unfounded. She was a quiet triumph. That someone like her could express hope, fearlessly and publicly, was more than alarming, it was persuasive. If she could believe, then who couldn't? For herself, Jean had never felt that certainty of inclusion before. Wherever this was going, it was taking her with it.

Jonas made home visits to the souls she collected, for which Ermeline bought him a new suit. 'I'm not here to make you feel better about who you are,' he told them. 'I'm here to tell you about who you could be.' He told them he would put their faith to good use, and they handed it over willingly, along with cash or personal cheques. Though receiving funding from Ermeline — who had a not-too-shabby remnant of a once-impressive inheritance — the Reverend required this additional source of income to realise his own dream: a rally to be broadcast on radio, announcing Success Through Spirituality to the world. The few disciples he had so far acquired would supervise the mass conversions that were sure to follow.

Jonas held a group meeting to welcome them to their futures, arriving with new hair; the feeble strands that covered his balding pate supplemented by thick swathes of glossy black. The congregation arrived certain only of the impossible, how it surrounded and controlled them. He told them their failures were mere rehearsals for success, he lifted blame from their shoulders and wiped doubts from their minds. God had a purpose for them, he told them, and that purpose was to succeed. They had only to convince Jonas they were ready, though the Reverend was terribly hard to convince.

Jean pored over the programme every night, memorising the first Step towards Success. She, in particular, had a long way to go. It was as she had suspected; wholesale change as a precursor to the attainment of bliss — nothing less. In anticipation, she let her mind wander over possessions, settling on a car one moment, then a television set the next; she spirited Gloria across the miles in an aeroplane and set them both on the ocean in a liner. She wondered what she would look like new; how she would look through Denny's eyes.

Jean recited the Steps as she cleaned, as she ran, as she lay in bed alone and let her eyes follow the fine cracks in the ceiling. Unlike a word that loses its meaning on repetition until it seems wholly unlikely, dogma gains in credibility, even — it seems — in probability. The Reverend had devised a programme of meaningless platitudes, involving recognising and utilising, surrendering and accepting. It was so brilliantly nebulous as to be unclear whether one was adhering or contravening. It was simpler than a fad diet and more complex than a treaty. It meant absolutely nothing and at the same time everything. Here finally was something Jean could work at. She saw why Ermeline couldn't leave religion alone — you could worry it like a scab that never healed.

The next meeting was open only to those who had progressed to the second step. Jean had continued to leaflet the disenfranchised and had even told Gloria that she had taken an interest in self-improvement; to stop now with so much ahead of her would be madness. But the steps were ruinously expensive — she wondered if she might work one off, cranking the mimeograph or delivering more converts. 'Does the Lord give credit?' Jonas asked in response to her suggestion. Jean didn't want to get left behind and wondered if any of Eva's other friends had difficulty visiting their own doctor. When she suggested this to Eva, she was warned against ambition and received an interim payment to ensure her exclusivity; and so Jean continued to advance.

There were slightly fewer converts at the second meeting, to which Jonas wore new teeth under his new hair, but he seemed delighted. He had fed them bunkum and the majority had returned with plates scraped clean, wanting more — they were his now. Ermeline was less enthused. She stood to the side of the makeshift stage in the small hall they had hired, surveying the crowd. Few carried Bibles, all carried brochures, and they looked to her a desperate, grabbing bunch more suited to a fire sale than a revival. She looked to Jonas, who nodded gravely and swept an arm out towards the crowd. 'Our flock, Miss Mildmay,' he said. 'Yours and mine.' Ermeline had never had her own flock before, and was instantly seduced again. Jean stood at the back, clutching her brochure as if it was a lifebelt. 'You are a step closer' were its first words. She felt it, and looking around knew everyone else felt it, too. 'I am part of something,' she thought.

'Welcome to those who are to continue,' Jonas boomed from the stage. 'I am honoured, yes, honoured to have you here.'

Jean felt her chest swell; the entire hall lifted as if buoyed by a gust of helium.

'You are the chosen. You have already proven yourselves worthy, so applaud yourselves.'

They did, and it felt good. Then they reaffirmed their belief in change. 'Change will make me different,' screamed one young man, almost frothing with excitement, and it was taken up as a chant. Jean felt it pulse in her breast. Take me with you, she thought. I want it too. The crowd was fizzing with the incredible freedom of saying it all out loud. I want, I want, I want. And there was no one to ask why, why should you? Jean used to think she had no right, but in the hall, with the massed voices swirling around her, unified in their grasping, their craving, she felt entitled. The war was over.

There was barely time for anything more after that. Jonas couldn't quiet them, and gave up trying. What he had to say was so much less important than what he had enabled them to.

They would carry themselves forward. At the end of the hour, they streamed out of the hall, dazed and elated. Too exhausted to speak, they did indeed feel as if they had left a little of themselves inside, ready to be filled up with the Reverend's transforming creed. Jean thought she might have to sit down and put her head between her legs. She wanted desperately to reach the next step; she felt that the air was running out, and she had to break through the surface soon. At the rate she was going, it would take her years to complete the programme; she wouldn't get what was coming to her until she was an old lady. She was nearing thirty as things stood. 'A new life can't start with the old you,' the Reverend told them. With this in mind, Jean accepted Eva's proposition.

On the night it was made, Jean's first Hollywood winter was giving way to spring, and there was something in the air. She would have sworn her steps were lighter, were it not for the aural evidence. Jean was returning late from one of the Reverend's sessions, and arrived home just before midnight to find Eva sat on her porch. Eva attempted to wave brightly, but her hand was shaking too much; the cigarette between her fingers painted little lassos of light in the darkness.

'Hey, you,' she croaked, as Jean drew near. 'Wanna help me help a movie star?'

Yes, Jean thought. I am part of something.

★   ★   ★

437

When Varga James was fourteen years old and called Margarita Phillips, she went missing from her family's farm. She was found, nine hours later, in a hollow, half buried in mud, with the germ of Eva already inside her. Two months later, Margarita was sent west to convalesce from a sudden bout of scarlet fever, and never returned home. She was visited often by her mother, who, after one extended stay, brought home another daughter, a blessing for her late middle age.

Eva was informed of her parentage when she was seventeen. The farm had long since failed — along with every other in the area — but the Phillipses were kept comfortable with Varga's money. The only thing Eva wanted for was a future, and it was decided that Varga would give her one. The only condition was that no one would ever know her real name and relation to Varga.

Varga was used to co-stars rather than daughters. She took Eva through a montage of shopping, beauty treatments, ice-cream sodas and movie matinees, and then ran out of ideas. The question of what Eva would actually do had not been considered. While Varga worked, Eva took dancing and singing lessons, despite possessing no gift for either discipline, and was sent for a screen test — Varga couldn't imagine what any girl would want more. But first, Varga had her doctors reshape Eva's nose and ears, to make sure no resemblance between them could be noted. The experience merely affected Eva's sense of smell, not her luck. Her long, lean face lengthened even more on camera, to the point where they chalked 'horse' on her test boards. The wardrobe department found her too heavy (she ate, at this time), the publicity department too shy. The script department was her last stop.

At the time specialising in shopgirl-hooks-millionaire fantasies, the studio retained a small army of female readers who selected works on behalf of millions of their straitened sisters, dreaming of love and comfort from behind glass counters, elevator doors and teller's windows. The readers were kept poorly paid to sharpen their eyes. Eva loved to disappear each day into a pool of fiction, but could not quite fit into the urban rhythm of what was required: tales that clattered along like heels clicking on a sidewalk. Her recommended submissions were always returned, her judgement in question. Head-scarves featured heavily in the stories she preferred. Orphans were forever drawing them tighter around their faces as they battled their way through snowstorms ahead of advancing misfortune. Eva wallowed as few had since the advent of sound, and was let go.

So she married. It was perhaps her least successful attempt to establish herself as an individual. Parker Brinsley started out as — and for the length of his brief career remained — the romantic interest in poor comedies, in which he would serenade the ingénue with his high, thin voice while comedians undermined them in the background. They met at a party — he had come hoping to seduce someone rich enough to finance his comeback. When Eva told him who her mother was, he turned his waning talents to blackmail. Their secret marriage lasted just a few weeks, until Varga involved the studio heads and he became their problem and they his. Eva wanted to keep his name as a reminder no one was interested in her alone, but was told she had already caused enough trouble. Mrs Brinsley disappeared with her husband and Eva went back to Varga. She learned to make cocktails, give injections and manicures, and be invisible on set and at home. As Varga's secretary and companion, Eva saw every day the life she had been judged unworthy of. Her attempts at making herself visible — fuelled by the cocktails she had learned to prepare so expertly — led to her eventual exile from the mansion to the desert. There she could break furniture and crash cars to her heart's content.

A hungover Eva had been summoned by the housekeeper the previous night; Varga was locked inside her bedroom, responding neither to phone calls nor entreaties shouted under the door. Bought at the height of her fame, Varga's mansion appeared to have been designed by a time-travelling narcoleptic. The Tudor hunting-lodge flavour of the exterior was forgotten in favour of Spanish colonial for the entrance hall. In the Renaissance reception room, a fresco slid back to reveal a Grecian screening room. The themes and periods did not bleed into one another; it was as if they had been commissioned between blackouts. The entrance hall was dominated by an enormous photograph of the owner, preserved behind glass. It, like the house, was from her peak. Her skin was flawless, it ran over her bones like cream over the back of a spoon. She didn't need colour, the glow of her skin made grey look alive. Some women were more beautiful in life than in pictures, but Varga had the alchemy the right way round. Mirrors disappointed her. Eva paused in front of the portrait, as she always did, to wonder how anyone could look like that. And why no one managed it for ever.

Varga had smothered her youth, like an overprotective parent. Even before it had started to slip away from her she had tried to embalm it; having her face pulled tight before it was loose, dying her lustrous hair a dull black before the grey could creep through. She had begun to mourn youth years before it left her, and when it finally did there was no more to be done. It was like trying to revive a ghost. And now her star was falling faster than her face. On the orders of the studio, she had, over the years, undergone two abortions and two facelifts and sued for one divorce. The other divorces were her own business. She had done every single thing they asked of her, but stayed young. Even the women that had loved her on screen weren't interested now she was old; perhaps because if Varga aged, they aged too.

Eva wondered what it would be tonight; what slight had sent Varga reeling. She had become as sensitive as a wound, just when she needed her hide to thicken: since she was no longer profitable, no one felt the need to be nice to her anymore. A photographic session the previous week had been disrupted after the art director called for a higher denier of stocking for the lens. Varga had challenged him to put the stocking over her head, and then swept out, knocking the camera to the floor as she did so. In the old days, the studio wouldn't have charged her for it, but these were not the old days.

Eva let herself into the bedroom, and eventually found Varga in the adjoining, mirror-lined dressing room; from that she knew something was very wrong. Varga was settled on the floor in a little nest of furs, with a hundred identical selves spreading from her like wings. 'This is a terrible room to get drunk in,' she deadpanned, a crooked lipstick smile continued to spread out from her own.

Varga pushed back the fur to reveal a gold dress that had been Eva's favourite as a young girl, she had watched the film her mother wore it in more than a dozen times. The dress no longer fitted her, and was crowned by rolls of skin as the pieces of her body expelled by corsetry searched for somewhere to go.

'Any tighter and that dress'll be wearing you,' Eva quipped.

Varga's lipstick smile turned down towards her quivering chin, the last of her courage spilling out of it. 'Be nice, darling. I'm finished. We're finished.'

Eva felt her throat suddenly dry.

'Is he back?' she whispered.

'No. Just all the other chickens, looking for a place to roost.'

Varga's latest film would be her last with the

studio. The remainder of her contract had been sold to a smaller outfit, along with some prop furniture and costumes. She was part of a job lot. The worst of it was that Varga had no better taste in accountants than she, or her daughter, had in husbands; loans had been taken against films not yet made and profits not yet counted. The mansion was mortgaged past its value and Eva's little rented house out in the desert was, on paper, a luxury ranch complete with swimming pool and putting green. Varga had been paying five times its worth. She couldn't borrow against the future and the past had made all the money it was going to.

'We're broke?' Eva desperately wanted to hold on to something solid, but her hand simply squeaked as it slid down a polished mirror.

Varga nodded. 'I won't even get any money for this picture they've sold me to. It's part of the deal. They were paid to take me away. You'd think I was an abandoned couch.'

'There's nothing at all?'

Shifting onto her hands and knees, Varga began to push against the mirrored doors. 'Where's the fucking bar? I closed it, now I can't find it. Find it, would you darling — mark it with lipstick when you do.'

Eva pushed against a long panel, which swung back to reveal a cocktail cabinet. When she had been allowed to live at the mansion, she had spent hours drinking among the mirrors, searching for the angle at which she might resemble Varga. She poured herself a drink, drained it, and then poured another, handing the bottle to Varga when she was done. 'What will we do?'

'I don't know. You could go back home, to Mother and Dad.'

'Back?' Eva was horrified. 'I can't go back, I'm not anything yet.'

'Time's run out, darling. You've had so long.'

'No. I need . . . We'll go to court.'

Varga snorted into her drink. 'We'll have to give our names, and our *ages*. You're thirty-one and I'm forty-five. Even reporters can add, Eva. They'll find out about us, and then what? With the files the studio has on me, I'd be lucky not to end up in jail. After all I've done for them.'

Eva had made her mother many promises over the years; they were scattered about like the worthless IOUs of an inveterate gambler. The harsh regimes of the sanatoriums failed to contain her, they appealed to her alcoholic masochism; the perverse pride taken in choosing and not yet entirely succumbing to such an effective method of self-destruction translated into the immense drive to remain addicted. To take the cold-water cures, the charcoal wash, the wrist and leg straps and then, on the day of release, to divert the station taxi to a bar was, to her, a kind of glorious triumph. But with no time left, it suddenly seemed very small, very wasteful. But she wasn't going back. No one went back like this. She would have to do something.

'Varga, how do you make them want you?'

'That's easy,' Varga shrugged. 'Have something they want, or something they fear.'

Eva's glass was warming in her hand; she

444

looked at the clear liquid and felt its pull. Love is possible drunk. Art is possible, and even probable, drunk. But revenge must be exact, calculated, sober. She thought she might base a clinic on it.

★ ★ ★

Eva and Jean sat across from one another, still inexperienced in each other's company, the forced intimacies of Eva's blackouts and Jean's petty frauds not translating into ease. Eva refused the offer of a beer, then wondered whether she would knock Jean down to get at hers.

Smiling awkwardly, they raised their glasses — Eva's filled with milk — in a toast. Eva had not yet found the words to begin and so drank in silence while looking round the room. Jean's house was smaller than her own; the kitchen was bare of feminine frills and additions, nothing of delicacy troubled the shelves or dish drainer. Jean was not made for porcelain. Four photographs were taped to the wall; in each the head of the subject was fully or partially eclipsed by the sun, the body clad in a two-piece bathing suit. The images gave Eva the creeps and she looked away.

She wondered how to begin. She knew all about Jean's recent conversion — Jean had left some leaflets in her home, and returned to find them hanging from the toilet-paper dispenser — and it worried her. Righteousness was infectious, in Eva's experience. But if Eva was apprehensive that Jean would not approach blackmail with the same equanimity with which she had conquered deception and pill-peddling, she was also certain that that there no one else to turn to. This realisation nearly finished her before she started. She was doing something reckless, and she was doing it without a drink; there was a lack of mitigation to this new existence. If Jean had known mitigation was what Eva was after, she could have sold her a brochure. Eva decided to plunge right in.

'I wanted to ask you a favour. It's something I need you to do for me. I can pay you three months' rent.'

Jean was decided. 'I'll do it.' She could be different now, not some point in the future that moved with the horizon — now.

Eva shook her head. 'No, you see, it's quite a large favour; you have to hear what it is first.'

'Oh.' Jean thought for a moment. 'I'll do it, though.'

Eva pinched her nose to stave off a headache. 'You might want to say no.'

Jean was unmoved. 'I don't think I will.'

Eva sighed. She looked at Jean, and decided to explain. She also wanted to hear it out loud, herself, perhaps to see if sense would come tearing in and put a stop to it all.

38

There were times when Eva thought it was a brilliant plan, and there were times she couldn't believe it was the best sobriety could come up with. She asked Jean to make another doctor's visit and prescribed herself some of Varga's pills; confidence had to come from somewhere.

Jean thought it was like something out of a film, and perhaps not a good one. But, despite her misgivings, she could feel excitement build, a rushing in her veins that told her she was on the move. 'You're the only one who can help me,' Eva had said, and that was enough for Jean. She convinced Eva that her alliance with Jonas and Ermeline would not prevent her from being useful and, above all, discreet.

'Don't they have anything to say about blackmail?' Eva asked.

Jean was sure they didn't. 'The Reverend says that wherever the money comes from, it's going to a better place.'

Eva smiled at this. 'Jean, do you know what a rube is?'

'No,' Jean replied. 'Is it important?'

If she had read more, she would still find nothing in her new Bible against what was about to be undertaken, just as there was nothing about adultery or murder. Covetousness was the permitted sin and the pursuit of earthly desires the attainment of bliss.

The studio that had bought Varga set her quickly to work on a Western shooting in another state. Eva's time was completely her own, but every moment of it was coloured by what she was about to do. She spent her days at the movies, immersed in lives better constructed than her own. She took eccentric routes home and went to the supermarket in dark glasses. In the evening, when the need for a drink threatened to burn off her hair, she sat at her typewriter, setting down all she could remember. Jean could hear the clack of keys well into the night.

She, meanwhile, furthered the dream of leaving herself behind. Jean had received half her fee up front; the Surgical Brace and Truss Company accepted a small, non-refundable deposit, Jonas accepted the rest.

An early heatwave weighted the sky; it hung low and discontented over the valley and the promise of rain could be felt in its clammy embrace. A combination of heat and atmospheric pressure can make it feel as though something must be about to happen, that the current state cannot continue unchanged. But what feels like momentum can just as easily be the beginning of a spiral. Last chances were being seized all over.

★   ★   ★

The estate was tucked away in the hills, and almost impossible to simply happen across; a modest little hut modelled after a French royal palace, it was filled with treasures both real and

448

imitation. Eva dropped Jean at the mouth of a tunnel that linked the house to the road, and was known only to those old enough to have danced with bootleggers on floors slick with illicit champagne.

'Give me ten minutes from when you reach the top. I'll come to the back of the house to let you in.'

In her blonde wig and Varga's gold dress, Eva looked like an award about to be given out. Her skin glittered with sweat, her eyes with fear. They had arrived before the hired waiters, before the greenest of the green actresses, before the most eager of the priapists on the exclusive guest list of the exclusive party. Former guests such as Varga were not expected to divulge the locations of these parties to minions, having too much to lose — but mismanagement had reduced too much to nothing.

It had seemed unreal to Jean, up to this point — a joke or jaunt. Now, at the head of the dank tunnel, she wondered what she had agreed to. There was time enough to get away, no one would know they had ever been there; the invitation was a password, and almost untraceable. But only Eva knew this. Jean nodded and crawled into the darkness.

Decorated along the same lines as Varga's, the mansion appeared to be the storage locker of a world-class looter. Eva checked behind statues, tapestries and mirrors before concealing Jean inside a plaster sarcophagus in a velvet-lined room; her job was to work the camera and not pee.

After an empty couple of hours, the room

filled quickly. It seemed that the party started elsewhere and stumbled in when sufficiently morally relaxed. Jean began to crank the camera.

As an Amazon, she had waded through the truth of people's lives. Bombsites were incorrigible gossips and laid bare the smallest detail of an existence to anyone that was passing; letters, photographs, a penchant for ladies' underwear — these things were offered up to the locality without a thought for the months, years, lifetimes spent concealing them. She had once gathered pornographic postcards from what was left of a rectory and saved a reputation from a difficult afterlife. She discovered madness, illegitimacy and adultery in records blasted from locked tin boxes. Her crew even came across the skeleton of a first wife, released from under guilt-covered floorboards. But nothing was as shocking to Jean as the living.

As the mass of bodies flailed towards pleasure, it looked to her like a room full of the dying. The small holes cut in the sarcophagus — originally to pipe air to the bandage-clad actor playing the mummy on one of his more sociable days when he met both a werewolf and a vampire — afforded her a curiously specific view of what was going on. Isolated body parts mashed together in fevered congress, often in combinations that taxed Jean's education and imagination. Sometimes she couldn't tell what it was she was seeing, other times she just couldn't believe it. On a small cinema screen, yet more people she didn't know were exposing themselves to her. She was caught in a deluge of exhibition.

Jean had never seen a place that shone so brightly on the surface and was nothing but darkness underneath. After a night raid, she might emerge in an entirely different world — familiar faces disappeared or were blasted into alien forms, and great spaces appeared where there had been dense humanity. She had got used to that, but she had never seen it done without some other force behind it. Here it seemed people could shed their skin as if it were a bathing suit and reveal the workings underneath at will. It took no vast conflagration to unmask them: they were ready as anything.

Wisteria had warned her daughter that there were some that would worry a cow in a field and when Jean saw the goat being led in she didn't doubt it. It had bags of wine strapped to its back and was chased around by those too drunk to catch it. Others took their refreshment from the surface of mirrors or in pipes and needles and were variously electrified or insensible. An older man, naked except for a pinny and high-heeled pumps, served small food from a large platter and was gently whipped for his pains. Eva had been too subtle in her warnings, but had been right to trust Jean. She had neither the vocabulary nor the desire to describe this scene to anyone. No one there seemed bound to be — the doors were unlocked and the windows were not barred — but very few seemed at all present. If Jean had seen a medieval painting of disembodied souls cavorting to their doom she might have had a point of reference. As it was, she began to count the tiles on the bits of floor she could see.

451

For what seemed like days, Jean stood and worked the camera. There was enough room inside the sarcophagus to change reels and she did so until they ran out, though the activities on show soon became monotonous in form and application. After she ran out of film she closed her eyes and concentrated on standing still. She had a single bottle of pop strapped to her chest and a long straw running up to her mouth. She didn't want to finish it all in case her bladder needed emptying so she took very small sips of the once-fizzy liquid and hoped she would not belch.

Jean felt her own perspiration settle in her pores. The mummy's box was suffocating her and her overalls were heavy with sweat. She continued to fold herself into unforgiving spaces, hoping once again to emerge in a changed world. But Jean was not buried, awaiting resurrection; she was merely trapped, like so many others, under the great weight of circumstance. She closed her eyes, but what she had seen was deeply etched. She tried hard not to imagine how it would feel to be used so joylessly, though her skin crawled of its own accord, as if it sensed the danger it was in. Jean had never felt such fear before. She had seen what these people did to each other in the name of pleasure, and could not imagine what they would do to her as punishment. She came close to wetting herself when the ancient coffin rocked to the force of one of the revellers trying to break in. But the half-clothed starlet couldn't work the clasps and, after knocking on the Pharaoh's chest for a time,

452

gave up and allowed herself to be carried out and thrown into the pool. Jean realised she had travelled far beyond the parameters of her understanding, and felt the terror of being surrounded by the wholly alien.

She was asleep, like a horse in a stall, when Eva came to let her out. Only a few cocktail glasses resting carelessly on the arms of chairs betrayed any hint of what had occurred the night before. Eva had covered her dress with a raincoat and wore a hat over her wig. She held a finger to her lips as she led Jean to the open window, and gestured towards the hallway; Jean strained to hear the sound of heels striking the floor. Someone was still dancing.

With Eva's hand tightly gripping her own, Jean ran from the house to the tunnel. She felt the urge to laugh bubbling up in her; she could feel it in Eva's shaking arm, too. By the time they reached the car, they were both convulsing with laughter which was wild and uncontained and filled with as much horror as relief.

Eva didn't stop the car until they were far from the hills and almost at the ocean; she thought she might need Jean to help prise her hands from the wheel. Jean changed out of her overalls behind the car and Eva dumped her wig and dress in a gas-station toilet; when they walked into a diner for breakfast they could have been two friends out for a Sunday drive — although they still twitched from the adrenalin of transgression.

Jean had not exactly imagined the minutes afterwards, only what the mission would eventually bring. Sitting in the normality of a booth, bathed in honest daylight, she was filled with the sensation of having got away with it; she was becoming lucky. It was stronger even than fear, she noted.

Once the waitress was safely back behind the counter — Eva had ordered for them both, she didn't want Jean to be remembered for her accent — Jean was free to speak, though she still whispered, in case the recently dampened hysteria returned and exploded in a shout.

'Where did you go?'

'I hid in a bedroom closet,' Eva whispered back, feeling as unpredictably giggly as Jean. 'I finally found a room that wasn't occupied, so I shut myself in the closet. It had bars, you know, slats, so I could breathe, and cases to sit on. A few hours later, somebody comes in and starts — you know. I thought they hadn't noticed me, then they asked me if I could see OK.'

'No!' Jean could not imagine such bald depravity.

Eva shrugged. 'Well, at least I could smoke then. And at the end . . . ' Eva paused as a fit of giggles overwhelmed her. 'At the end I applauded. I didn't know what else to do. God, I knew things would get a little hot, but I had no idea. So how are you, was it rough?'

Jean felt as if her hair could dust the sky, and imagined she looked like an exploded comedian, with a trick cigar at the corner of her mouth. But she was having fun. It was a shock to realise it.

'All right, I suppose. Bit of an eye-opener, wasn't it?'

Eva laughed, a genuine throaty laugh full of relief and half-chewed food. 'Well, yes,' she said when she could. 'That it was. I'll bet you never imagined such things went on.'

All Jean knew was that she was weirdly glad of what she had been able to do for Eva that night. It was a muddy, dirty way to dig herself in, but she had nothing else. Something bound them now, and it was too filthy to be denied.

'The film, that's going to help, is it?'

Eva nodded. 'Would you want people to know that's what you got up to?'

Jean frowned. 'If that was me, I'd be glad my mother was dead and my children not born.' She swallowed, and took a chance. She was enjoying her first friendly conversation in weeks, and hated to ruin it, but she wanted Eva to know that she knew. More importantly, that she wouldn't tell. 'I think it's very nice of you to do this for your mum.'

Eva turned to her, eyes wide.

'I saw a photograph, that you left on the floor,' Jean explained. 'You have the same smile.'

Eva shook her head. 'God damn, I should be more careful.' She paused, suddenly aware of how little it mattered at that moment. 'You know, that's our only photograph together? I looked different then, though I never did look much like her. And since then . . . well, let's just say I was supposed to be discreet. You're the only one to notice. I guess no one looks twice at the assistants in this town.'

'I thought you did her dialogue.'

Eva smiled. 'Oh, English,' she said, with

something approaching affection.

Jean blushed and changed the subject. She was helping Eva, at least; that was not a lie, and she was not a fool to believe it. 'Lovely day, isn't it? It's nice here; I really miss the sea.'

'Is that where your home is?'

'Not anymore.' Jean took a napkin and wiped her hands. 'Thank you for breakfast. What do you reckon, my treat tomorrow?'

'Tomorrow?'

'Yes. I thought I'd pop by. See how you are.'

Eva was suddenly serious again. 'Jean, I don't think you should come over. It's not done yet, don't you see? Things have to stay normal. We have to stay normal.'

That was hardly the point of it for Jean. And she had hoped she would get something more from this than money. 'I understand,' she said, barely able to cover her disappointment.

Eva touched Jean's knee, under the table. 'Here, take the rest of the money now anyway, you've certainly earned it.'

Jean looked down at Eva's hand, clutching the money, and couldn't think why she didn't now want to take it. She couldn't say she had been misled, she had just hoped for too much.

'And promise me something, Jean.'

'What?'

'Don't give it to them, Ermeline and the Reverend. Spend it on yourself.'

'But it is on myself, in the end.'

'Sure,' Eva grimaced. 'In the end.'

Eva made it hard to believe in anything, and yet Jean knew in her heart that she was looking, too. Everyone was; the Reverend had confirmed it.

'I have to change,' Jean said, firmly. 'It could be next month, or next week now I've got the money. I can't wait any longer.'

Eva rolled her eyes. 'Orgies and Bible class. You know something, English? I think you may be the type to do well here, after all.'

Part Five

BEGINNING

39

As her investment in her soul deepened, Jean got behind on the rent. Her additional sources of income were drying up: Eva could not match Varga's appetite for prescribed narcotics and had yet to run out, no further acts of blackmail were required and the trees remained stubbornly free of fruit. Jean took to pocketing stray coins and single bills found trapped under seat cushions and in clothes that were to be washed. She had finally lost her honesty, having never before transgressed purely for her own sake. She told herself that these were invisible thefts, easily stood by the unknowing victims — though she wouldn't have taken so much as a penny from their conscious hands without earning it first.

But the end was nigh. She felt as though she were running downhill, gaining speed as she shed control; legs clattering, arms wind-milling, brain spinning. At night, lying still, she could feel the wind push back her hair and whistle through her teeth. She craved work but made a poor job of it, her movements quick and careless, her judgement skewed. She spent extra hours covering her mistakes and was not sorry to see them go, all her time was waste, until The Day. She gained an appetite for the city, dreaming of its stores and streets, seeing herself amongst people, unnoticed, unremarked upon. It was already happening at the meetings; each convert

461

was so focused on the vision of him or herself remade, they barely noticed their surroundings — even when surrounded by Jean. She had spent a lifetime trying to hold herself back, in check, to minimise harm — but she was the Church's responsibility now. It was unstoppable: she was going to change.

If Jean was mobile, Eva found herself paralysed with power; the enormity of what she had done cut her off at the knees. She didn't know how to make phone calls that couldn't be traced, or write extorting letters with the requisite menace. If she went into an office carrying the film, what was to stop anyone from simply taking it from her and throwing her in jail? Her life suddenly seemed like someone else's very bad idea. The canister sat at the back of her refrigerator, from which she imagined waves of sickness radiated; nausea seized her every time she passed it. She swore to herself she could feel its malign influence seeping into the walls and thought about ordering in liquor, anything that would suspend time and outcome.

Jean kept to her usual hours, as agreed. They were still bound, and tightly, but without ease. The facility of that morning in the diner was mimicked but didn't convince; it was as if Eva was behind glass and having to mime to be understood. Everything was a little too pronounced. Then Eva found out that Varga's location shoot had been delayed, and began to suspect that she would never see her scheme's end; she would be in the precarious state of unfulfilled blackmailer from then on. She began to pack.

Jean found her kneeling among a stack of cases that would shame a touring company. Eva was indiscriminate, clothes went in with utensils and were topped with phonograph records. Jean felt the colour drain out of her; they must have been found out.

'Wh . . . what's happening?'

Eva looked up from the large trunk she was filling with dinner plates; she was wearing all four of her silk kimonos at once, and her arms from wrist to elbow were smothered in bracelets. 'Nothing. I'm practising. For life on the run. I've done this five times already.'

'You're not going anywhere?' Jean didn't think she could be abandoned again so soon. She wanted someone to see her different.

Eva shook her head and threw up her hands, the bracelets clinking against each other. 'Absolutely nowhere! I can't do anything. I'm stuck.'

Despite Eva's agitation, Jean couldn't help but feel a little pleased at this. She had done what she did to help Eva, but also to bring her close. Even if Eva herself didn't feel it.

'I'm here,' Jean said. 'I mean, I'm here to help, if you need me. It doesn't have to be . . . you don't have to pay me.'

Eva sat back on her heels and stared at Jean. She seemed to be evaluating her as if she were a familiar object that had just exhibited a surprising function. 'My God. You would have done it for free, wouldn't you? You would have done the film for free.'

Jean blushed and looked away, she hated being

so transparent in her need for people. If she could just do without them, as she was so clearly supposed to, marked the way she was, things would be much simpler.

'You would, wouldn't you?' Eva continued, disbelieving. 'I thought you were reliable, but . . . Well, you sweet sap.'

Eva seemed about to reach for Jean's hand, but abruptly switched to the pack of cigarettes resting on the table. She had been wanted for herself, even as she was unsure what that was, having defined herself with props and substances for too long to remember. She lit a cigarette, holding the smoke in her lungs until she had control of herself again. Eva wished for cruelty, or indifference, at which until recently she had been skilled. She had begun to slip at the same time this curious woman had washed up at her feet.

She exhaled, and felt none of the steel return, just curiosity. 'Why?'

Jean thought hard, she wanted the words to behave themselves on the way out. 'Because I can't be for me alone, can I?'

Eva opened her eyes wider, as if trying — and failing — to absorb the sense of the remark through them. 'Why ever not?' she asked.

Jean opened her mouth, and then closed it again. She had no answer. So she offered to make them both some tea.

While she was in the kitchen, Jean looked through Eva's cupboards. The refrigerator was empty, as usual — Eva's appetite had receded further since she replaced her liquid diet with a

464

capsule one — but some ancient, dusty tins remained. Jean selected three, of which only one was missing a label. The nightworker had earlier, and unknowingly, sacrificed some bread and cheese, and even Ermeline would go on to contribute a few vegetables and some butter. Jean was amazed what she could fit into her overalls without anyone noticing. It wasn't enough to satisfy her, but that, after all, was the point of her teachings. She wasn't supposed to be satisfied anymore. Her stomach growled and she knew there was want in her; she had come so far, so quickly.

Jean grimaced at the sweet tea — she had run out of sugar so put more than double the usual in the cups, for energy — but Eva didn't seem to notice. She took a pill from a small gold case and chased it down with the syrupy brew. As she lit another cigarette, Jean noticed how yellowed Eva's fingers were again. She had done little but sit and smoke since the party.

'How much longer, do you think?' Jean asked. 'Before it'll be done?'

Eva freed one arm of half its bangles and spread them across the table. 'A day, a week, a month. Who knows? I can't do anything without Varga. How can I strand her out there? I don't know what to ask for. She was supposed to be here. I was going to make it a gift: the answer to everything.'

Jean wanted to reach for her, but knew that the time when she might have given Eva a hug had passed, if it had ever come at all. So she asked: 'Would it make you feel better to come to

465

a spiritual meeting?'

Eva's left eyebrow swung up to her hairline and two exquisite curls of cigarette smoke shot from her nostrils. 'It most certainly would not.'

Don't worry, Jean thought. I'll come back for you. She was certain that Eva would appreciate that; though the Reverend Hatchard would have appreciated it more if he knew.

Jean, at least, did not have long to wait to be saved. Jonas had announced the Success Through Spirituality rally, and not a moment too soon. Though her faith was one of indulgence, her life as a follower was tending towards the ascetic and it was a somewhat reduced Jean that made her way to the boardwalk for the much-overdue day of reckoning. She saw this as a good sign.

On what would turn into a hot, sunny Saturday, she rose, lightheaded, with the dawn. She repaired the dress that Gloria's sewing circle made her, patching in fabric culled from a pillowslip at the arms and neck and nipping in the waist. She washed her hair and scrubbed her skin as hard as she dared. Dressed, she dabbed powder on her nose and rouge on her lips. Outside, she was hope. Inside, she was starving. Before leaving, Jean checked her reflection in the bathroom mirror. 'Goodbye,' she whispered.

The brightly painted buses that ran to the beach were more festive than the norm; boarding one, Jean felt she was about to go on holiday. The boardwalk had long been home to an ever-changing roster of mediocre entertainments: dancers, mediums and psychics; would-be crooners with their backing bands of part-time mechanics and chemistry teachers; demonstrators extolling labour-saving gadgets or foul-smelling liquids with fantastic stain-removing properties; and a flat wooden rink where records played over a tannoy and young unmarried couples and children rolled around on rented skates.

A marquee housed the dancers and the bigger names on the band circuit. Something happens to air under canvas, the consistency thickens with cigarette smoke and humidity, while the oxygen thins. It is ideal for religious meetings, and this was where the Reverend would launch his crusade. A small, independent radio station broadcast live from the boardwalk every weekend and had agreed to add the Reverend to their 'local colour' section of the programme. A committee of microphones crowded a trestle table to one side of the stage, manned by a harried-looking technician who was trying to fend the public off.

The sign outside said 'Change Your Life — see inside' and 'Success — Guaranteed'. The phrases were duplicated on the cover of the most recent brochure, under a photograph of Jonas. Jean arrived early, having barely given a glance to the amusements she passed. She and the other faithful were to set the stage and shepherd the curious through what passed for doors. Jonas had also taken the precaution of engaging some extras, who were told to push their way through, loudly proclaiming that they could not be held back from the good deal that was on offer inside. Jean studied the faces of the people filing in, they mostly had that look of needing directions but not wanting to appear a tourist. That look of life. Jean knew it; she had been like them, afraid to ask the way in case the person she asked took one look at her and demanded to know what the hell she thought she was doing here anyway and to get the hell out. If there wasn't anywhere in particular she was supposed to be — and if there was, it had been blown to bits years before — then everything was trespass. She wondered who had come because of her heartfelt leafleting; she didn't recognise any of them. Or rather, she recognised them all. They looked the same: there was something small and easy about them. She didn't think they were people who could afford to lose what little they had, which had to be a good thing. Everything to gain, the Reverend said. Jean felt her stomach tighten a little and decided it was excitement.

Ermeline sat fidgeting in the front row, her gloved hands rolling over each other as if she were trying to keep hold of a gerbil. In recent days she had entertained doubts about the Reverend — doubt in itself being quite alarming to her, as one born on the path to righteousness, and doubt about a man of God positively heretical. But she had heard less and less about God as the mission had progressed. Her inheritance had dwindled as her doubts grew; the Reverend had new clothes, new teeth, new and almost entirely convincing hair. But she, as yet, had no ministry to rule over with him. The meetings had been loose and unsatisfactory, and still no date had been set for the building of their

468

church's permanent home. Surely, she thought, they had collected enough money by now. Ermeline had envisioned two large white chairs, simpler than thrones but just as imposing, set on a stage in front of a vast congregation housed in a gleaming marble hall the size of an aircraft hangar. This foetid tent was not what she had expected her hundreds of dollars to bring her. She squared her shoulders and tried to remember the last time she had seen Jonas pray of his own free will.

Ermeline initiated the prayers at the beginning of each meeting; Jonas said that he preferred to save his energy for the Message and was likely to get so carried away with speaking to God that he would forget to deliver his words to others. But once or twice she had snuck a look at the Reverend and found him not as a man of the cloth should be. One time she was certain she saw him smirking at his reflection in a wall mirror while all around him heads were bowed. Then there were the words. His was not the language of holiness. When returning from a meeting one night, they had driven past a vast billboard on which a beautiful actress advertised toothpaste.

'That's what we need!' Jonas cried. 'A star. If it makes them feel better to use the same toothpaste as one of the chosen, imagine how it feels to use the same God!'

Ermeline was all for inducements — an ancestor of hers had passed out blankets, beads and smallpox in an attempt to convert the savages — but to manufacture God along with toothpaste, to squeeze Him into a tube and pack Him into a box, this was too much. She was beginning to have her doubts that Jonas was even Christian. She had pulled the car over to the side of the road and demanded an explanation. Why, could he tell her, was he acting as if he had invented the Almighty for the purpose of this Church and not the other way around?

'We are here to serve *the Lord*, Jonas. You cannot promise God and deliver toothpaste. The people will know the difference.'

Though he wanted to push her face through the windscreen, Jonas backpedalled furiously, apologising for using the crass language of advertising in the pursuit of salvation. He explained that the late nights he had spent studying such material in order to properly diagnose the spiritual malaise currently affecting society had coloured his language, but never his mission. He suggested they alight from the car there and then and pray for reaffirmation. Ermeline assented, but kept him by the roadside for half an hour just to be sure. As the gravel dug into his knees, Jonas promised himself that he would be rid of Ermeline as soon the Church was properly launched. But he didn't forget the billboard.

★ ★ ★

By six o'clock the tent supports were creaking and the air was as thick as broth. For anyone at all to come inside on such a day, they had to be desperate. The Reverend was relying on it:

470

desperation was the vast resource that would fuel his ascent. The sides of the tent could be rolled back to let in air, or kept closed to make sure nobody got a free look; Jonas had instructed that only the front of the tent should be open. He wanted passing trade to be able to see in, but not too much; best to let them think they were missing out and push forward for more. By the time they reached the front they would be in such an anxiety of consumption they'd hand over the money just to get it out of their hands. The crowd swayed as one, absorbing each surge from the hinterland, rolling with it. The radio technician set up a cordon of folding chairs and was using a limp newspaper to swat anyone who got too close.

'How much longer?' a man asked Jean, his wife draped over his arm like a damp towel.

'Not long now,' Jean replied. 'We're almost there.'

★ ★ ★

At six thirty, there was a whir of machinery and two huge fans at the back of the stage came to life. Usually, they were used to lift the skirts of the dancers but today had been angled at the crowd. The Reverend Jonas Hatchard swept on as if powered by the breeze; the cool air washing over him and down over the congregation. The faithful broke into applause, which quickly died down. They wanted to hear more than anyone.

'Thank you,' he said. 'And welcome to the rest of your lives.'

Jean saw an entirely different man to the dry old stick she had first encountered; he gleamed with health, with the kind of well-being money brings. He carried a leather-bound brochure and a sheaf of pamphlets that he placed on a white lectern. Even the firecloth, with its crude renderings of half-naked dancing girls painted on it, couldn't diminish his air of purity. He inspired a kind of awe. Jean felt her lips part in anticipation, her breathing slow and her neck extend forward, her toes flexed as if balanced on the edge of a kerb. The rest of her life. She had been studying for weeks, and this was the moment it would all become clear.

'So what are you selling, you old buzzard?'

Someone swept in by the general flow of people, and unconvinced by the strange-looking bird in the expensive suit, was jumping up and down to make himself heard. There were giggles from the crowd. He didn't look like a reverend, didn't wear the collar, so they felt no compunction about gently mocking him. They needed to, almost; they were looking for some way to vent a little of their excitement and their shame at being so needy. There was a definite atmosphere of suppression, pent up as before a fight or a race. From his previous life, Jonas knew just how many so-called good people — the numbers used to astound and amuse him — lived on the edge of sin and envied its trappings while decrying its practitioners. He knew what they wanted and what they weren't prepared to do to get it — the necessary. Well, he would show them the way. The Reverend smiled, leaned his elbows on the lectern and addressed the back of the room.

'What is it you're looking to buy?'

The man stayed down this time. He didn't want to answer in case he found himself to be at an auction and suddenly in possession of an expensive antique, something useless and curlicued that couldn't be returned. (It was a particular fear of his, he believed that auctioneers lay in wait for unsuspecting citizens, trying to trick them into outrageous purchases with a sly nod or wink.)

'No, really, tell me.' The Reverend cast his net wider, looking beyond the heckler to those around him, who were also trying to avoid Jonas's penetrating gaze. 'What is it you're looking for?'

The man bobbed up again. 'I don't want anything from you!' He was sweating, gripped by the irrational fear that he was now the owner of something gilded and French, probably a chair.

'And I don't want to sell you anything, friend. I just want to know what it is that you want. And then I'm going to tell you how to get it. What is it that you want? What is it that I can help you achieve?'

The crowd was entranced. The Reverend's rich, dark eyes so full of concern, his voice so full of compassion, the heat settling on them like a wet blanket. No one had ever asked them what they wanted. The Reverend had hit upon a simple truth — when it came to what to want, there were too many people telling and not

473

enough asking. And he knew it would be enough for most people just to be asked.

The heckling man was torn between fear and desire; he could feel the crowd willing him to answer, urging him to get the secret from this strange, hypnotic speaker, but the image of the chair was now so fixed in his mind he feared he might scream for it. Jean sensed a shift in the room — she had had to learn to gauge the mood of groups at a young age; she was not the sort to be subjected to unilateral attacks — and this was not violence, but an oddly constipated tension as if the entire gathering was trying to hold in wind. Ermeline's hands were in overdrive, a cylindrical blur of white. Only the Reverend was calm, his absolute sense of purpose acting on him like air-conditioning.

'Don't you want to know how you can turn your life around, achieve everything you've ever dreamed of?'

To the left of Jean was a woman caught in the sag between firm youth and loose age; neither old enough for exemption nor young enough for inclusion, she hovered painfully in that desperate stretch of time that is only interested in running out. She dreamed of love. She had on a new sundress, but a week's worth of grease settled in her hair. She had been approached by a follower in a laundromat where she had been watching clothes not her own turn over on themselves. The woman was clutching a leaflet and had obviously already worked herself up into quite a state over the prospect of it coming good. The heckling man's silence was going to cost her dear

474

and she knew it. The Reverend knew he was going to be rich when he heard her yell, 'I want to know!'

'Of course you want to know.' His eyes snapped on her in a second. 'You see other people, not always better people, enjoying more and you think, why?'

The woman nodded vigorously; she had often seen and thought just that, it was true. The Reverend knew her heart.

'But the question should not be *why*. Did God ask *why*?'

No one in the tent seemed sure. A few opened their mouths only to close them again, others gripped their chins. Ermeline wondered who God could ask, and why, indeed, would He.

'No, He asked Himself *how*. *How* can I show mankind the way. Now I am saying to you, you need to ask yourselves *how*. *How* can I find the way. There is no *why*. You're good people, hard-working people. You go to church, pay taxes, and still . . . where's the reward? In heaven? Certainly. But what about now? God says believe in Me and you shall have heaven. Faith brings rewards, everybody knows that. I am on a mission from God. I say believe in Succesa Through Spirituality and you will have Heaven on Earth! There is no reason why you should not have everything you desire. Now, my dear, what is it that you want? You have to tell me before I can help you.'

She was the kind he needed, the kind he hoped for. A lifetime of unhappiness had yet to extinguish the belief that happiness was her right and due and was being held from her by forces unknown. Those with a limitless amount of belief that stubbornly resisted the proof of experience, they would never learn — and he never wanted them to. He had them believing he was the one who would draw back the curtain to reveal the hiding place of the life they should have had.

The woman touched her dress, then her hair, then her mouth. The dress had meant nothing but crackers at lunch for five days; her hair was starchy from a badly performed home permanent; her mouth hadn't received a kiss in two years. She had come for a walk today to show off the new dress, hoping that what she had paid for it would be recouped in a dinner, a movie or a Sunday drive that would lead to something more permanent. So far it had not resulted in even a single admiring glance. She could have spent the money on a fine dinner and a dozen or more movie tickets, falling in love as many times in the safety of the theatre.

'I want better,' she said, almost to herself. But Jonas heard it. The crowd heard it. It flattened dissent in an instant. Even the already faithful turned to look at her, in renewed recognition. What they wanted had brand names, currencies, locations, but really it was just 'better'. Better than this.

'I want better,' she repeated, firmly this time, and was applauded. The war was over. It was no longer enough just to have survived; there was no merit in simply existing. It had to be better.

'Now,' Jonas leaned towards her a little and she responded in kind, 'let me hear you say you

476

deserve it. Let me hear you say you deserve better.'

'I do!' she cried. 'I deserve better!' The crowd applauded again; and one thought formed in and rose from them. If she does, then so do I.

Jean's stomach seemed host to a colony of bats rather than butterflies, so heavy was the beating of wings inside her. Everyone here was like her, desperate and alone and without answers. They were her and she was them. And still she couldn't explain the sudden lead weight of doubt in her.

'Excellent! You see? Belief. That is what our Church is about. It's a Church of man! It's good to want. It's natural to want. God wants you to want!'

Jonas was shaking with emotion at this point; the surge of power he felt going though his body was unlike anything he had experienced in his days of specialised pleasure and narcotic experimentation. He had busted the dam of their desires and they couldn't wait to tell him every sad little yearning that rendered their colourless lives all the more unbearable. And the beauty was that once he had convinced them they could attain that particular want, it would no longer be enough. The Steps Towards Success could lead all the way to the sky.

'What more do you want? Do you want proof of what Success Through Spirituality can achieve — what you can achieve? Here it is! Welcome, please, Reggie Baines from *Time of Your Life*!' The Reverend flung out his arms and the crowd cheered as if the President were being inaugurated in front of them.

Reggie Baines Junior hosted *Time of Your Life*, a very successful radio quiz, soon to cross over to television, in which members of the studio audience tried to correctly identify a year through a piece of music, a newspaper headline or popular catch-phrase and were rewarded with appliances supplied by the sponsor. Reggie liked to be whipped.

It was his misfortune that he had been arrested in a raid that had also collared individuals of a considerably more sordid disposition than himself, and the judge was threatening him with complicity in their crimes. Reggie had not appealed to Jonas for help, but Jonas had extended a request for information regarding such arrests, particularly those of personalities involved in radio or television, and had arrived at the cells offering succour. His own past made him a poor blackmailer: there was at least as much dirt lying around on him as there was on anybody, and to stir it up only necessitated fresh laundry for all. But he was in a position to offer help to those who were in dire need of it and unlikely to receive it from any other quarter. In return, they would publicise his Church, make some modest claims about its role in their own success and continue to enjoy that success without the threat of ruin and disgrace hanging over them. Jonas had welcomed Reggie to the fold and paid off the judge.

Reggie was not the best Jonas could hope for. Though there were many people who would like to be him, there were, sadly for Jonas, many who could manage the feat on their own. If they only knew the system. But everyone had to start somewhere, and good disciples were expensive. Someone who sold toothpaste, that's what Jonas really wanted. But because Reggie gave away expensive prizes every week, a lot of people assumed he could personally afford to do so and he would seem successful enough to the majority.

Reggie Baines Junior bounded on to great applause, which he immediately dampened. Reggie's solemn face was at odds with his sky-blue striped suit. He wore the kind of clothes all radio hosts wore at public appearances to suggest the rambunctious personality that was, on air, produced with laughter cues and slide whistles. The crowd calmed, he looked as if he was about to lead them in prayer.

Perhaps this was when the veil would be lifted, Jean thought, casting the doubt as nerves. She lurched forward, her eagerness to hear overtaking her balance. She had to put her hands on the shoulders of a man in front of her who nearly collapsed under the weight. 'Back off!' he hissed, but he was too rapt to even look behind him, and she regained her footing without starting a panic. Steadying herself against one of the supports, Jean looked out over the sea of faces, sweat-shiny and hopeful, every one. She had not been wrong, she told herself. She had not been wrong to think that she could be changed. Everyone else here thought it too. They were not unlike her.

'I used to believe in God,' Reggie intoned, eyes to the floor, ears tuned to the expected gasps that were readily released. Then he lifted his head, pointed his fingers at the roof and grinned. 'But the Reverend Jonas Hatchard has shown me that God also believes in me!'

There was uproar. Reggie hurled buttons into the crowd that bore the words 'God Believes in Me' and they were snatched up and pinned on with such ferocity that several shirt pockets were torn. Jonas signalled Ermeline and she pushed two cases of brochures onto the stage, obedient despite her growing alarm at the irreligious nature of proceedings. Reggie held one aloft and declared:

'This is my Bible! This is where the answers were waiting for me and where I found my future. This gave me the strength to believe, to realise and to become. And it can for you too! It told me to leave behind the person I was, because that guy was a bum! It told me to find out who I wanted to be. It showed me how I was going to become that person. By the time I finished, people, by the time I finished I had a job on radio. And I'm not done yet!'

Reggie Baines Junior had a talent for spinning out dead air, noted when he followed his father into the technical side of the business and was unexpectedly called on to fill in for an electrocuted announcer. While his father fixed the circuits, Reggie described the view from the studio window. It was decided he was a radio natural. He had been on *Time of Your Life* ever since, and regarded the move to television as his just reward for years of tedium: the gateway to a world of fabulous earnings and national fame.

Jonas had discovered him weeping in his cell. To Reggie, at least, the benefits of Jonas's Church were bona fide.

Jonas regained the stage. He shook Reggie's hand, smiling, and duplicated his gesture of pointing at the ceiling. 'This is what God does,' Jonas was saying. 'Not your God, but mine. Under exclusive contract.' People from the crowd were crying out now, demanding to know what the steps were and how they could begin. They surged forward, dollar bills in their outstretched hands, then receded, clutching their futures between two glossy covers. With each brochure, Jonas asked, 'What do you want?' and after receiving the reply would proclaim, 'Here it is!' and hand over the glossy publication.

Ermeline's suspicions crystallised at the top of her boiling brain. The brochures being handed out looked markedly different to the set she had been given by Jonas, in a leather folder embossed with golden angels. These carried no mention of God that she could see. Perhaps He was inside. She grabbed at a brochure that was being passed overhead, but had it snatched away by an irate matron who was Ermeline's match in weight but a class above in viciousness.

'Wait your turn, lady!' the rival barked, and bounced Ermeline from the front row with a practised jut of the stomach. Once Ermeline was loosed from her moorings, she was at the mercy of the crowd, squeezed through the ranks like a drop of oil through cogs, ending up at the back, abused and exhausted. She could only watch as Jonas rode the wave of need cresting at the front.

'Those already in the Church,' he shouted. Hands waved in the air in response. 'You have arrived at the start of your journey. Those who have yet to come to us?' More hands as they helpfully identified themselves. 'We are waiting for you. Don't be late, I don't want to leave without you!'

He dazzled them, he flattered them; he grew wings and danced over the heads of the congregation. Wanting is as good as getting, he told them, you just have to learn how to want. He didn't say what happens when what you want doesn't want you.

The air was thick with want; Jean felt as if she was suffocating on the desires of others. People who had fought their way to Jonas once were going back to confess some more, worried that they had started too small and would be held to an opening bid. Cars and jobs and refrigerators became love and beauty and youth. The Reverend had unleashed an unstoppable wave of desire that could never be satisfied. Nausea clutched at her stomach. The current of need lifted Jean away from the edge of the crowd, drawing her deeper. It stirred up her blood and poured memory back into her veins, Denny pulsed in her again. People were screaming out ever more personal details; good-for-nothing sons and whore daughters and cruel mothers and absent fathers and fat wives and violent husbands screamed their inadequacies to the sky and pleaded with Jonas to cure them. It was a competitive frenzy of failure.

'We are all worthy,' he told them. 'Cast off that

failure, join the Church of Success where failure does not dwell. Just to join, is to put yourself on the path.'

They were happy, Jean could see that. The people were happy, they were coming away from the front of the crush, clutching brochures, feeling good and hopeful and reassured. Others struggled to take their place, the crowd churning like water as the satisfied and the hungry converged. This was what she wanted to be: smaller, thinner, fatter, richer, average. Their wants were her wants: more, better, sooner. Everything she deserved, for everything she was; a trade. Jean looked down at her shaking hands, at the furrowed skin of her arms that told her it could be a world without consequence. She thought of Gloria, unprotected by beauty; Wisteria unhindered in her malice; and what strained at the surface of some perfect skins, in a velvet-lined room.

Jean could feel an internal tide turn. She wanted to pull away from this; it made her scars crawl. She looked at the people around her and saw herself, ravenous, greedy and wasteful, bent on destruction. There was more desperation here than she had ever known. And the Reverend was stoking it; with him she would never stop wanting, never stop believing there was something better waiting for her, just out of reach. Looking down at her body, she sought the reassurance of solidity, but her dress hung loosely on her and her wrists looked thin and weak — she was no longer familiar to herself. Instead of triumph, she felt fear. She wanted to remain, suddenly. What did change hold? Underneath the ruined skin and the excellent muscle, what longing would there be? She might be everything he didn't want, might rid herself of everything he had wanted, and yet still not be free. And the world, with its peculiarities and its fancies — how could she be certain of it?

The Reverend's words seemed hollow in the din. It hardly mattered anymore what he was saying; hysteria had taken over and was now the force guiding them all. Jean listened as if for the first time. 'Want it!' he cried. 'Name it! Receive it!' Assuming it could be captured in a word. Assuming that she could. Cars, vacations, radios and refrigerators — all that can be manufactured. Let us have them, the crowd was saying. And let them be enough, Jean thought. She had tried so hard not to be consumed by a longing that could have no relief, but it was in her like a virus and it was stronger than her. She coursed with the pain of love gone rotten from being made to no one's bidding and stored to no purpose. Her whole body suddenly woke up angry, with pins and needles in her limbs and her heart. Everything she had denied herself came crashing through at once, and she felt as though she might explode, that her skin would split from the force of desire raging in her and torrents of unused, useless love would cascade from her, burning like acid. She wanted, and it made no difference. It was as useless and empty as belief.

'I'm going to speak to every one of you,' Jonas was shouting over the excited babble of those who believed they had purchased more than promises. 'This is only the beginning.' Jean waded through the outpourings of desperate souls, their words clinging to her like strands of a spider's web — she felt them catch in her hair and break on her sleeve. She was smothered in want and still it was nothing to her own. She had no money to hold out to Jonas and she had all the pretty brochures she could read and find to be worthless; she just needed to form the words, in a voice that could be heard in heaven.

'I want not to want!'

It was as if time froze and she existed outside of it. Everyone looked and no one spoke; only her sobs were audible, only the movement of her grief-racked shoulders disturbed the thickened air. She was raw and wounded and obvious. Jonas felt every word he had ever known evaporate from his brain; there was nothing to say in the face of this. He could feel the crowd willing him to answer, to tell her that she was wrong, that it was good to want, that the absence that pained her now would be filled. That she only had to believe. But he could not answer. All eyes had turned from Jean and were now on the Reverend, silently urging him to help her, as a wounded animal should be helped, by being put out of its misery. But he had no bullet for her. She had pulled the curtain back and seen nothing at all.

'I . . . I want to be free of it.'

'And . . . I will free you, sister!' In his panic, Jonas reverted to the language and intonation of his father. 'I will free you. Just tell me what you want. One of our earliest followers, ladies and gentlemen, overcome by the occasion. Remember, Jean, you *can* ask for yourself, it is *good* to want, to *crave*. Don't deny yourself!'

'No!' Her body trembled with the force of the reply and Jonas's smile died on his face. 'There *are* things I can't have. And wanting them is too much. I'm not here for a car, or a swimming pool or gold bloody teeth! There are things I will *never* have. There is too much in this world for me.' She was begging now, desperate for whatever magic he could conjure. 'Please! I just want not to want, anymore.'

The Reverend Jonas Hatchard was frozen in the horror of looking at something true and incontrovertible when the sound of wood splintering broke like thunder above them and he only had time to scream a few words.

'My God, what have you done?!'

★ ★ ★

Accounts of what happened next conflicted. None of the people attending the meeting suffered more than bruises and anxiety, but a cloud of confusion settled over the incident that was never fully dispelled. Some said that the big, strange woman in the red, white and blue dress had reached up and pulled the tent down around them. Others that a small earthquake had hit at that precise moment, the work of an angry and insulted God. One extremely nervous young man swore blind that the big, strange woman had actually exploded. Jonas said it was sabotage, plain and simple, and urged the

486

attendant police officers to interview Jean. At that same time, two terrified teenage boys were debating whether to confess to their prank, which had involved attaching one end of a rope to their kit car and the other end to the main tent support, and then driving like hell. But to everyone that was inside, Jean was at the centre of it somehow.

Little chills the blood more effectively than the groaning and cracking of wood moving against its will. Though they knew perfectly well they were in a tent, on the boardwalk, by the beach, the sound plunged every person there into a mine that was caving in. Ermeline led the screaming, while Jonas commanded the faction that ran in circles. Jean, who knew what it was to be buried alive, blundered out of the side exit like a rogue elephant escaping the circus.

Behind her, the collapse was total. The mission now resembled a punch-up under a pie-crust with figures flailing beneath the downed canvas. Bystanders rushed to help, lifting the edges of the tent so that Jonas's congregation could wriggle out like worms from a rotten core. A chain of people formed; rink attendants, lifeguards and pretzel-vendors passed along iced water to revive the stricken, dousing an unfortunate few.

Jean felt the chaos diffuse her, until she was no more than a shadow. She crept away, drifting through the crowds, uncommonly dreamy and light-footed, passing almost unnoticed. She felt like a spirit, untethered to the earth and humanity. Then, above the sickly sweetness of sugar and sweat, she caught the sharp scent of the sea, and home. She had her direction. She left the boardwalk and let her feet sink into the sand, which felt as cool as a dry palm in the evening air.

Everything seemed sharper away from the smothering fog of the tent. There had indeed been a change: she was now a thief and an accomplice to crimes she didn't even understand; her money was gone, her home was certainly lost and her hope had been stolen. That was what want had showed her. To have nothing is not always to have everything to gain, sometimes it is just to have nothing. She felt one last impossible request form: 'I want never to have done wrong,' she thought. But it was too late. It was all too late. She had not even enquired after the price of a bus ticket back to Gloria, and could never admit to her friend that she was waiting to become new before she saw her again. Gloria wouldn't understand, and she wouldn't now be able to explain. There was nothing left.

Once, Jean had dreamed that she was transformed by darkness and became a giant night creature, pale and terrible in the moonlight. She lived in the sea during the day and would emerge when the sun went down, the wetness clinging to her body like oil. She would roam about the town, peeling the tops from houses to get a look at the people inside, fascinated by the atoms of their lives. They would stir under her gaze, perhaps throwing off their bed covers, which Jean would gently replace, lifting a corner with a silver-green fingernail as long and curved as a scythe. She would watch over them, her little neighbours, entranced by their funny little ways. Then she would sit on a hill as if it were a footstool and comb her hair with a telegraph pole, enjoying the moon on her skin as if it were the midday sun. Before the sun rose she would return to the sea; existing only as the last dream a person remembered before they woke.

But she had looked into people's lives and found no room in them for her, and it had become too hard to exist only for herself; she was more than she had need for. The time had come to return.

Jean threw her tennis shoes behind her and let the sand gently lash her bare feet as she walked. She stopped to inhale the scent of the sea, flooding her lungs with childhood and home, and felt an impatient dig at the back of her mind.

'Mum?' It had been so long, Jean couldn't be sure. Her lips barely moved as the thoughts were given voice in her head. 'Where have you been?'

'*Waiting,*' she heard Wisteria reply. '*For this.*'

'Let's be off, then,' Jean said, out loud.

The smell of the sea got stronger. Jean looked forward to the feel of salt water against her legs; more crisp and alive than bathwater or rainwater, it could feel as rough as paper until you were under it, then it was like blankets and down and kisses. It felt like the only thing that was meant to be, all the rest was accidental and over with. She was after all only doing what her mother had tried to do, what she had fooled herself out of in the desert. It was not so much suicide as a very late abortion.

With Wisteria on her shoulders, Jean stepped into the sea. It ran up over her toes and then scooted away into the sunset. Seconds later it was back, tagging her and then running away. There was no mistaking its invitation. She was in no hurry and stood at the ocean's edge enjoying the game, waiting for the right moment to join.

The sound of sirens drifted over her on its way out to sea, and she guessed the police had arrived. In matters of structures falling down, it was only a short while before someone looked for her involvement in some capacity. At least she wouldn't now go to prison. She could hear the faint cries of those still trapped under the canvas. The boardwalk was its usual blur of colour and noise, but the colours were from searchlights and flares and the noise was screaming. Jean sighed for the world she was leaving, realising it would only thank her for leaving it alone. She waded out into the deeper water and it kissed her knees in welcome. Something wanted her at least. She was going back to where she should never have started from, back home to where she could have come to this just as easily and sooner. She would put an end to want.

She turned to take one last look at life in all its disastrous glory and was rewarded with the sight of a lone figure, staggering on the sand; a refugee from the boardwalk disaster, she supposed. His white hair was as wild as a physicist's and his white suit-coat flapped around him as he waved his arms madly in warning or greeting — Jean couldn't tell which. Outlined by the neon fire of the boardwalk lights, he looked like a crazed prophet come to advise her of the world's end. Jean was transfixed; there was no place she could go where weird would not follow. It was devoted to her. Resentment bloomed; there might well be one thing she could do with proficiency, if anyone would let her get on and do it.

'Stay back!' she shouted. 'This is my business here. Nothing to do with you.'

Gasping, the white-haired man reached the edge of the ocean and held up a hand as if begging her attendance. Then he doubled over, clutching his knees as his lungs clutched at air. Jean thought he was a goner, but when he reared up again after a few seconds of wheezing, his face was a picture of joy and his arms were open as if to embrace her and fate.

'I sing the body electric!' he cried, with all the air left in him. 'And you, dear lady, could power a small city!'

And with that he bowed, jerked, grabbed at his chest through his suit jacket, and pitched face forward into the wet sand.

40

As the white-haired man was lapped gently by the tide, Jean looked out at the sea and wondered if to keep going made it murder. Then the water reached his nose and lips, bubbling around them.

★ ★ ★

Elijah Porter regained consciousness as Jean was tipping him into one of the sunchairs that could be rented by the hour. Behind them, in the twilit distance, the tent had been pulled back almost into place and the last of the dazed congregates were being dragged into the air. Jonas was just visible in the searchlights, a sleeve torn loose from his handsome suit and his shop-bought hair hanging from one side of his head as if the top of his skull had been opened like a biscuit jar.

Porter looked up to see the mighty Jean stood over him, her hands planted firmly on her hips, her strong jaw jutting forward as she contemplated the scene of chaos that was happening close by them. He felt moved again — as, it transpired, he would often in her vicinity — to cry out, as if in the presence of the divine. He flung his arms wide, and from the reclining majesty of his sunchair, addressed the goddess before him.

'Goddamn it! If I'm not dead and this isn't

heaven, then what is an angel doing before me?'

Though his voice boomed, surprisingly audible for a man apparently near death just minutes ago, Jean looked down as though she had heard an ant whistle for her attention. He was from very far outside her experience.

'You what?' she demanded.

'No, you what? What you?' he retorted playfully, even flirtatiously. 'You couldn't be an old man's dying apparition, could you? In that case, finish me off and send me to hell, for I've had enough of this cruel world!'

Jean remembered that responsibility never could be accurately measured before being taken on; she had obviously rescued a madman. She decided to ascertain his physical condition and then have done with him. She would find a quieter stretch of beach after that.

'You look a bit off. Does your chest still hurt?'

'No, but my heart aches at the sight of you. I've been looking for you my whole life, you gorgeous creature. Let me buy you your weight in beer and oysters and tell you how I'm going to enrich both our lives. I'm not trying to take advantage of you; I merely want to bask in the presence of my saviour. I have identification. See here.' He opened his jacket and pointed to a pocket wallet. 'Elijah Porter, showman.'

Jean stared at the man in white; he was crumpled and discarded-looking, as if she had hauled him out of a wastepaper basket. That he could think she might be worried by him made her want to smile. Her stomach had given a growl at the mention of food. Knowing that time

493

was now finite made Jean feel generous with it; she couldn't waste an hour she was only going to spend dead, and a bit of food might help her sink faster. But she had to get away from the scene of her latest crime.

'Not here. But somewhere with lights. Bright lights. And you pay for the food first, then I eat. And I don't want any funny business.'

'Ma'am,' Porter attempted a bow from his half-prone position, 'you honour me.'

Born in another century, Porter trailed a lost era behind him, one in which hucksters such as himself travelled on wagons and brought wonders to towns that were devoid of such things and had heard only rumours of their existence. Now, it seemed, everybody knew everything and had seen it all, and his kind no longer cluttered the back roads of the country. He had beached himself on the coast after vaudeville had died, the barnstormers had crashed and the circuses had gone more or less legit. He turned professional at eleven, exhibiting his own webbed toes, and was sixty-seven years old when he saw Eugenia Curnalia (née Clocker) and got a premonition of success so strong it gave him palpitations and temporarily deprived his brain of oxygen. In her, he could see the future, even as she was close to denying herself one.

Jean's appetite was ignorant of her decision to no longer exist, and was raging by the time they reached a restaurant. They sat outside as Jean had not been able to recover her shoes from the beach. If this is to be my last night, she thought, why shouldn't it be strange? I will die as I have lived. Being small didn't matter so much now — tomorrow she would be nothing at all. Elijah watched with pleasure as she tucked into a hotdog — Jean had rejected the offer of oysters; to her they looked tubercular, something spat from a diseased lung — and drank from a large glass mug filled with beer. Despite herself, Jean could not help but smile back.

'Feeling better?'

'Yes, thanks,' she mumbled, through wads of dough and meat. 'Didn't realise how hungry I was.'

'What were you doing out there, my dear — if you don't mind me asking?'

Jean put down the hotdog she was holding and worked on swallowing her food. Porter persisted.

'Did you have something to do with that snake-oil show on the boardwalk?'

She eyed him suspiciously. 'Are you the police?'

'My dear, I am not the police. I'm not even a concerned citizen. I am, however, on your side.'

Jean wondered how to put it into words. She decided to be to the point, as little enough of it made sense to her now. 'They said they were going to give me a new life. But it turns out I didn't want one. Then the tent fell down.'

'Excellent. A new life, you say?'

'Yes. Sort of. I don't really know now. It seemed all right at the time. I gave them money, and they gave me a brochure. I was going to find out how to be different, now I suppose I'll never know.'

'Well.' Porter took another hotdog from the platter and placed it in front of Jean. 'It seems I got here just in time. I wouldn't want you any different.'

'Sorry?'

'I want you to work for me, Miss . . . what is your name, my dear?'

Jean hesitated, it just seemed a name was one more thing keeping her here. If he didn't know, he couldn't tell anyone when she was gone.

'Very well' — he seemed unconcerned — 'I shall call you Venus. She looked a lot like you, I imagine. So, is it Miss or is there a husband?'

Jean shrugged. 'Gone. I thought if I changed . . . '

Porter shook his head and tutted. 'Fool. What a man destroys without knowing. So, you're broke.'

Jean nodded.

'And keeping that delightful form all to yourself.'

Jean didn't know what to say to that, so nodded again.

'Work for me, then.'

'Doing what?'

'Not doing, Venus. Being. But first, let me tell you who I am.'

★   ★   ★

Elijah Porter had spent fifty-six years amassing and losing small fortunes; at times owning an entire circus, at others no more than a change of clothes. He had come out on top more often

496

than not and had seldom ended up broke through a bad business decision; he had been robbed, married and drunk, but he had rarely been wrong about his audiences. Perhaps because he was among them.

While the wounded were borne away from the disaster, and Jean ate her way through several more hotdogs, Porter expounded his philosophy to his latest discovery. He told Jean about the world, as he found it. A world that in the last few years had seen more wonder and horror in a single day than he could have produced in a hundred years of showbusiness. One that had seen the bounds of terror breached so many times that ordinary people now looked for reds under the bed and little green men in the sky — anything than look at their fellow man and try to guess what was in his heart. There was a need for new forms of fear; it was somehow less terrifying and more pleasurable to be scared witless by one of these than by what already existed. After all, one knew that beings from outer space weren't really on their way to vaporise Earth, but one couldn't guarantee what one's neighbour would do given a uniform and free licence. Jean pulled up a sleeve to scratch her scars, and Porter was immediately fascinated.

'From the war?'

'Sort of. Gas explosion, right at the beginning. I didn't get bothered after that. I s'pose I was immunised.'

'Yes.' Porter seemed to like that way of putting it. 'Yes, I suppose.' He reached forward and, holding Jean's wrist with one hand, ran his other palm over her forearm. It felt oddly affectionate to her, as when a grandfather ruffles a boy's hair. 'You know,' he said, suddenly wistful, 'sometimes it's good to be an old man with no one to care for.'

Jean understood; she couldn't have stood more loss. He let go of her arm, relinquishing it with a gentle pat, and continued with his oration.

'Folks don't want to know the truth about themselves right now. They've had too much of it, in my opinion. They want us to disguise it, serve it up in a rubber costume with a mask on top. Well, OK, then, that's what we do.'

With a glass of beer halfway to her mouth, Jean paused. 'We?'

★ ★ ★

Porter used to make his living giving people what they wanted; now he wanted to make them scream for what they feared. He felt it was the right time, and he was the right man. He had come to this city to make his dreams reality, as so many had done before him. Only he had come with cash.

A life spent in and out of hotel rooms, boarding houses, the warm reading rooms of public libraries, brothels and bars had given Porter an eclectic education on which he was constantly trying to improve. He read partially, enthusiastically and without censure. He had perused Hatchard's fliers with interest; there was something in them that reminded him of the old days, so he came to the boardwalk to see what there was to see. He had also recently been delving into the psychology of mobs, and any meeting that pulled a tent down was of interest to him. Certain types of entertainments had been his specialty and he had made it his business to find out all he could about this field. He was not only looking for new acts and possible rivals, but past glories and present understanding. Then he'd spied Jean, quietly making her escape.

In her, he saw something for which he had been searching for a long time. She was an exaggeration, but not a gross one; an anomaly, but one that conformed to the same pattern of perfection as her brethren — only on a different scale. She was a step forward, he thought, rather than a stumble sideways or back. She was not of this world, but not of another or the next. She was incredible and yet conceivable, the essence of horror.

'Do you read, Venus?'

Thanks to Cousin Leonard, Jean never knew how to answer that question. She set aside her plate, and simply nodded, using the excuse of her overstuffed mouth not to answer out loud.

'Excellent. I read everything, though never all the way through. Evolution!'

She started, the tone, not the concept, taking her by surprise.

'There's a theory. Evolution! Filling the gaps in nature, forging new paths down which the rest of us follow. Freaks, my dear. Do you get me?'

Jean shook her head. She rather liked, if didn't

quite understand, the white-haired showman. The company and the food had proved more cheering than she could have imagined. The sea still called, but went unheard.

'The freak shall inherit the earth! Blessed are the freaks! Freaks, those that survive, have to be strong, adapt into the gaps left by uniformity, from where they will flourish! Aaah, beautiful, beautiful evolution. Freaks are the way forward, freaks are the vanguard, I should say. Where they lead, only then can the humdrummers follow. You follow?'

There was a glimmer of something in what he said, a memory of magnetic flaws drawing Jean to them. Bars and straw and people, and the feeling of having found community. He knew — somehow this man knew.

'I think I do.'

'I knew you would! Nature abhors a vacuum, my dear, particularly in a town where everyone gets their nose fixed. Conformity is just around the corner. Can you imagine a world where everyone thinks the same, eats the same, drives the same car and lives in the same house? Well, it's coming. People are erasing themselves.'

Porter lit a small cigar and watched the smoke divide into circles in the still night air.

'People used to travel hundreds of miles to see a two-headed calf,' he sighed, suddenly nostalgic. Sitting across from Jean stirred memories of a brief romance he had enjoyed some forty years before, with one of the few female strongmen on the circuit. She had been much shorter than Jean but as broad and muscular and had worn a lilac tutu as she bent iron bars around her powerful neck. It hadn't been a serious affair; the first time he went to raise his voice to her, Porter realised he was afraid to and, seeing no equality in such a match, called the whole thing off by leaving town in the dead of night.

'I once saw a plane sticking out the top of a house,' Jean offered, keen to have an oddity to contribute. 'They pulled it out and the house fell down.'

'Exactly.' Porter understood. 'Remove the magical and the mundane falls apart. I think the mundane became too strange to cope with and there was no room for the magical, the truly magical, for a while. I don't mean tinsel and miracles and snow in July, but the strangeness of nature and the unpredictability of life. A two-headed calf can bring that right home.'

Jean felt a sudden surge of affection, as if she had found a father. 'Yes, I suppose it can.'

'And here we are in a place where odd is a crooked tooth. No wonder things are in such an unholy mess. Well, I've run on, as I have a tendency to do, so let's get down to business. I want to offer you a job. It's a new age and I think you can be the embodiment of it. You're something people haven't seen a lot of, and I can tell you that what they've seen bores them senseless already. They're ready for something unexpected. I'm going to make movies, Venus, and you're going to make them with me.'

Jean was appalled. Either the man was mad or spiteful. She looked at him with terror and disbelief in her eyes and he simply nodded, his

501

expression one of delight. She realised he was serious, or thought he was.

'But what would I do?'

'Be, my dear. Be.'

'But I don't understand.'

'Well, let's worry about that later. First, take a look at this.'

Porter took a home-made comic book from inside his suit. It was the property and creation of his other recent discoveries, Prestwick Garner and Simon Blumenthal.

One of Porter's many weaknesses was for single-room museums, the display of an individual's predilection and passion appealing to him more than a gathering of significance. It was at one such place that he had met the two young writers, and struck up a conversation over a jar containing the pickled remains of what purported to be a merbaby. Friends and writing partners since their asthma-ridden childhoods, Garner and Blumenthal had explained their view that such aberrations were extraterrestrial in origin and showed Porter the home-produced comic books they were hoping to sell to a publisher and later develop into a series of inexpensive movies in which ideas would take the place of stars. Porter was impressed. He had then impressed the pair by declaring that if they could make him want to see their movie, he'd put up the money to make it.

Jean looked at the lovingly coloured pages. They had been divided into frames and each one was a small masterpiece of detail and desire. The story tracked the progress of an alien woman

— human in most characteristics; though her skin was silver-green, her breasts were dual and enormous and her face carefully made up — who had crash-landed on Earth and been enlarged to terrifying proportions on contact with the atmosphere. Over the carefully etched pages, she embarked on a murderous rampage in an attempt to locate the materials needed to fuel her return home and was finally brought down by the military who used top-secret soundwave technology to shrink her to a size they could kill. The scientist who had devised the method of her destruction stood over her in the last frame, his head hanging down on his white-coat-covered chest. An oblong box contained his poignant words of regret.

'It was a creature of misfortune,' Jean read aloud. 'A hostage to its nature, but we had to destroy it before it wiped us all out.'

Tears welled in her eyes and she quickly pushed the comic away before drops of salt water splashed onto the paper. She had trouble speaking, but something needed to be said. 'I think it's the most beautiful story I've ever read.'

Porter replaced the book in the inside pocket of his suit.

'You see, people have been dreaming of you.'

'No,' Jean whispered.

'Yes.'

Porter loved what he did. He loved taking money from people and shocking them in return, knowing that they needed him to do it, to help them live in some small way. And he loved finding others like himself. Like Jean. A quirk of nature unaware of her potential, until he handed it to her and she wept, as if something precious and lost had been returned to her. Something she had given up all hope of seeing again. His life had made him money and made him happy and nearly got him killed a few times and he couldn't imagine a better waste of time than it had been.

'Yes. They have, they have been dreaming. But my eyes have been open. I've been looking, and I've found you. Will you say yes? Will you submit to their gaze, will you glory in strangeness? And will you take seventy-five a week?'

Jean felt dizzy; the combination of food and adulation was too much for her. She thought of the studio she had glimpsed when delivering the pills to Eva, how she'd thought then that she had found the secret centre of things. Wondrous chaos. Images from the comic book took flight in her mind, she saw herself with silver-green skin, red lips and flowing black hair. She saw herself destroy. The circus had finally come for her. Porter was inviting her to take her place among those who defied the conformity others sought, those who had no choice but to do so. He was going to let her in. Let her return. Jean suddenly knew she had been waiting for this and that she was not going back to the sea, but emerging from it, finally.

'How did you find me?' Her voice was barely there, drowned in relief. Porter smiled and patted her hand.

'I've never stopped looking. I knew I would find you, but I just didn't know where. The world had to turn a little to bring you to me.'

Jean felt fresh tears streak her dirty face. She wondered if this was why she had always to be alone, so she wouldn't be missed when the time came. It made more sense than anything else so far.

'My name's Jean,' she admitted.

'Well, Jean, it's a pleasure. But I have to tell you, though you'll be the star, you'll always lose. You can be strong, but you can never win. You can be strong as long as you don't.'

'Yes,' said Jean. 'I knew that.'

41

Jean left the boardwalk with what she had travelled there for: possibility. Porter gave her a small cash advance and the assurance that he would settle her rent with Pace, then come for her when the time was right. 'Lots to prepare, worlds to create!' were his parting words.

The fiasco that Success Through Spirituality became gained a small mention in the next day's local newspaper; the two teenagers had confessed to their prank, so Jean went back to bed to recapture the hours of sleep she had lost waiting to be arrested.

That afternoon a truck arrived and Ermeline's vast collection of oddities was decanted into it. The boxes were worn out and loosely tied, and soon a trail of artificial legs, doll's heads and stuffed woodpeckers led from the door to the truck. The first leg to fall caused an upset: the mover yelled and threw the box he was carrying to the ground, but as more of Ermeline's peculiarities escaped, the men became blasé and improvised a game of baseball using legs and doll heads.

After the collapse of the rally, Ermeline had been dragged to a first-aid station where she was pronounced unharmed. It did not begin to describe the state of her soul. She shouldered her way through the wreckage, seizing on every man in a suit with hair not his own, until she found Jonas — perched on the running board of an ambulance, swathed in a blanket. The euphoria of omnipotence had drained away and he was as twitchy and vicious as a junkie between fixes. Ermeline trembled before him; righteous anger activated the dampened flounces of her dress, giving her the appearance of a bird about to moult. At first she feared she might not find the words, but when Jonas turned to her with an unrepentant sneer, they tumbled out in a biblical flood. She called him a swindler and an apostate, an affront to God Himself; the servant of the devil and the master of destruction. When she was done, even her lips were drained of colour; she was white with hatred.

'An affront to God?' Jonas would have spat on the floor had he spit in his mouth. 'Take your God — a consolation prize for the losers.'

'Consolation?' Ermeline was scandalised. 'You speak of consolation? What is my consolation? You have *abused* God and *taken* my money!'

'Yes,' Jonas admitted with a smile. 'And your God was very helpful in getting it for me. He makes a great bag-man.'

Then he began to laugh. He threw his head and his wig back and laughed through his brand-new teeth. Ermeline felt the cold hand of ruin winch her underwear tighter, and knew she had followed her last holy man.

The removal truck left Phuture Homes for a small coastal village, where Ermeline was waiting. She went on to assume a new name and open a boarding house with what remained of her inheritance. Having little industry and fewer prospects, the village was becoming home to various radicals, free-thinkers and general misfits pushed out there by the homogenising effect of the times. Ermeline housed all she could. The favourable rates she gave to atheists and the immoral led to her great popularity among artists and writers who drew on her like no cleric she had ever met. She never managed to convert a single one, but enjoyed many years of lively argument and a sense of spiritual satisfaction unknown to her before. Her collection of Bibles was eventually donated to local schools; her store of legs and other miscellany decorated the boarding house and added considerably to its atmosphere.

Jean watched the truck go and then set off for the drugstore, where she made a collect call to Porter. She was to do this every evening until he was ready for her. Be patient, he told her, miracles were being worked. It was what Jean needed to hear and she went home happy, to wait. She decided not to tell Gloria about Porter's offer, preferring to wait until it came properly true. Instead she wrote long letters full of detail from their old lives, which comforted Gloria and made Jean glad she had not renounced every part of herself chasing some promise that rode the breeze. She had been trying so hard to give herself a reason to go on that she had forgotten what it was to have Gloria, to have been rescued by the tiny child with sugar-encrusted fingers, how it had changed her more than fire and glass. What Gloria required, she would from now on put safely aside. What was left, was up for grabs.

Jean wished she could ask Eva's advice about Porter — Eva would know if things like this really did happen — but she hadn't seen her since before the rally. More from habit than duty, she went to Eva's house on her usual day and found it locked and empty. Eva reappeared two days later, announcing her return by driving into her own porch; Jean was woken by the sound of timbers splitting.

*   *   *

Varga's death had released Eva from her inaction. She had once told Eva that it was only when she saw herself on screen that she knew she existed. It was only then that she could finally shake the mud from her hair and see the bruises on her body fade.

When the Western returned from location, Varga and the rest of the cast were invited to watch the footage in a rented screening room. Varga was playing a saloon hostess who had seen better days, and the director had seen no reason to be kind. The make-up was harsh, the lighting bad and the film stock inexpensive; but it was still all true. The screen had become a mirror, stripping Varga of her remaining beauty and leaving her exposed. It was as if she had ceased to exist.

In her hospital bed, the taut movie star regained the looseness that had been cut out of her; Varga's face sagged a little at the jawline and her tired body softened and sank into the bed.

She looked to Eva, for the first time, like someone who could have given birth to her; someone Eva could perhaps hurt and disappoint more than anyone else. Eva reached the hospital too late, the overdose had taken possession and Varga would not wake again; all the unsaid things she had brought with her would have to be taken away again. Instead, she held her mother's cooling hand and wondered who would be responsible for her now.

The reporters began to gather at the first hint of death, guided by the same instinct that alerts keen old women to the funerals of strangers. The studio sent the production head responsible for enforcing the studio's moral code, and a press agent to deliver flowers and ultimatums. 'We'll have to tell them something. The truth is always best.' His voice was thick with mock concern, and a certain helplessness, as if he wasn't about to throw Varga's body to the wolves.

Eva was prepared. She sent the press agent out and took the small canister of film from her purse, placing it on the bed that contained her recently deceased mother. The remaining executive sighed; home movies always depressed him — this would be the sixth he had dealt with in a year. He yearned for the days when cameras were too cumbersome to conceal. Eva pressed her toes down so she could feel the floor through her shoes and be sure it was still there. There were so few things she had to get right, fewer still that she had managed to. But she would come good in the end, she had to.

When she left the hospital, Eva went straight

to the nearest, darkest bar she could find, and mourned Varga until she couldn't stand.

★ ★ ★

Jean pulled on her overalls and went outside to see what could be done. She found Eva slumped over the wheel of her car, the front of which was folded back on itself like a rumpled napkin. Jean carefully lifted Eva's head, which was unbloodied.

'I'm all right,' she murmured. 'I just didn't want to stop.'

Jean helped her indoors, bathed and dressed her, and then forced black coffee down her. In the case of losing a loved mother, she didn't know what else to do. They sat in the bare kitchen, coffee and cigarettes on the table between them. Eva shivered from a cold Jean couldn't feel, and kept pulling the neck of her sweater higher.

'It'll be a heart attack,' she said, her teeth chattering slightly. 'And the funeral will be f-fabulous — that's a guarantee; as long as the film goes into a vault, and stays there. Varga will be safe, I will be safe and their pervert head of production will be safe. It's a marvellous game: we hold knives at each other's throats and see who sneezes first. Anyway, it's done. I can't save the house, but it'll be auctioned quietly, not by the bank. I even get to live there till it's sold.'

'You're leaving?' Jean flinched at the whine in her own voice; she would have to do better. After a pause, she tried again. 'What will you do?'

Eva looked pleased with herself. 'I'm going to write a book. About Varga. It'll be a cautionary tale — they love those here; no one ever learns anything from them. But you never know, this time . . . It'll get turned into a movie, of course — that's really the point — but you can't get the good stuff in movies, the dirt; that's for the book.'

Jean sat down to join her. 'But, after all you did?'

'I said *they* couldn't publish. This is *me*, her daughter. Who else has the right? It's my revenge, and her little bit of the afterlife; she would have wanted that. I know she would have. Except I'll change her name. And the ending, maybe. The ending wasn't quite right. I didn't get it quite right. Definitely the name, though. What's in a name, anyway? What does it matter whether you're Eva Witter, or . . . or plain old Gladys Phillips.'

'Who's Gladys Phillips?'

Eva laughed, a short, sharp bark. 'Me, that's who. Terrible, isn't it? My grandmother named me. And then my mother did, nineteen years later; said I wouldn't get anywhere with a name like that. I've been Eva Witter for a dozen years, and it still feels like Gladys Phillips didn't get anywhere.' Eva flicked the ash from her cigarette into her coffee. 'Now, what d'you say we get a real drink?'

It had not taken long to flush the few weeks of sobriety from Eva's skin. She was drawn and grey again. Jean hoped she would be allowed to feed Eva something.

'Do you think you should?'

'Yes.' Eva was emphatic. 'I do. Now, more then ever, is a time to feel less and drink more.' At this she slowed, and the cigarette between her fingers twitched. It was momentary, like a second of film at the wrong speed, and then she caught up. 'Glasses. You get them, I'll mix. Liquor's in the car, the back, thank God — should be in one piece. You don't have to run off to one of your meetings, do you?'

Jean shook her head. 'No, I'm finished with it.'

Eva couldn't disguise her amusement. 'Oh, really? So what happened? Ermeline excommunicate you for knowing me — or was it the pills?'

'I don't think they'd have cared,' Jean said, truthfully. 'It was nothing to do with me in the end — I was neither here nor there.'

'Oh, Jean. So, how much did they take you for?'

'Everything,' she admitted. 'But it's all right. I've got a job.'

'Doing what? Not another scam, I hope?'

Jean hesitated. Did she really want Eva to tell her it wasn't true, that Porter was not what he seemed; that she had been taken in again. 'Oyster bar,' she replied. 'On the boardwalk. I'm in the kitchen.'

'Well, good for you. We'll celebrate. Back in a tick.'

Jean wished Eva could have waited a few days more, then someone would see her be wanted and put to good use. If that's what was going to happen. Instead, over morning cocktails, she decided to ask, as obliquely as she could, what to

513

do. Eva, after all, had been the one to say she had a chance.

'Eva, how *does* someone do well here?'

Eva's smile pushed into one side of her face only. 'Oh, this one I know: have something they want, or something they fear.'

42

When Porter was ready, he sent a taxi to Phuture Homes. Jean had stayed still and a slim shard of lightning had come to her. She had no idea what was to follow, boarding the cab with the same feeling as when she had boarded the boat that brought her from England. But Porter knew. She was to be herself, only exceptionally so.

On arriving at the small collection of outbuildings that Porter had rented as his studio, Jean was delivered into the care of Guillermo the costume designer, who was known to everyone as Gill. He was tall, slim, on the pretty side of handsome, and unafraid to touch her — he ran his hands along Jean's arms and across her waist as a precursor to measuring her. The combination of the professional and sympathetic pressures he applied delighted her skin, and made Jean feel slightly closer to her old self, her best self, the one that had taken pleasure in small things. As instructed, she had spent her cash advance on steak and ice cream, and Gill clicked his tongue appreciatively at her form. He had prepared a costume based on Porter's estimations and would only have to alter it a hair — there was so little budget for waste. When he finished taking her measurements, Gill squeezed Jean's waist to show he was pleased with her, and Jean was flooded with a memory of Frankie, who had also possessed the gift of kindnesses

515

conveyed swiftly and lightly.

There was nothing known about what was happening to her, nothing familiar or explicable, and yet Jean felt safe again — back in the tumble of benign disorder — even when Gill stripped the clothes from her back and left her standing naked in the odd little room.

For two years, Gill had been performing as Carmelita, the Last Known Virgin of Guadeloupe, at a supper club known to a select and fastidiously dressed clientele. For this weekly engagement, he made his own costumes — exquisite copies of gowns taken from fashion magazines or Technicolor spectaculars. For shoes, he favoured wedge heels for balance and ribbon ties for the way they accentuated his slim ankles. These were made for him by a discreet, well-established firm with a wide-ranging clientele. Returning to the costume cupboard, he produced a pair in this style for Jean, lately worn by himself in his Cuban-themed revue 'Havan-a Heatwave'. They were bright aquamarine in colour, shimmering silk at the toe and heel. Touching the moulded sole of one, Jean understood why he had kept her naked waiting for them. She didn't want to see herself in anything else.

'A lady just isn't dressed without her shoes,' he laughed, as he helped Jean climb onto the magnificent objects. Jean could only think of the coalman, who had died never knowing such things existed.

'Oh,' she whispered. 'He'd have loved these.'

Gill assumed she was speaking of some past

516

love and smiled sympathetically before turning away to find the rest of her costume.

'I knew they'd fit; we're practically the same size. Now,' he proffered a shimmering bodice. 'Let's finish you off.'

Three inches of cork separated Jean's toes from the ground and her heels were hiked six inches over them; if she had pushed at the boundary of the possible before, it now lay in pieces at her feet. Her hair was concealed by a flowing black wig, the planes of her face had been sharpened with make-up and clear tape had been applied to her forehead and temples, pulling back her large round eyes into exotic, feline shapes. Her skin was covered with metallic paint and she wore a boned bathing suit covered with silver mesh that sparkled when she breathed, which she barely could. Full in the bust and bottom and slender and curved at the middle, she was two glittering teardrops joined.

Porter had gathered his employees — his writers, crew and unique extras — in the courtyard that was the parking lot, backlot and storage area of Porter Productions. Guillermo helped Jean through the doorway, then joined his colleagues, leaving her alone in front of them all. She wobbled on top of her heels and squinted against the sun, waiting for judgement.

There was silence; the first word had to be Porter's, everyone knew that. Jean watched him for some sign of approval, not wanting to believe he had brought her here on a lie. He stepped forward, bowed before her and produced poetry from his magpie brain.

" . . . Euclid alone

Has looked on Beauty bare. Fortunate they

Who, though once only and then but far away,

Have heard her massive sandal set on stone.'

Welcome, Jean, welcome to our family.'

Porter kissed her hand, held it aloft as if she were a victorious Olympian, and then turned to his cast and crew.

'Now! Who has a hard-on and who wants to piss his pants?'

Every person present, male and female, put both hands up.

★   ★   ★

He took her by the hand and led her past a wall where a glittering backcloth had been hung to dry — 'The universe, my dear,' as if he were offering it to her — to a blanket-lined shed containing a model city culled from her dreams. Most of the buildings were simple blocks, but a few had more detail; roofs that lifted off, revealing tiny plastic people inside, and toy cars in garages. It was the most elaborate plaything Jean could imagine, clearly made to resemble the city they were in. Now she could finally see where everything was meant to be. The rest of her new family filed in, the last one closing the door and sealing the darkness. Jean was alone in a spotlight. Porter explained what he wanted her to be and do, and she thought she understood.

518

She just hadn't realised there would be a camera.

Crosses of black tape marked where Jean should place her feet. Two of the crew held her steady while she lowered the fabulous shoes onto their starting positions, and then withdrew, leaving her precariously balanced over the imagined ordinary lives beneath. Jean wished the underwear they had provided her with was fuller in its intentions — she didn't like the idea of standing over the fancied town in anything less than knee-length knickers — but she put aside her objections and raised her head. It was then that she looked into the eye of the camera. That something half her size could be so threatening was a surprise — it trained its beady glare on her and she froze. Jean suddenly felt wiped clean, the certainty of her form dissolving; she could remember nothing of her purpose. Porter tried to soothe her.

'Perfectly natural to be nervous, my dear. Forget about us. Just relax and be yourself.'

Her self. She wished she could produce whatever that was. The self of the body was what Porter seemed to want, but she was not everything it promised.

Jean had been instructed on where to step, where to look and when to move, and she fulfilled every request carefully; Gloria had trained her to take direction well. But something didn't happen. Jean couldn't disappear into it, as she had wanted to all these years. She was not, it turned out, enough.

She tried, over and over again, to be the creature they wanted. She wailed and thrashed around, nearly toppling over several times; members of the crew would rush forward and push her back onto her shoes. But she didn't convince. Her power diminished, rather than grew. She felt it ebb away. 'Aaaaargh,' she mouthed, feeling miserably tame. 'Aaargh. Aaaaarrrrrgh.' It was not the sound of horror, it was the sound of a sick bullock. She had spent too long dampening the terror in her, the capacity for violence. Porter thought he might need a cattle prod.

After five wretched minutes during which Jean discontentedly lifted and replanted her feet as if she were stepping in hot manure, he ordered the camera be halted, and took her aside. She tottered carefully on Gill's loaned shoes towards a corner of the set, where she leaned against an oil drum and waited, dejected, to be told to go home. Not only could she not change, she could not be what she seemed to be. She was nowhere.

'Now, my dear,' Porter offered her a cigarette, which she took. Her make-up left traces of silver on the tip. 'I need you to be frightening, that's all. Do you think you can do that for me?'

Jean's life was defined by fear. The fear of doing harm, the fear of having them turn on her in greater numbers than she could repel. Others were her worry. Their fear was her responsibility. Jean shook her head.

'Something might happen.'

Someone might run into a tree, or have a stroke, or just fade away into nothing.

'Exactly.' Porter was all patience. 'We want something to happen.'

'No. Something bad.'

'Or something very good? This is pretend, my dear. Nothing bad can happen here. You can let it all out and it just floats away on the breeze, no harm done. There is nothing you can unleash that can't be contained.'

Jean was unconvinced. She looked past Porter at the crew waiting for her return; no action of hers had ever been of interest to so many people. Jean diverted her glance to the hurriedly made city, commissioned once her dimensions had been discovered; she let her eyes fall to the make-up nestling in the delicate channels that criss-crossed her arms and felt the expectations of others touch her with every breath exhaled. They'll send you away if you can't do it, she thought. This is what there is to lose. Hold on to this, for at least one day. Hold on to being anticipated, being watched without blame, being painted with silver tones and wrapped in glittering gauze. This is unlike anything else that will happen, she reminded herself — and she had to match it to remain. And if she could not be contained, then she would be responsible.

But how to go about it? Years of docility lacquered her. Of all the things burned and broken by time and circumstance, it clung on; the fear of herself was set deeper than bone. But if she knew it to be true, she couldn't remember ever devising it; it was hereditary, like some disease of the blood. Jean realised that she suspected far more than she knew, more than had been proven. If her mother had told her she couldn't walk, she wondered if she would ever have taken a step. She had reined herself in for so long, believing the only thing to do, the only safe thing, was to endure, to avoid doing harm. But she had forgotten intent; she had to believe she had some say in the matter.

Porter led her back to the miniature city and held her by the wrists as she climbed into its centre.

'Please, for me,' he whispered, as he surrendered his grasp. 'Scare the piss out of them.'

Jean took her place in front of the crew. Porter, as intent and anxious as a surgeon, mopped his brow. He could not believe that she would be useless, a sleek and fabulous liner that sank on its first voyage.

Jean closed her eyes and concentrated on the feel of the bodice gripping her torso and the heavy make-up that made her aware of every inch of exposed skin. What is this body's limit, she wondered. Find it, Porter had told her, find something in you and push it out, let rip, just holler for all you're worth. She knew what Wisteria would have said: 'All you're worth? Not bloody much on this account.' Jean had not considered deeply why she had been punished so brutally for being born. It had seemed obvious enough. Jean had disappointed her mother in so many ways, but the main one she hadn't guessed at — she had never properly used her strength. In her lifetime, Wisteria had entertained the fantasy of being as large and unstoppable as her daughter, enough to punish everyone who had ever looked at her sideways. Enough to tear the beauty from them and render them less than herself. She would level the world and bring it lower than she. She would be noticed. To Wisteria, Jean was a disgrace. She had not even been a decent instrument of her wrath, ill disposed as she was to random cruelty and overwrought vengeance. 'All bulk and no use,' Jean remembered her mother saying, though all she did was work.

Jean pictured Wisteria — the never-young face and bowed little body — and tried to think what it would be like to be her. She would have to lose her strength, teeth, height and hope to get close. She would have to dig herself back into the house, with its chilly rooms and strange odours that emanated from wardrobes and plugholes, any dark space. She would have to lose everything that had made it possible for her to get out, that had made her the one who would survive. It was the most terrible spell that could ever be cast, one that would change her into Wisteria and leave her there. Jean felt a tremor pass through her chest down to her stomach; no more than an insect skating on water, but the tension in it was familiar. It wasn't her fear, it was her mother.

What Wisteria could have done with strength. She had tried to draw what she could from her daughter, but Jean's was a selfish body, gathering all its resources to keep going in the face of the onslaught that was her childhood. Jean looked at herself through her mother's eyes, and saw something not worthy of what she had been given. Wisteria was not afraid of her daughter;

she was disgusted with her. Through those pale and watery eyes, Jean saw an unused weapon, impotent and pacifist. She felt her mother build in her until she was all rage.

Wisteria loathed the girl who could have taken anything for herself and refused; she loathed the very meekness she had beaten into her, it had been too easy to do.

The scream of Wisteria's life was ready to be given voice; she could feel it rise from her gnarled toes, through her barely fleshed ankles; gathering speed, coursing up her thighs and into her withered womb, scorching her bloated stomach and coated lungs; finally to her lips where it burned in impatience to be heard. She threw back her head and screamed it free. In the town at her feet, she saw where her life had been pissed up the wall, where she had been born into shit and travelled nowhere but down. She felt the misery of impossibility, compounded by the knowledge of what could be. In each house she saw someone with something she wanted, something that should have come to her; she plunged her hands into their lives, tore the roofs off their houses and crushed the little people between her fingers, watching the smugness run out of them down to her elbows. She opened her mouth wide and let the fire of her disappointment scorch everything in front of her, then ground the ashes underfoot. She raised her arms up to the cruel sky and roared her frustration with fate and design and everything else that had conspired to make her so unexceptional, so undeservedly. She was everything nature could unleash and more, directionless, irrational and insatiable. Because whatever came to her now would come too late.

Jean felt as though she were climbing free of her own skin; there was no limit to how high she could reach — her body would allow it. The city beneath her feet could not contain her, no city could — she had been liberated. She soared, then plummeted, in perfect control of her inescapable limbs. She slammed her foot into the meagre houses that would have her shrink to fit inside them; the pure achievement of her would have been enough to flatten them, she knew. She roared with the pleasure of command; joy licked up her veins like flame on a trail of gunpowder. She had feared destruction, but discovered power. She could transform, she could change, she could be anything.

The end of it was like waking up to a noise only dreamt — sudden, inexplicable quiet. In Jean's nostrils and on her tongue there had been fire and blood and glass and metal, and suddenly there was cool air that carried a breath of the ocean. Her legs shook and her fingers twitched as spent rage dripped from them — the last of Wisteria. Jean was in total possession now; her body responded to no call but her own, held no one's shame but her own. The assembled spectators were silent. They looked at her and she looked back, wonder on both sides. Against the silence, Jean thought she could hear her scars sing again. The pitch of wartime couldn't be sustained; it was like a high C, beautiful but shattering, screaming out against the roar of death. This was low and content, somehow familiar, as though something in her had been tuned to a long-forgotten station. Looking at the assembled faces, she could see that she was what they had been waiting for, what they had hoped would exist. She belonged, because they wanted her to be theirs. Porter was right, the globe had to turn a little. It was why she had to leave England. Countries were not her destination, but worlds.

They might have all stood there for an hour if Porter hadn't recovered his senses and shouted: 'Cut!' Twenty people exhaled at once and Jean fell onto her backside, as if knocked down by the collective breath. She was dizzy at the thought of how easily she could have missed it all; of how easily things had been hidden from her unquestioning self and would have remained so. Porter called for a blanket and slowly approached her with it; he was a little afraid she might go off again with him in range. Jean looked around. The city was a cushion of toothpicks beneath her and the beautiful shoes were scuffed. She hiccuped, and fancied a last little bubble of spleen took to the air. Finally, she knew what she was for.

'Did you see it?' she asked. 'Did it really happen?'

Porter wrapped the blanket around her shoulders. 'It did, my girl,' he replied, beaming. 'You destroy, and you create. You truly are a goddess.' He gave the Herculean shoulders a squeeze. 'Just tell me you can do it again.'

Jean smiled. If only she had known earlier, she could have done it all along.

'You bet,' she replied.

Jean was to be revealed at the drive-in. Porter had a trailer made, the juiciest pieces of her scattered through it — the whole remaining a tempting mystery — with the words 'Never Before Seen' splashed across them. The trailer drew cheers and whistles, feet were stamped; her breasts were applauded as though they had performed a heroic rescue. All around Porter's car, she was being screamed for. When the title, *Vashtara, Queen of Destruction*, flashed up, a voice shouted, 'Destroy me, baby! Destroy me!' Jean had dominion over them already. Every yell from the waiting crowd sent electricity through her body and made her head spin. They were waiting for something new and strange, something to excite them beyond reason; and so was she. When she finally appeared, they were ready for her.

Above their heads, there was only Jean, and above her the stars — there was room for little else. She could not have been contained in a theatre, a screen against the sky was required. On it, Eugenia Clocker finally became so vast as to disappear, leaving a wondrous creature in her place. Among the audience, she saw the effect she remembered from her youth, the disorientating improbability of her. But here they gave themselves over to it and didn't fight; they wanted and allowed her to overwhelm them. She gave shape to their shapeless fears, and they loved her for it. Restless energy spilled from the cars: the young and already jaded were excited again. There was no worshipful silence; screams and laughter greeted her; lewd suggestions were hurled; music played and wolf whistles carried across the dark. Jean felt a surge of life pass through her, almost lifting her from the seat.

'You're killing them, just killing them!' Porter crowed.

In front of them, she stood astride a city on fire. Jean had to tilt her head back to see her own face; it was a marvellous thing. Her body seemed both hewn from rock and as supple as water, she flowed in and out of her costume. The crowd screeched with delight as she popped humans into her mouth like candies. They applauded when she overturned tanks with a flick of her platform heel, and if they cheered loudest when, finally, she was brought down, they had at least understood her till then. She was just trying to survive them.

The ending was her favourite part; she would remember it long after her memory of the rest had faded to nothing. Her body lay in the smouldering ruins of the unnamed city, finally reduced to almost human size and weakness by the experimental sound weapon. The rugged scientist, whose shirt had disintegrated revealing a hairless, well-muscled chest, stood over her lifeless form and spoke gently the words that had first struck at Jean's heart on a night she had thought all was lost. She was a creature of misfortune, a hostage of nature. Jean cheered louder than anyone to hear it. Then she cried.

Seeing herself on screen, Jean fell in love. And knew it absolutely for the first time. This was the world that could take her; she needed the approval of no other. It was unexpected how almost beautiful she became in her abandon; her person mutated to one without fear and without limitation — she exercised her capability to the full and brought civilisations down around her. That was what she was for: possibility, to illustrate what could be. It was more than beauty; Jean was her own republic.

Part Six

CHANGE

43

After her triumphant unveiling, Jean was taken to a bar where Chinese lanterns cast a warming glow, an effect matched by the cocktails she consumed. She was placed on the wooden counter, her head pressing into the nicotine-stained ceiling, and applauded, sung to, adored. Porter declared her his saviour; Gill named her 'Monstruo Hermosa' — Beautiful Monster — which, once explained, made her cry again. The writers Garner and Blumenthal composed a limerick in her honour, which she heard while perched on a pool table, with them crouched at her feet. 'If I am to die,' she thought, 'let it be now.'

Porter had billed Jean only as '?', wanting to preserve the mystery of his discovery — and he thought both Curnalia and Clocker to be as ugly as a hammer blow. By the light of a red-paper lantern, he unfurled a poster, showing Jean as an Amazon queen: her wild hair threaded with vines, animal skins barely covering her body. She looked unstoppable, carnivorous, gorgeous — the fulfilment of her body's purpose. At the bottom of the poster, in bold yellow letters tinged with crimson, it read: 'Adelia Fury in *Amazon Rampage*, Coming Soon'.

'That's me,' she whispered. 'Yes, that's me.' Porter had the name painted onto the door of one of the rickety outbuildings of Porter Productions.

After one sold-out week, the run of *Vashtara, Queen of Destruction* was extended by a month and the drive-in chains booked *Amazon Rampage* before it had been written. Porter set Jean to work on her second feature.

Her first film set the template for the rest. Jean would go on to play aliens, irradiated housewives and the patchwork creations of mad scientists (for which they left her scars uncovered, going so far as to trace over the lines with make-up so she appeared horribly piecemeal). Porter would take Jean to the desert and film her clambering out of craters that she was supposed to have created by crashing into the Earth's surface with her spacecraft, or by tunnelling up from below. Or the Botanical Gardens would double as a planet full of exotic fauna whose venom could cause abnormal growth in a human or provide the birthplace for a gigantic extraterrestrial. But once Jean's origins were established, she would rage, her clothes would shred and she would eventually die extravagantly. She was not exploited in any way that she saw; she was not the freak because she was not beautiful enough to be the sweetheart. She was the freak because she was strong enough to be.

Though Jean might have once wished she could be average and loved — the two had been bound up in her like gum and hair; it took an age to separate them — she was not now ashamed, or even shy. She was the wildest performer Porter had ever seen. The camera captured the way her body pulsed with the thrill of her own power; she seemed to beat like a heart. And while her costumes revealed her, there was no invitation in it. Jean remained unassailable, needless of protection. She was no longer the benighted keeper of her body, struggling to satisfy its demands and conceal its nature. She was the proud exhibitor of a wonder.

When she wasn't being filmed, Jean moved scenery and painted sets; she helped dig the holes in the desert that she was filmed climbing out of. People like them, explained Porter, had to build the world each day. The circuses he travelled with used a tent not only for shelter, not only to marshal and control a crowd, but to create a place in which such things as they could exist, and rule. And to make sure there was no trace of it left to disturb the peace once they had gone. Many of the people he employed lived in trailers, always ready to move at a moment's notice. The world they built was peculiar to them, made to exist alongside rather than within the other. The centre of things was a dangerous unknowable place; thousands had come in search of it and found it hollow or full of nails. It was best, he said, to exist a little off of the centre, where forces both benign and malign are weaker and less attention is focused.

Porter had secured the use of a water tank through dubious means — a card game with studio security guards was suspected — and wanted to make the most of it. While Garner and Blumenthal constructed the story of an Amazon queen whose island people had recently been discovered by a couple of hapless male explorers, Jean was stitched into a flesh-coloured bathing suit and repeatedly lowered to the bottom of the tank, from where she would attempt to swim gracefully skywards.

At the end of a long day of trying not to drown, a shrivelled and shivering Jean was dried, wrapped in a bathrobe and a raincoat, and driven home. Once there, she immersed herself in a hot bath, soaking off the last of the itchy metallic paint that gave her skin a piscine glitter. Flakes of paint lifted off her and rose to the surface of the water where they formed a brilliant scum, broken by the bend of her knee, the slope of her breast and the dune of her stomach. Jean let the heat lull her into a half-sleep; she closed her eyes and saw herself doubled, tripled in height, straddling a city on fire, the flames only warming her imperishable flesh.

She hadn't allowed herself to be curious for such a long time. She hadn't wanted to wonder if the things her husband had allowed her to feel could exist without him. But now, she had a suspicion they could. She had seen the power her body possessed; not just to harm, or terrify. Her skin was now warming independently of the water; in her mind, the fire crept higher up her body, the flames like tongues on her skin. Her fingers trembled as they slipped below the surface, grazing ridged skin that was alive to sensation. It was time to stop saying no to things, she decided, with or without knowing what saying yes meant. She didn't want to do without him, she just couldn't help but find ways to manage.

She discovered her male fans often had literary aspirations. They would write long, sometimes painstakingly illustrated letters — story suggestions for her next film were frequently enclosed, though these rarely amounted to anything more than costume suggestions. In the case of genuine script ideas, Porter would present them to Garner and Blumenthal as an inspiration that had struck him in the night, and leave it to them to make something of the fantasies of her public. Few of them lived alone, sick mothers and dependent sisters were a common theme.

The man who would be her first affair brought her a sheaf of story suggestions (he had no talent for dialogue but a genius for creating worlds that might spawn women of Jean's proportions and appetites) and six red roses. They met on the boardwalk and took a room in one of the hotels that had guestbooks full of Smiths and Does. (He couldn't stay much past nine, his mother had been bed-ridden for fifteen of his thirty-five years and the burden of caring for her rested with him alone.) Once inside the room, the first thing he did was to drop to one knee and kiss Jean's feet; he would have happily stayed there had she not given her permission to advance. She lost count of the number of times he said thank you, and politely ignored his tears.

The succession of men was not particularly rapid; there was more curiosity than hunger in play. Some had outlandish hopes: that she would be adorned with fins or scales, or able to summon her alien hordes to transport them to the stars. To them, she was a vehicle to another fantasy as well as a dream contained. But there seemed no expectation in any that she would see them again. She was assumed to be a transient creature, like her screen self. Jean certainly gave no indication of requiring more than temporary company. Her life was too hard won to share. She wanted it for herself alone, at least for a time; to get the wear of it before it had to give to accommodate anyone else.

They said they worshipped her, and she wanted to see what it felt like to be worshipped. Jean found it to be not at all bad. It was not being loved, it was not loving, but it wasn't at all bad. Though her body wakened in the company of these men, it didn't sing with quite the same force as it had with her husband, or when she was Adelia, and no longer bound by humanity. She understood that there had to be balance; she would not be allowed it all. She was used to living only a part of life, and feeling the absence of the rest.

44

Porter would blame himself for what happened.

★ ★ ★

The strange empire of Porter Productions grew as the public appetite for oddity and paranoia increased. Jean wondered where they all hid until he found them. Perhaps most were like her, in plain sight but unnoticed by the majority who saw only deviation rather than the beauty of the way in which the norm had been deviated from.

His offices entertained a constant procession of those fortunate enough to be have been marked out by nature when sheer luck had passed them by, while Porter himself continued to roam the natural gathering places of the rare and unclassifiable. A man whose progressive skin condition had left him with a bald, ridged scalp, fiercely pointed ears and webbed fingers was practically hauled out of his car by the elderly Porter after he had the good fortune to stall at a cross-section near the eagle-eyed impresario. Garner and Blumenthal were ordered to produce a screenplay about an underground race of lizard men who had stashed their eggs in desert caves in preparation for the fulfilment of their world-domination plan. Jean would be their queen.

The specialist magazines devoted fevered

pages to Adelia Fury and her unusual build, which was occasionally attributed (by Porter, who scattered stories like seeds among the fan writers) to the result of experimentation by a scientist dedicated to winning the war through the use of an outsized female army; other times to the effect of a comet on a land girl, caught in an open field by a shower of mutating radiation from the sky. Her films became minor events; things of importance to a growing audience fascinated by the possibilities held within her costumes and without the known universe. They would flock to her scheduled appearances at drive-ins and pulp-book stores, and thrust forward their magazines for signing.

Jean herself collected all the fan rags, and the publicity photographs; so much of her life had escaped, she was determined to document as much of the remainder as she could. She bought a camera and snapped pictures of her Porter Productions family at work; she even pasted up photographs fans had sent of themselves, sometimes dressed as her. A hefty girl of the Midwest (a disproportionate number of her fans came from the dairy states) had artfully recreated each of her costumes to date, using little more than foil, old sheets and garden twine, then photographed herself in what looked like a barn, acting out Jean's roles. That photomontage took pride of place over Jean's television set.

Schooled in deprivation and the seductive danger of want, Jean had taken the first real money she had earned and used it to make the ground under her feet as solid as possible. Pace's predictions were finally proved correct: the road did come and the rent did rise, but by then Jean had bought her house from him. She filled it with her pictures, a radio, and the television, which she watched, while dressed in her overalls and drinking a beer, on Sundays and late nights after filming.

Across the valley floor, the half-finished skeletons were now homes filled with life, and Jean was unable to run riot through the night to where her screams wouldn't be heard. But it was her day job now to get up to such things, and the need diminished. Grass had managed to take hold and snake its way round the little white houses; thanks to a new irrigation canal, it was even green in places. Avenues of trees were planted and cars lined up to park under them. Phuture Homes was on its way to becoming a real suburb. Jean loved the strange, determined order of it, and what a poke in the eye to truth it was.

She knew no one there to any measure on a scale of intimacy. There was nothing desperate for her to delve into; no one needed her. Those that were aware of what she did were simply more likely than others to leave her alone. It was a very respectable suburb, which Jean felt she deserved. In fact, it was all so wonderful, that she was not altogether surprised when it came under attack.

Jean had heard of the Committee, but knew only that everyone else was afraid of it, not why she should be. It was the early days, when there were still enough party members to go around;

they would not come for the merely different for some time. Porter said he should have known better, that it was his fault for sending Jean to the centre of things; the smug little village in the middle of the enchanted forest, where things unusual were slain or enslaved, never appreciated.

A studio executive had seen her rampaging as an Amazon and, impressed by her physique, approached Porter for a loan; he wanted Jean to play a female gladiator in a biblical epic, and be sent into the arena to terrorise Christian martyrs. The offer was received with some excitement, though Jean herself had reservations — she thought she was being put up for adoption. Her annual contract with Porter was approaching its end — he'd offered to make it for a lifetime, but Jean wanted to sign every year; she liked being reminded that she was wanted. He had expected her to be thrilled that she would be joining a big-budget production; instead she burst into tears. Once Porter had explained to her that a loan was just that, and that she was to be returned after a few weeks spent with another studio for more pay, Jean was happier — though she signed the next year's contract early, just in case.

With her new-found wealth, Jean had installed a telephone and permitted herself the occasional luxury of Gloria's voice. She decided to personally inform her of her own newly conferred legitimacy, and to remind Gloria that she herself had trained Jean for the genre, all those years before.

When Gloria first heard that Jean had become a film star, she broke finally with fantasy. She and it had been outstripped by events. Gloria had spent all her energy pursuing her own creations, though the distance between them never diminished. Jean had again challenged her idea of what could exist, but not in the way she expected. Gloria decided to stop falling in love with need, and want what she might have. It was, after all, a terrible waste to die without having loved and been loved.

It started with the white-haired boy that could pass for her own, the child with which she had deceived her parents. Loving the child's mother had made it one less lie. When only a girl, Gloria had rescued Jean, choosing to love where no one else would; it had taken all the courage she had. At the age of twenty-nine, she found herself quite the girl again.

Gloria wrote that she had moved in with a friend, leaving Sally free to sell the house for medical bills. It was a kind of truth; there was a convenience to the situation that helpfully masked the coup that was happening inside Gloria.

She had always wanted the certain kind of love, the kind returned on the first glance, the kind laid out in books and song, to be memorised and re-enacted, with feeling. Jack had loved her at first sight, and she him. But, too late, Gloria realised she wanted to be known. With Theresa, she discovered for the first time what it was to love without the certainty of return, without even a blueprint. It was like falling. A war widow, Theresa had room in her house and her life for a friend who was as committed to her son as she was. After three months of living with Theresa, Gloria realised that the sensation of being near her felt like air rushing past her head. It was only when Theresa received Gloria's kiss without a word, without a tremor, that she felt her stomach leap at the halting of her descent.

Gradually Gloria purged the other lies from her life, she had her marriage to Jack annulled and told Jean that she had had enough of make-believe; it had served her appallingly. She would care for Jack as long as he lived, but she would not be his wife again; nor anyone's. She declined Jean's offer of a train ticket west, saying that she had real problems and real pleasures enough to deal with where she was, but should Jean ever use the train ticket herself, she would find a bed kept aside for her — as ever.

★   ★   ★

The biblical epic would be the first of Jean's pictures Gloria could see, and she was thrilled at the prospect. (The others were shown in a neighbouring town at a somewhat seedy picture house where married women — even those who no longer cared tuppence for marriage — were not seen.) She promised that she would buy the first ticket to go on sale.

The publicity shots of Jean that were in

544

circulation did not fit what the studio had in mind. She was occasionally pictured hoisting a man above her head — Porter employed light, nimble men, ex-rodeo clowns usually, that she could lift or hurl through paper walls without straining herself — and was deemed a little too terrifying, even for a gladiator. The studio wanted to promote Jean as a fantastically proportioned but still very much of-this-earth war heroine, and requested any pictures she had from that period of her life. Gloria thought she had just the image.

Jean had been cropped out of the photograph when it appeared in the local paper on the anniversary of victory. But Mrs Smith bought a copy direct from the photographer, and so Jean, in her red crêpe-paper dress with a white hammer and sickle across the chest, was restored. Mrs Smith had sent the photograph to her daughter in America, where it was put in a drawer and forgotten, hidden under a layer of pristine baby gowns. Jean told her to send it to the studio directly to save time and Gloria, ever ignorant of petty hatreds, did just that.

Jean was being fitted for her costume — a custom-made bronze breastplate worn over a short white shift; a wig of blonde curls and strips of leather that criss-crossed her legs from ankle to thigh — when the letter was opened by the secretary of the publicity department. While the photograph was being couriered to the legal department, the wardrobe mistress was recording Jean's measurements onto a file card, remarking that they added up not so much to a standard size as an equation for which there was no solution. As the picture made its way to the vice-president of the studio, Jean's measurements were on their way to a central medical office from where a diet plan would be issued to ensure she did not exceed the recorded dimensions for the duration of the shoot: the breastplate was an immodest work of art which cost more to the production than she did and they didn't want to have to remodel it. Two hours after the photograph arrived on the desk of the vice-president, Jean was sent home, still wearing the bronze vest.

Porter drove her; she had called on him for help, suddenly vulnerable again. In the convertible, the sun heated her metal-covered chest up to an unbearable degree, but Jean was grateful for the encasing bodice; beneath it she was exposed gut. Her heart, repaired by belonging, had been rent. Porter looked as though he might cry.

'What do they have on you, honey?'

He knew that their kind often had unexpected weaknesses. An oddity of the exterior would be twinned internally, a weakness in the heart or brain or lungs. He had lost many friends that were dear to him, but it hurt more to lose them like this, to have them lured, trapped, then skinned. Jean shrugged and drew on her cigarette. They had shown her the photograph and she had seized on it with joy — precious proof of her and Gloria — and asked if she could have a copy, too. They told her what the picture showed was unacceptable, that, if reason won out, legislation would soon be coming into force against it, that she was a fool to parade so openly and would have to suffer the consequences. She didn't know they thought she was a political undesirable; Jean thought her own self had finally been outlawed.

45

Jean's appearance in front of the Committee escaped official record. She was ushered into a small office to testify in front of a panel of just three. As the lead freak in socially and morally dubious creature features, captured on camera parading in honour of the mother country, the ideological enemy, she was to be no more than a formality. (Her part in the biblical epic had already been recast with a Swedish swimming champion possessed of terrible teeth but impressive shoulders — though her voice would have to be dubbed due to a resolute accent.) Porter assured Jean that clever things could be done with false papers and noses, but she had never been able to hide very well — she wondered why she had spent all those years trying — and faced the hearing alone. Though her suit was dark and conservative, Jean made sure her heels and hat were high. She would be unmissable.

They were evidently not of the first rank of interrogators: a circuit judge and the heads of the studio's public relations and legal departments. The elite got to question the real movie stars; it was often their only chance to meet one and places on the bench were hard-won. As usual, something lesser had been put aside for Jean. She realised that there would be no debating the outcome; she was to be processed, not pardoned. There was a long introductory speech prior to the questions and she did her best to listen; though no television cameras were present, the judge had rehearsed for broadcast and could not be dissuaded from addressing, at length, an imaginary national audience. As his diatribe against the infiltration of the industry continued, Jean's attention was distracted by the certain knowledge that she had seen him before — in high heels, a pinny and little else. She closed one eye to approximate the effect of looking through a hole drilled into a mummy's sarcophagus, and any doubt was removed.

As a judge, he was known for his leniency and was rewarded for his understanding — for example, in the case of a promising young starlet whose career would otherwise be ruined by having backed over her maid when driving drunk — with occasional forays into the hidden world that fascinated him. Jean wondered if the goat would make an appearance.

There had been times when Jean overlooked the ammunition fate had handed her — Wisteria's death at the hands of another was testament to this — but she had been utilising her gifts of late, and had grown in confidence and wisdom. A body is a thing to be enjoyed; consequence is not necessarily to be feared; and blackmail can be very useful indeed. She thanked God for Eva, wherever she might be.

Asked to stand, Jean did so. Placing her hand on the Bible, she swore that she would tell the truth, the whole truth and nothing but the truth. Then Jean took a step forward, with her hand raised.

'Do you wish to approach?' The judge wished he could peer down at her, but even on a raised platform she dwarfed him.

Jean's smile was at its broadest. 'Yes, please, I do.'

On reaching the bench, she took off one of her shoes and placed it in front of the pinny-wearing judge. She knew of only two places in town that could make shoes to her, and his, size and gambled on him knowing them both, too. The name of the establishment was clearly visible, written in gold on the instep. Though Jean's shoe was a later model, it was not significantly different from the pair that the judge had worn with his pinny, being black patent with a rounded toe.

'You may think you know all about me,' Jean said, slowly and deliberately. 'But I know *all* about you.'

The stenographer was dismissed and an arrangement come to. According to a statement from the studio that hardly anybody bothered to read, Jean was thanked for her cooperation but was unable to give the Committee any useful information and so was dismissed without formal interview. Privately, it was recommended that she take an extended vacation, and deliberate long and hard on any return to the business. The judge was quietly dropped from the ranks of investigators, as well as the invitation lists of the parties he had favoured.

She did have luck, she always had. But it was so extreme in nature as to be balanced only by utter disaster. Anything less and her life would spin out of control.

46

Arriving home would make it real. Jean asked Porter to drive as slowly as possible, and they were at a crawl when Phuture Homes finally came into view. She spotted the figure on her porch before Porter did, and placed a hand on his wrist to direct his gaze.

'Do you see him?'

'Sure. What do you think, studio? Federal?'

Jean shook her head. 'He's my husband.'

Porter whistled through his teeth. 'Well. Some days God just takes a big shit, doesn't he?'

When the studio let her go, she was too dazed to feel anger. It took seeing him on her porch to waken it. Porter had slowed to a stop in front of the house and Denny walked down the steps and out into the light, shielding his eyes from the glare. Porter hesitated before killing the engine.

'Do you want me to run the bastard over, kitten?' he asked. 'My eyes aren't what they used to be, could easily confuse a pedal, an old man like me. They'd just take my licence and call me an old fool, unless I kill him, but I think I can manage not to.'

At that moment, Jean could not have given similar assurance. It was as if there had been a trade, the self she had built for the man she had loved, and she had not been consulted. If it had been a choice, she didn't know that she would have made it. After a few moments' consideration, she refused Porter's offer and told him she would be all right alone.

He kissed her cheek and whispered a final piece of poetry in her ear. 'No coward soul is yours, my dear,' he assured her. 'Never forget that.'

As Porter's car disappeared from the road into the heat shimmer of the highway, Jean tried to think what she would do. Her suit was clinging to her and she wanted to kick off her shoes and stand under cold water. She didn't want this to be happening now.

Watching her, Denny couldn't think how he had gotten away in the first place. If she had chosen to hunt him down, he didn't doubt she could have found him. Perhaps he hadn't run, as he thought, she had simply let him go when his nerve broke, letting him think he was escaping inevitability when he was heading straight for it. It had felt like the only thing to do at the time; the life he could stand only because she was in it was still one he despised. He had woken, suffocating, his body streaked with lipstick and powder. His first conscious breath took him all the way to the door. The next, away from her. It would be ten miles before he didn't have to force the air into his lungs. But he was close enough now to smell the perfume on her skin. The pressure to speak was like fingers around his throat.

'How . . . how are you, Jean?'

She was unprepared for his voice; it washed her away. There was awareness, not apology, in it, and she had to wait for words to trickle back to her. She felt her fingers lift, as if on a current of air, and tucked them into her palms. She was too curious for the feel of him, to see if she knew the grain of his skin as she once had. Her own flesh was crawling with reminiscence; it knew him still. She wished to be again encased in armour; he pierced her too easily.

'I'm fine,' she replied, never having found adequacy in words. She wanted her anger back, it was at least defined. Now, she was spinning.

'Can I come in?' he asked.

Her permission was required, though he had been able to waltz freely and unbidden into her mind a hundred times over the years. She wondered what she should say, and what she would. She couldn't believe that he was again close enough to touch, or to strike. When he left, she nearly died. He had made being alone unbearable, when it was the one thing she had no choice but to bear. She had not considered what he might bear. She had assumed that, for him, the cut had been clean and cauterised; she assumed the only grief had been hers. She wondered if she could feel it all again, from the first day to the last. If she had been made strong for a reason, did that make it an obligation?

She nodded, and unlocked the door; the action itself seeming so strange in front of him. He took a step towards her and, despite herself, she flinched, stilling him — apart from his hands, which were shaking. She could see the nicks and scars of labour on them, the stains of countless cigarettes. She studied him, taking in the curl of his hair, the sweep of his brow, the map of her heart. She could smell his scalp, his breath; things that had been as familiar and exotic as engine oil and roses. She had missed his scent. There were rules here, conditions. She should demand information and see that it satisfied her before she granted any more favours. But she didn't care for words. Before she said or could hear anything more, she had to know that he was real; nothing was as important as the feel of his skin.

She placed her hands on his face and he felt his head lift from his shoulders and float between her fingers. She felt the stubble on his cheek, the roughness of his sunburned skin; he looked worn and mistreated, and in her heart she felt something cramp, swiftly and painfully. She had once wanted him to be weak because she could not conceive of someone whole and perfect needing anything from her. It made her sweat to remember how she treasured the nights he couldn't sleep, how she had savoured his pain because she could soothe it, and welcomed horror into her bed because it would bind him to her. He leaned against her, arms hanging redundant at his sides, while she held him, tenderly, but without commitment. She couldn't think why he had come back, why he would return to a marriage that had been built on straw, a few sunny days a hundred years ago, when death made anything possible. She had governed her life by what was appropriate then, by what was due from her as a survivor of it. She had asked herself often enough what would be due to this man who came back from a war, to her. She told herself everything. Anything. All. And she had never denied him a thing. She had derided every moment of boredom as ingratitude. Every flash of pain as churlishness because she was at least alive. It was what she was for, she used to think: compensation. It was what Wisteria had made her for. But what, she wondered, could she still owe him? He might only be tired and poor, she thought, with no more reason than that. Perhaps he would tell her, and then she would know if it mattered.

'What do you want?' she whispered.

He was silent for a moment, then replied: 'This.'

He had seen her on screen, and couldn't go on after that; having tried to stay away long enough to figure out a reason for leaving her behind. Watching her, he knew that reason was never going to come. He had wanted it to be something other than fear that drove him, something unique and unanswerable. He had wanted to be free, but found himself instead adrift; the world had proved too usual, and he had found he had no gift for it alone. Then he realised that she had held him not to a future, but to the earth. He felt less, without her; tasted less, sought less and was satisfied with nothing. But because there were things she could not make worthwhile, he had left. Because he didn't know how to do anything but run, he ran. When she appeared on a screen in front of him, he decided to see it as permission, and made his way home.

'What else?' she asked. 'There must be more.'

He shook his head. 'I just want to come home. I can't sleep without you, Jean.' He raised his eyes to her; they were desolate, like the ground after a fire. 'You're the only peace I had.'

She knew of worlds within worlds, and always had; he had found one in her. Nothing was supposed to touch them after it was all over; they were supposed to have already lived through the worst of it. But it wasn't enough. It couldn't always be. They had to let something hurt, be bad, be disappointing. She had thought he was her maker once; she had thought the two of them would have to be extraordinary, love being so fantastical and unlikely for some that it requires explanation, rules and commandments. She had not considered that it could be a freak, an evolving, adapting thing that can cling to a barren surface or lie dormant deep beneath the skin where it waits for a form to assume, for a place to thrive. Nature, after all, abhors a vacuum.

He put his arms around her, gripping her tightly; it was as if a memory had dug into her flesh. What did she want beyond reminiscence, she wondered. And what did it matter? If there was no tomorrow, she could stand it; she had yet to find what could finish her. His head lay against her chest, cradled in her palms; she felt tears spill through her fingers and run down her veins, lighter than blood. It was her decision to make.

Is this love? she thought; his face trembling against her hand, as rage and pity and regret beat through her palm. How terrible it is. She did not forgive him; she was sure of that. She did not yet know how to forgive and still love. She did not forgive her mother; she did not forgive the bomb that had killed Frankie and her children; she did not forgive Jack; she did not forgive Paul Bradshaw; she did not forgive herself. But she knew this: she could crush Denny's skull between her hands and it would be wrong; she would be punished. She chose not to exercise the full potential of her strength because she had been taught not to. But she could break him inside, in that moment, by denying him. That, of all things, was allowed. Love makes little gods of us all. It awards the power to shatter the existence of someone who, by loving, has made themselves glass. She might have used it as casually as a child pulls a cat's tail had she known earlier it was hers. But by the time Jean realised, she was herself clear and fragile.

Epilogue

Jean saw no option other than to become a refugee. The ordinary was no longer bearable, and everything is strange in motion; she could hide there. She gave up the little house and bought an enormous, gleaming trailer, christening it the Monstruo Hermosa. After the studio threatened legal action over her failure to return the Roman breastplate, Porter settled with them and made Jean a present of it; she fixed it to the prow of the land yacht.

Porter labelled what was happening a routine rout of the interesting and unusual; the routed would flourish in some new and fortunate place and the town would wither and decay without them. As a farewell outing, he took Jean to the drive-in to see the glossy melodrama that had succeeded them. It was Jean's choice of movie; she wanted to see what they had made of Eva's book. It had, not unexpectedly, become the tale of how a caring industry tried to save a troubled, doomed individual. It made Eva a lot of money.

'All this bland perfection,' Porter sighed, gesturing at the beautiful people on screen. 'What is it but the stagnation of art?'

'Will you keep going, do you think?' Jean wondered if there would be a home for her to return to, or if it was all exile from now on.

'Of course, always. Even if they shut us down, we'll crop up somewhere down the line. In some

558

other form. Evolution, remember? Forward with the freaks. I have some very interesting possibilities to develop. And we'll be waiting for you, don't you worry. Just keep moving, my dear. Keep moving.'

No one saw them off. They left at dawn, when it could feel more like escape than retreat. Jean wondered how it might have been if Denny had come back a day earlier, when she was still marvellous. It had never been easy, with them, to separate motivation from circumstance.

★ ★ ★

She discovered the child eight weeks into their journey. After six months, it seemed to fill her from chin to kneecap like some vast tumour or undigested meal.

From under the shade of a tree, she watched Denny pack their things into the trailer. They stayed no more than a few weeks in each place; long enough to rest, not long enough to be known. Inside her, the child stirred, as eager as its mother to get going; Gloria was waiting for them. The last of their possessions disappeared inside, and she thought of Porter, building possibility where none had existed then folding it down into a box and moving on; another world demolished, another to be found. She never again wanted to be fixed and finite. Denny worked without his shirt, and on his back she could see the recent outline of her hand, branding him hers again. Jean rubbed her belly, feeling the enormity of the change held within.

She would not only survive, but be survived; her existence would mean something to someone now, good or bad. Life had her.

Denny turned to face her, and she saw uncertainty strike him; it passed over them both as often as clouds. How long would it last, they wondered, this odd, hungry thing fed with their warmth, their breath, their fear? When would it reveal them as fools, hiding naked from the world behind a sheet of glass? A god would envy love for the resilience of its followers, and balk at the level of proof they require. They have belief, but no faith.

Then he smiled, and raised his hand, making small circles in the air with his index finger. Time to go. A tiny foot struck at Jean's side and she clutched her stomach.

'Breathe,' she whispered. 'Breathe.'

We do hope that you have enjoyed reading this large print book.

Did you know that all of our titles are available for purchase?

We publish a wide range of high quality large print books including:
Romances, Mysteries, Classics
General Fiction
Non Fiction and Westerns

Special interest titles available in large print are:
The Little Oxford Dictionary
Music Book
Song Book
Hymn Book
Service Book

Also available from us courtesy of Oxford University Press:
Young Readers' Dictionary
(large print edition)
Young Readers' Thesaurus
(large print edition)

For further information or a free brochure, please contact us at:
Ulverscroft Large Print Books Ltd.,
The Green, Bradgate Road, Anstey,
Leicester, LE7 7FU, England.
Tel: (00 44) 0116 236 4325
Fax: (00 44) 0116 234 0205

MISSING YOU ALREADY

Pauline McLynn

At a remote railway station in Norfolk, Kitty Fulton runs the ticket office and her pet project is the lost and found. Nothing gives her more pleasure than to reunite possessions with their rightful owners. It is an experience that remains elusive in her own world as with each passing day her mother's Alzheimer's pulls them further and further apart and, on top of this, she must endure the disintegration of a close relationship with a childhood friend. When Kitty feels her life can't get more complicated a series of extraordinary events challenges her notions of duty and fidelity. And in struggling to find the answers Kitty embarks on a journey that questions the importance of life and the way we must live . . .

THE SUMMER HOUSE

Mary Nichols

The Great War; 1918. Young lady Helen, daughter of Lord Hardingham, is persuaded to marry Richard. But her soldier husband returns to the front leaving Helen to wonder just who it is she's married. Then Oliver Donovan enters her life and she's in love for the first time. Oliver returns to his regiment — and is never seen again. When Helen is left with his child the baby is taken from her and given away for adoption. Over twenty years pass; a second war is ravaging Europe, and Laura, Helen's daughter, is also caught in a tragic love affair and left expecting a baby. Gradually the truth about her parentage is revealed, old wounds are healed and, with Helen's support, Laura learns to fall in love again.

HUNGARIAN DANCES

Jessica Duchen

Karina's life was once mapped out for her — she was meant to follow in the footsteps of her Hungarian grandmother, a world-famous violinist. Instead, she's a teacher, a mum and wife to Julian, a very English husband who's not always in step with her. But when disaster befalls her best friend, Karina feels forced to question the very foundations of her existence. Encouraged by a chance encounter with a like-minded musician, she begins to delve into her grandmother's Gypsy past, and to discover the secrets of her Hungarian family history. Life will never be the same again. Like most people, Karina isn't sure the life she chose was the right one. But she is willing to take drastic steps to change it.

SHATTERED LIVES

Bernardine Kennedy

Orphaned as children, sisters Hannah and Julie were either ill-treated or left to their own devices. Hannah was always the more sensible of the two and now, happily married with a steady job, her determination to succeed has paid off. The same cannot be said for Julie. Easily led by the wrong crowd, she drifted apart from Hannah when she fell pregnant at fifteen and the sisters eventually lost contact. Now, with three children from three different men and surviving on benefits, Julie is living a life of misery and drug addiction. She needs help and it's up to her sister to step in, but in doing so Hannah discovers to her horror that her own life might not be so perfect after all . . .

TESTIMONY

Anita Shreve

At a New England boarding school, a sex
scandal is about to break. Even more
shocking than the sexual acts themselves is
the fact that they were caught on videotape.
A Pandora's box of revelations, the tape
triggers a chorus of voices — those of the
men, women, teenagers, and parents involved
in the scandal — that details the ways in
which lives can be derailed or destroyed
in one foolish moment.